T0157987

Amber's Ambitions

Janice I. Meissner

authorHOUSE®

AuthorHouse™
1663 Liberty Drive
Bloomington, IN 47403
www.authorhouse.com
Phone: 1-800-839-8640

First published by AuthorHouse   06/13/2011

ISBN: 978-1-4567-5338-2 (sc)
ISBN: 978-1-4567-5336-8 (hc)
ISBN: 978-1-4567-5339-9 (e)

Library of Congress Control Number: 2011903843

Acknowledgement:

I am profoundly grateful for the time and love of my husband, Louie, whose extensive work led to the completion of this book.

I want to acknowledge Jean Setne's devotion spent in reviewing the manuscript.

While this story is about love,
the love actually occurs in a
dimension where the
understanding of the inner
actions with people is
more recondite and difficult
to grasp.
However, in the *Greater Realms*
Love is all that exists.

Amber's Ambitions

Amber Breddgeforth walked into her sorority house with her dear sorority sister Miranda Gaterr. They obtained their mail. Amber found one important letter from Professor Robert Phillips at the University of Texas in El Paso, known as UTEP.

Amber squealed, shrieked, and shrilled her way to her desk as she read the letter of acceptance into the Business Management program for a Masters Degree. This meant Amber was seeking to fulfill another ambition to work someday in business. A native Oklahoman, Amber graduated at the top of her high school class. In a week, she would graduate *Summa Cum Laude* from Oklahoma State University at Stillwater. Her next goal was to immediately leave for school in El Paso. She wanted to complete her Master's degree in less than a year. Her attitude toward learning exceeded that of many of her immediate family members.

Amber had light colored hair with some red strands which gave a glow to its shoulder length. She parted her hair high on the right side. Ancestors from Scandinavia provided her fair skin and features except for her hazel eyes, which came from her father's side of the family.

Not only her hair commanded attention, but Amber was 5 feet 8 inches tall with a very slender build. The animation Amber used when talking made people listen to her. Amber was generous with her time in helping her sorority sisters; therefore was well liked.

This career-driven lady spent three days at home after graduation, then loaded her new car, a gift from her parents, who delighted in her tremendous achievements. They were thrilled at her high school graduation where she had won top honors which included a fully paid scholarship to OSU.

She carried with her bed linens, bath supplies, a toaster, microwave, and an electric skillet. Everything else was furnished in her efficiency apartment.

Once Amber arrived in El Paso, after obtaining the key for her apartment, she sat on a love seat and called her mother, relating she had arrived safely and thanked her mom again for the car. She was tired from the drive, mainly because she was not used to driving that distance, but the car needed unloading. She was thankful her mother had packed some snacks with peanut butter and fruit. She especially enjoyed the banana. After eating, Amber fell into bed.

She slept late the next morning, then dressed to meet her professor. Amber wore a crinkled printed skirt with violet flowers on a white background. Her fine sleeveless top was the same violet color as the flowers. Amber's favorite color was violet. She wore no hose, but had open toed flip-flops with an inch cork heel whose top was graced with three flowers, the center one being violet.

Before she left, Amber looked through her purses (shoes and purses were her downfall) to find a shoulder one whose color would go with her outfit.

She parked as close as possible to the building where the professor had directed. Arriving thirsty, she found a dispensing machine with water.

A long discussion ensued with Professor Phillips, who was taken with her enthusiastic eagerness and drive. Amber was asked to help with pre-registration for an up-coming seminar on business management, finance, and crisis in business, which was to be held the following month. Amber accepted the job, showing interest and enthusiasm.

The weeks passed as Amber applied herself toward her goal. Because she had accepted the pre-registration job, Amber met other students.

She found herself among more males than females, but none of the males attracted her. She thought most were self-centered and sex-driven, except one, a kind gentleman from India who was studying for an advanced degree in Business Management and Accounting. She and Marshara Gudura did research together in the library. To relax, they went to movies. Amber paid for her ticket. Marshara was likeable and a gentleman. Both were helping with the pre-registration seminar plans.

On Friday morning of the seminar day, Amber was dressed in a light violet rayon dress with slip-on shoes. She wore no hose because of the heat.

As she walked toward the main door of the business building, Amber was wearing her name tag. She carried a shoulder purse the color of her dress and a note pad. In the sun, the few red strands in her shoulder-length hair glistened beautifully. She had very white skin with lovely features and hazel eyes, which glowed when she interacted with people.

As she walked, a gentleman noticed and admired her from upstairs. He had flown into El Paso and rented a car to attend the event. His family business had paid for his expenses. He noticed this lovely violet-clad lady thinking, *She is quite tall. I must meet her.* He quickly walked to her and extended his hand.

"Good morning, I am Armand Rambulet. I read about this seminar in a professional journal. My family business sent me. I am looking forward to this conference very much. How about you?"

"My name is Amber Breddgeforth. I consider this conference to be a part of the research I need for my master's thesis, *Business Crisis Management,*" she answered.

'Wow! That's your field?" he exclaimed. "Our business needs someone with that knowledge."

The hall lights dimmed announcing the attendees were to take their seats in the auditorium. Armand asked, "May I sit beside you?"

"If there are two seats together," she answered. They found two seats near the back of the hall. She opened her notebook and prepared to write. When the lecture began, Armand was amazed at her concentration level. She listened carefully to the lecturer and took far more notes than he.

Armand was distracted by Amber, wondering about her home; where she came from; what type of family she had. He recognized she was very attractive and studious. However, Amber was intent on nothing but the lecture.

During the break, he positioned himself to watch as she came from the lady's room. He thought, *I wonder if she would have dinner with me tonight, just a simple meal somewhere near here?*

She did not approach him, instead went directly to her seat. He thought, *Oh now, the cold shoulder treatment. Ugh. I'm not going to let this behavior impinge my thoughts or feelings toward her.* He went into the room, took his seat and asked, "How did you like the first segment?"

"It was fine however, this next portion is where my interests lie," she remarked.

A thought came to him. *Do not feel she has been impertinent. Her*

3

thoughts are on the lectures and what she can learn from them to help her with her thesis.

Amber took copious notes. At times she concentrated on the lecture as though she were rolling thoughts in her mind. When the time came for a lunch break, he asked, "May we eat together?"

"That would be fine, but I want to greet some people first."

"I'll find a place for us in the lunchroom. What would you like to drink?"

"Bottled water, please."

Their meal was served buffet style. He purchased water, then found a table and waited for her. When she entered the room, he went to her saying, "Please, you go through the line first."

"Thank you," she remarked, obtaining a tray, plate, and napkin-wrapped silverware, then she selected her food. He followed.

To the cashier he indicated, "I'll take both checks."

Armand led her to the table he had chosen. When she put her tray down and her purse on the chair, he invited, "Madam, it's my pleasure to seat you."

"Thank you so much. Are you obtaining important information for your business?"

Before thinking, he blurted, "I am too awe-struck with you, Amber."

Embarrassed, she explained, "I am a student here learning a great deal. I am sorry if your attention is diverted. I do not intend to impede your energies. Please, let's talk about what we've heard."

Instead, he asked, "Where is your home? Please tell me about yourself."

Thoughtfully, she answered, "Both my father and brother are mechanical engineers. My mother is a nurse. They all live in Oklahoma City. I always disliked the climate there and came to UTEP for my advanced degree. This school favored me because of my good grades at Oklahoma State University in Stillwater. Please tell me about yourself."

"My mother and father are graduates of the University of New Mexico in Albuquerque. My brother has a degree in law, while my sister, who is two years older than I, has a degree in business. I obtained my master's degree in business from the same university."

After lunch, they returned to their seats to learn the fundamentals of business which was boring for him. Amber continued listening and writing. He quickly reached the conclusion he had met a very intelligent lady. At the final break, he asked, "Amber, may I have the pleasure of entertaining you over dinner tonight?"

"If you desire, I would like that very much."

That afternoon Amber and Armand walked to their cars. On the way to the parking lot, Armand chatted about where Amber would like to have dinner.

He had obtained the address of her apartment. In his motel room, he dressed in a fresh blue shirt and wore a deep blue tie with white diagonal stripes, a pin stripe suit, and shoes which shined, shimmered, and shone in the late afternoon sunlight. He looked every bit the part of a successful businessman who had a great deal to talk about with the lady he had just met. He was 6 feet 1 inch tall, slender with blue eyes and light skin with a hair style done especially for him. His fair skin came from his French ancestry.

Over dinner, they questioned each other about the lectures they had heard. Armand was clearly aware of how intent Amber was to obtain her master's degree, and how anxious she was to use her knowledge. She explained to him her schooling grades with added drive to obtain her scholarship. All her parents had to pay for was her sorority expenses and miscellaneous school needs. In discussing her grants, he observed, "Most people think they are only for athletes."

The next day at the seminar, they sat beside each other and ate lunch together. He took her out to dinner afterward. He noted she was becoming more personable. He witnessed sparkle and twinkle in her eyes as she described the lecture on financial crises.

Amber asked, "Just how do you rescue a business when you hear about the exigency too late?"

"I believe that the chief executive officer needs to be eviscerated from the business, because he did not conform to the goals of the overall business direction, which the other officers held.

In a small business like our family's, we hold weekly meetings to make certain we are all on the same track. We apprise each other of what we are doing."

They enjoyed their dinner, mainly talking business. Armand took Amber home. At her door, she agreed to meet before the noon banquet the next day.

Seated beside each other, Armand met Marshara. They talked about financial techniques for the treasurer or controller of a company.

Armand was picking up tips to help him assist a company with which he was struggling because executive officers made errors which had become troublesome, placing stress on all the employees.

After the banquet, they walked hand in hand to his car. He opened her door and offered her the seat belt. While driving her home, he asked, "In three weeks I'd like to return and take you out to dinner on Friday evening. No doubt I will be late because I must put in a full day before I leave to catch the plane coming down here. Will you be available?"

"Certainly, but I'll be steeped in work and may not be very sociable," she responded, as she squeezed his hand adding, "Thank you so much for your enjoyable hospitality. Please call me when you arrive home."

Armand called Amber Monday morning after he'd been at work for a while. She was on her way to the library. She thanked him for his pleasant company and for their meals.

They were comfortably conversing when he interrupted, "I must cut you short. A client is here. I'll see you on Friday, July 18th. It'll be after nine p.m. Goodbye."

Amber worked in the library until after five p.m. She'd put in a long day which was typical. She spent Tuesday with Professor Phillips, discussing and giving him details of what she had written. He suggested special areas which she needed to enlarge upon.

After their meeting, Amber went directly to the library. She wore flats and shorts because of the heat. Amber continued her diligent work day after day, including Saturdays. On Sunday mornings she slept in.

In one conversation she told her mother she wanted to stay on campus over Labor Day weekend and on Thanksgiving, too. She agreed to spend the Christmas holiday at home.

When time came for Armand to fly to El Paso again, Amber had asked him to please help her in the library on Saturday, the 19th. He agreed. She suggested that he dress comfortably with shorts and sport clothing. Armand agreed that shorts would be all right for study, but when he took her out to dinner he would wear a suit.

Amber quietly greeted his arrival saying, "I see you made it. I'm ready." She locked her door and slipped the key into her purse. She added to Armand, "I see you are still in a suit, but by the way, you look especially handsome."

He answered, "I observe you're in a dress, but it's not violet. However, you are very attractive." He opened the car door and handed her the seat belt. Once he was inside, he asked, "Where shall we eat? Why don't you direct me."

At the eating establishment, he helped her out of the car, took her hand, and opened the restaurant door. Inside he asked for a booth. Amber scooted into the seat first. He slid in beside her. As she fidgeted with her purse he put his arm around her and drew her close. His right hand gently turned her face toward him. He leaned his head a bit and gave her a soft, gentle, tender touch, and kissed her saying, "I would be more than happy to help you tomorrow, my dear lady."

When the waiter appeared, Armand asked for two glasses of champagne. He then looked at Amber and queried, "I hope you like what I just ordered."

With a scowl she replied, "I hate the stuff," then quickly broke into laughter admitting, "Champagne is my family's preferred drink. Any brand will do."

That began a more delightful evening than Armand ever imagined. He found that, although serious, Amber had a great sense of humor.

It was nearly midnight when they left the restaurant. When Armand opened the car door for her, he placed his body so she had to kiss him. When she was seated, he handed her the seat belt. He drove to her apartment, took her hand and walked her to the door. When the door was open, she went inside. Armand followed.

She put her purse on the table, then their eyes met. Armand put his arms around her in a full embrace. He kissed her again, this time in a lengthy, affectionate, gentle greeting. He hoped there would be many more to follow. Releasing her he asked, "What time tomorrow?"

"Would nine thirty be okay?"

"That'll be fine. I'll eat breakfast at the motel." He gave her another kiss on her cheek as he left, saying, "Goodbye."

Once outside, Armand did a quick two-step. In the car, he told himself aloud, "That was great!"

In the meantime, as Amber prepared for bed she thought, *I've been kissed and embraced by other men but there was something different with Armand.* She went to sleep thinking about this new man.

The next day, she greeted him with an embrace. He carried her laptop and notebook in his left hand while holding her hand with his right. They took a short-cut to the library. Armand wondered why Amber's purse (which was the one she used for classes because it held more) was so puffed out and seemed to be heavy. He thought, *There's no way I will carry that thing for her.*

Once in the library's reference section, they sat side by side. Armand placed her laptop on the table. Amber put her heavy purse on an adjoining chair, then pulled out two water bottles, a small note pad, pens and paper, which was a little crumpled on the edges. Amber was all set. She then handed Armand the note pad, which contained the names of books she wished him to find for her references, while she typed information she already had.

He examined the book names on her list. Leaning toward her, he whispered, "Amber, you'll have to help me get started on this. Where do I look?" She took his hand and they moved to the area where the reference books were kept. He brought two books to the table and began leafing through them. When he found a chapter she wanted, he left the book open and pushed it aside.

He went to another book, one about financial and fiscal policies. This one spurred his interest with information needed in business. Amber finished her typing and turned to the chapter Armand had obtained for her. She typed the book's name, author, chapter, and page, often typing portions of the exact passages which the author had written. She was working so energetically, she did not realize noon was approaching. She was surprised to hear Armand whisper, "Amber, it's time for lunch." She packed up her things. He carried them to the eating area in the student center where they ate their lunches.

During their mealtime conversation, he leaned to kiss her on the cheek. He told her more about his family business and how his grandparents were still somewhat involved. His eyes flashed very blue when he related what he was reading in the reference book which she would use next. He admitted, "I'm learning some new information myself."

She felt very happy. She realized his mind was being challenged. They returned to the library and remained there until after four, then left for her apartment. Placing her paraphernalia on the table, Amber poured glasses of water for them. He embraced her. She suggested they sit on the love seat. His arm around Amber made Armand feel good. They discussed where to go for their evening meal. She mentioned there was to be a campus play that night. "Would you like to see it instead of a movie?" she asked. They decided that would be their evening's entertainment.

She embraced him before he left, suggesting, "We're on campus. Almost anything goes for clothing. Please do not wear a suit. You would stand out like a sore thumb. I'll wear something casual."

"Okay, that sounds good." Armand was off to his motel room. He took a short nap, showered and donned a polo shirt and suit trousers. He didn't have a pair of slacks with him. The next time he would be better prepared.

Amber was in a sun dress with *aubergine tattersall* lines. More of her arms, back, and neck were exposed. She was remarkably beautiful because her white skin was more exposed, which made her hazel eyes glow.

Armand embraced her before going to eat. The usual kisses followed prior to their being served. With a toast, Armand pledged, "To us."

Amber's eyes twinkled, 'Thank You'. She was thrilled for his help today. She appreciated his willingness to assist her. However, at this point in time, Amber did not realize how taken Armand was with her. He was a kind, gentle, caring man who was not interested in anything more than being with her. On this happy occasion they watched a humorous play with plenty of banter. They enjoyed their evening very much.

On Sunday, they each slept late. Armand arrived and took her to lunch. They, spent a long time talking about what she planned for the week and what he would be doing. Armand agreed to call her when he arrived home.

She related, "I'm going to spend Labor Day weekend here, working. I'll have easier access to the references I need."

Hearing this, Armand agreed to fly down and help her, after spending a full work day on Friday. He departed with a warm embrace. On his way, he stopped at his motel and made a reservation for the Labor Day weekend. He asked the motel clerk, "If I send a box here with my name on it, will you please hold it for me? Then I'll not have to wait for luggage at the airport." The agent agreed to his request.

On Monday he called Amber, telling her he was at work and would return on Friday evening of Labor Day weekend and would take her to dinner. Amber appreciated his thoughtfulness and thanked him for his help and a wonderfully happy weekend. She ended her comments by saying, "Please keep in touch. I'll do the same and be ready for you."

With Armand at work, Amber steeped herself in her thesis material. The time passed quickly. She felt she had about one-third of her work finished.

When August 29th came, Amber was dressed in her violet *tattersal-* lined dress. She had purchased violet barrettes, which held her hair in place so when Armand kissed her, he didn't have to push her hair aside.

Armand arrived to find Amber with her purse over her shoulder. She looked beautiful. He immediately put his arms around her, embraced, and caressed her. Over dinner Armand wanted her full attention. He stated,

"I am happy to help you on Saturday, but I hope Sunday can be reserved so we can go to a movie."

"I'd like that, but I would like to spend a couple of hours typing on Sunday afternoon. You would be welcome to stay at my apartment until I finish."

"Good, I'll heckle you so much, you'll want to be with me, loving me." He gathered her in his arms in the booth before their drinks came. "Amber, I like your barrettes. Their color is the same as your striking dress. How do you get all these colors to match?"

"I have a sense of color. I do not need to have a dress, blouse or skirt with me in order to match something I am considering."

"That's a real talent, " Armand marveled.

"I haven't told you, but my parents will be here for Thanksgiving. I told Mom I'd spend Christmas with them," she announced.

"I have a request. Please come to Albuquerque and spend New Years Eve and day with me. I want you to meet my parents and family. I'll purchase plane tickets for you. Then you can fly back here. There is no way I want to be alone on New Year's Eve."

Amber was happy to agree with his wishes.

After their meal, he returned Amber to her apartment. With embraces, he left for his motel. He told her he would sleep late. She suggested he come to her apartment for brunch.

When Armand arrived at her place, he brought a lady's briefcase for her laptop, notes, and special items. He explained he was tired the previous night, because he had worked long hours. Amber became teary-eyed and broke into sobs. She had never had any man be so concerned, attentive, and who would spend so much time, energy, and money on her.

She looked carefully at the case, opened it, looked at each compartment, and ran her hand into some of them. She looked at Armand who admitted this present was his wish for her. She complained, "You didn't need to spend the money." As tears rolled down her cheeks she threw her arms around a waiting Armand who stood, silently observing her every move.

Armand enfolded her in his arms asking, "Please don't cry. I bought that briefcase because you need something for all your gear." He wiped her tears continuing, "This is a happy time."

Taking a deep breath, Amber thanked him, then said, "I'm hungry. I'm certain you are too."

She micro-waved bacon and hash browns, while scrambling eggs with cheese which made them very good. She gave him a banana, orange, and cantaloupe with blueberries on top. She pressed the bacon on a paper towel and served the eggs and hash browns, asking him to sit.

"Not until I seat you."

There was room in the tiny kitchen for only two chairs. They sat with their shoulders touching. She made toast with peanut butter and jam. She served juice asking, "Would you like some coffee?"

"Certainly."

She poured bottled water into one of her only two cups, and put it into the microwave. When it boiled she added instant coffee. Armand ate as if he were hungry. He realized she had only the barest of essential dishes. The bowls were filled with fruit. She laughed, "If you want cereal you'll have to eat the fruit first."

"What would you like to do tomorrow?" she asked.

"Whatever you'd like."

"I had thought of driving to the *Chamizal National Memorial*. Ben Barnes, who is from here, says it is worth spending some time there. I'm not certain about the name or what it commemorates. I've been told there is a nice park, so it should be interesting."

"I didn't bring a cap. I'll need something. What about you? Do you have something to protect your skin?" he offered.

"No, but we can stop at the mall for headwear of some kind."

Amber washed the dishes. She had no dish drainer, so Armand drained each piece for a time, then placed them on paper towels to dry. She replaced her kitchen equipment and wiped the sink and counter top.

Then Amber turned to her briefcase. She put her laptop, notebook, and extra pens in it. Armand took the filled case. With her purse and two bottles of water, she locked her door and they were off to the library to study.

Many hours later, Armand leaned over and whispered, "Amber, it's four o'clock. May we wind this up?"

"Sure, but please let me finish this paragraph."

On the short-cut to her apartment, Armand became serious and asked, "Amber, how much longer do you expect me to help you?" She removed her hand from his, then stood looking at him stating, "That's up to you," as she leaned to kiss him.

With her briefcase in his left hand, he enfolded her in his arms and held her in a lengthy embrace. When he released her, he looked into her eyes. The blue of his met the hazel of hers, blending into questions which could not be answered at that moment.

He asked, "May we take some time to talk at your apartment?"

"Of course."

At her place, Armand held Amber in a lengthy embrace. It became so long that Amber's lips became tired. She withdrew her face from his stating, "Armand, I believe you want something from me to which I cannot consent."

"Amber, that's not true. All I want is to be able to hold you, embrace and kiss you from time to time. Look, I came down here of my own free will. I have a reputation to live by. My family expects me to be honest, sincere and kind to everyone with whom I come in contact. That includes you, Amber."

He continued, "I'm sorry I did not thank you for that wonderful breakfast. My dear lady, you certainly know how to take care of a guy's hunger." Then, because she was still in his arms, he gently kissed her again.

With her face close to his, Amber murmured, "Armand, I can say this for certain. I am fond of you. I have never been this near any man for this long." She took a deep breath. Looking into his eyes continuing, "The more I'm around you, the more joy you bring to me. Please give me time. I must finish my thesis. I cannot, and will not, allow anyone or anything to get in the way of my goal. I hope before Christmas, with your help, I will have it three-fourths finished."

With their faces nearly touching, looking into Amber's eyes, he asked, "After your goal of finishing your thesis, and graduating, what do you plan for your next achievement?"

"I'd like to find a job and work in a business. That's why I worked so hard in school. I do not want to get married and be tied down with babies. I've never been around them, so why would I want to help create something which would be in the way of my goal?"

"Do you think it would be possible to be married and in business without children, for at least a few years?" he pressed.

"I suppose, but the correct person would need to be with me to help make that decision." Armand kissed her, then suggested they go to dinner. Back at the motel, he dressed in a suit, then went to pick her up. When she opened her door, she was again dressed in that same *aubergine tattersall* sun dress, which had an underskirt, giving the dress body and added fluidity. The skirt enhanced the red-violet lines, which became more saturated while the *aubergine* faded as her body moved.

This all brought naturalness of color. The dress had a built-in bra which fit her perfectly. The dress came to mid-calf making her look taller. Armand could do nothing but embrace this beautiful woman, of whom he was becoming more fond each day. Of course he checked to see any breast revealment. He wondered *How could that dress not reveal any more than it does?* However, what little he saw was terrific.

As usual, he assisted her in and out of the vehicle and opened the door of the eating establishment. He asked for a booth. This evening Amber was prepared for his advances. After an embrace, he asked, "What would you like to drink?"

"We are in a part of the country where margaritas are wonderful. Why not have them?"

After the drinks were ordered, Amber renewed the conversation which had begun in her apartment. "Do you understand where I am coming from?First wanting to finish my thesis as quickly as possible; secondly, to graduate; and thirdly, to work in business. That's what all this training has been for. Didn't you go to work immediately after finishing your master's degree?"

"Yes, I must admit, I was lucky because I knew where I would work."

"That will be another goal, to find the job which will suit me, one which would utilize my talents." They drank to each other's happiness. Amber did not let Armand become too serious. He did not need to tell her of his attraction to her. She felt his magnetism, however, Amber was holding back. She didn't want him to think she was completely enamored over his apparent gentlemanly manner toward her.

Their whole evening was delightful. They both enjoyed being together. Amber suggested sleeping late, then she would make breakfast again before they went looking for caps and hats. She explained her extra food needed to be eaten.

Breakfast was tasty and enjoyable. Armand thought, *Could this actually be something I could experience again with her, say six months from now?* He helped her clean the kitchen. Both were wearing shorts and athletic shoes. Amber guided him to the mall where they found a blue cap for him and a brimmed hat for her. Back in the car she directed him to I-10 east of downtown El Paso to the proper exit for the memorial.

At the Chamizal, they walked in the park then went into the building, to discover how the Rio Grande had meandered between Mexico and the United States many times in centuries past. In 1964, President Lyndon Johnson met with the Mexican president Adolfho Lopez Mateos and agreed by treaty, that the present course of the river would become the permanent boundary, regardless of where the river would wander in the future. The memorial was built to commemorate this important treaty. A large park was made around the memorial on the border, where the U.S. flag and the Mexican fly on their own side of the Rio.

When they had done enough sight-seeing, they left to find a place for lunch. As they ate, Armand kissed her several times while they were sharing a pleasant conversation.

As they drove back to the UTEP campus after lunch, Amber cheerfully thanked Armand for his help the day before and their noon lunch.

Instead of her apartment, Armand drove to his motel.

"Why are we here?" she interrogated.

"Please come in with me," he asked as he helped her out of the car. Amber became belligerent over what was happening. He took her hand. She said nothing until they reached his motel room door.

Visibly annoyed, she stomped her right foot and raised her voice. Conspicuously angry, she shrieked, "NO ARMAND, NOT THAT!"

Now, inside the room, Armand thrust his arms around her in a full embrace. By this time tears were rolling down her face when Armand insisted, "No, it's not that!" He wiped her tears, and continued, "I could not take advantage of you. That's what I would be doing. However, Amber, would you please lie down beside me? Just pretend we're on a blanket under a shade tree, embracing each other."

Continuing to shriek, she quickly left the room and headed for the car. He immediately began to apologize, "I'm very sorry I did not ask if you would agree to my proposal. I am so sorry I upset you. I guess I took for granted that you knew me well enough to understand, I could not harm you in in any way. It's obvious you are very upset."

"TAKE ME HOME!" she demanded.

"Of course."

As he drove toward her apartment he contritely admitted he had made a terrible blunder. He thought, *I love this woman so much I cannot let her be angry to the point she would not go to dinner with me.*

She opened her apartment door and allowed him to enter. He thought, *I hope what I said made her feel better. Now she is on her own turf. Perhaps she feels she has more control. I realize she does have more confidence here. I would do anything, anything for her embraces. The feel of her hands around my shoulders is something I am not willing to give up.*

After she placed her purse on the table, Amber turned to him, with arms outstretched. He lifted her face to meet his and tenderly kissed her lips. When her arms went around him, his eyes filled with tears. After their faces parted, he led her to the sofa where he continued to be repentant over his aggressive behavior.

"Please listen to me, Amber. I am not ready for any intimate contact with you or any other woman. Shoot-fire, I'd hardly know what to do, to be quite frank. Something such as this renders me incapable of any action." He continued to kiss her cheek. "Amber, I am too enraptured with you. I cannot bear to see you angry."

"Armand, you have found how I react when threatened. I will not allow you or any other man to use my body against my will."

"Amber, let me ask you this. If my actions had been on a blanket in the park east of the campus, would you have been threatened, lying beside me?"

"No. That area is open. Children could be playing nearby. You see, the closed door and bed bothered me. I've had too many men try to come on to me. I cannot stand that."

"How do you want me to treat you in the future?"

"Just as you are doing now."

"Don't you think, as time passes, our fondness will grow stronger?"

"Perhaps, but I will not allow you to interfere with my goals."

"Do you date other men?"

"I go to movies with Marshara, but we are only friends. I pay my way. He only takes me, that's all. Besides, why do I need another man to complicate my life? At this point in time, you are all I can handle."

Still in each other's arms, Armand kissed her again, reflecting, "Good, I don't need to worry about competition. Before you ask, back home I have no girlfriends. I find my life complicated enough coming here to be with you. I don't need any more complexity added to my life. Should we get ready to go and eat?"

After a gentle embrace, Armand went back to his motel to freshen up. When he returned, she was dressed in a violet crinkled skirt and top with step-in shoes. She wore violet barrettes in her hair. In the restaurant she was not quite as talkative as usual. Armand found himself carrying on the conversation. When he asked her, "What are your thoughts?"

She replied, "I've been thinking, perhaps we need to break up. What's happening to us is because I will not take the time to become serious."

"Oh, no. Please Amber, no, no."

"Armand, it costs you a bundle to come down here. Then you insist on paying for meals and any bills."

He kissed her cheek, stating firmly, "That's my choice. There is no other place I'd rather be. I want you to know, I have learned my lesson. Your thesis and graduation come first."

"Yes, Armand, please give me time. I admire you. I appreciate all you have done for me."

"I'll continue to help you." He finally flagged a waiter and asked for two margaritas. The two continued talking about their relationship. Amber told him that in the morning, she wanted to work at her apartment.

"Then, how about me coming over? I'll bring the *El Paso Times* and read while you work. Would that be all right?"

"That'd be fine. I would appreciate you being near."

When the drinks came Armand raised his glass and pledged, "For us," as they touched their glasses he kissed her.

After they had eaten, Armand drove her home. The two spent the rest of the evening talking about how he needed to react to her. He had learned his lesson about what not to do.

He told Amber he expected to visit her every three weeks. He reminded her that she was to spend New Years Day and Eve with him.

Chapter 2.

Time passed quickly for Amber as she struggled with her work. Her parents visited her for Thanksgiving. They had not seen her small apartment. The door flew open after their knock. With tearful greetings, she hugged her mom and dad, and thanked them for their financial support. Her small quarters made them realize Amber did not live in a spacious place. Her dad remarked, "Even a spider could not survive here."

"Dad, don't mention spiders. You know I am scared to death of them."

Her father then asked, "What about this man who flies to visit you?"

"Dad, he is wonderfully kind and helpful. When he comes, he assists me a great deal. I am not smooching or going to dinner and movies with him all the time he's here. He is a very affectionate twenty-seven year old. I've told Mom he's a businessman from Albuquerque. His whole family is involved in their business. An older brother is a lawyer. His sister has a degree in business as well. I understand they have their own nearly new building."

Her dad then asked, "What about the love issue?"

"Dad, that's the hard part. I've told him I must first finish my thesis and graduate. After that I want to work."

"Amber, finding work is another big thing."

"I know, Dad, but I can't think about that now. Today I worked all day, some at the library, and the rest of the time here."

"That's good. Let's find something to eat. After that I'd like to see a few pages of your thesis."

Her mother added, "I would too. After we eat we can go to our hotel room where we can stretch out. We have a room with two queen sized beds." Amber procured some of her efforts, locked her apartment, and left with her parents to eat. While in the car, she admitted she did not take time to do much grocery shopping. "There are some things I need. I would like to make breakfast for you before you leave."

"How will we all fit in?" her dad asked with a smile.

"We'll make-do, Dad."

"How is your money holding out?"

"My funds are okay for now. I'll ask when I need more. When Armand comes, he buys whatever I need. He doesn't let me purchase anything. He won't even allow me to pick up the waiter's tip when we eat out."

Her mother observed, "He sounds like he is rather domineering."

"That's a characteristic your mother understands well," her dad smiled. After dinner, Amber provided a finished portion of her thesis for them to read in their motel room. Just as her parents suspected, Amber fell asleep on the other bed, while they read some of her efforts.

They were impressed as always, with her work. Her father knew she had struggled extremely hard to have as much finished as she did. Her thesis revealed she had data on working with, or helping small companies. He was so impressed he spoke out loud, "What Amber has in this thesis needs to be applied to Wall Street. Is it any wonder that workers are laid off when a business goes abroad? It's time some good business practices are applied to banks and lending institutions, too."

"Just as I thought, this is great material," her mother admired.

When Amber awoke, her parents praised her enthusiastically for her work. Her mother went to the closet and brought out two outfits which she had purchased from their favorite dress shop.

Amber's eyes gleamed as she gazed at the garments. Her eyes filled with tears.

Her mother mentioned that the tags were still on the dresses, so one or both could be returned if she wished.

Thrilled beyond words, Amber took the dark colored blue-violet dress with violet buttons into the bathroom and put it on.

When she came into the room, she looked as though she was a violet portion of the rainbow. The skirt, being light weight, had generous folds so it flowed beautifully as she walked. She turned when her dad spoke, "If that doesn't turn on your man, nothing will."

"Dennis, for heaven's sake. Is that all you men think about? If he is in business, his mind can't be on Amber all the time."

"A twenty-seven year old man may be in business, but if he spends the bucks to come down here, he's looking for a wife," her father argued.

"Dad, you're not telling me anything I'm not aware of. However, I have planned to finish my thesis and graduate. If he is able to stand beside me and wait, that will show whether he believes in my goals or not. That too, will confirm his love for me, after which you will know is authentic.

"He graduated and went to work immediately. As a man he could do that. After my graduation I want a job and be able to work as a woman. Why can't women do the same thing as men?"

"As your mother, I hope you make your goals, otherwise you will not be happy. Armand must realize you are a strong woman, with definitive goals."

After this discussion, Amber took the other garment, which was a dark brown dress with a jacket of the same color, but had gold *tattersall* lines, the color of her hair. This outfit was definitely for the working woman. Quite naturally she looked the part, (except for no hose and casual shoes) when she came into the bedroom.

"Mom and Dad, thank you so much. These dresses are really gorgeous. Dad, will you please take me home?"

In the car her father advised, "Don't be a pushover Amber, just do your thing."

"I will Dad, I promise." Her father helped carry her partial thesis, which she had in binder form, and her new dresses. "What time tomorrow? I want to work a bit more," she asked.

"We'll call you before we come." They embraced as they parted.

After her relaxing evening, Amber went to bed feeling warm and fuzzy like the coating of a peach, a real feel-good sensation. She ate a light breakfast, then worked before her parents called to pick her up. Amber directed them to a cafeteria for lunch. Amber chose pumpkin pie for her desert, something she had not eaten since last Thanksgiving, when her mother had purchased one for their family gathering.

While eating, her parents said they wished to see more of El Paso. All they had seen was the I-10 freeway corridor. Her father asked Amber to drive so they could see the sights better. She explained, "I don't know that much about the city but if we could find a city map, you could direct me." They purchased one.

"One thing which is unique about the city," she revealed, is that the

Franklin Mountains divide the eastern and the western areas of the town. We are on the western side here." This conversation began an adventure for all of them to explore her city.

Amber first drove Mesa Street to Park Avenue then to I-10. She wanted her parents to see the Chamizal National Memorial. She explained this name came from a desert plant called Chamizal, which formed impenetrable thickets called Chaparal. The plant was eradicated from the area before the memorial was dedicated during President Lyndon Johnson's term. Mexico and the United Sates agreed that the present site of the Rio would be the permanent boundary in the future. The flags of each nation fly on their side of the river. The threesome spent some time there. Amber then drove back west on the freeway to Schuster, to Mesa, as her father guided her to Rim Road which wound high on the Franklins, becoming Scenic Drive. Beautiful views of the city lay beneath them.

Her father then directed her to US 54 which they drove north to Trans Mountain Highway from which they saw very impressive, glorious, spectacular mountain views. As they headed west, they saw a narrow waterway in the distance, the Rio Grande.

From there, they took the freeway back to Mesa Street and stopped for salad and soup. After eating, Amber drove to a supermarket to buy food for her parents' breakfast before they left. After a long afternoon and early evening of exploration, they were glad to get back to her apartment, where they left the food. Her parents returned to their motel after sharing goodnight hugs.

They all enjoyed sleeping late. Upon arising, Amber donned slacks and flat leather shoes. They would spend most of this crazy day after Thanksgiving in frantic and strange confusion. It was the biggest shopping day of the year. Amber and her mother wanted to shop. Her father left them to themselves and found a coffee shop where he spent the morning.

In a kitchen store, Amber and her mother found a dish drainer, towels, and dish cloths. They spent more time looking than buying. In a dress shop, Amber found a couple of tops she liked. The weather was getting cooler; she needed long sleeves.

Growing hungry, they found her father and ate in a nearby restaurant. They checked movie ads in her dad's newspaper and went to a show. After a quick supper, her parents went to bed early. The next morning they would head back to Oklahoma City.

The morning was still dark when Amber's parents arrived at her apartment for breakfast. As she micro-waved bacon, her parents sat at the tiny table sipping juice. Amber ate standing up. She heated water for coffee, made scrambled eggs in the frying pan and put hash-browns on paper towels. Warm rolls and bowls of fruit completed their breakfast. The three talked about the full-day's drive which her parents faced.

They parted with loving embraces. Amber finished the left-over eggs and bacon and made coffee for herself as she reveled in the memories of a happy reunion and two new, lovely dresses.

When the kitchen area was clean, she worked with her computer at her small desk. Then Armand called her to find if she had enjoyed the weekend with her parents. "I'll be down in two weeks," he promised. This added to her happiness.

She worked until lunch, then ate. Then she put her laptop, papers, and water in the briefcase. With her purse over her shoulder, she walked to the library where she worked the entire afternoon.

Back in her apartment, she warmed a microwave dinner. After Amber ate, she pulled her wall-bed down and was soon asleep.

The next two weeks passed quickly. Amber continued to work steadily. Armand would arrive tonight. She expected his call any time. He had called just as he was boarding the plane. Amber was dressed in her new violet dress and wore violet open-toed strapped shoes.

Armand was delighted to see her as usual. He quickly embraced her praising, "Amber, you are one beautiful lady." She grabbed her *ambergine* leather shoulder purse and they left for dinner.

The conversation over their food was deep.

Armand's conversation was very serious. He wanted to know how she felt about him. Without telling her, he had ordered amethyst and diamond earrings for her Christmas present. Then, hopefully next year, he would present her with a ring in which the same stones were set. Their wedding rings would also be amethyst and diamonds. She would wear a beautiful brilliant cut, purple necklace on her wedding day.

In a serious embrace, Amber spoke. "Armand, you have weakened me. I care a great deal about you. I see you as loyal and willing to do almost anything for me."

"You have that right."

"I must admit, it has been difficult for me to concentrate so hard and know there is a gentleman who wishes to marry me. Am I correct?"

He kissed her, then asked, "How long must I wait?"

"Please let me finish my thesis; have it accepted; and graduate. Armand, you know I want to work."

"I believe all that is possible."

After their drinks arrived, he continued , "Amber, because your degree is what it is, there will be an office for you in our building. You will be able to work twelve feet from me."

She was flabbergasted beyond words. With tears rolling down her face, what more could she say? She thrust her arms around his shoulders and embraced him, finally finding words, "Thank you so much for your benevolence and your beyond-description job offer."

Smiling, he interjected, "Remember, I have not said what your salary will be. That must come from my family."

Their food only satisfied their stomach needs. There was far too much to talk about. They were planning their future. This made Armand feel on top of the world. He had won his lady. Now it was time for him to wait for her. That would not be easy; but he could plan his proposal. With these thoughts in mind, they drove to her apartment where, sitting on the love seat in each other's arms, he began to discuss religion.

She responded, "Armand, ordinary religion is mostly a derivation from the true path of guidance, which must come from within. You must have had some sense of my thoughts on this matter."

"Oh yes; I feel the same way. However, my color is blue. Will you be able to live with that?"

"Part of the *Etheric* world is blue. It is a color badly needed by many evolving spirits here. I don't like to use the word 'soul'. To me the word should be *spirit*. We all have a spiritual nature," Amber emphasized, "Religion is a hurdle we do not need to cross."

"Armand, your thoughts on sex in marriage, please."

"I'll try to respond but it may be somewhat lengthy. First, the man must be very attuned to his wife. From what little I have read, I understand marriages fail because of money problems and secondly, the man neglects to be tender, loving, and tuned to his wife in the intimate moments leading to satisfaction for her. I understand that the man becomes more fulfilled when he is able to bring her with him. That's what I have read."

He continued, "Of course I have not experienced anything like that, but it's my understanding, when celebrated in marriage with the person you love more than anyone else in the world, it's something to achieve together."

Armand added, "Please stay with me. When sex is performed, there is a possibility of the woman; that means you, Amber, could be impregnated. I believe I read you well enough, and you have spoken about not wanting babies, because you desire to use your mind in work: we say, forget babies.

"However, something needs to be done. An operation on you would be expensive. You could take the pill. I know medications are available for me; but I believe an operation on me is the most reasonable answer. If we change our minds, this procedure can be reversed."

He took a deep breath, then kissed her on the lips, in a long show of affection. He released his lips from hers, then looking directly into her sparkling eyes, asked, "Am I right on?"

"Absolutely, unequivocally, and unqualifiedly, yes."

More kisses followed. This evening's conversations lasted until the early morning hours, which meant a late start for Amber the next day. She told Armand, "Sleep in, then call me. I'll fix us breakfast."

In the morning she suggested, "I've been thinking, in the future, I'd be glad to pick you up at the airport. Then you wouldn't need to rent a car. Would you like that?"

"I would accept your offer, if I could drive you home and pick you up. I must continue courting you."

"Okay, that would work. My goodness! You have a strong desire for courtship."

"My dear lady, have you just realized that you are the one I wish to go through life with? When you have submitted your thesis, let me know. I'll come down that weekend."

Amber admitted to herself, she had heard a proposal. She pondered, *That means I'll receive two proposals.*

The conversation continued as she cleaned her little kitchen. Armand admitted, "I'll give you an idea of what to wear when that time comes." Amber said nothing.

As she studied, the week-end went Armand's way for a change. Her phone rang. It was Ben Barnes, who wondered if Armand would like to go to a basketball practice with him. He mentioned, he had seen the two of them together yesterday. Amber explained to Armand she felt this would be a good idea. "I'd be able to work all day."

Armand embraced her as he left saying, "I'll see you at five tonight." At noon Amber made herself a peanut butter and jelly sandwich on toasted bread. She drank a small amount of orange juice, knowing that too much Vitamin C interferes with the ingestion of vitamin B-12 which is critically needed for the immune system.

While the men drove to the campus, Armand asked Ben where there was a really nice place to eat. He admitted, "I want to propose to Amber. We are not much for loud music. Certainly most restaurants do not turn me on. Do you know of any really high class restaurant near here?"

"The first one I think of is a beautiful old, ornately decorated, elegant place in Mesilla, New Mexico, maybe 40 miles from here."

"That sounds great, Ben. If I drive down from Albuquerque, would you bring Amber and meet me there?"

"Armand, I would be happy to bring her and Marshara on a Friday night. I know Marshara would be glad to join us. The two of us could be on our way after we meet you."

"Golly Ben, that's a terrific idea!"

Ben instructed, "When you drive down, traveling south on I-25, turn right on University Avenue. Turn right at the second stop light and we'll be in the parking lot."

"Wonderful Ben. Could you arrange for some singers and guitarists to play for a half-hour or so?"

"Sure Armand! I have the phone number for the place. My parents eat there quite often."

"Terrific! Here is my business card. If I do not answer, leave a message."

"Armand, you must be excited. I know I would be. Amber is a very pretty woman."

"That's very true. Not only that, she's headstrong. She plays hard-to-get, too," Armand related with a smile.

"I see her as pleasant, but the love-deal must be reserved for you. She is really smart and applies herself," Ben responded.

The discussion about Amber stopped when they reached the Don Haskins Center. Then the two men talked about sports.

At five, Armand picked up Amber, who awaited him. One thing he had noted about Amber, she was always ready. He never had to wait. With an embrace, he praised, "I thank you for your promptness."

"You're welcome," she answered

At the restaurant, after he had ordered margaritas, Amber asked to please be let out of the booth to go to the restroom. *This is unusual.* He thought, *It has never happened before, but I imagine she is having problems with her menses.*

When she returned, he arose to let her in the booth asking, "Are you okay?"

"Yes, for now. As you may have expected, it's that time of the month which I hate with a passion."

"I cannot imagine what women go through just to be a part of the reproductive process."

"You have learned what I think about that process. It's asinine. Oh, let's talk about something else!

"I'll leave a week from Monday to be with my family for Christmas. Then I'll fly to Albuquerque to be with you. By the way, thanks for the tickets."

"I thought that was the only way I would have you with me."

"That's nonsense; she responded, as she mussed his hair.

"You have learned to irritate me. I don't like my hair mussed. What a rascal," he chuckled as he kissed her. When their drinks came, they toasted their future. With their meals ordered, she asked, "How does your family celebrate Christmas?"

"Very traditionally, but minimizing religion," he answered. This conversation was followed by politics, with definitive opinions being offered, as always. The evening was lovely because it produced more bonding.

The next day, after taking her to lunch and back to her apartment, he returned home. Amber stubbornly persisted with her thesis.

Before her trip, Amber needed to pack a suitcase and would carry her briefcase. For her plane flight she would wear a slack suit with a long sleeved blouse and soft leather flats. Amber laid them out the night before her flight. She had to be at the airport at five a.m. She was in bed early the night before. Her alarm rang at four.

At the airport she had to walk a long way after she parked. Amber pulled her suitcase with her purse over her right shoulder and carried her briefcase. She was surprised to see so many people at the airport at such early hour. She paid the fee for her suitcase at the airline counter. Security personnel opened her briefcase. Her purse was X-rayed. She passed the inspection for boarding, after removing her shoes. She thought, *What a mess to have to go through.*

Then her thoughts turned to Armand. *He has to go through this nonsense every time he comes to see me.* Once airborne, she worked with her computer until just before landing. She was greeted by her happy mother, who was warm and enthusiastically cheerful to see her only daughter, the youngest of two children.

The next day the two women went shopping. Since Armand would be taking her out on New Years Eve, Amber's mother thought she needed a party dress. Amber felt the ones she tried on were too revealing. Patricia insisted, "My dear daughter, what do you think he expects?"

One dress Amber liked was blue with crystals on the bodice and a dotted skirt, which flared with lots of fabric in motion as she walked. The bodice was cut low with narrow straps, revealing some cleavage. The dress had an open back and was zippered at the waist. The garment looked great on Amber. It would be her Christmas gift from her parents.

As a token of her love, she purchased perfume for her mother. She continued looking at clothes and found some slacks. She would need them next week.

At home after grocery shopping, Amber helped her mother prepare their evening meal. They discussed Christmas Eve and Day activities.

Later she took her dress out of the plastic to look at it, then sorted through her stash of shoes which she had not taken with her to school. Among her footwear was a pair of silver strapped medium heeled shoes with little beads on the top. They had an open heel and toe, perfect for the dress she would wear.

On Christmas Eve, after the preparations for following day were finished, her father made margaritas for them. Amber's dad wanted to hear more about this man in her life from Amber herself, not what Patricia had told him.

Amber related, "He is six foot one, slender with light brown hair which has a special cut, and is combed back and held with gel. His eyes are blue and captivating. When he comes to see me, he always wears a suit, but changes into shorts and polo shirts once he is with me. His older brother is the lawyer for the family business and has two children. His sister and her husband both have business degrees and work in the family business, as does Armand. With a little luck, I'll be aboard in the future."

Her father laughed with, "I guess business meets business."

The next day her niece, Sue and nephew, Raymond burst through the door shouting *Merry Christmas*, with her brother, Wendell, and her sister-in-law, Lily.

Because many preparations were proceeding in the kitchen, Amber took Sue into the living room where she held her and read from a book she had bought as a present.

After they were all seated, her father said a prayer and conversation began. A typical Christmas meal was served. Amber had made a gelatine cranberry salad. They all enjoyed mashed potatoes and gravy over the white meat of turkey. The dark meat was reserved for soup the next day.

Lily brought pumpkin pies. Amber enjoyed her desert, sitting beside little Sue, and helping her eat.

The opening of presents created a mess and exclamations of joy and happiness. Amber showed off the dress she would wear on New Years Eve. Seeing that, her brother admired, "If that won't knock the socks off that guy, nothing will!"

She coyly remarked, "That's the problem. He has already tumbled. We'll see what happens after I submit my thesis."

"How's it coming?" Wendell questioned.

"Fine. My goal is to submit it in February."

Her father questioned, "Amber, are you missing a gift?"

"I did expect something from Armand." Her father proceeded to his den, and returned with a small gift-wrapped box. Attached was a card which read, *Merry Christmas. Enjoy the contents.*

Hurriedly, she opened the box while everyone was still seated at the table. When she saw the earrings, Amber burst into tears. She was so emotional, her mother took the box and passed it around for the adults to *ooh* and a*ah* over. Amber gained some control over her emotions when the box was returned to her.

She took her old rings from her ears and replaced them with deep violet dangly earrings, surrounded with diamonds. No one knew what kind of stone the dark one was, but the earrings glistened, glimmered, and glittered as she tossed her head.

Her brother promptly announced, "Mom and Dad, prepare yourselves for a wedding--and not an ordinary one either. Plan a *whoop-de-do* party, because we have a businessman entering the family. It looks like a slam-dunk affair is in the near future."

Amber was still choked up. She waited until her brother's family left and the kitchen and dining room were put back into normal order before calling Armand.

Armand answered her ring. Amber began weeping and softly murmured, "Thank you so much, sweetheart. I am wearing them. They are so beautiful, I cannot thank you enough." She regained more composure, and asked, "No one here knows what kind of stone the dark violet one is."

"It is a round cut, dealers here call it 'brilliant'. The stone is an Amethyst, the side diamonds are *Baguette* cut. I hope you enjoy them."

"Armand, you did not need to go to such expense."

"You are worth it my love. Than you for the picnic blanket. Eventually, we will be able to lie on it in the park, if the weather is nice."

"Of course. Did you have a good Christmas?"

"It was fine. But I'd have been happier if you had been here."

"I'll be there in four days. Armand, please be patient. I love you."

"That I must do, goodbye, my love."

Amber's 'I love you' sent him out to his car, to sit and ponder about her engagement ring. He decided to talk to the jeweler, thinking, *I'll feel better if I get that in the works.* Because his purchase had been so recent, the jeweler went to his desk to find notes which Armand had given him earlier. The jeweler suggested a ring and any other jewelry for her would look better if the stone cuts and settings were all the same.

He also suggested, "Continue the *Baguette* cut for the diamonds. The shape of the amethyst in the earrings is round. Therefore, I'd continue that shape. Now, let me give you an idea how you can enhance the stone with diamonds."

He took Armand to a back room. At a table, the jeweler began drawing saying, "Diamonds of different shapes can be used. In fact, I personally prefer a setting which is enhanced by varying diamond shapes." He drew the ring in its actual size so Armand could alter the size and setting if he desired.

Armand was so captivated, he was surprised when his phone rang. His father ordered, "You have a client waiting." Armand left quickly, telling the jeweler he would be back after work to finalize his decisions.

After work he returned, becoming engrossed in what the jeweler was telling him as he described different diamond shapes around the primary stone. Armand decided the diamonds should be set asymmetrically around the main stone, on both sides. He wanted six round diamonds and three *Baguette* cut ones in the center of each side. He knew the size and color would determine the price. The deep amethyst color was in all of his choices. The jeweler's stones were from Brazil.

"I want you to have the ring design finished by next February 14th. It will be her engagement ring. In addition to that, I want wedding rings for Amber and myself in yellow gold like her earrings. Finally I would like you to design a necklace with amethyst and diamonds as a wedding gift."

As the men talked price, in the back of his mind Armand thought, *I'll not be able to make as many trips.*

He left a deposit, went home, and plopped on his king-sized bed thinking about what he had just done, as he fell asleep.

Amber was due to arrive on December 30th. Armand had a client and could not break away to pick her up at the airport. His mother volunteered to go instead. She knew Amber would be recognizable because of her height and light hair.

When Amber emerged from the baggage claim door, Celeste Rambulet was on the sidewalk waiting. She introduced herself and told Amber of the last-minute change in plans. The two women embraced and Celeste offered to carry Amber's briefcase. They chatted continuously on their way home. Celeste thought this was a good way to introduce Amber to their family. The succeeding conversations covered more about Amber than the Rambulet family.

Celeste informed her that she was planning a New Years Day dinner for all the family, including Armand's grandparents. Arriving at the Rambulet home, she showed Amber her room. After she used the bathroom, she had to dispose a menses pad. She growled to herself, "Having this at a most inconvenient time is a pain. I wonder where I can get rid of it?" She wrapped it and took it back to her bedroom and put it in her suitcase. She hung up her party dresses, the violet one which her parents had bought for her, and a green one. The crinkled-skirt she left tied up in her suitcase to maintain its crumpled effect.

When she finished with her dresses she went to the kitchen where Celeste was working. She asked for a place to dispose of the package in her hand. Celeste showed her the waste basket, stating, "Isn't that a pain in the you-know-where, that we have to deal with? I believe our evolution here is turned upside down. We need to use our minds instead of that sex-thing. I don't agree with this system at all. The *Great Mind* made a mistake. That's my opinion."

Amber agreed. After she washed her hands, she offered to help. Celeste remarked, "I hope you don't mind. There will be just the four of us, so we'll eat in the kitchen."

Amber responded, "I have no problem with that," as she set the table and helped make a lettuce salad. Then she carefully measured the ingredients. Celeste had instructed her to put the ingredients into a small bottle for their salad dressing.

"I hope you like scalloped potatoes. They are our favorite around here," Celeste asked.

"I love potatoes in any shape or form," Amber answered.

Armand's father was the first to return home. He rushed to her with outspread arms, praising, "Amber, you're all that Armand described and then some. Welcome, welcome! Did you have a good flight?"

"Yes. While in the air I worked at my laptop. Even with interruptions this week I have managed to do a little more work on my thesis."

"When do you expect it to be completed?" he asked.

"I am hoping right after Valentine's day, or at least before the first of March. Armand has been a big help for me."

"He told us you were progressing very well. Did you enjoy your Christmas?"

"Yes, particularly thanks to Armand's gift. I love my earrings. I wear them no matter what color dress I have on."

"Yes, they are beautiful. He gave us some of the details he had worked out with the jeweler."

Celeste looked at Amber's earrings more closely while Amber held her hair back. "Indeed, they are gorgeous." Then she questioned, "I wonder what has happened to Armand?"

He soon burst into the house and ran to Amber, embraced her, and lifted her off her feet, turning round and round, holding her tightly.

Amber pleaded, "Please, that's enough." She noticed he had fresh after-shave lotion on, a new shirt, and likely a new suit too.

"I'm glad you're here," she whispered softly.

"After you two complete your *lovey-dovey-ness*, we're ready to eat," Celeste announced.

Francis made drinks. They clinked glasses toasting, "To Amber and Armand." Delightful conversation and tasty food followed. Amber particularly enjoyed the baked fish and scalloped potatoes. The time passed quickly.

The kitchen was cleared and the family retired to the living room to learn more about Amber, and she about them. The family all had to work the next day. Celeste asked, "Amber, would you like to sleep in tomorrow morning?"

"Would I ever. I'll make lunch for you and dinner too, if you wish."

"I would be thrilled to come home to a home-cooked meal. What a delight. The kitchen is all yours. Snoop until you find what you desire. Good luck, because my cupboards need cleaning."

Amber slept late, dressed, then went into the kitchen for meal preparations. She drank juice and, while eating toast and pondering what to prepare, her mother phoned. Amber cut the conversation short, thinking, *Please give me some breathing room, Mom.*

After her mother's call, she opened cupboard doors to determine what line of food was in them. She began with a brownie mix. After the brownies were finished, she found a pan in which to heat canned soup.

She realized that the refrigerator was loaded with things she felt probably were reserved for New Year's Day. Amber thought the cheese looked good. After she had eaten the last slice of bread, she felt there must be more around. In the laundry room she found a fresh loaf in the freezer.

Okay, grilled cheese preparations coming up, she thought, as she set the table. She felt it was wonderful that Celeste would allow her to prowl in her private domain. Few women would permit someone else to snoop in their kitchens.

In the cupboard she found powdered sugar and cocoa and decided to make frosting for the brownies. She mixed cocoa, sugar, and butter, then added coffee a little at a time until the frosting consistency was correct.

As she slowly heated the soup, she began to brown bread on one side in a large skillet. When toasted, she turned the bread over, added large slices of cheese, and browned the other side.

Soon three hungry people entered, each wanting a little more attention than the other. Armand was so pleased to see Amber content in the kitchen, at least for a day. He watched as she finished her toasted cheese sandwiches.

She embraced him and suggested they be seated. Armand seated his mother, then helped ladle soup, while Amber gave each a sandwich, dripping with cheese, and made another batch.

Armand seated her saying, "God, this is good!" as cheese dripped from his chin. Francis muttered his thanks with cheese on his cheeks. Amber arose, cut the brownies, and brought a plate of them to the table.

Celeste commented, "That box of brownies has been in the cupboard for ages. I hope they taste okay." With Amber's frosting, they were soon devoured.

After the meal was finished, the women discussed what Amber should prepare for their evening meal. Celeste planned to come home early, mainly so the women could have some time together.

Amber cleaned the kitchen, then worked at her laptop until four p.m. She was setting the table when Celeste came home.

The women prepared the meal together with discussion of many topics, including Amber's thesis. Celeste told her that they were unusually busy due to the weak economy. Businesses were looking for cost-cutting measures, instead of having to discharge people.

The meal was ready when the men arrived. Armand greeted his ladies warmly, remarking how great it was to have hot, home-cooked food.

After the kitchen was cleaned, Armand took Amber to his townhouse. She did not know where he lived because they had always found other things to talk about.

His home was nearly new, located not far from his parents' home. She found he had no furniture except one bedroom set with a king-sized bed. The kitchen had an eating bar and two stools, no other furniture.

"Armand, you need more furniture. The place is bare," she observed.

"That's because I'm never here except to sleep and have breakfast. Most nights I'm either at my parents' home, or my brothers' or sisters' places. On weekends I work out, swim, and find something to do away from here. This place needs a woman's touch."

"I'm not certain about a woman's touch, but the place does need furniture."

"So it needs furniture. That can come later."

Armand then drove back to his parents' home where they talked for a short time before he returned to his house to sleep. He promised to take her out for dinner and to a movie the next day. His parents would dine out somewhere as they normally did on Friday evenings.

Amber was content to sleep late, eat something, and work on her lap top.

Armand called saying he would pick her up at six.

She bathed and dressed in the new violet dress her mother had bought at Thanksgiving. Amber looked striking because the dress color emphasized her light skin and hair. She was ready when Armand arrived. He was delighted to see her, and swept her into his arms, embracing her.

He was taking her to a very decorous restaurant, which he thought was the best in town. He had taken other dates there, but this night he felt he would enjoy the atmosphere more than ever. He was with the woman he deeply loved. That would make a big difference.

Amber was very relaxed. She conversed on and on about how pleasant his mother was and how she enjoyed prowling in his mother's cupboards.

Finally Armand turned her face toward his directing, "We need to talk about our future."

Her hazel eyes glazed with green when she was excited and playful. Amber acknowledged, "Sweetheart, we need furniture."

"My love, you will choose that. Now, please come closer to me." He kissed her as she put her arms around his neck, which was what he wanted. She kept her arms around him for a lengthy period, then looked at him saying, "Our food will be here soon."

"You always break up our embraces. Are you going to continue to do that?"

"Armand, most of the time we are in public. I'm a little more private than you are. Remember, we have embraced time and time again while we are on the love seat in my apartment. Those times have been lengthy. I believe part of this problem is that you need more reinforcing than I do," she whispered softly.

The remainder of the evening was warm and delightful, with an excellent dinner.

When they arrived at his parents' home he embraced her goodnight quietly, because his parents were asleep.

The next morning, Amber awoke hearing voices. She dressed and went to the kitchen to eat with Celeste and Francis. She was still tired. They told her about their advice to Armand, when he was considering purchasing his townhouse. "We insisted on two bathrooms with three bedrooms. The fact he has no furniture is due to our urging him to hold off."

She thought, *Thank heavens. I do not like his bed or dresser.*

Amber also asked about women he had dated. He never had become serious with any of them. Then Francis quipped, "He's never given any woman beautiful earrings like those you're wearing, Amber."

"I love them. Armand will not even allow me to pay the waiter's tip or small things like that."

"Armand can be strong-willed. We believe the same may be said of you. It's going to be interesting to see how two head-strong people get along. So far, it appears to be working," his father smiled.

When the kitchen was in order, Armand's parents left to shop for groceries. Amber napped. With the door closed, she did not hear them when they returned home.

She awoke and went into the kitchen to help prepare food for the next day. Celeste had asked if she would make a gelatine salad.

Amber found the ingredients, heated water and prepared the gelatine, after asking Celeste if she had any cream cheese.

"There is at least one package in the 'fridge', Celeste answered, adding, "That and store-bought bread are two things we are going to have to live without because Eleanor, our daughter-in-law, whom you will meet tomorrow, is becoming a health-food freak. Be prepared for remarks about sugared gelatine, corn sugar, and cream cheese. All soft cheeses contain a bit of aluminum from their processing."

Amber thought, *This is all part of dealing with different individuals in families.* His parents ate lightly. Amber had a small bowl of soup then went to prepare for her special evening with Armand, who would arrive at seven.

After she was dressed and replete from head to toe, she came to where his parents were sitting. Their mouths were agape. Armand's dad exclaimed, "My god! Amber, you will sweep Armand off his feet even more than he is now! Celeste, we must prepare ourselves."

When Armand's car approached, Francis suggested, "Amber, please duck into your bedroom." He closed her door. When Armand entered the house, he expected to see her. Instead, with great animation and fluster, his father spoke lovingly, "Son, may I present to you, Amber Breddgeforth." She followed him into the living room.

Armand put down a hair corsage, attached to a hair clip he carried and greeted Amber with tears in his eyes. He buried his face to one side of her cheek, so his parents could not see his emotion.

His parents joyfully watched as he took the corsage from its package, and gave it to Amber. She pulled back her hair on the left, and placed the flower, exposing her earring. This action impressed Armand. Holding Amber's hand as they left the house, he bid his parents, "Goodbye. We'll see you next year."

Then they were off to dinner, dancing, and merry-making to welcome in the new year. Armand hoped that the new one would be the year in which he would marry his lady, who had so totally captured his affection.

He and Amber ate a good meal toasting each other with margaritas. She caught glimpses of him stealing glances at her bodice. She purred sweetly, "I've skin exposed, which evidently you admire."

"Yes, indeed, my love. All I can say is that you certainly know how to enrapture me."

When their meal was finished, their drinks had relaxed Armand. He wanted to dance stating, "My love, I will hold you close in hopes I'll be able to lead you properly and you'll be able to follow. It's been a while since I have danced, and never with a lady more lovely than you." He stretched his left arm to hold her hand. His right was on her bare back. Tepid, haptic sensations flowed through his body. They took their first steps. Their bodies moved smoothly with suavity allowing her dress to enhance their movements, which were polished and planned, with bodies closely pressed.

During their dancing, he whispered sweet secrets to her. She returned his remarks. Occasionally they would rest, sip more of their drinks, then continue dancing.

Their evening progressed until midnight. The crowd yelled, screamed, threw confetti, blew noisemakers, with whoops, hollering, and shouts, *Happy New Year* in the first moments after midnight. Lengthy kisses and embraces between the lovers followed. He whispered, "To our new year."

Amber did not answer. She was growing tired and put her head on his shoulder, breathing in the exhilarating whiffs of his after-shave lotion. She closed her eyes thinking about this evening. She never believed she would fall in love with this man whose persona she found intoxicating. She wondered how she could return her mind to finishing her thesis and completing school.

He guided her off the dance floor to the exit. Once in the car she began to weep. She was releasing tension from an evening which one could only dream about, being away from school and her thesis.

Concerned, he parked in a lot and went to her side of the car. Opening the door he requested, "Please sit in the back seat. She scooted into the seat while he climbed in and locked the car. With his arm around her, he put his face next to hers, kissed away some of her tears, and embraced her.

Through her tears Amber mumbled, "How am I going to be able to crack the books and finish my work?"

"My love, I'm sorry if I am interfering, but I want you to do your thing. If you don't finish, you would regret your decision for the rest of your life. Besides, I know your job depends on getting that degree."

He held her in his arms holding her right hand. "Do you feel better now?"

She softly murmured, "Yes, thank you."

He opened the car door and helped her into the front seat again. On the way to his parents' house, they conversed about their wonderful night and holiday.

When they arrived at his parents' home, he opened the door and kissed her goodnight reminding her, "My love, I have to wait. Now you need to hurry."

She took off the flower clip and quickly prepared for bed. She wasted no time because she was tired. As she went to sleep, she remembered this delightful night.

She slept late, then dressed in a green high-collared garment, green sandals, and prepared to assist with the meal preparations.

Francis and Celeste had also slept late and were at the kitchen table when she entered. Francis stood and greeted her marveling, "Wow, you look terrific." Grabbing a box of cereal, Amber began relating what a wonderful time she had enjoyed last night. Sitting at the table, she related how noisy the place became at midnight. "I'm used to quiet and peace, not noise-making."

Celeste had two standing rib roasts in the oven. Potato peeling was her next priority. Jennifer, his sister would bring vegetables, Eleanor, his sister-in-law, was bringing desserts and home-made bread.

At three, Armand arrived with a chocolate torte, which was put in the refrigerator. Amber left her room and came to meet him. He embraced this green-clad lady who looked like a princess.

Jennifer and Ronald were the next to arrive. They embraced and welcomed Amber. "What a delight to finally meet you," Jennifer responded.

When Eleanor and Jeffory arrived, Gabrielle and Gilbert were beautifully clad, Gabrielle in a dress, Gilbert in a suit. When Armand's grandparents arrived, they too were well-dressed. All the men wore suits and ties.

The men finished work in the kitchen, while the women relaxed in the living room with drinks. When the call came to eat, everyone came to the table while Francis brought the food on a cart. Being the guest of honor, Amber was seated at Francis's right. Celeste was seated at the other end of the table.

Francis offered a short spiritual thanks for the new year and the joy of family. Then the food was served. The conversation was lively with the grandchildren offering their thoughts, as the food was consumed. Everyone was hungry. The food was devoured in short order.

After they had eaten dessert, everyone pitched in to help with the cleanup. Francis was in charge of storing the leftovers. Amber played with Gabrielle. She found her to be a delightful youngster. She was happy to be able to know this child better. The women gathered in the living room. Conversation flowed freely.

When Armand came in, he related, "Tomorrow, Amber flies out. I need some time with her tonight."

They left. He drove to a lighted business parking lot and stopped under a light. He opened her door and helped her into the back seat and locked the doors. He thought it was the only option he had to be alone with her before they all retired. He planned to take her to the airport in the morning, before work.

In their last moments alone, Armand expressed his devotion, relating how her coming into his life had changed him drastically. He held her in an affectionate embrace and kissed her repeatedly. When she reached around his head with her arms, this gesture especially pleased him.

She purred pleasantly and softly, "Armand, no man has affected me like you. I love you, sweetheart." He expressed his love openly as he helped her return to the front seat. He drove to his parent's home to allow Amber to tell his sister and brother's families goodbye.

Back in the living room, Amber seized the opportunity to greet them all by offering, "The next time you see me will probably be at our wedding. Armand understands I must complete my thesis; have it accepted; and graduate. After that it will be Armand's turn."

He embraced her in front of his family, and looking into her eyes, he growled, "I must wait and she must finish that damned thesis."

The household resounded with laughter. The family parted and Amber went to bed. The next morning after breakfast, he took her to the airport.

They parted with many *I love you's*.

Chapter 3.

*O*nce on the airplane, with her seat back, she reflected on her experiences. The last few days had done wonders to give her confidence Armand was indeed the gentleman she loved.

She never took her computer out of the briefcase. Instead she focused on what she needed to do, beginning tomorrow. In her car, she called Armand to tell him she was on her way home. He responded, "Thank you for letting me know my love."

She unloaded her car. Once inside, she unpacked her suitcase and hung her dresses, including her New Years Eve dress. After that, she grabbed a glass of water. Sitting, cross legged with her feet over one end of the love seat she called her mother, who was very irritated she had not called her earlier.

Amber's explanation was, "I'm so sorry, Mom. I know you knocked yourself out to make me look spectacular. I appreciate that very much. I was with people I had never been with before. I wanted to focus my attention on them. They are very down to earth and wonderfully thoughtful, like Armand.

"I met his sister, Jennifer, and her husband, Ronald, who have business degrees and work in the company. Then I met Eleanor and Jeffory. He is a lawyer. They have two beautifully-mannered gracious children. The family gives them lots of attention.

"Our New Year's Eve was delightful, Mom. I've fallen in love with him, but my thesis comes first you know. Tomorrow I'll work all day here unless I need to look up something. I'll call you sometime this weekend. I love you. Bye bye."

Amber bought a few groceries so she would be able to focus on her work at home.

Armand did not call every day. She used her computer continually. He knew e-mails would be useless. She focused on the task at hand, carefully watching her typing and sentence structure. At this point she felt that the activity was just plain drudgery. However, at the same instant, she realized she was crafting words and theories proving her ideas were indeed, a production which had taken nine months so far. She would need another month to finish.

Amber was managing her time well. She called her mom on weekends, but on Friday nights, Ben, Marshara, and she went to movies. They all were struggling with their own theses.

On Saturday evenings, Armand would call, spending an hour talking with her to fully recharge his battery. "I'll be down the last weekend in January."

"When you come sweetheart, I want you to carefully read through the options concerning a business which is facing failure. I believe in most cases, something from a firm could be salvaged. There are ways out of insolvency.

"My routine is to mull over ideas, thoughts, and concepts, then committing some of them to paper. I'm finding that this writing has so many pages, I'll need to put it into some other form. When you wrote your thesis, did you find the pace drudgery at times?"

"Not only that, it was a pain in the butt!"

That statement made her laugh. "I guess what I'm doing is preparing to publish what I have labored and plugged along with for these many months."

"My love, you are nearing the final production. I'll come down and help. I think I'll drive this time. It's less expensive."

"When you come don't rent a motel room. There's an empty apartment down the street. No one will be coming this late in the year. Maybe they will rent it to you, for just using the bed. I have an extra set of sheets you may use. You could eat with me."

"That sounds like you know how to conserve funds. My love, we will make a good team. Good night for now, I love you."

"Goodnight. I am looking forward to your visit."

Amber was doing no unnecessary twaddling in her typing. Facts were divulged in detail, whose function was to prove her points. What she was working toward, was revealing her professionalism. True, she was going through a day-by-day grind, but she was able to concentrate, and hand-craft her document which, when finished, would be hard-bound. Her parents insisted on that, even though the cost would be higher.

When Armand arrived, she had procured the key for the empty apartment. Their embraces were numerous before he went down the street to unload his suitcase from the car.

While waiting, she made a lettuce, tomato, cucumber, and onion salad. *Onions are good for us. Forget the after-taste and what it does to the breath,* she thought. She began browning hamburger, then added the rest of the onion, tomato sauce, corn, and baked beans. When her food bubbled, she added tacos. Seeing Armand walking up the street, she applied lots of cheddar and white cheese. When the cheese melted and formed a crust, they could eat.

When Armand entered, he embraced her with thoughts of, *I wonder if this is part of the future?*

Her hot dish was superb. They both ate hungrily, while talking happily. They were together for another weekend, even though he would be spending some time reviewing her latest work.

When she told him her thesis was very nearly finished, his thoughts sprang into action. *I must have that ring finished. I'll check with the jeweler as soon as I'm back home.*

As he read her work, he found one area which needed a few extra sentences to explain her concepts. She accepted his proposed changes with a flourish and a cheek kiss. After that he found another void in her writing. Otherwise, there were no problems.

The next night, their entertainment was a silly movie. After such concentrated effort they said, "Why not relax?"

On Sunday she fixed breakfast and spent more time typing. At noon he took her out to eat. Her small apartment was getting to him. He did not want to read any more of her thesis, either.

After eating he took her to the mall. She wanted to go back to her apartment but Armand had a better idea. "Wouldn't you like to do some window shopping?" In the mall, on stools, drinking specially flavored coffee, Armand admitted he was proud of her and her perseverance. He told her the thesis was great, she had done a fine job. They shared lots of affection before it was time to take her back to the apartment and him head for home. As they parted, he embraced her saying, "I'm not coming back to see you until your thesis is finished, completed, and accepted. Goodbye, my love."

Driving north he turned off the freeway at the University Avenue exit in Las Cruces. He took note of the ramp he would be exiting and noted the traffic lights and the shopping area where he would meet Ben, who had told him he had talked with the beautiful old restaurant's management, had contacted musicians and a photographer. However, they all needed a date before finalizing their availability. Ben didn't have that information at that time.

Amber worked in her routine, crafting the final pages in strain and toil which could only be understood by others who had finished, or were going through this labor to its end. Only they could understand the effort which was spent.

When she finished, her neighbors heard her shouts of "HURRAH HURRAH", in exuberance. "IT'S DONE!" She took her work to Professor Phillips, who would review it and have other professors evaluate it as well.

She returned home and called Armand, shouting, "I've submitted my thesis. It's finished. HURRAH."

His answer came swiftly. "I'll be down this weekend. I'll drive." This meant he must make the final payment on the ring. Armand called Ben saying, "Plan to have the musicians this Friday night at six-thirty p.m." His plan was being completed. Ben would drive with Amber and Marshara to meet him.

Armand then contacted the place for dinner, and ordered chocolate and flowers to be delivered. Over a noon hour, he rented a tuxedo for himself and drove to the jewelers to obtain the ring and check on the beginning work for their wedding rings and her necklace.

Before he left work the Friday before Valentine's Day, he called Amber and asked her to look especially pretty. "My love, Friday night will be our night. Ben and Marshara will bring you to Las Cruces. Please be ready for them by five-thirty."

Pretty in a new dress, she responded, "I will, and besides, I love you."

They ended their phone conversation with more *I love you's*.

Armand then called Ben, giving him the final details. He left work early in order to arrive in Las Cruces by six-thirty. He became more excited the closer he came. He exited on University Avenue, he spoke to himself, "Just a few more minutes."

He was thrilled to see them waiting for him. He embraced his love, then helped her into his car. He followed Ben and Marshara to the restaurant in Mesilla, which was a big help for him. On the way, he lovingly emoted, "You are stunningly beautiful."

"Thank you, "you're handsome in your tuxedo."

"Yes, I wanted to do the evening up right."

When they arrived at the old, but elegant place, a hostess seated Amber in an area to the right of the entry, in an antique-filled room. Armand asked to look at the table which had been reserved for them. The musicians were waiting. Red roses were in a vase near the chocolates. He went to Amber and helped her arise. The hostess led them to their table, which by then, was the center of attention for everyone in the room.

The photographer began to capture pictures. Armand seated Amber, who now had tear-filled eyes. He kneeled on one knee, holding the ring in his left hand. Using his right to steady her finger, he asked, "Amber, my love, will you marry me?"

"Of course," she murmured quietly. They embraced as the musicians began their guitar serenade singing and playing love songs. Amber was too overwhelmed to hear them. They played for a half-hour, while Armand and Amber drank to their future and they waited for their food to arrive. Their conversations centered on the question of when they could be married.

"It will be after graduation. Weddings take lots of time to prepare properly. I will not be hurried. I don't have a calendar with me, do you?"

Armand obtained a small one from the waiter. Together they studied it. Amber suggested, "Would the first Saturday in August work?"

"Oh my! Yes my love," as he embraced and kissed her.

As this thrilling evening progressed, Amber began to notice the beautiful ambience of the restaurant. Gold leaf covered the ceiling; mirror frames; heavy draperies, and gilded chandeliers were beautiful in the low light. This was a perfect place for a proposal. "Armand, how did you find this place?"

"Through Ben." This statement ended with another kiss. The photographer left when their meal arrived. Light rays flashed from Amber's ring as she moved her hand. "Do you like it?" he asked.

"Of course, because you gave it to me. It's exceedingly beautiful. You gave a ring with my favorite color. Oh, thank you so much," Amber mumbled softly, then threw her arms around his neck in a full embrace.

The ring had a large, deep violet stone and was surrounded by diamonds in varying sizes enhancing the brilliance of the center stone.

"Now I have a bride to-be. I'm elated." Occasionally, their conversation was disjointed at times, from their excitement.

"Thank you for the flowers and candy."

"You're most welcome."

The happy couple left the eating establishment rather late, heading for El Paso. On their way, Amber asked, "What kind of a wedding do you want?"

"A big family one."

"Being the only daughter, I know we will have a lovely wedding, which will mean tuxedos for the men, including the ushers."

The next morning they slept late. Armand ate breakfast with her. He asked, "What will my wedding expenses be?"

"You only pay for my flowers; but tux rentals and anything else you wish for your attendants are up to you, and of course, the honeymoon."

"I'll enjoy planning that."

"The first thing to do, is start lists." Soon their conversation drifted back to her thesis. She asked, "How long do you think Professor Phillips will take before he calls me?"

"That's hard to determine. The number of other theses he and his associates need to read, will make a difference."

"I know Ben and Marshara are still working on theirs. I don't know if anyone else has submitted one."

The lovers ate dinner out that night, followed by a movie.

The next day, he left for home after dinner.

During her wait, Amber called her mother often in the evenings. Many of their conversations covered wedding plans. They exchanged ideas.

Her mother had begun a list of what she would like to see done on Amber's big day. She found a judge who would perform the ceremony.

For Amber, the wait was becoming unbearable. When she tried to call Armand during the day, his phone was disconnected, which meant he was with a client. He answered her calls in the evening.

In March, he drove down again. The weather was pleasant. On Saturday, he purchased chicken salads, french fries, and cold drinks to eat on the blanket she had given him. Amber had no problem lying beside him, with their arms around each other before they ate. Other people were in the park.

To have her beside him in a loving embrace, after they had eaten, was a dream come true for Armand. He held her so close to his body she could feel the hardness in his abdomen. He wore briefs with his penis upright.

This experience made Amber ask questions about what he expected from her when they were married. "What, when, and how much sexual activity are you expecting?" she questioned.

His emotions were no different than they had been previously. She caught him off-guard. He brought her face close to his and softly answered, "My love, I do not know. Much of our loving of each other will depend on your romantic feelings. However, I realize it will be up to me to help generate those feelings. So far I have not been disappointed."

Armand emoted, "I think much depends upon my approach to you. To make our marriage work there must always be consideration of your emotions. I believe timing in intimacy is as important as understanding the other's feelings at the moment. From what little I know, I believe much of the initiating falls upon the man. Most men rush into those precious moments much too rapidly."

Amber added, "I admit, I must do more reading, since I have little background in sex, I will need to be prepared, otherwise I'd be ripped apart."

He kissed her saying, "My love, that will not happen. When a man loves his spouse, that's not possible. I love you too much. I want to spend the rest of my life with you. Therefore, rushing our experiencing of each other in marriage would be a huge mistake. By the way, after I go back, I'll have my operation. Is that okay in your mind?"

"Of course. That's the easiest answer."

She kissed him all over his face. He kissed her back. Flirting with each other and sharing deep thoughts took most of the afternoon.

She then asked, "How did you come to pick the design and the stone of my ring?"

"Since you are such a violet lover, I did not think a diamond would suit you. I worked with the jeweler and we both played around with the stone, shape, and cuts. Incidentally, our wedding rings are in the works, using the same stone which means I'll wear your color. Our wedding rings will be *Bezel* set with colored stones and diamonds together. I chose yellow gold because I like that better than rose or white. Needless to say, I spent some time thinking about our rings. The jeweler was a big help."

"Sweetheart, I will pay for your ring. That is my gift to you. I want other women to know that THIS MAN is taken." She tickled his chin, put her hands over his eyes, then kissed all over his face, ending on his lips.

Armand had to admit, he was loved and embraced. The day was becoming cooler. Amber helped him fold the blanket. She took their lunch remains to a garbage container. After the drive to her apartment, Armand went to his rented room to freshen up. As usual he took her out to dinner.

The next day, Amber fixed breakfast. They spent the day away from her apartment. In the late afternoon, he returned her home, then left for his drive back to Albuquerque, and work on Monday.

Later, Amber spent her spare time with Ben and Marshara. As they ate in the student center together the men could see that she was extremely happy.

The men plugged along with their work while Amber anticipated a call from Professor Phillips. She became so keyed-up over not hearing, she went to his office. The professor asked, "Do you have time?"

"Yes."

The professor directed, "In one place in your dissertation, you put in why a crisis occurred. That's not clear. I understand your conclusions."

Amber explained her thought processes as she wrote that portion.

"One page would be sufficient to clear up my question," Professor Phillips directed. Then he prepared to leave. She departed for her apartment, thinking over what she had neglected, and how it could be corrected.

Amber spent the evening adding to her thesis, realizing she had made a silly error. Finishing her correction, she added a typewritten page, using both sides of the paper, and made a copy for the professor.

She went back the next morning. Professor Phillips, being very authoritative, agreed that her added comments were necessary. He congratulated her. "You have now successfully completed your thesis. I will reward you with your master's degree. I suggest you go to the print shop and obtain a day and time for the printing of your work. Please make copies for all the professors in the department including me, of course."

He shook hands with her. Amber's enthusiastic body language and emotions burst out with, "Oh, thank you so much." She went off to the printer, calculating how many copies she would need. She remembered her parents wanted a copy, and they insisted that it be hard bound.

Continuing, she thought, *In addition to my copy, Armand and his father will each want one."*

She set a date and time at the printers. As she walked, she was so giddy, kicking her long legs swinging them at times, she nearly interfered with other people on the sidewalk. She hummed a tune which included 'Mama Mia', a song which the singing group ABBA had made famous years ago. Time did not matter. She was thrilled and excited.

She arrived at her apartment and relaxed on the love seat, drinking water. She called her dad at his work. He responded, "Did you have it hard-bound?"

"Yes, Dad, it'll be done next week, I'm so excited." She then gave her Dad the date of graduation finishing with, "Dad I love you."

Hanging up the phone, she shouted aloud, "I DID IT--I DID IT!"

She called her mother, whose line was busy. She left a message on her answering machine. She then talked briefly with her brother, Wendell, who praised her for her endurance.

Unable to help herself, she then called Armand. When he saw her number on his caller identification, he knew why she was calling at this time of the day. He responded with, "My love, you are bursting with news."

"Oh, Armand, my thesis goes into print next Tuesday afternoon. I am so excited I can't contain myself."

"Congratulations! My love, you have a job waiting, but your salary is undetermined at this point in time. I'll come down next weekend. You'll need to select office furniture and equipment. The firm will wish to use the next three months to pay for your purchases."

"My goodness, Armand, my ambitions are coming true. What a thrill."

"I must run, my love. Don't burst your seams. I love you."

"I love you too."

Three weeks passed rapidly. She assisted her friends and some of the professors, to kill time until Armand came. When he arrived, he made certain they went to the park with box lunches. They teased each other in their joy. She tormented him by covering his eyes then kissing him all over his face, except his lips. He patiently waited until she found them.

Though fully clothed, he found haptic sensations in his abdomen with his mind working overtime, imagining such encounters after their marriage.

In Armand's mind, there was absolutely no question that he loved her, and that she loved him equally. He questioned to himself, *What would living with her for a year bring? Will I love her more? Will she love me more?*

He enjoyed her attention, but eventually she grew tired. She lay quietly on the blanket waiting for him to say something. Finally she queried, "Are you day-dreaming sweetheart?"

"Of course. I've never been happier. Just think, in three weeks, you'll be graduating. I'll fly down. We can load your car for our drive to Albuquerque. We'll drive back on Sunday after graduation. You can stay for a few days before you go back to Oklahoma City to continue making wedding plans." He felt very loved.

Finally the Friday arrived for him to fly to El Paso for her graduation. On the plane he thought back of all the phone calls he had made. As she worked on her thesis, she did not answer his e mail messages.

She was waiting at the airport. They ate dinner at a steak house not far away. He took her home, then went to his motel not far from the campus. He ate breakfast with her. They spent the morning strolling in the campus and walking in the Haskins Center, where the graduation exercises would be held.

Amber became more excited the closer her family came to El Paso. Getting ready for the ceremony, she dressed in her apartment then went to Armand's motel where he was waiting for her. He helped her out of the driver's seat and to the passenger side. Then he drove to the motel where her family would be staying.

Chapter 4.

The night before Amber's graduation, in the dining room of a hotel on the west side of I-10, close to the campus, Armand met her mother, Patricia; her father, Dennis; her brother, Wendell; his wife, Lily, and their children Sue, aged four, and Raymond, seven.

Armand was sociable. The family could see the affection he had for Amber. He held her hand as much as possible. The family saw her beautiful ring. She explained their wedding bands would contain stones cut from the same amethyst which was in her diamond engagement ring. They talked until the children were put into bed. Armand had purchased a cuddle toy for each, thinking this may help them sleep better.

"I will come to your home when Amber needs me to help plan our wedding. My love, please don't ask where I'll be taking you on our honeymoon." Kissing her he continued, "I want to surprise you, as well as have time together for our first two weeks."

Dennis expressed, "Honeymoons are important because that's about the only time you have together until the kids are grown."

Armand answered, "I've undergone a vasectomy. Amber has expressed very strongly to me she wants to work and not be tied down with babies. I agree with her."

He continued, "Since I believe I know what you are thinking, I have not been intimate with Amber. For one thing, I know she would have said 'NO'. That action would show I did not respect her personhood. I would have lost her."

"Mom and Dad, Armand is a gentleman and always has been. He

certainly went out of his way to court me. I was impressed, not just with his conduct, but because of his own self-esteem and knowledge of what he desired in a wife. I respect him so much, I cannot find words to express my affection for him."

Continuing she said, "There's a park not far from the campus where we would go, sit on a bench and talk. Sometimes we would just contemplate or meditate. Like me, he has no affiliation with any religion. He has deep respect for his personhood. That's why he respects me. We are made for each other. There is nothing we have not discussed."

While she was speaking, Armand looked at her with a warm loving bond of affection. In his mind, there was no one for him but her. After these conversations, Amber left her sweetheart and family, returning to her efficiency apartment.

The next morning, wearing a deep blue-violet, princess-style dress to make her look taller, with violet sandals gracing her feet, she ate breakfast with Armand and her family.

She donned her cap and gown in Armand's motel room. She gave him her car keys. He dropped her off close to the graduation ceremony. A short distance away, Armand found a drive-in eating establishment. He talked to the manager asking if he could park the car in their lot. A little conversation with a generous tip assured a place for her car.

When he arrived at the *Don Haskins* center, swarms of people were entering the area. He spotted Amber as he climbed the stairs. She had told him in what row she would be seated, near the main aisle. Thinking ahead, Amber had found a red rectangular card for Armand to hold up so he could be spotted by her family. Armand found seats and was soon joined by all her loved ones.

Amid the pomp and circumstance, they heard Amber's name announced, to receive a master's degree in *Business Crisis Management*.

After the ceremony, Amber waited for the crowd to clear so she could greet her family before they left for Albuquerque. Her parents had obtained rooms in an Albuquerque motel for that night. Armand embraced her with a kiss purring, "Congratulations, my love."

Arm in arm, they walked out together. Her family faded into the many departing bodies. Armand took her hand and remarked, "You will never believe where I parked."

"Armand, In this mob of people, parking must have been very difficult," she declared.

He walked slowly allowing her to keep up with him. She had trouble holding her cap in place, so he carried it for her. "I was thinking proudly of you graduating with honors at your first commencement, before you started at UTEP," he stated.

She spotted her car in the fast-food lot and exclaimed, "Armand, how were you able to park here?"

"My love, it's money along with love that makes the world go round," he smiled, as he helped her into her seat. In the car he asked, "What would you like to do now? I'm not hungry. How about you? Let's go to the park. We can sit on a bench and talk our hearts away."

"That sounds wonderful," she sighed, removing her gown.

With an embrace and a long kiss, Armand marveled, "Wow, you are stunning in that violet dress." When she released her lips, his eyes were twinkling with confidence and self-assurance, which she admired so much.

He embraced her again, "Golly, I won't have too much longer to wait."

"What about tomorrow?" she asked.

"When do you want to leave?" he queried.

"Let's pack the car tonight. I'll collect my personal belongings and meet you for breakfast. After that we can head north."

"Sounds good." They went to her apartment. Both carried her belongings to the car. The trunk was packed, after which they put suitcase on the floor. Her dresses filled the back seat almost to the windows.

This effort made them hungry. They went to a restaurant on Mesa Street. They toasted each other, then talked until Amber became tired. She drove to his motel, then returned to her apartment.

On Sunday morning, Amber greeted him. They ate breakfast together. He paid the bill, insisting, "I am still courting you, my love. I hope I never get over my happiness of being with you."

"I hope so too."

She settled behind the wheel for the drive to his home. After a brief stop, Armand drove the rest of the way to Albuquerque where their arrival was impatiently awaited.

Amber had dressed in light-weight violet slacks with a yellow top. Her slip-on shoes had a cork heel with violet and yellow flowers on top. For ease and comfort, she had pulled her hair back with violet clips. She wore the amethyst earrings which Armand had given her.

Celeste and Francis were watching for them. Hurrying out the door, his mother greeted Armand. His father welcomed Amber as they entered the living room. Celeste suggested that Amber stay in their guest bedroom.

"Phew! I need a little time to catch my breath," Amber admitted. "I'll return to Oklahoma City to work on wedding preparations. As we drove north we confirmed our wedding day will be the first Saturday in August," she offered. "But only Armand knows where we will be going on our honeymoon. He refuses to tell me. Armand, I will need to know what kind of clothing to pack."

"Shorts, swim suits, skirts, and blouses should do."

"Then it will be warm there?" she queried.

'Yes, for sure."

For their honeymoon flight, she would pack summer clothing in a suitcase which Armand would ship to where they would stay. He needed to pack his own things later. Since the other family members had not arrived, Amber and Armand decided to go to the townhouse to unload her car and hang up her clothes. Later she would determine what to take with her to Oklahoma.

They returned to his parents' home. Soon his brother, Jeffory, the family attorney, with his wife Eleanor and their children Gilbert, and Gabrielle, came. Finally his sister, Jennifer, and her husband, Ronald arrived.

After a pleasant Sunday dinner with plenty of conversation, Amber revealed some of their wedding plans to the family.

The families returned to their homes early enough to prepare for their work day tomorrow. Amber and Armand cleaned the kitchen, permitting his parents to relax.

Amber had not been in Albuquerque other than to pass through. Armand drove around to acquaint her with some of the streets east of I-25 and north of I-40. She remembered he had turned off I-40 on Tramway. They had driven this street to his parents' home on a short street with a queer name in a new area. His parents home was nearly as new as his townhouse.

Amber had directed Celeste, "Please do not cook anything for our supper. We'll put something together when we return from our explorations."

Armand was feeling on top of the world as they drove.

Amber explained to him she wished to select some furniture before she left to go home. At this time nothing was in his townhouse except bedroom furniture. She would have selected something different. After a wonderful sight-seeing ride, they ate a light supper. Armand then went to the townhouse to sleep. He would come to the house for breakfast before his parents departed for work.

Chapter 5.

The next morning Amber dressed in her crinkled violet skirt with a printed violet top. With her hair falling to her shoulders, they left for the family business, *Rambulet and Associates, Inc.*

In Armand's car, they traveled west on Montgomery Boulevard east of I-25. The *Rambulet* building had smoky-glossy sides with four stories of office space. It was rectangular, with entrances in the center of three sides. The freeway was on the fourth side. The doors led to lobbies and elevators. The center of the building was completely open, permitting light from a large glass roof prism to illuminate the entire atrium.

Offices were placed on the outer walls, allowing each office to have an outside window. In addition to the elevators, wide beautifully carpeted orange and yellow stairs led to the upper floors. Entering, Armand asked, "Would you rather take the stairs, or the elevators, my love?"

"I'd like to climb," she answered.

The family offices were on the top floor. Amber greeted his parents, each in their own office. Armand showed her his office, which had a lovely desk, chairs, shelves and a computer with all the necessary software.

"Oh Armand! Your office is beautiful," she marveled.

"Thank you. The empty space next door will be yours. You may select your own furniture later."

"Wow! My mind is overwhelmed," she exclaimed. "I noted that my office overlooks the freeway. Armand, this building is beautiful."

"That it is, my love. It takes a lot of family people, working shoulder to shoulder to make a business work," he explained.

They went back to his office. She asked, "Is there anything I could do now?"

"Please pull up a chair. I'll turn on my computer. You can follow the information if you like." He explained what he was doing at the time. He turned off his computer saying, "You'll be doing something similar to this."

They spent the morning together, then walked hand-in-hand to a nearby café, still talking about their future. With a gentle kiss on her cheek, Armand spoke, "I love you."

"I love you, too sweetheart," she replied.

At lunch they discussed furniture, first for her office, then for the townhouse. "Armand, when we come home from our honeymoon, I don't want to come to a house with no furniture."

"Which pieces do you think would be the most important?" he asked.

"Probably living room items. Sofas, side chairs, and lamps, would give that room some life," she suggested. They recognized that they must purchase more pieces over a period of time.

After lunch, they departed to shop, first for office furniture, which would be a business charge, and then furniture for the house. Armand stated, "My love, I'll be happy to purchase furniture for us," thinking *I guess I better hold onto my credit cards.*

After the purchases were made, on their way back to the house, Armand urged, "I don't want to see you drive back to Oklahoma City unless the weather is good. There is enough worry over travel, without being concerned about the climate, too."

"I agree. I'm not looking forward to going home except to make wedding plans," she answered. Armand went back to work while she stayed at his parent's house. They carefully watched the weather reports. She talked with her parents' more often than she had done when she was in school.

The furniture arrived at the townhouse. Amber directed the delivery men where the pieces were to be placed. Afterward she packed a suitcase to take home. She showed him a two-piece bathing suit, which made Armand whistle.

When they returned to his parents' home she decided to drive to Oklahoma City the next day, if the weather permitted. The next morning, Celeste and Francis bid her goodbye. Amber promised to call Armand when she stopped for lunch. He filled her car with gas and gave her several hundred dollars, for emergency use.

"No, sweetheart, I can't accept this money," she argued.

"Please my love, take it. It will help ease my worry."

"All right, if you insist. I plan to drive the whole way. I'll stop only for food and gas. I'll call when I arrive home."

He kissed her warmly, and embraced her, holding her more closely than he had ever done, stating, "My love, be careful and always stay alert. I-40 has some terrible traffic."

She was on the road by seven to eliminate some of the city congestion. Once on the freeway, she put the car on cruise control, remained alert and did not listen to the radio. She kept her eyes moving constantly. At Amarillo, she called Armand when she stopped for lunch. He was glad she had progressed that far.

"I find it hard to keep my mind on my work," he declared.

"I've moved right along but I'll be glad to reach home and kick back," she admitted.

"I'll be happy to hear you've arrived."

After she ate, Amber stopped at the ladies room and used clips to pull her hair back. She filled the gas tank and was on her way. In the car, she called her mother to report her progress. Patricia admitted they were certainly thinking about her.

At Weatherford, she stopped for a walk, a break, more gas, and a snack. As she walked, she called Armand to report her progress.

"My love, I'll work late tonight. Please call as soon as you arrive home," he asked.

"My home is on the west side of town, actually in Bethany, north of I-40."

"Be cautious and careful, my love. This separating must stop," he insisted.

"You're correct. I'm ready to get in the car for the final push. I'll talk to you tonight, hopefully around seven, six, your time"

"Oh sure, the time zone change. I'll have to remember that when I come to see you."

"Goodbye, sweetheart."

"My love, I love you. Goodbye."

She whispered, "I love you too."

Amber pushed her car, making good time. At ten minutes after seven, she pulled into her parents' driveway. She gave a big sigh of relief.

Her father, who had been watching, opened the garage door. She called Armand, saying, "I am in the driveway. Dad has just opened the door. I love you. I'll call tomorrow around breakfast time. Over and out."

Armand thought, *That's Amber, direct and to the point, but by golly, you know where she stands on any subject.*

Amber slept late. Armand was at work when she called. He remarked, "I thought you had all ready forgotten me."

"Sweetheart, I was exhausted."

"I'm sorry, I did not mean to be curt. Please forgive me," he begged.

"I'll take a few days to rest up, make dinner, then begin to plan our big day. I'll need you and your families' measurements. Please relate this information to them, " she requested.

"I'm already so darned lonesome I don't know what to do with myself. Last night before I went to sleep I patted your side of the bed. I'm wanting you near," he affectionately related.

"Oh yes, you have talked about nearness before. I believe I understand what you mean, but how near is near?" she asked, laughing.

"My love, you know the answer to that question. Why must you tease?" He didn't find her remark funny. He was serious and she was not.

Finally she spoke, "I can tease because of the distance between us. Tell me how you're doing? How long have you planned to work and where will you eat supper?"

"I'll work late because I'm lonely. I'll fix something simple at home," he replied.

"How do you like the furniture?"

"It's fine, but what the hell good is it when you are not here to enjoy it with me? Who in bloody blazes wants to eat by himself all the time?"

Amber realized he was missing her terribly and was depressed. "Please, sweetheart, when you are home, start to make a list of people you want to invite. Have your parents do the same. Tonight I'll e-mail you. Keep busy, I'm lonely for you, too. Besides that, I love you. Goodbye, sweetheart."

"Goodbye, my love."

After that conversation, Armand walked around inside the building. A question came to mind. *Where do we go on our honeymoon?* Over his lunch hour, he went to a travel agency and obtained some booklets on places to go. He wanted a location which had a golf course. Neither he nor she had played golf for a long time.

He was reading brochures when he remembered to check his e-mail. Sure enough, she had written, *Mother insisted that I keep all the money which I didn't use. I used Mom's credit card and went grocery shopping. I made supper for us which delighted my parents. They asked me to greet you. It was wonderful to relax and day-dream about you and me, together finally. Though, when you think about it, we have known each other for a year, sweetheart. I love you. I wish I were in Albuquerque because I hate the sticky, humid, lousy climate here. I'll e-mail you again tomorrow. I love you.*

The next day at work, he e-mailed her relating, *I was looking at advertisements from resort hotels. I've not reached any conclusions. However, when I do, you will not know my decision.* His e-mail note was surrounded with red hearts.

Amber felt she needed to look for a gown. Her mother suggested the store where they usually purchased their clothes. Amber called and arranged for a meeting before noon on Saturday.

At the store, Amber and her mother looked at gowns. She was careful in her garment selections and was not interested in trying on one gown after another. She had definite ideas and could make decisions quickly.

One particular dress interested Amber. Her mother insisted she try on this expensive garment which was tightly fitted white satin. Over that was a slinky, flimsy fabric which would give movement and flowing fashion to the garment. The bodice was covered with ruffles of satin folded, then stitched. Sparkling beads were sewn into the fabric and scattered in other areas to catch the light.

Once Amber was dressed in this beautiful gown, both she and her mother thought the dress was fabulous. Her mother announced, "You are a stunning lady, in a gorgeous garment."

Amber had purchased white satin shoes the previous day which matched the gown perfectly.

Noon time came. Amber asked the clerk if they could eat lunch before looking at any more wedding accessories. The clerk agreed, saying she would begin to make some pre-selections for her. During lunch Patricia called Dennis regarding the gown. It was costly. She wanted to make certain she would not be growled at for going overboard with these purchases.

Amber felt a little awkward and stated, "Perhaps I need to work awhile before this event."

"Don't be silly," her mother remarked, "You know your father and I always talk over any large purchases. You are our only daughter, it's our time to splurge. Your father recommended we go ahead."

After lunch, the next selection was a veil. The clerk had several veils pre-selected. Amber did not want to try on very many because they would muss her hair. The clerk helped her put on the gown again. She placed a veil on Amber saying, "This is my first choice." She had the fabric folded in front permitting the back of the veil to fall below her shoulders. Then she lowered the front. The top of the veil was held in place by a small cap-like form with beaded netting, like the bodice of her gown. The two looked beautiful together. Amber wanted to look taller because her husband-to-be was over six feet. She asked if there was a tiara which could be attached. The clerk replied, "Please let me look." The clerk returned with several, asking, "Which of these would you like?"

Amber selected one and put it on top of her veil. She was pleased. The fabric hid where the tiara was placed. The clerk thought Amber had made a good choice. She asked Patricia, "What do you think?"

"My daughter's choice is fine. I compliment you on your veil selection." Amber was now fitted and looked ever so much like a bride. The clerk opened a door to the bridal room for a photograph. Her dress needed no alterations. She was a perfect size ten.

Amber wanted to hold something. A prayer book or man-made flowers were available. She wanted neither. Patricia asked Amber, "Will white lilies do?" Amber felt they would be suitable.

Her mother went to a nearby florist where yellow, orange and red lilies were on hand, but no white ones. She settled on a beautiful white catalaya orchid, which the florist put into a plastic bag to protect it from the wind. Her mother carefully carried this beautiful flower to her precious daughter thinking, *I hope Armand is indeed a gentleman deserving of our daughter. Sometimes the heart becomes caught-up in love and does not see hidden problems.*

Seeing the orchid, Amber burst into tears saying, "Mom, I did not want anything this expensive."

"Honey, they had no white lilies or roses. It was this or nothing else."

After drying her tears, Amber was photographed standing, holding the catalaya after her veil had been lowered. Her mother thought, *she is going to be a beautiful bride.*

Amber was divested of all her selected finery. Her mother placed the flower back into the bag. The gown and veil were properly packaged for Amber and her mother to carry.

When they arrived home, her father remarked, "Did you buy out the store? My god! Women take forever to shop. I'm glad I stayed here."

As the women were carrying in the beautiful purchases, Dennis made lunch.

As Amber showed her father the purchases he remarked, "By god Amber, you better look good in that outfit, or I'll be mad as hell! I hope Armand will be worth it. Patricia, why in hell are you holding that flower?"

"Dennis, I am holding it carefully because it was expensive. I have to determine what I can put it in."

"I must say, it would look good on you," he grudgingly agreed.

Amber hung her gown and unpacked the veil. She laid it on her bed temporarily, and went into the kitchen where her mom was still standing, holding the orchid. Amber went to the garage, obtained a food cooler and added ice cubes. She carefully laid the flower, with the glass tube into which it had been placed, into the cooler. "That should work," she announced.

Dennis thought to himself, *Good gosh, this is just the beginning. I better get used to money flying to the credit card companies. All this because my daughter has found a man she says she cannot live without. Just what in hell does he know about what fathers go through! Shoot fire, he has not even asked me for Amber's hand.*

"Amber, Armand ticks me off," he spouted in his annoyance.

After their meal, instead of e-mailing she called Armand.

"Hello, my love," he answered, rather surprised, "What have you been doing?"

"I'm so excited. We purchased my gown and veil today. I'll be so beautiful you'll be awe-struck," she exclaimed.

"My darling, I am love-struck with you," he lovingly replied.

"Sweetheart, Dad is so mad. In fact he said he was mad-as-hell, because you have not asked him for my hand."

"Indeed, he's correct. I've been so moon-struck by you I have not thought of him, and a father's ego. I need to come over soon and rectify that situation. How about next week end?"

"That sounds fantastic sweetheart."

"I'm lonely. I forget what I am doing. I'm making mistakes. I must go over my work carefully. All of this is due to you, my love," he emoted, "I'll fly. I won't attempt to drive. I'll arrive as soon as possible for a couple of days with you. I'm out of this world in love with you. I'll purchase tickets tomorrow," he stated.

"That'll be fine sweetheart. We can make plans together. I'll have a list prepared. Bye bye. I'll be looking for you."

"Goodbye, my darling wife-to-be." He called later announcing, "I'll arrive at six, your time next Friday evening. I'll return on Monday afternoon. I love you. Over and out." (He wanted to beat her to the punch with this comment.)

She drove to the Will Rogers Airport to meet him. Before leaving home, she had prepared their evening meal. Earlier she had made a salad and set the table.

On the flight Armand mulled over in his mind where to take her for their honeymoon. He went over points for each of the resorts he had considered. None suited him completely.

She waited in her parked car because Amber wanted him to embrace her in a slightly more private area. When he walked out of the terminal she shouted, "Over here Armand!" She was jumping up and down in a dress he had not seen.

He was wearing a gray suit, white shirt with a blue tie and cuff links. Putting his suitcase down he enfolded her in his arms, kissing her with so much strength she tried to back away. He continued to hold her. His lips slid from her mouth to her cheek, finally freeing her. "My goodness, you were lonely," she uttered.

"You're darn right. It's frustrating to have a wife-to-be yet still be alone."

"Honey, you need to learn a little patience," she urged, as they walked to her car, hand in hand.

On the way home, he asked about tornado shelters. She told him, "When Mom and Dad built the house, an underground cement shelter was part of their plans. We reach it from a small basement partition. I'll show you," she said.

"Good, I won't have to worry about that."

"My parents' home is nearly new. They had it built after I started to college when they were certain they would not have to pay for my schooling. Winning that scholarship was terrific for my ego. Here is our street. The house is on the right, with the double car garage. Using her electronic opener, the door lifted.

She added, "We listen to weather reports carefully. We have good *Doppler Radar.*"

"That's good to hear." He climbed out of the car as she pushed the button to open the trunk. He retrieved his suitcase and grabbed her again requesting, "I need another embrace."

After their hug, with his small suitcase in one hand, holding her with the other, she led Armand into the house. Her parents were delighted to see him and welcomed him warmly. Amber showed him the guest bedroom with its attached bath.

"When you have refreshed yourself, we'll eat," she offered.

She helped her mother put the meal on the table.

Armand seated Amber's mother, then Amber. He was allowed to serve himself first, then pass the food on to her father.

He noticed there was no liquor served. When he took Amber out, especially when they dined, they always had a drink, usually champagne.

The conversation flowed over dinner. She told him what she wanted to do the next day. Once they finished the meal, he and Amber tidied the kitchen.

Armand concentrated on how he would ask Dennis for her hand while he helped rinse the dishes, working beside her.

When they finished, Dennis was seated in his favorite chair with a book. Armand went to him, kneeled on one knee asking, "Mr. Breddgeforth, may I have your daughter's hand in marriage?"

Her dad was taken aback by this sudden request of his soon-to-be son-in-law.

"Yes, of course, Armand."

Armand arose and embraced Amber tenderly in the presence of her parents saying, "I love your daughter very much. I go nuts being alone."

After breakfast the next morning Amber, Armand, and Patricia went to the hotel to arrange for the ceremony, and then a ballroom for the reception dinner and dance. Her mother signed for these affairs.

Amber then drove them home where her father had prepared lunch. She thought, *This is terrific on Dad's part. I want Armand to show the same concern after we are married.*

After lunch Amber and Armand went shopping for a tux. He realized she was going all-out. His tuxedo would be white with tails, tie, and the works. He was also fitted for white shoes. While shopping, Patricia told them, "Go back to the hotel and work out a menu, design your cake, and remind them children will be present."

Amber asked Armand, "How many guests do you think will come?"

His answer was, "Perhaps fifty. More may come if hotel sleeping arrangements could be made."

She suggested, "Since the first Saturday in August is our day, why couldn't we have a family get-together on Thursday night with those who want a little vacation? We could have rooms blocked off for families."

"That would be great," he exclaimed.

At the hotel they met with the chef to arrange for their wedding dinner. They directed, "Non-alcoholic drinks only, because children will be present."

The chef asked, " How many people will be in attendance?"

Amber looked at Armand, saying, "I would suggest 150."

Armand agreed, "I think that number would be fairly close."

They determined their cake would be three-tiered, topped with white wedding bells. The groom's cake would be chocolate with cherries.

At the registration desk, they asked for fifty rooms to be set aside for out-of-town guests.

Next they stopped to order invitations, then went to the photographer. Their visit with him took so long Amber called home saying, "We're just finishing. We'll call when we are on the way."

Going through all this fuss and detail made Armand feel good. He was becoming more at ease. *Certainly Amber is in control,* he thought, *but when hasn't she been in command?*

When they were in the car, Armand called, informing her parents they were on their way. In the car she asked him, "Why did you want cherries in your cake?"

"My god, Amber, I am so sorry! I did not think of that! Mom makes a very good chocolate-cherry cake, which is a favorite of mine. Please call the chef and insist he omit the cherries." With a deep breath, he growled, "That was a horrible idea. See how important you are to me. I make mistakes all over the place."

"Yes," Amber replied, "After we are married you will have all the cherries you want!"

"Indeed, but what a woman," he sighed. Hand-in hand, Armand opened the kitchen door for her. He kissed her mother on the cheek, then went to refresh himself. Dinner was ready.

Their dinner was late because of their delay at the photographer. Her mother admitted, "Our attitudes and ideas do not matter. We both want Amber to have a beautiful wedding, and special day." Patricia was interested in what they had decided for food, rooms, cake, and invitations.

Their dinner conversation turned to the idea of a family gathering on Thursday. Her parents felt this was a good idea. Children could swim in the hotel pool. As they talked, Armand learned that Dennis had been raised on a farm in Garfield County.

"I graduated from Enid High school. At the University of Oklahoma I earned a degree in Mechanical Engineering. After graduation, I accepted a job in Oklahoma City. I'm still with the company. I'm glad I am, or I would not be able to pay for this wedding which is going to occur."

Amber laughed, "Dad, that's what happens when you have a girl baby, or was that all Mom's fault?"

"Amber, my daughter, you know who determines the sex of a child. I cannot look elsewhere. I determined your sex perhaps, but your personality and individualism are yours, and yours only. You predetermined those characteristics before coming into earthly existence. In fact, you were encouraging your mother and me to have sex, because the entity which was to be you, was looking at us. In other words, you wanted us to be your parents this go-round."

Amber hugged her father leaving a kiss on his cheek saying, "Dad, you are terrific, but please don't beat up on Mom over bills which result from our event."

"I've never beaten your mother. If anything, she beats-up on me," he laughed.

Armand chuckled over the remarks being bandied about. He blurted, "Am I causing a family quarrel?"

Dennis quickly spoke, "This is just a family discussion. What kind of disagreements occur in your family?"

"Oh, my parents really can argue with minute details, mostly over business. Sometimes I am able to intercede," Armand added. "So often, a difference of opinion is based on incorrect data. My family business will be set straight by your lovely daughter, who captivates me completely--well almost totally," he smiled.

Dennis admitted, "Armand, I've been observing you. I know you are smitten just like I was. When we men fall for a lady we move heaven and earth to obtain her, which almost always includes asking her father for her hand. Yes, I will be delighted to place her hand on yours, after which, you pay the bills."

"Dennis, I'm certain you're correct. I've bought some furniture she selected for the town house. I've already determined she does not like the bedroom set and the bed I now sleep in," he admitted.

"Armand Rambulet, that statement was not nice. Dad, I guess I must admit, when the right man comes around and one is smitten, then one must put up with the undesirable characteristics along with the good ones." Amber scolded.

Standing straight and tall, Armand responded, "Amber, I will so overwhelm you with my love-making technique, you won't care what bed you are in, or what city or state!"

Now Amber's face became flushed. He lovingly embraced her, then looked at her parents, saying, "See what I mean?"

Laughter resounded. Dennis retorted, "My dear daughter, you have your hands full with this man. Since he is your choice, you cannot blame us."

After dinner Amber took Armand to the Murrah Federal Building Memorial site. He was immensely impressed. The sight, particularly of the tiny chairs commemorating the children who were killed in the attack made him weep. Facing the reflecting pool, he quietly prayed. Standing beside him, Amber did the same.

Hand-in-hand, they silently walked to the car. Once seated, Armand admitted he had never been so moved. "However, I have not seen that many memorials either."

She asked, "Would you like to see the Cowboy heritage museum?"

"After the Murrah Memorial, I'm afraid I need time to reflect. May we go back home?"

Amber saw the quiet, reflective side of him for the first time. She knew he enjoyed talking about esoteric happenings. In her mind, she thought, *perhaps he is remembering how he met me and escorted me so well in a past life. Now I am escorting him.*

Having accompanied her in a new experience, Armand realized no other woman had ever been so understanding and loving toward him.

Back home in her living room, they discussed the memorial. Armand reflected, "Something like that is so powerful, the good energy which is there is overwhelming. I really felt the need for prayer."

She responded, "You know we both believe in prayer, but I do not want the trappings which all brands of religion bring with them." After a pause she continued, "I've been stupid for too long. It's time for me to wise up. I am assuming you will be the one to help me this time around."

He replied, "So far, I believe I'm helping you. With a lifetime ahead of us, I hope we will be able to meet whatever challenges lie ahead."

On Monday, Amber took him to the airport. He embraced her passionately saying. "I can't do this many more times or I'll go nuts."

With her arms around him, Amber hated that they had to part. She reasoned, that's the way love works. As he waved goodbye, he called, "Don't forget to call the caterer."

In her car, Amber's thoughts were about the man she was engaged to marry. So far he met her every expectation, but what he had said last night caused her to wonder, *No way will I be a sex slave once we are married. Perhaps I need to clarify my thinking to him again.*

Her thoughts continued, *He knows I have not slept with any man. I know what I expect of him. Does he know what to expect of me? I doubt very much if he could 'con' me into not caring where the bed was, or in what city. His power was showing, which was all right, but marriage is a give and take situation.*

Once back home and into his work week, in his spare time Armand determined he would take her to San Diego for their honeymoon. He reserved a honeymoon suite for one week. The following week, they would spend the night wherever they wished. These plans kept him high on life. He could settle his mind on his work because time was winding down.

He received wedding invitations to address, which kept him occupied after work.

Amber's next e-mail notified him she had talked to the caterer. No cherries in your cake, sir. Her mother had procured an official to marry them and had arranged for a time to talk to the florist. As only she could do, she wrote, *Hang onto your wallet. You must buy the flowers I will carry. I love you. Amber.* She entered a smiling face. (☺).

In another e-mail she wrote, *I have written invitations, talked with my girlfriend who works in St. Paul. You will like Delores. My friend Miranda is from Dallas. The girls will wear gold dresses. You and the men will wear gold cummerbunds. I love you.*

His e-mail reply was, *Madame, what else do I need to do? I love you. Armand.*

Her response, *Bow to the east once in awhile. I love you, Amber.*

He purchased tickets to visit her again over the July Fourth holiday.

She had placed the flower order and had given the florist ideas for a background and how the corner of the Will Rogers Room in the hotel was to be decorated. She had visited the department store and selected china and stemware, along with daily dishes and glasses. She had the name of the clerk and department number, as well as the store phone number to ease the purchases for people who were not able to visit the store in person.

The last e-mail he received before he left was, *Please think about music. What do we want played or sung as people are being seated? Also, have Jeffory, Eleanor, Jennifer, Ronald, and your niece and nephew send their clothing measurements. They must be in our wedding party. I love you, Amber. Over and out.*

Chapter 6.

*A*mber met Armand at the airport to begin their July Fourth holiday. They were delighted to see each other again. After embraces, going to the car Armand announced, "This will be the last visit I'll fly. In three weeks, I'll drive to be with you until our big day."

"We're receiving invitation responses. I'm beginning to feel excited," she emoted, "Have you given any thought to music?"

"Yes, I've written down some ideas."

"Good. I need help. What music will we use when we walk toward you? I've met with musicians and for now told them to use some of their own songs. This 'marching' music has me stumped, though."

"Really, this shindig is more your doing than mine. I'm afraid I can't help you."

Later, just before Amber went to sleep, she thought of a neighbor who played the flute. She would ask him to play the waltz from *Romeo and Juliet*. Then she thought it would be great to have that aria sung. Thinking more, she decided to have the aria sung before the ladies walk toward the men.

Her parents had planned an old-fashioned Fourth of July Celebration. Patricia decided that would be a good way to introduce Armand to Amber's family.

The lovers peeled potatoes for salad. Her mother planned to make a crock of baked beans. Cabbage had been purchased for slaw. Wieners and hamburger would be grilled.

Grandma Breddgeforth was bringing Waldorf salad. Patricia's mother and father were bringing wiener and hamburger buns.

Wendell, Amber's brother and his wife Lily, would bring carrot cake. Armand helped Dennis clean the garage. The patio would be put to use grilling and serving. Armand was happy to be a part of this hubbub. He was thrilled to be able to wear shorts and comfortable clothes. The humid weather made his clothes stick to his body. He thought, *No wonder Amber complains about the weather.*

The weekend flew by. Armand enjoyed being a part of her family. He was doing his best to create a good impression. He made certain he seated Amber and was affectionate with all the family.

Armand met cousins and Amber's niece and nephew, Sue and Raymond, who remembered seeing him at graduation. Armand joined them in throwing *Frisbees* or playing ball. The exercise made him warm and he left to go into the house to wash his face and neck, thinking, *before I crawl into bed tonight I must shower.*

Family members left and everyone else went to bed.

The foursome awakened with a mess to clean up. Armand pitched in. After breakfast, tables were taken down allowing the cars to be returned to the garage. Storms had been forecast. Only heavy rain with strong wind gusts came. The patio was cleared before the clouds let loose.

Armand vacuumed the living room, while Dennis cleared the dining room table. Amber was at the sink loading the dishwasher while her mother handed dishes to her.

Cleaning took most of the morning. Amber's parents were very appreciative of Armand's help. They could see he had drive, which a businessman needs. The more they saw of him, the greater respect he garnered in their eyes.

When Amber had finished, she went to Armand, who was still picking up and kissed his cheek. He stopped, placed his arm around her waist, purring, "Just like home. A woman's work is never done. They work and toil and receive no respect." His eyes glittered with thoughts of his lady.

After lunch the lovers sat on the sofa talking about food, music, band, dancing, invitations, and tuxedos. Yeah, just like I don't know where we will be going on our honeymoon. Armand, that's not fair. You would not like secrets kept from you."

"All right my love. We'll be able to golf. There is water. The weather is nice. It's Southern California," he divulged.

She put her arms around him, "How wonderful." He told her family he had chartered a private jet for his family to fly to Oklahoma City for the wedding and return to Albuquerque on Sunday. "We can fly with them, then catch our flight to San Diego."

"My god! Armand, that'll cost an arm and a leg," she exclaimed.

"My love, it beats driving all to pieces. Besides, we will need both of our cars at your home to bring wedding gifts back. I'm not looking forward to that chore. At least we will be in tandem. I'm glad most of my clothes are with you all ready."

"I must admit, when I am lonely, I go and touch your clothes. Then I feel better," he admitted.

"I think we are both ready to say 'enough' of this back and forth business. Now it's plans for the ceremony," she reflected.

After Armand left to return to New Mexico, Amber checked with the neighbor who played the flute, asking him to play the waltz from *Romeo and Juliet* at her wedding. Honored to be asked, he accepted.

She found an operatic soprano, who had studied with an opera company in the east, but who presently lived in Oklahoma City, to perform her music.

When these details were settled, she drove to the hotel making certain the men and women would have a place to dress. From there she went to the department store to direct the clerk in what hotel room to place the ladies' gowns. Next she visited the tuxedo store, giving them the room number where tuxes should be delivered. She felt this idea was better than having the men pick up the tuxes at the store.

Finally, at the florist, she asked for two tall white candles for the bride and groom to light during the ceremony. This was a detail she had almost forgotten, but it was an important one. She felt people needed to know they were committed to each other and that neither one had ever experienced a sexual partner.

Downtown, she grabbed a bite to eat, then went to the limousine office to make certain they had the times and location correct. She looked forward to the limo ride to the airport. She told them, "The final trip will be to the airport's private jet area."

While downtown she went back to the department store looking for a larger shoulder purse and a large beach-type bag she could carry on planes.

Her parents were at work. She arrived home late, but in a short time she had the meal well started and the table set.

Over their meal, her parents marveled about what a fine man she was marrying. They were happy to have met him.

"Mom and Dad, he is honest, sincere and always respectful. These qualities are not easily found these days."

Amber was delighted her bridesmaids were flying in on Tuesday night before their big day. She told both of them they would stay at her parents home. Armand would have an opportunity to meet and talk with them. He would arrive on Monday.

The weekend before the wedding, all three thoroughly cleaned the house. Simple food was prepared. On Sunday, they went out to dinner. At the meal Amber spoke, "I must check to make certain tuxedos fit the boys and the gowns fit the girls properly." Later in the day, she called Armand asking, "Please don't forget our rings."

"I have them, my love," he replied. That night he was so excited he put the rings in the jacket he would wear on the plane and put the garment in his car. He could not forget those rings. Amber had sent money for his, which pleased him so much. He knew she was an outstanding lady. He packed a small suitcase he would carry aboard the plane. After that he showered and went to bed with his mind filled with marvelous events which were going to happen this week. *Ah yes, I will have won my bride. From here on, she will be with me,* he thought, as he fell into a fitful sleep. He was too excited to sleep deeply.

He awoke at 4:30 a.m. He thought, *Shoot, since I can't sleep I'll get up and put on my shorts. I know it will be humid over there I might as well get started.*

After a very early breakfast, he shaved and put his equipment into his suitcase. His cell phone was attached to his belt. He double-checked everything, making certain he had all that he would need for the week and climbed into his car.

Wasting no time, he was on I-40 a few minutes after five. He settled into his car and joined the traffic flow. Time passed rapidly. He was thinking of his bride-to-be, but it was too early to call. At eight Amber's time he called saying, "I left shortly after five. I'm passing Tucumcari now. I'm heading your way as fast as this vehicle will lawfully take me. I love you or I would not be going to this extreme."

Amber answered, "Be careful, sweetheart. Call when you are close and I'll guide you to the house." Because her mother did not have a recipe for chocolate-cherry cake, Amber called the *Oklahoman* Newspaper food editor who found one and e mailed it to her.

After receiving his call, she immediately began the cake, checking the recipe carefully. The final addition was maraschino cherries, which she cut in half. Tonight she would tease Armand about his cherries. Her parents who were at work, knew nothing of this story or what she had planned.

Patricia and Amber had shopped for groceries the previous day. The refrigerator and freezers were packed. After returning home they prepared menus. Amber was free. She felt that cooking at home was less expensive than eating out and it would give her something to do.

After the cake was made she prepared a gelatine salad with multiple colored layers of cream cheese and cherries. She planned to give her sweetheart cherries in every shape and form, including a cherry pie ordered from the local café, which they would pick up tomorrow.

She made a bite to eat for herself at noon. She had not heard from him. *"Where is he?"* she wondered. Soon she answered a call from him, "Hello sweetheart, where are you?"

"I'm at Shamrock, Texas ordering lunch," he responded. "I've gassed up. As soon as I eat, I'll continue the grind. I'll give you a call when I'm almost there. You can guide me to the house. I love you."

"Goodbye, sweetheart, I've been working in the kitchen. I love you. Over and out."

Armand continued his drive. She grated cabbage for tomorrow night's salad. Amber then went to the store and purchased steaks.

Back home, she set the kitchen table with place mats and dishes. She then prepared the dining room table, using fancy place mats and good china for this special meal tomorrow evening.

Her mother arrived, still in her nurse's uniform as Armand's call came. Amber directed him, "Sweetheart, take exit 143, then turn left going under I-40. Continue heading north on Rockwell Ave. At 30th street turn left. Call and I will direct you to our home."

Amber had made a hamburger hot dish and green beans in a dish with onion rings, which she liked. She then became excited and went outside to watch for him.

When he saw her waiting, his heart skipped a beat. He climbed out requesting, "Please put your arm around my neck." He kissed her and picked her up, carrying her inside, greeting her mother on the way.

Patricia greeted him saying, "Welcome, we are certainly thrilled to have you here safely."

"I'm immensely happy the time has come for me to be with Amber. I about went nuts over there by myself."

Patricia responded, "I believe plans are finally coming together."

When he went to his car, Patricia put an opened book on his bed and returned to the kitchen. She did not know what Amber had prepared. Checking the oven she was happy to see the hot foods which were beginning to smell 'yummy'. On the counter sat a lovely cake with chocolate frosting. She knew Amber had been busy.

Dennis arrived while Armand was removing his suitcase and overnight bag from his car. The men embraced outside. Her father held the door for Armand.

Once in the bedroom, Armand saw the open book. He went back to his car for trousers and a sport jacket and placed his jacket partially over the book so it would not be noticed by anyone passing in the hallway. He refreshed himself. The food smelled good.

He joined Amber in the kitchen saying, "My love, I need another embrace." She kissed him requesting, "Sweetheart please be seated."

He quickly retorted, "Not until I seat you, my love."

Everyone dug into their food hungrily. "This is delicious," Armand praised. Her parents had worked a comfortable day. Everyone was happy and contented. When their meal was finished, before dessert Amber asked, "Sweetheart, could we see the wedding rings?" He placed the ring boxes beside her plate while she and her mother cleared the table. They returned with the dessert. He seated both ladies. Amber noticed the boxes, quickly opened them and became teary-eyed. Her mother agreed they were very special.

Eating dessert, Patricia stated, "Armand, I feel honored to be seated by you."

Dennis rejoined, "After a while married life is just that."

"Dad, I hope not."

Then Armand asked, "My love, what am I eating?"

"That's chocolate cherry cake. Since you like cherries, you shall have them even before our marriage," she smiled.

Armand's face became very flushed but he said nothing.

She continued, "Armand wanted chocolate cherry cake for the groom's cake. I said no to that nonsense. He now has his cherry cake and our wedding day has not arrived."

Amber and her parents laughed. She had one-upped her love. Armand was quiet.

After the meal, with the kitchen in order, Armand asked Amber if she felt like a walk. She agreed. On the walk, he embraced and kissed her several times, then announced, "I don't like being embarrassed before your parents."

"I'm sorry sweetheart. I could not pass up that joke." As they walked, he did not mention the book. Back in the house he placed a polo shirt over the book so she could not see what was underneath if she came into the room.

Her parents retired at nine. She and Armand talked until ten thirty then went to bed. Patricia and Dennis left for work before the lovers were awake. This night both would be home early to meet incoming guests.

Her sorority friends would stay in bedroom with single beds. In the afternoon Armand drove his car, which was larger than Amber's, to pick up her friends. Amber directed him to the airport. The first to come was Delores from St. Paul. An hour later, Miranda arrived from Dallas. On the way home, the car was filled with bubbly excited conversation. This was the first wedding party for both visitors.

Amber's parents were home when the giggling, wise-cracking girls bounced out of the car. Armand carried their bags into their room. "Ladies, enjoy your space as much as I do mine," he offered.

He took time to read the chapter of Patricia's open medical book. The subject covered proper cleansing before intimacy. He felt it was appropriate information. He went to Patricia in the kitchen and thanked her for the advice. Patricia asked, "Armand, are you taking saw palmetto extract, pumpkin seed, or something for your prostate? Begin to treat yourself now Armand, so when you become middle-aged your prostate will remain its normal size, without enlargement."

"Yes, I have read about prostate problems. My urologist related to me the need for supplements. I've been too sedulously occupied to shop for those things. Thanks for your suggestions."

"Please take time after your marriage to help your body," she suggested.

Amber and Armand had forgotten to obtain the cherry pie. Dennis went after the dessert, not mentioning the oversight to anyone.

Amber came into the kitchen. Both Armand and her mother indicated they were doing fine. Dennis started the grill, which was soon ready for the steaks. He took individual orders for how the meat should be prepared saying, "When the steaks are finished, I'll put them on your plates immediately."

Armand helped Patricia put potatoes, vegetables, and condiments on the table. Individual salads, prepared by Patricia, at everyone's place.

Armand requested all the ladies remain standing until he could seat them. Patricia was seated first, followed by Amber and then the two guests.

Dennis finished the steaks as ordered, serving his daughter first. His wife was next, followed by the guests then Armand and himself. Conversation overflowed. Everyone felt his steaks were delicious. The men listened much of the time while the ladies chatted.

Dennis requested the ladies remain seated while he and Armand cleared the table. Having been around the kitchen long enough, Armand knew where the leftovers were to be placed. As Armand cleaned plates he saw the forgotten pie. "Oh my gosh, we forgot to pick up the dessert."

"You kids were so high on life, I went for it after you returned."

Dennis cut the pie into six identical pieces, impressing Armand with his accuracy. The pieces were served with ice cream. Armand served his bride-to-be first, then Patricia, the ladies, his father-in-law, and himself last.

Amber noticed Armand was enjoying every bite. She smiled, "More cherries for you, sweetheart and it's still not our wedding day."

The ladies giggled but Armand was furious. Excusing himself, he took his plate into his bedroom and shut the door thinking, *Let them laugh. There's much to be said about purity.* In spite of his anger, he found the pie delicious. Still angry, he removed his jacket from the book, put it on the dresser and lay on the bed with his feet off the end.

He pondered, thinking deeply about his ignorant statement about wanting a chocolate cherry cake for the groom's cake.

A knock at the door aroused him. "Sweetheart, may I come in?" She opened the door before he answered. He was arising from the bed. "Darling I am so sorry I offended you," she murmured, with her voice breaking. She sat beside him and placed her arms around him, now crying, "Please forgive me. I was rude and crude. I was way out of line," she wept.

Instead of embracing her he quietly sat on the edge of the bed thinking.

She leaned to kiss him. He gave no response. She stood, bent and kissed him on the lips. He too, was weeping.

He finally asked, "Please, no more jokes about cherries. It's not funny, because I am the object of raw humor. That's a put-down. I'm not disrespectful of you. Please don't be of me. I've not seen this side of you Amber, making statements like you just made, that is not humor. It's gutter language, common fifty or one hundred years ago. Statements like that lower my esteem of you."

Continuing, "I don't want to be married to a woman who will poke fun or put me down whenever she can find wiggle room. That's not love, it's seeking power over me. Yes, I have great respect for myself. I have always lived a positive life. I want people who are upstanding and forward-looking around me. Amber, humor has its place but not at the expense of someone you supposedly love."

Amber rubbed his back and hugged him asking, "Please forgive me. Oh! Please forgive me. . ."

Her father knocked on the door wanting to speak with her. Before leaving, Amber kissed Armand on the lips saying, "Believe me, I do love you. You are a gentleman. At this point I am not lady enough to be your bride."

Still crying, she went to her father. They walked into the kitchen where Patricia was loading the dishwasher. Her mother blurted, "The first joke was funny, but you have put him down. That is not humorous. Amber, you are a damn fool to belabor jargon which is as old as the hills. You have put your father and me in a terrible position. Just what do you want in life?"

Her dad entered, "I for one, think this is terrible. It is an affront to his ego and his personhood. He is one terrific individual. I am going to talk to him. Have you apologized?"

Through her tears, Amber nodded, "Yes."

Patricia spoke again, "After all this planning and expense, we certainly don't want him to become so furious he would leave. We cannot let that happen. Dennis, after you talk to him, have Armand come and converse with me. He is a tremendous person. It seems we have a non-thinking daughter. If she were younger, she would be paddled."

The girls came into the kitchen asking if they could help. Patricia did not want any assistance, as she was still tearful. "Amber, go and entertain your friends," she directed, while she quietly intoned spiritual words to help raise the vibrations in the home.

Dennis went to the guest bedroom, leaving the door open. "Has Amber apologized?"

'Yes," he replied.

"How do you feel about her apology?"

"Clearly, I had not seen this side of Amber. I do not want to be the source of jokes or put-downs. I don't think that shows love. Instead, I believe it shows an attitude of, *I am superior to you,*" he stated emotionally.

"You are correct in your thinking. I feel the same way. We have spoken harshly to Amber. Her mother gave her hell and so did I. What can I do to make you feel better?" he asked.

"Your coming in here has helped me regain my composure," he answered.

"Amber's mother would like to talk with you in the kitchen. She has words she wants to share with you," Dennis invited.

Armand took his fork and plate to the kitchen. Patricia quickly wiped her hands, put her arms out to embrace him. "We cannot permit an emotional situation to drain our energies. It's love energy we all need." She held him in a long embrace, saying, "So often we overdo a good thing. I have spoken harshly to Amber. I don't know how she is doing, but I hope she feels terrible. Would you like to help me finish these dishes?"

"Of course," he agreed as he handed her more dishes for the dishwasher, asking, "I'd like to change the subject. I have not seen your basement or storm shelter which Amber told me about."

"When we finish, I'd be happy to show you. We check the weather every night. Depending on conditions, sometimes the TV weather channel is on all day."

Once the kitchen was clean, Armand and Patricia went downstairs. A table tennis setup filled the center of the room. A door led to a small concrete bunker, in which were two single beds, a battery powered radio, water, some snacks, flashlights and jackets. Armand was impressed. Patricia continued, "Please don't worry about us."

"After seeing your shelter, I certainly will not."

"Would you like to play some table tennis?"

"Certainly."

They batted the bouncing ball, having a great time. Patricia realized this would help Armand relieve some of his stress. Soon, Dennis came down to play while Patricia went to the living room to find her daughter who was being soothed by her friends.

When she saw her mother, Amber spoke with her sentences breaking, "Mom - I'm - so - sorry."

"Amber, you need to understand Armand's anger. I believe he loves you and you, him. However, do not put him down--ever again," Patricia spoke firmly. "We were fearful he would leave because his respect for you has been damaged. Amber, you may think you have caused him pain, but you have hurt yourself more."

Speaking more firmly, Patricia continued, "Amber, quit acting like a spoiled brat. Become the lady we thought you were."

Then addressing Delores and Miranda, "Girls, whatever relationship you have with a gentleman, be kind and loving. But this does not mean giving your personhood to that man until marriage. Respect is so necessary and something which Amber forgot. Girls, why don't you go downstairs and play some table tennis. Armand and Dennis are down there now. The four of you could play while I speak further with Amber."

Patricia took Amber in her arms saying, "My dear bride-to-be. You are a nervous wreck. We all make idiotic statements once in awhile. You need to forgive yourself or you will not be able to enjoy the days ahead. My goodness, you cooked up a storm, which shows love all over the place. You have every reason to be the happiest girl in the world." Her mother rubbed her back saying, "Please forgive yourself, Amber. If Armand had not forgiven you, he would have driven away in a huff. That's not the case. Please apologize again to him, then forget the whole incident."

When her mother went downstairs she met Armand coming up. Patricia spoke, "Amber feels horrible."

Armand heard a voice telling him to go upstairs to Amber. She sat, curled up on the sofa. He gathered her into his arms. "I have forgiven you, please forgive yourself."

She put her arms around him and coiled in his arms. He quietly held her firmly. Then he kissed her warmly and gently assured her, "I love you Amber."

"I love you too, my sweetheart."

He gave her his handkerchief, which she used to wipe her tears and nose. She pushed back her hair, which had fallen over her face as she wept. He invited, "It's nice outside. Could we walk around the block? No further. I'm tired and I'm certain you are, also. We'll be able to relax a little more."

Hand in hand, they walked. She told him where some of the neighbors were employed. "We live in a wonderful area. People are friendly and care about each other."

They returned home, hearing the sound of ping pong balls bouncing in the basement. The foursome came upstairs to the living room where Armand held Amber warmly in his arms.

Delores related, "I have been going with this guy. I guess he is like all the rest, he wants me to move in with him. I asked him, "What do I receive for security?" Duh. His silence ended that affair. One would think that education would make a difference. Not necessarily. I believe it's family ties and upbringing which instill moral principles."

Miranda expressed, "I've had problems with men too, though I have not gone with anyone long enough for thoughts of living together. I too wonder where equality lies?"

They spent the remainder of the evening discussing their activities and asking about Armand's work and his family business. The conversation continued until Amber yawned.

Patricia bid them goodnight with, "Everyone sleep late tomorrow. We'll have a good breakfast. Then your day is free to do whatever you wish."

After breakfast, Amber took her friends shopping at the mall. When they left, Armand embraced Amber and Dennis growled, "Women and their shopping."

Dennis invited Armand to join him at his work, introducing him to people who would be attending the wedding on Saturday. They ate lunch in the company cafeteria, chatting with people on their break. This was wonderful for Armand. He was a people-person. The employees were well-educated. They asked Armand about his work and family business.

They returned home to find Patricia preparing their evening's meal. The dining room table was set with different place mats and china. She asked Armand to prepare some kind of a drink to serve before the meal. Armand saw an unopened bottle of champagne saying, "Mother, as far as Amber and I are concerned, this is the ticket."

"Good," she replied. "We like champagne too. That's why the bottle is here." She found glasses and put the bottle into the freezer to cool quickly.

Three giggling women arrived, clutching bags of purchased treasures. The two girls went to their bedroom with their valued things. Amber embraced her sweetheart and offered him a package murmuring, "I love you," before breezing to her room.

The tie was blue with darker dots of different sizes. His gift made him realize her wedding gift was still in his car. He thought, *I need a shirt to wear tomorrow night. I forgot about the family dinner. I was only thinking about the airplane ride.*

He went to her room greeting her with, "Do you think tomorrow morning we could look for a dress shirt for me to wear? I forgot about your dinner tomorrow night."

"Sweetheart, I'd love to take you shopping. Perhaps we could go where I purchased your tie. Do you like it?"

"Of course, because it came from you. Thank you."

The next morning Amber called her beauty shop to make certain all the ladies' hair and nails could be done before the ceremony. She called the limousine service checking to see if their times were correct.

Armand realized he needed to check with his good friend and buddy, Ralph and his wife, Lisa. He found they were ready for their flight. Armand had served as Ralph's head groomsman when they were married two years before.

After breakfast, the lovers left for the clothing store. As she drove he thought, *It is wonderful to be with her.*

At the men's shop Armand purchased a blue shirt, his favorite color. His blue cuff-links set off the shirt beautifully. Then they double-checked at the photographer and florist. Armand saw Amber's bridal bouquet in the cooler. He paid his portion of the flower bill.

Meanwhile Patricia took the two girls to a strip mall where she normally shopped for clothes. Dennis stayed home because wedding gifts and packages were arriving at the house. He made lunch for the shoppers.

After she returned home, Amber lay on her bed thinking, *My goodness, I haven't written my vows.*

At her father's desk, she obtained paper and pen and began to write. Finishing, she made a copy for the clergyman.

Both her parents noticed how 'antsy' Amber was becoming. However, she ate a good lunch.

Their rehearsal was scheduled for five p.m. The meal for all guests would be at six.

Armand lay on his bed feeling good about the day. He was certain tonight would be wonderful. He would be happy to see all of his relatives and Ralph and Lisa.

There would be seats for him and Amber on the plane which would return them to Albuquerque.

Armand showered, shaved, and applied lotion. Then, dressed in his suit, trousers, new shirt, and tie, he looked at himself in the mirror thinking *I look the part of a new groom.* He reclined in his room. All he needed was his jacket.

A knock on his door revealed Amber asking, "Sweetheart, are you ready? Oh my, you look nice." She received a warm embrace.

"Amber, you're a knockout. You are absolutely beautiful in that violet dress." It flowed as she walked. The long sleeves had ruffles at the wrist and around the hem, which came slightly below mid-calf. Her violet sandals matched the dress.

He took her into his arms smiling, "My love, we don't have much longer to wait."

The limousine arrived to take them to the hotel. The girls were giddy and bubbly. Armand and Amber sat quietly in the back seat. His arm was tightly around her.

At the hotel, they were greeted by relatives who had come from several Oklahoma cities. Others came from New Mexico, along with his family who had flown in.

Armand's niece and nephew said they thought the plane ride was really nifty. He told them they needed to thank their grandparents for the airplane ride.

The wedding party assembled. The official came and asked for copies of their vows.

Patricia sought the chef. Many relatives came into the area and took seats. The florist's background was in place. The rehearsal went smoothly with all the bridal party in attendance. Hand-in-hand Armand and Amber walked into the lobby. He introduced his bride-to-be to his friends and relatives. Amber's cousins, whom she had not seen in years, were present to offer their congratulations.

The chef announced to Patricia, "Dinner is served." She came to Amber and Armand asking them to please start the line. The wedding party would follow. Parents of the bridal couple came next. Because of her nervousness, Amber ate little.

The gathering soon became a happy party with relatives all over the place. Children ran back and forth until their parents settled them down.

At the microphone, Ralph gave Armand's background, discussed his schooling and professional societies. He tantalized those present with stories about how smitten Armand was over Amber and the flying trips he had made to El Paso to see her. He related how Armand had shown him her engagement ring.

Ralph ended by saying, "I see they are holding hands. Evidently they wish to stop this madness and get married."

Dennis then took the mike. "Once you have finished your meal, please feel free to meet Amber's relatives and friends. Welcome and thank you and thank Celeste and Francis Rambulet for their part in this evening's festivities."

Voices blended in dozens of different, happy conversations as relatives talked with one another, or with Armand and Amber. The long enjoyable party was still going strong when a limo returned to take Amber and Armand to her home. Dennis informed Celeste, Francis, all the family members, and Ralph and Lisa that limousines would be available on Saturday morning at the hotel, to bring them to the Breddgeforth home. After lunch the women would be taken to the beauty salon in the limos. From the beauty shop, they would go the hotel. "Thank you for coming. Goodnight. We will see you tomorrow."

Chapter 7.

After a hearty breakfast, Amber took a bath. She dressed in panty hose white satin shoes with shorts and a white front-buttoning blouse. She wanted nothing to interfere with her hair after her veil had been placed at the salon.

At 11:30 a.m. limousines brought family and wedding party members to the house. After lunch one limo took the women to the beauty salon. Lily had a video camera and took many shots.

After her hair was finished, Amber's veil was positioned and held in place with generous amounts of hair spray and many hairpins. Then her tiara was put on top of her veil with fabric covering the sparkling jewel-like coronet. She laughed, saying "I certainly must look strange in shorts, high heels and this veil."

When all the ladies were finished at the hairdressers, a limo took them to the hotel where final preparations would be made. In the limo Patricia protected Amber's tiara from being bumped. Amber was uneasy, hoping they would arrive at the hotel before the men.

A bellhop showed the ladies the room where they would dress. Amber had her gown with her. The dresses for the other ladies were hung on a rack. While they dressed, they heard the men arrive making lots of noise and wise-cracking.

The women were not acting like meek, quiet females either. They were laughing, cackling, and making jokes. Amber gave a small box to Gabrielle for her Uncle Armand.

A short time later a box for Amber was delivered.

When she opened her gift, Amber found a beautiful amethyst and diamond necklace, then broke into tears. The women waited on her hand and foot. Patricia realized that her daughter was still very uptight. She ordered a soft drink brought for Amber. Patricia thought, *this girl has had very little to eat. She could possibly faint. We can't let that happen.*

Amber drank some soda which made her feel better. She was then assisted into her gown. The girls zipped a small train to the hem of her dress. *This lady is outstandingly beautiful,* her mother thought. The two mothers had corsages pinned to their gowns while the girls received baskets of flowers from the florist. Finally, Amber was presented with her bouquet of catalya orchids. She became tearful again.

Her mother opened the door. Now they could hear music. Eleanor watched from the women's dressing room. When she saw the minister enter, followed by the men she told everyone to take their places in the hall.

Amber's father stood waiting for her. She told him, "Dad, you look handsome as the dickens."

"Doesn't your mother look beautiful? But Amber my dear daughter, you are more than beautiful. You would make any man's heart go pitter-pat."

Amber's mother had been seated first. When the opera singer finished, the flautist began to play. In the hall, Eleanor, Miranda, Delores and the other ladies waited, followed by the boys with wedding rings on pillows, the flower girls and finally, Amber on her father's arm.

Flowers were everywhere. When Dennis and his daughter neared the dais, Armand came forward to be near the minister. Dennis placed Amber's hand on top of Armand's. Again shivers were surging through his body. Armand looked at his bride-to-be through her veil and saw a stunningly beautiful lady, who, in a few minutes would be his wife.

The minister said a few words about each of them. They lighted their individual white candles as the minister indicated this action was a sign of purity.

The time came for her to declare her vows. She began "I, Amber Cassandra Breddgeforth wish to make the following statements about you, Armand. I find you to be devoted, loving and always kind, considerate, and understanding. I take you as my loving h-u-s-b-a-n-d. . ." Armand reached to steady her. He was concerned.

She began to wobble with her voice breaking. Eleanor quickly gave her bouquet to Miranda and took Amber's arm as she asked for more soda.

The minister asked the ushers to bring some pop for the bride. Armand never took his eyes off her. He also had the jitters.

Amber lifted her veil to drink as Eleanor held her arm. Amber regained her composure after what seemed like an eternity.

She then continued, "Armand, I need you by my side to go through life with me. Obviously, I need you to steady me when I am too nervous to know what to do with myself. I am yours and yours only, my dear sweet man. I give you this ring as my outward sign I am married to you. Armand I love you with all my heart."

Taking a deep breath, looking his love in the eye, Armand began, "I, Armand Randolph Rambulet, declare to you, Amber, when I first saw you, my heart was smitten and I fell head over heels in love with you. You know I need you, because, without you, I make mistakes all over the place."

These remarks made Amber giggle. He continued, "You are my better half. Amber, I declare there has never been anyone else. I belong to you. I love you more than mere words can state. I now present this ring, which shows you belong to me and I belong to you."

The minister concluded, "Armand, you may kiss your bride." Eleanor and Miranda helped lift her veil over the tiara enough to enable the bride and groom to embrace.

She took his arm. Music began as they walked to a waiting limousine to take them to the photographer's studio. During the ceremony, the photographer had captured many candid shots. In the studio, Armand insisted on a photo of Amber by herself. After the photo session, Eleanor released the train from her gown, permitting Amber to walk comfortably with her groom.

Back in the limo, The newlyweds embraced several times. He sighed, "I am glad that's over with."

Amber related, "I lost my cool thinking of the sad cherry events."

Kissing her warmly, he urged, "Please forget those incidents."

When the limo returned them to the hotel he stated, "I have taken your slack suit and overnight case along with my sport jacket and slacks to our room."

The newlyweds arrived at the hotel to cheers, whistles, and tinkling of glasses. They stood to greet their guests. Other members of the wedding party were free to meet people individually, not in a reception line. Amber knew the children would become antsy and would not be comfortable in a situation they did not understand.

From Armand's standpoint, today was the beginning of the rest of his life with Amber.

The chef asked Patricia and Dennis to invite the guests to be seated.

Ralph sat next to Armand. Eleanor was next to Amber. The remainder of the party took seats near the newlyweds. Ralph stood and asked the guests to raise their glasses in a toast to Mr. & Mrs. Rambulet. Speaking to the wedding party he praised, "Young men you look elegant, young ladies you are beautiful. The wedding party is expertly adorned."

Continuing, "Those of you who have not greeted the bride, make certain you notice her lovely necklace. Amber, you are breathtaking. Armand, my friend, you have made yourself quite a catch." Wiping his brow, he expressed, "Whew, your bride is stunning."

This encouraged Armand to give her another kiss. Throughout the meal the newlyweds often kissed each other. Armand whispered, "My love, on this day you've exposed more skin than I've ever seen."

"My handsome heart throb," she whispered, "You are looking at my bosom, but you aren't seeing anything, really."

"Of course, I'm looking. I know I'll see more later," he smiled.

Daniel, Dennis's brother, went to obtain his vehicle. After he had filled his car with wedding gifts, he took Dennis home to procure his car for more gifts.

Amber and Armand cut their cakes. The chef placed pieces of each cake on both of the newlyweds' plates. As they ate their pieces, with a twinkling, devilish look in his eyes, Armand whispered, "Mine would have been better with cherries."

"Now who's rubbing the cherry bit into the ground?" she growled.

"I'm sorry. I know there will not be an opportunity like that again," he teased.

When they were finished, the bride and groom arose to carry out several gifts.

"Dad, will you please bring my violet purse and beach bag when you come back?" she asked.

"Certainly," her father replied.

Armand went to the dressing room, grabbed the hangars they had used and gave them to Dennis. Several men helped them move their regular clothes to cars.

In the room where the ceremony had taken place, the band was setting up for the dance. Chairs were moved off the floor.

Patricia came to Amber asking how she was feeling. "Mom, I was tied in knots. I was afraid something would go wrong. I was the one who was out of it. I don't think I was far from fainting. Now that I've eaten, I feel fine. Thank god it's all over. I can begin to relax. When Dad gets back, I want to dance with him before I dance with anyone else."

Armand came with more hangers. He asked her, "Just for a break, why don't we go up to our room? I can rid myself of these. I'm certain your parents will be charged for any unreturned hangers."

Amber thought, *That's the businessman part of him showing.* He hugged and kissed her in the elevator.

"While we are in the room, would you please help me so I can use the bathroom?' she asked.

"Yes. What do you want me to do?"

"Please hold up the back of my gown. It's slippery--I'll pull up the front."

"Goodness my love, what a process," he chuckled.

When she was washing her hands, he told her she was very beautiful. "My love, you have so smitten me I'll always be under your spell."

"My dear husband, I will not control you. You are the one who does the controlling. I may influence however," she smiled.

"That's what I really meant he retorted, as he embraced her with a long kiss.

Her father returned with her purse and beach bag. Armand gave Ralph the key to their room so he could take Amber's things to their suite.

The dance began. Armand enjoyed every step with his bride. He whispered to her, "This night has been a long time in coming." She then danced with her father.

The dancing progressed until midnight. Then Dennis took the microphone, thanked the caterer, the hotel staff, the musicians, and the florist. With his bride beside him, Armand thanked everyone for their gifts. "You won't hear from us until three weeks from now at the earliest."

Amber then asked, "Who would like to have the orchids? They are in water picks and may be taken." She carefully handed the flowers to guests, explaining, "If I wore one it would only become crushed. Keep them watered and cool. They look fragile, but they are long-lasting. They do not like heat. Goodnight everyone."

She took her husband's hand. Together they walked to the elevator. Again, he embraced her when they were enclosed. Reaching their room he opened the door, then asked, "Please put your arm around my neck." He flipped her gown up in the back and lifting her, he asked, "Hold on and push the door open with your feet."

In the room he placed her on her feet and took off his jacket. "Now, my dear lady, what can I do for you?"

After kicking off her shoes, Amber went to the bathroom and tried to determine the simplest procedure to remove the veil from her hair.

"My love, please sit on this chair." He poked and felt with his fingers to determine where he could begin the procedure. "You have so much hair spray, your hair feels like horse hair." One by one, he removed the pins until the tiara could be lifted. He then carefully removed her three-piece veil.

Unzipping her gown, he saw her bosom for the first time. She finished stepping out of her garment. He removed his outer garments, then went to where she was seated, removing her panty hose.

"My love, I need an embrace." She lifted up his undershirt and rubbed his back. "Oh Amber! That will put me to sleep," he stated sweetly.

When they finished in the bathroom, Armand turned off the light. "Please, may we have a nude embrace before we go to sleep?" (She could not help noticing his erection.)

Amber met his request, rubbed his back, and kissed him all over his face. Once in their sleepwear, Amber coiled up in his arms and fell asleep. He slumbered off smelling her hair spray and perfume.

The phone awakened them at seven-thirty. With affectionate embraces, Armand went to shower. She dressed, then tried to adjust her hair agreeing, "Armand was correct, it feels like animal hair."

They ate breakfast while enjoying each other's company. Wendell came to pick up the tux, her gown, and things they were not taking on the plane.

The limousine arrived shortly. They bid goodbye to her parents and all the family members and friends who had gathered.

His family plus Ralph and Lisa rode in limos to the airport for their chartered plane to Albuquerque.

Two seats were left in the back for the newlyweds.

In Albuquerque, everyone left for their homes except Amber and Armand.

Chapter 8.

The lovers ate a light meal and waited for their plane. Before boarding the aircraft, they each went to the bathroom. Both agreed, a seat which did not move was much more desirable than the aircraft facility. Armand admitted, "It's hard enough to guide the urine stream when the stool is fixed, but with the plane's motion, that's something else."

She asked, "Why is the urine stream hard to control? Can't you guide it while you are holding yourself?"

He smiled, "My love, I'll show you when we reach San Diego."

"Sweetheart, I have to 'back in'. Can you imagine how difficult that is?"

"I had not realized how women went to the bathroom until our experience in the hotel room. I can see being in heels and all dressed up would make it much more difficult," he agreed with a chuckle.

Amber whispered, "All you men have to do is hang it out, do your thing, and zip up. I have to wipe myself before pulling up my panties and slacks. Today I have on knee-highs. In time, you'll see all the nonsense we women put up with; like our periods. Then of course, our men like to probe quite often." She finished with a kiss on his cheek.

Looking straight into her eyes, he quietly stated, "I am looking forward to uniting our bodies. That's what marriage is all about. I've saved myself for you, as you have done for me."

Still looking at her he continued, "Did you know your mother left a book open on the bed? She wanted me to read the chapter on intimacy. It emphasized the great necessity for cleanliness, particularly man's hands and sexual organ. I have a special glove the urologist gave me, along with lubricating gel. I did not tell your mother I was aware of the need for this type of preparation. My doctor told me your ob-gyn would give me hell if you contracted a bladder infection. He said, 'That's why so many women develop these difficulties.'"

She responded, "I've never had a bladder infection. No doubt there is pain and illness. Sweetheart, that I do not need. I want to be able to work in your family business."

Their plane began its decent into San Diego. A taxi took them to their resort. Upon arriving, Armand helped her out of the cab. The front desk clerk confirmed their reservations. A bellhop, carrying their luggage led them to the honeymoon suite. In their rooms, Amber looked out the window exclaiming, "This place is beautiful!!" as she put her beach bag on a chair.

Armand paid the bellhop, hung his coat, unzipped his bag, and changed his clothes.

"Amber are you hungry?" he asked, as she hung a skirt.

"Oh yes."

"Let's eat in the dining room. We can finish unpacking later."

Their table had a wonderful view of the ocean. He sat across from her, allowing him to hold her hand and admire her rings. A waiter arrived requesting their order. Armand asked for a bottle of champagne.

"What are you trying to do, get me drunk so you can have your way with me?"

"My dearest love, I could not do anything which was against your will, especially where your body is concerned!"

With a glitter in her eyes she purred, "I was just checking."

The champagne arrived. Armand toasted her, "My darling Amber, this is the beginning of our lives together."

"Thank you. I thought the sound or Mr. and Mrs. Armand Rambulet had a nice ring when the person at the desk announced our names."

Hearing these comments, Armand kissed her left hand. He was delighted to be with her. They could do whatever their hearts desired, whenever they wanted.

Amber watched the ocean, the people swimming in the pool, and the fabric umbrellas over tables around the pool, which undulated in the ocean breeze. She watched a huge naval vessel moving in the bay.

Their conversation turned to their wedding. "I was really concerned when you faltered as you said your vows."

"I was tied in knots. I had been worried about what could happen if someone goofed, but I was the one who went to pieces. I've never been so nervous. Armand, our marriage must work. I couldn't go through an affair like that again!"

"When two people love each other, they work on their marriage together. We both must understand what the other person is thinking."

Armand's second toast to her was sweet and dear. He told her their life together was just beginning.

The food arrived as they continued to watch darkness settle over the ocean, while ships and boats scurried in the water. The swimming pool area was flooded with light.

Finishing their meal and champagne, they then went to their room. The expense of the meal would be put on their final bill.

In their room he asked, "My love, may I undress you?"

"Only if I can do the same to you."

Their evening together away from family and friends began with tender love strokes.

Then Armand remarked, "I'd like you to watch me urinate. You may then understand my statement on the plane."

She watched commenting, "I can see that directing the stream does take some care. My you're well built and certainly are all man."

"That manliness is useless unless it serves for mutual pleasure."

Naked under the sheet, they caressed each other extensively. This was satisfying to both. Then Amber asked, "Sweetheart, I'd like to look at your scars."

He flung the sheet off, spread his long legs apart as he held his penis aside. "Please have your look-see. I'm all for you."

She carefully handled his scrotum, looking at the scars from his surgery observing, "No wonder you were sore."

He answered, "I hope this ceases any pregnancy worries. My love, I'd like to begin the process of helping you to accept me."

"I guess I went through all those machinations so I could be your wife. However, I hate to spread my legs."

"Let's see what I'm able to do."

She watched him carefully wash his hands and don a latex glove.

"My love, please lie on the left side of the bed. This will give me enough room to sit at your torso."

He stroked her body with his left hand. She wiggled. He asked her to continue her movement, which made it easier for him. He finished, saying,

"My love that's enough for tonight." He hugged and kissed her until she yawned. They donned their sleepwear.

In bed he put his arms around her. He moved enough to be able to place his hand under her pajama top, murmuring, "Oh, my goodness my love, your feel fills me with wonderment. I don't know what to say to you, except good night my love."

The next morning, Armand planned to shower, but Amber wanted to take a bath. "That sounds wonderful," he exclaimed. As she removed her PJ's he poured champagne in glasses and climbed in the tub with her.

"'My love, I toast you."

"Thank you," she purred as she sipped her drink.

With a wash cloth he began to soap her body, using the resort's bar.

"Please let me obtain soap I brought. There are only a few lathering materials which my skin will tolerate." She handed him a bar of her special soap commenting, "You have earned the honor of cleansing me."

His hands moved over her beautifully smooth body with her lovely, well filled bosom. He tenderly moved his hand over each breast. She watched the male part of him enlarge before her eyes.

With her bath completed, it was Amber's chance to wash him. "Please, sweetheart, turn so I may cleanse your back." When she finished his back she asked, "Please allow me to wash your chest."

Her touch was so exceptional, his maleness continued to expand. She washed his arms and torso, then went to his groin. She grabbed his penis, marveling, "Enough expansion, you will explode!"

Laughing he joked, "My love, your feel is special."

She purred, "Just wait, there is another portion of me which has a special, special feel." She dried herself as he let the water out. Dripping, he embraced her. They were thrilled as their nude bodies blended. Amber thought, *Armand is a special man.*

After breakfast they left to explore the area. Amber enjoyed window shopping. Holding hands they peered into shops. They walked all morning. A rest in a café with soft drinks gave them time to watch people. At noon they found a place for lunch.

While they ate he asked her, "Amber, do you plan on this kind of thing all afternoon?"

"I am looking for a place where I can find a shower cap. I am certain you would like me to shower with you sometimes."

"I would enjoy that very much my darling," he emphasized with a smile.

They returned to the resort about four. In their room they sank into bed in each other's arms for a nap.

When they awoke, Armand suggested a shower and a good meal. In the dining room they were thrilled to watch the sun set into the ocean. They were thoroughly enjoying their precious time together.

"My love," Armand stated, "Isn't this like a dream come true?"

"This place is wonderful," Amber answered. "The food is great and the setting for our first hours and days together is very special."

With his hand over hers, he asked, "May I proceed tonight like I did last night?"

"Yes, I believe I need to satisfy your sexual desires or that penis of yours will explode," she laughed.

"My love, a penis does not explode. It becomes very erect. You think you've seen an erection--wait a short time. We will feel a new experience."

Before they slept, Armand carefully repeated his procedure.

Amber awoke in the middle of the night. She kissed him on his cheek. He turned over and embraced her. "Are you all right?" he questioned.

"I was lying too close to you when I awoke and thought I'd kiss you. I'll move away and go to sleep again."

Drifting into sleep he thought, *She is with me at last.*

The next day was a repeat of the previous one except Amber found a clothing shop and a dress she really liked. However, she was in shorts and walking shoes. She requested the garment be put aside.

In a footwear store she tried on many shoes, finally finding one pair which would go well with the garment she had seen. Amber explained to Armand, "That dress and these shoes are for work. Most of my present clothes are something college kids wear. They are not suitable for a working woman. Sweetheart, I like these shoes. Will you purchase them please?"

"Of course my love."

Hand in hand, they returned to the dress shop where she tried on the dress. Armand's reaction was, "My love, you look spectacular in that outfit."

"Thank you."

"Yes, I'll buy the dress for you. Oh! what men go through to satisfy the woman they want."

Amber hummed happily. Armand carried her purchases thinking, *What I want from this lady, money cannot buy.*

He was not putting one over on Amber. Resting on a bench she whispered, "I know what you have in mind for tonight. I am with you Armand. You are my one and only."

Looking into her hazel eyes, he sighed, "I thought our coming together would be a hard sell. I've gone through hoops for you."

They returned to the resort, rested a bit, swam, and ate their evening meal watching another unbelievable sunset. They held hands as they sipped champagne. He asked, "Now that I have prepared you, do you think you could enjoy our uniting? I think this event will be special for both of us."

"Armand, I honestly don't know," she replied.

After they entered their suite, Armand held her in a very warm embrace, kissing her with a passion she had not seen exhibited before. Now she was his wife. She thought, *I will find out what married life is like.*

He showered and prepared himself. She was naked in bed awaiting his approach.

When she saw his very erect penis, she blurted, "How are we going to make your idea work?"

Kissing her ever so tenderly, he rubbed her body with his left hand, enjoying the haptic sensations he was obtaining. Armand asked, "My love, please take my penis. I want you to insert me into your body."

Amber was shocked. She did what he asked. He continued to stroke her more lovingly than ever before. What a magical happening. What a precious time. He was feeling something he had never felt. The warmth of her body was special.

He whispered, "My love, please move. I'll move with you. Do you feel anything?"

"Nothing except I'm being probed by a very large bratwurst."

He chuckled asking, "Please be serious."

He touched her homologous area to his. This quickly changed her attitude. She drew him toward her. Her hands stroked his body, as she emoted, "Oh ARMAND! . . Oh goodness! . . Oh, my! . . Oh . .Oh . . Oh!"

Armand was breathing deeply and blowing out short breaths. He held her with his left arm, his body was supported by his knees.

At the apex of his experience, short bursts were thrust from his penis, which Amber clearly felt. He pulled her toward him holding her tightly. He finally spoke, "Amber, my love, what an experience!"

"Man, oh, man! you worked hard to deliver those ejaculations," she marveled.

"Have you ever had feelings like that, before?"

"Of course not," she answered. "Armand, I have not had that much time to see your whole body. You have had far better glimpses of mine than I have of yours."

She continued, "I know you told me your penis size, but to see you fully erect and stiff as a board took my breath away."

"Now that you have experienced me, what did you think?"

"All I can say is that you were tremendously loving and gentle. You certainly knew how to lead me--and you say you have never experienced this before?"

"Amber Rambulet, I could not put on an act like that. You know I am not an actor."

He continued, "I did a lot of reading. Besides, I asked the urologist some pointed questions. I'll ask you again, Amber. What did you think of our first encounter together?"

"My experience was more fantastic than any I have ever read about in books. Armand, your technique was wonderful. I felt loved in as deep a way as possible. No doubt that was because we both agreed to go through the machinations of a wedding ceremony, which cost Mom and Dad a goodly sum."

Once in their PJ's he held her closely, emoting, "Our ceremony was beautiful. My darling, you were so stunning. My eyeballs about popped out. Then, before we went up to our room, you gave your bridal flowers away." He laughed remembering, "I paid for them."

She sat up and put one leg over his torso. She then sat on top of her husband stating, "Because you were so smitten how could I have worn one of those flowers as a corsage? The large blossoms would have become crushed. I thought someone else could enjoy them. I had other things on my mind, like getting to know you."

She leaned forward kissing him warmly. His arms were around her. Amber tried to tickle him but found he was not ticklish except in his groin. He was squirming all over the bed with exaggerated movements to gain her complete attention. He then pulled her forward and gently laid her down.

He was loving her tenderly when the phone rang. They were shocked and frightened. No one knew where they were.

"Hello." The hotel desk asked if they would take a call from Eleanor Rambulet?

With a deep breath, Armand said, "Yes."

"Armand," his sister-in-law spoke, "I hate to disturb you and Amber, but Dad had a heart attack. He is in pretty rough shape. We took him to the hospital after work."

"Is Mom with him?"

"Yes. So is your brother."

"I'm sorry to hear this."

"We debated whether to call. If Dad does not pull through, what would you want us to do?" Eleanor asked.

"I'll keep my cell phone on tomorrow. No matter where we are, I can be reached. As for what to do, Mom knows Dad's wishes. Just follow them. Think positive. I'm going to continue my honeymoon regardless. Remember, life goes on. Before you know it, we'll be back at work pulling our weight. Dear Sister-in-law, we love you and Jeffory, Gabrielle and Gilbert, too. My love for Mom and Dad goes without saying. Goodnight. Thanks for calling."

Amber had her legs crossed, sitting on the bed in a *Lotus* position. Her arms were on her legs with palms upward. Armand joined her.

She began to intone. *Dear Energy of love, please send special energy to Francis Rambulet this night. I ask that energy from the Ethers protect and surround Francis Rambulet.*

Armand felt this prayer was very special and added. *I ask that love energy be sent to my mother and that of protection as well. May those energies also be with us, as Amber and I continue our time together.*

When he finished, he embraced her with generous kisses. "Please my darling, sleep well. We must continue our lives together, regardless of what blows we must take in the gut."

With this, he turned to sleep.

Amber awoke to hear the sound of Armand in the shower. He emerged as she was applying make-up to her beautiful hazel eyes. In his nudity he embraced her. She could not resist 'tweaking' his manliness. They dressed, ate breakfast, and were on their way to visit museums.

While in a cab, he called his sister. He found their father had been taken to the operating room last night. However, he was in his hospital room again this morning connected to numerous tubes and machines.

"All right Jennifer, have a good day. By the way, how did you find where we were?"

"We called all the travel agencies until we found the correct one. They would not tell us where you were until we told them why we wanted to contact you. I'm glad we were able to get through. You and Amber have a good day."

"Tell Mom and Dad we love them and are thinking about them. They are in our prayers."

The newlyweds spent the entire day visiting art galleries. Amber carefully looked at prints. Armand discouraged her from making any purchases there. He felt shipping such works would be a gamble. "My love," he stated, "I realize there is nothing on our walls, but art can really set us back. Remember, we are starting our lives together. What we want takes time."

Amber realized he was correct. She did not pressure him further, which he appreciated. They stopped at a florist and ordered a dozen red roses sent to Francis. They thought that would cheer him up and let him know they were thinking about him, even as they were engaged in a very important portion of their new lives together.

Another day was spent swimming. Armand enjoyed having Amber in the water with him. She allowed him to throw water on her because Amber needed to wash her hair. She commented, "Armand, you will be happy because we can shower together and be very close."

He wondered if she would allow another special sharing of their bodies tonight. In their room he asked, "Would you wash your hair in the shower?"

"Of course. I knew that's what you would want."

Armand enjoyed the shower with her. He was happy to be able to touch her body, run his hands down her back, then kiss with more water splashing on him than her.

When her hair was washed, he handed her a towel which, after drying her hair, she put around her, exposing her bosom.

He dried himself then went to her as she was toweling herself. He gently caressed her bosom, kissed her neck, then lips, asking, "May we become one again?"

"Please let me dry my hair and set it. Then I will come to you asking for your special love," she agreed.

He thought, *She certainly knows how to inflate my ego. I hope that continues after we are home.*

No phone calls interrupted their time together this night. Before sleep, they planned for their day tomorrow.

After a week had flown by, Armand called for a rental car and checked out of their honeymoon suite. This enabled them to visit sights further away from town. Their first drive was to *Cabrillo National Monument.* Then they visited *Sea World.* The next day was spent at the zoo.

At the koala exhibit, Amber was giddy and excited, especially to see the white koala. "Look Armand, their eyes are pink. They could never survive in the wild. But aren't they just dear? It would be wonderful to cuddle one." She continued her monologue as Armand, allowed her to 'run off at the mouth'. He enjoyed seeing his love excited.

They walked, rode the train, walked more, and snacked. Before they left, Amber insisted on stopping at the gift shop. He thought, *I'll not get out of here without paying a bill.*

He realized she had been excited before. But in the shop she 'went ballistic'. Amber jumped up and down seeing a stuffed white koala toy with a baby on its back. She insisted, "I'd like that, Armand." She then found plastic drinking glasses, salad plates, and other plates with koalas on them. "Armand, they would be nice for company," she announced.

Continuing her shopping, she spotted napkins decorated with koalas. His response, "Aren't you going a little overboard with your koala bit?"

"Now Armand, after last night, I believe I deserve something," she smiled with her hazel eyes dancing delightfully as she handed him the stuffed toy.

He thought to himself, *I guess in marriage, our wives do not let us forget they are not free. At least this lady of mine is not.* He smiled at the thought.

"Why the stuffed koala?"

"Oh, to make our bedroom cozy."

"All right, as long as it is not on our bed," he insisted.

With eyes ablaze, looking directly into her husband's, "That bed you mentioned is ours--yours and mine. No koalas allowed."

He paid the bills thinking, *Anything for my love, within reason.*

After a delightful day, a wonderful dinner with champagne and words of love, they made their way to a different motel.

Amber was ahead of her husband. She knew she would accept his advances without a word of complaint. Armand arranged for their boat ride. Amber really let loose with emotion. He had never felt her so relaxed. He was delighted.

In their PJ's ready for bed, Amber stated, "That was my payback for your being a super honey."

Armand held her tightly as they said goodnight.

The next morning after breakfast, they returned to San Diego to visit more museums. Amber asked, "Armand, I think it would be nice to take a boat out to look at the city from the water."

"That's a great idea my love. Let's find the boats and get their timetables."

The next day, Armand arranged for their boat ride. They wore sun shades; Armand with a hat, and she wore a head-scarf. Both were in light jackets.

Returning from a pleasurable ride, Armand opened their motel room door, agreeing that they had honeymooned in a beautiful city.

Chapter 9.

On the plane going home, Armand told Amber, "My love, if you had not been so alluring, sexy, and beautiful, I would not have been able to perform on some of these past nights." Amber smiled at his remarks and kissed his cheek. They napped, then awoke when the plane descended and quickly deplaned. Outside the terminal they caught a cab to his parents' home. Armand wanted to check on his father; but he knew his mom would also be home.

Francis was delighted to see Armand. Amber hugged him as they exchanged thoughts about Francis' recovery. "He'll now be eating less fat," Celeste insisted.

Armand chuckled. His mother had been on his father's case for years. "Mom was right Dad, we must listen to our women or we're doomed."

Francis added, "I can see these past two weeks were needed to settle you down."

"We'll be at work on Monday," Armand stated.

Francis suggested, "Armand please determine what project Amber will work on."

Celeste directed, "Armand take your Dad's car. The doctor told Francis he could not drive."

At home, thinking of the purchases she had made, Amber remarked, "I cannot believe I bought all those things."

With his eyes sparkling, he commented, "The bill for shipping all that stuff home was a big one, but my love, you are worth every penny."

"Only a penny. That's not much."

"To a tightwad like me it's a lot," he smiled as he leaned to kiss her.

They helped each other undress. Both nude, he embraced her in the bathroom, asking, "Are you in the mood tonight?" They loved each other. The next morning they slept late. Armand was finally happy to have her with him in the bed which he had occupied alone for so long.

Armand began breakfast while she set the table. Before he shaved he called Jeffory, who was happy to hear they were home. Armand told his brother they were going to take it easy and they would both be at work tomorrow.

Jeffory told Armand he knew their mother needed help at work. "Amber should be a great help when she begins."

"She sure knows how to tell me what to do," he smiled.

"Armand Rambulet, you're awful!" Jeffory heard Amber's irritation in the background on the phone.

After he hung up she went to him, mussed his hair, and planted kisses all over his face while he was trying to shave. While she was brushing her teeth, she shoved some after shave lotion to him saying, "This stuff makes me sexy," she purred as she raised her shirt to reveal her bra.

When he finished shaving he replied, "You make me very sexy too, my love."

With her eyes flashing desirously, she suggested, "More this morning?"

"Of course. We don't want to become dull around here," he smiled. They took plenty of time to share themselves with each other.

In mid-morning they went to his parents home and brought wedding gifts back to their house. Unwrapping them, they wrote thank-you notes, and put the gifts away.

One box contained a vacuum cleaner, which Armand assembled and used immediately. He cleaned the whole house, which really needed more than a single once-over.

His Rambulet grandparents gave them a series of limited edition plates in frames. Amber remarked, "Sweetheart, look what your grandparents gave us. Aren't they beautiful? Where should they be hung?" Amber had one in her hand and went all around the house, finally determining the dining room was a suitable place. She watched as Armand hung them. "Oh, Armand, how nice. This house needs something on the walls."

Jeffory and Eleanor had given them a beautiful beige and brown soft green printed comforter, with sheets, pillow cases, and an assortment of decorative pillows. As he helped her make their bed, Armand noted, "This place is beginning to look like home."

Gabrielle, their niece, had a package of spatulas, wooden spoons, a wire whisk, and an assortment of turners for burgers, pancakes, and the like. Gilbert, not to be outdone, had given them measuring cups, spoons and a collection of spices.

A large card was attached to a box. Opening it, Amber was ecstatic. "Armand come and see what your parents gave us!" It contained a check for $5000, They opened the box to find a collection of mixing bowls. "Oh Armand! she added, "We can buy a new bedroom set and put the one we are using in the guest bedroom."

"If that is your heart's desire, it's fine with me."

Jennifer and Roland, in coordination with Jeffory and Eleanor had given them four sets of bath towels and two bath rugs, which matched the bedroom ensemble.

Armand made a snack while she unpacked more boxes. Place settings of their bone china made Amber squeal in delight. "Armand, you are one loved individual," she exclaimed.

Ralph, Armand's best man and his wife Lisa, gave them an eight place setting of dishes for daily use.

After they had eaten, all the dishes were put in the dishwasher except the bone china.

They both agreed it was time for bed. Amber put out her crinkled skirt with violet blouse for tomorrow. She would wear her violet sandals. On his valet chair, Armand hung a suit and the other clothing which he would wear.

Embracing her he said, "It is wonderful to be home and together. What you are doing to this house is tremendous. This place really needed a woman's touch."

As he held her she looked up at him saying, "This place will do until we have a home," and she kissed him.

"You don't like this place? Remember the dining and living room furniture you had me purchase, which set me back quite a bit."

"It's only the bedroom furniture I don't like. I must say, the comforter and accessories help a lot. I can't complain about the other furniture. You were a sweetheart," she said with a kiss, while rubbing his chest under his pajama top.

He returned her kiss, turned on his side thinking, *I could not be happier. What a woman I married. I hope she is always as attentive to me as she is now.*

The next morning they left for work in his father's car.

Amber was happy to see new office furniture and computer equipment ready for her use.

While at work, Armand called his dad. They briefly discussed what projects would be suitable for Amber.

Armand quickly found she had a wonderful stick-to-it concentration as she worked on a business problem for a client company. At noon, they walked to lunch. Armand was between his mother and his wife. Jeffory and Eleanor joined them. The two had met when she was a legal secretary. Jeffory worked full time. Eleanor answered phones part-time when their children, Gabrielle and Gilbert, were in school; she was with the children when they were home.

When they left work, Armand drove to a furniture store, where Amber suggested they look for a bedroom set which would suit her taste. She found what she was looking for along with a new mattress which was not made with cloth and wire coils.

Armand realized his wife had definitive ideas. She knew what she wanted. She did not take long to make up her mind. He observed, *What I was thinking would take all night, she selected very quickly.* After a brief stop for supper, they purchased needed groceries.

Once at home Armand asked, "My love, may we have some special time together?"

"Of course," was her answer.

With their day complete, they turned to sleep.

The next day, Armand and Amber took his father to lunch. Celeste would eat later, following a dental appointment. Amber told her father-in-law her new furniture and computers were just what she expected. They worked until six then returned to his parents' home.

Frances stated, "A neighbor of mine brought over a big beautifully wrapped box this morning for you before we left for work. It's in the guest bedroom."

Amber's response was, "Armand, we're going to have quite a time getting all the thank-you notes written."

Amber phoned her parents saying they would fly to Oklahoma City on Friday night, and leave early Sunday morning, driving their cars back to Albuquerque.

The week flew by. On Friday evening his parents took them to the airport and asked to please keep them informed during their drive back home.

Amber's parents met them at the Will Rogers airport. In her parents home they found the guest bedroom filled with many boxes. Armand and Amber had to transfer some of the packages into their cars before they were able to sleep in the bed.

On Saturday morning after breakfast the car loading began in earnest. Clothes Amber had left were put on the back seat of her car. Then gifts were placed wherever they would fit. She felt they would have many place settings of their bone china from the many boxes. Her parents had purchased a twelve place set of sterling silver in the same pattern as her mother's, which pleased Amber.

In the evening the newlyweds related the experiences and sights they had seen in San Diego. "That was a lovely place to visit," she told her parents.

Continuing, Amber said, "Once we're settled, please plan to fly over and visit us. We will do the same and come back here when we have time."

Watching Armand dote over their daughter, Dennis stated, "Don't ever lose that admiration you are showing for your wife, Armand."

"The more I am with my beautiful lady, the more I love her. She is one terrific person."

"By the way Amber," Dennis said, "I had your car checked because I did not want you to have any problems on your drive home." She thanked him warmly.

Her parents told the children goodbye on Saturday night, because Armand and Amber were planning to be on the road before five.

When they arose at eight, Dennis and Patricia dreaded seeing Amber's room and the guest bedroom empty. They had asked Amber to please call when they arrived home. "We believe you have some lovely gifts."

When they arrived in Albuquerque, Amber and Armand both phoned her parents. They unloaded her car, the smaller one. She was anxious to have her clothes hung again.

As Armand brought wedding gifts into the house, she put food into the microwave for warming, which permitted her to help Armand.

They prepared for bed immediately after eating. They were both very tired from the long drive. Armand was especially exhausted, as he had been concerned. In heavy traffic, her car, which traveled behind him, occasionally was lost from his sight. He would call her cell phone to be sure she was all right. Eventually she would catch up with him.

After they kissed goodnight, Armand thought, *I would not like to make that trip again. That thoroughfare, I-40, has very heavy traffic.*

They began their work at eight and quit at five. At home, Amber began their evening meal. They both changed into shorts, shirts, gym shoes. After they ate and the kitchen was placed in order, they tackled the writing thank-you notes.

When all the wedding boxes had been opened, Amber found they had ten place settings of bone china, an eight place setting of stemware, a bread machine, a steam cooker, plus beautiful pots and pans with glass lids from Jennifer and Ronald. These gifts were in addition to the others they had received previously.

A happy Amber insisted that Armand buy a hutch because space was needed to store these precious gifts.

They settled into work and home life. Armand gave his lady as much love as she would accept, which was often.

Some days they worked long hours. One day she stated, "I worked with your dad for awhile. I must admit, there are times when one needs to get away from the desk and think. Your family building is great for walking around and taking a quick break."

He agreed with her. Then she began again, "Do you remember me mentioning Marshara Gudura? He called me asking if we could use someone with a master's in *Business Math*. I have not talked to your parents. I wanted to feel you out first."

Amber made dinner while Armand set the table. As they ate, Armand said, "Your friend sounds interesting--but he better not be interested in you."

"Oh Armand! you know I only have eyes for you," she emoted.

"I know you look at other guy's crotches."

"Oh! None can compare to yours sweetheart."

Their meal was nearly finished when out of the blue, he asked her, "Do you think you will feel lost, not being able to have our own children?"

"Absolutely not! I am certain your parents would feel badly if there were to be no grandchildren to follow in their footsteps, except for your brother's two." She continued, "As for grandchildren, in my family, my brother has taken care of that. I don't know if they plan any more children. Time will tell. How about yourself? What's your gut feeling? Are you going to be disappointed?"

"Our working hours would not be conducive for young children. I would be a poor parent. Work comes first. However, I hope down the road, we could find--say two children; but for now we're just getting to know each other. Our sexual experience is paramount, as I believe it must be with newlyweds, especially husbands. Amber, you have added a completeness to my life, which I did not know could be so wonderful."

"The same goes for me," she sated. "I believe in a relationship, both people must be committed, not just to the relationship, but in putting their partner first."

He responded, "I grew up knowing Dad loved Mom and vice versa. They believed what ancient philosophers taught, that one male and one female constituted a family."

She added, "I know my parents abhor sexual promiscuity. That is why I have such strong feelings about sex. I've made vows to you I would never undo. I could not live with myself."

He asked, "Now that we are one, have you changed your mind?"

"Absolutely not. I love you more as each day goes by. Now sweetheart, let's get ready for bed." She responded with a yawn. In bed, she murmured, "I love you."

A family meeting was held to answer Amber's question about Marshara Gudura. Would it be wise to consider hiring him? The meeting concluded with a unanimous directive for Amber to call him with an offer, because she knew him. They felt her call would be more important than one from Francis or Armand.

Amber realized it took lots of energy on the part of the family members to run their business. She enjoyed the work, but did not care for the long hours. At times when she was free she wondered, *Under our conditions of work, how could we become parents? For now that is a question for the future.*

When Armand finished he came to her. She had closed down her computer and was writing notes to herself. He helped her from the chair and embraced her saying, "I love you."

"I love you, too sweetheart," she replied.

On the way home she told him, "Marshara was delighted to be offered a position. He asked when he could start work. Based on our decision at the meeting I told him October first."

She immediately started their meal. He took her purse to their bedroom. He then prepared a wonderful lettuce salad for their meal including an apple cider vinegar, honey, and olive oil dressing with herbs. In a bottle he shook the mixture vigorously to blend it well.

They realized one good thing about their work, the desktop computers stayed in their offices. After the meal was finished and the kitchen cleaned, they went into the back yard. "Do I meet your expectations?"

"Without a question," she smiled.

They sat quietly thinking and pondering these ideas for some time before they decided it was bedtime. They cherished each other's affections.

Weeks passed. The two put in long hours at work. Amber's menses came. She had forgotten to purchase feminine products the last time they were in the store. "I need to drive to the drug store. Do you need anything?"

"Let's eat first."

During the meal he asked her, "How do you feel?"

"I feel fine. It's just the disgusting bleeding every month."

"My love, isn't that better than being pregnant?" he questioned.

"Yes, but you men get off easy," she bitterly responded, "Afterward, the men are able to zip up their trousers and walk away."

"Not all men do that," he insisted.

"I can thank the *Great Energy* I have you," she marveled, with an embrace.

"I'll clean the kitchen," he offered.

"Good, I'll be right back." She closed the garage door as they always did.

On her return home, at the intersection of Candelaria and Juan Tabo Blvd, in the left lane of the street, with a green light, her car was impacted on the left rear side by another vehicle which had sped through the red light and struck her car causing it to spin around. The fuel tank ruptured which caused the gasoline to burn.

The other vehicle's left front was crushed so badly the driver had to eject himself through the passenger door.

Amber quickly gathered her purchases, purse, and exited the right door of the vehicle she had enjoyed. She was trembling severely as she called 911. Amber could barely carry her purchases across the street where she sat on the ground under a tree in fear that her car would explode.

Police, fire equipment, and rescue vehicles quickly arrived. She barely noticed that the driver of the other car was walking in circles. The fire department's extinguishers made a huge 'swishing' sound. A policeman approached her asking her name and address. He then called for an ambulance. Amber was trembling so terribly, the officer had difficulty in understanding her. She shook from head to toe. She was so upset she had not thought of Armand until she was asked. "He's at home," she stated. As she was being put on a stretcher, she called Armand, her voice quivered, "I -- am going -- to the--hospital. Another car -- plowed into my car."

"Good Heavens! I'll be on my way as quickly as I can," he uttered.

Before the ambulance left, a policeman told her, "Don't worry, Mrs. Rambulet. Tell your husband to meet us at the University Hospital. You need to be thoroughly checked." In the ambulance she vomited violently, realizing she was suffering from shock and trauma, difficulties she had never experienced before.

Armand called assuring her, "Our next door neighbor, Gil, is driving me. Where are you going?" She handed her phone to the lady who was attending her. "Mr. Rambulet, we are taking her to the emergency room of the University Hospital. Please meet us there. She needs to be completely checked because she's in shock. All we know is that it was an auto accident."

When the ambulance arrived at the hospital, doctors and nurses hovered over her asking questions. "Does your head hurt?"

"Yes." They checked her arms and legs asking," Any abdominal pain?"

"Yes, from menstrual cramps."

When Armand arrived, he was taken to the emergency room. Seeing him she was still shaking uncontrollably. Hospital personnel gave him Amber's purse and purchases. Slowly she sobbed, "Armand, M-Y C-A-R C-A-U-G-H-T F-I-R-E!" Armand rubbed her shoulders and kissed her forehead.

She was given a sedative and taken away. Later he was taken to a ward with white curtains between the beds. A chair was placed beside the bed for him to wait. After Amber was x-rayed from head to toe she was brought to where Armand was quietly seated.

He was very apprehensive not knowing what specifically had happened. He sat in meditation while she slept.

Finally an MD came to him saying, "She has not been injured. She was suffering only from trauma. She can be released." Hearing the doctor talking to Armand, Amber awoke.

Gil was waiting, which pleased Armand. He helped his love into the car, holding her while she rested her head on his shoulder. At home they thanked Gil profusely for his help.

It was two a.m. when Armand helped her undress. With Amber in bed, he put the clothes she had been wearing on a chair, quickly donned his sleep wear and fell into bed.

He awoke at seven and called his parents relating, "Amber's car was hit in the back by another vehicle, hard enough to rupture the gas tank, which caught fire. We spent much of the night in the hospital. Amber was frightened, but not hurt. She is still sleeping. Don't expect us until late this morning," he announced.

"Both of you sleep as long as necessary. We'll expect you when you feel like coming in. We're happy you called," his dad responded.

Armand returned to bed. Amber awoke at 8:30 to find him still sleeping. She put on a robe and reclined on the sofa. She went over in her mind the experiences of last night. *It all happened so suddenly. I did not see that guy at all. Where was he? He had the red light. All the other cars stopped. He did not. Did he come from a nearby bar? My little car is a goner. I'm glad I am all right. I was so happy to see Armand there.* These thoughts raced through her mind as she heard the commode flush. Armand kneeled with his arms surrounding her and gave her a kiss.

"My love, I was overwhelmed. I am so glad you are all right. I had some very anxious moments. Can you explain what happened?"

"All the cars ahead in the left lane were stopped at their light. This guy must have come out of a bar. He should have turned in his turn lane, but evidently went straight ahead and must have been going very fast when he hit me. Thank the *Great Energy*, he hit my car in the rear rather than into my door. The car spun around. Flames leaped up. I had to exit through the right door. Even though I was in shock, I had the car keys, my purse and purchases in my hand.

"Because I was fearful the car would blow up, I sat on the ground behind a tree after I called 911. I noticed this character from the other vehicle walking around in circles. The fire trucks came and two firemen put out the flames. When a policeman came, I was shaking so badly I could only give him the details very slowly. He motioned for a paramedic to come. The policeman told me not to worry. I was so upset I just shook all over. The next thing he asked me was, 'Where is your husband?' I answered him very slowly, saying you were at home.

"As I was being placed in the ambulance, they asked for our phone number. It's funny, when you are under severe stress, your mind doesn't work. I was shaking and could not remember. I threw-up in the ambulance and was still shaking when you came."

Then with a smile, she changed the subject. "Sweetheart, those were very expensive menses pads and what a terrible way to obtain a new car."

He helped her arise and dress, then fixed breakfast. As they ate, she marveled, "My dear, that experience was so horrible, I did not realize I was hungry until I drank that apple juice. Now I'm famished."

"You must be starved if you vomited in the ambulance."

After a large breakfast and a second piece of toast she went to the bathroom to prepare for work. She smiled, "I am sure glad my package was saved for me."

"The emergency room nurse gave your package to me," he responded, "Do you feel well enough to go to work?"

"I'd go bonkers here at home. I'll call Mom and Dad from work."

She called her Mom first, then her Dad and her brother.

Armand left a message for Jeffory to check on what accident details he could obtain from the police.

Celeste came into Amber's office and the two women shared a loving chat. When she revealed the details to Celeste, Amber asked, "Mother, please relate this information to other family members. I don't want to talk about the accident any more."

Almost immediately, two policemen entered her office. "Good morning, officers," she greeted. As she shook their hands, Jeffory approached, note pad in hand.

Amber began, "Officers, my morning certainly has been better than last night. I was frightened beyond words."

Armand came to her door asking, "Are you all right, my love?"

"Yes," she answered.

The officers had a good idea about this blonde, intellectual woman's personality. Obviously, she was very aware of her world. Amber answered their questions, hating to go through the trauma again. She told Jeffory she was glad to have him present. After they had discussed the details, Amber asked the officers about the man who hit her.

"Mrs. Rambulet, he was very inebriated. He's in jail."

Jeffory insisted, "That's where he needs to be."

The officers left. Her brother-in-law returned to his office. Armand came to her office asking, "Madam, would you please go to lunch with me?"

With a smile she put her computer in standby mode. He helped her from her chair and gave her a kiss.

Hand-in-hand, they walked to lunch. The sunlight made her feel better. A brisk wind from the southwest blew her two-tone green dress in folds revealing a light weight fabric, which billowed the skirt. The garment danced in the wind and gave an additional glow to her hair.

Sitting at the table, he held her left hand admiring her, thinking, *she could have been killed, but somehow the Great Energy agreed her parting time had not come to pass.*

Amber related she felt comfortable with her brother-in-law present as the officers questioned her. Jeffory wanted to make certain she said nothing which would incriminate herself. She again related to Armand, "I didn't see that car!"

"My love, from now on we must let the police do their work. The insurance people will need to pay up."

"Armand, I have been thinking. Do we need two cars? We're usually together. We could save quite a bit of money."

"My love, that's up to you," he answered.

"We work in the same place. My needs are different now. We are not going to be driving to El Paso, or Oklahoma City. I think this would be a good idea for now. We can earnestly begin saving for a house."

"I would like to purchase some exercise equipment with money from your car, but I would want most of the money to be banked. We could trade my car in on a new one," he suggested.

"That sounds good," she answered, as they arose to return to work. She complained, as the wind continued to muss her hair.

Armand embraced her on the sidewalk. "My love, you are beautiful. Your hair looks good. It shines like the dickens. You wear a golden halo."

"Oh sweetheart, you're prejudiced," she answered as she embraced and kissed him on the cheek when he opened the door to their building. Hand in hand they climbed the stairs to their offices. "My love, don't forget to call the insurance company."

"Armand, do I have to?" she pleaded.

"I suppose I could make that call. Have you told me all the important information in case they ask?"

Amber struggled as she relived the night of pain and terror to her husband.

Driving home at six he reported, "I called the insurance people this afternoon. They may call tomorrow for more details. Luck is on their side. We do not need to rent a car."

After they had eaten and the kitchen was in order, they went out into their back yard. Gil saw them and inquired how they were doing. Again, Armand thanked him, saying, "That night, I was not fit to drive, I was too uptight."

Amber told him, "The other driver was drunk. He now occupies a jail cell."

Armand added, "My brother was at the jail today. If he finds anything more, we will hear."

Amber answered her phone. It was her mother inquiring how she was doing. "There has been a lot going on in your lives, hasn't there?"

"Yes, there certainly has Mom. Armand would like to talk to you."

"Mother last night, I was very apprehensive and concerned when I heard she was in an ambulance going to the ER. Her speech was slurred and difficult to understand. I was very worried. It was a fantastic relief to find she was shaken up and traumatized, but nothing worse. She had a good day today. When the police officers came to talk with her, my brother was present taking notes on what she told the policemen."

"That's good Armand. Your business is fortunate to have a family member who is also a lawyer."

Amber took the phone and finished the conversation with, "Goodbye for now, Mom. Thanks for calling."

Some time later their thoughts turned to Marshara who would be joining *Rambulet and Associates, Inc.* Armand called him to find what kind of a computer he wanted.

Marshara answered giving his needs. They discussed his work and briefly what he would be doing.

A new computer was ordered and delivered to the building, along with a new keyboard for Francis. Office furniture for Marshara arrived shortly before Armand and Amber left for the Memorial Day weekend in Oklahoma City.

Armand had a good time talking with Amber's grandparents, Dale and Ida Breddgeforth. Her grandfather had plenty to say about his experiences during World War II. Armand commented, "I think wars are a waste of energy in all respects, but what can be done when nations or people will not talk with one another?"

Amber's mother had told relatives not to ask Amber about her accident. Instead, she talked about her wedding gifts and honeymoon. She mentioned their china and stemware and related the good time they had in San Diego.

"We planned to play golf, but there was so much of interest to see we had no time for a game."

The women began to giggle and Amber's face became flushed. She answered their humor with, "You all know what married life is like. Do you think my marriage would be any different?"

When Armand heard the women giggling, he went to Amber saying, "My love, are they giving you a hard time? Let's go for a walk."

Outside, they both realized how they were being needled. She said, "Armand, it's a nice day. Let's keep walking. There is a lake a few blocks from here. We can sit on a bench and enjoy each other. Let Mom and Dad wonder where we went."

In the park, she sat with her legs in Armand's lap. They talked about business and enjoyed their conversation. He asked, "Amber, don't you think it is unkind to pester us about married life?"

"Yes, I do sweetheart. I told them they knew what married life was all about. What made them think ours would be different?"

"My family would never act that way," he muttered.

Changing the subject she noted, "I love the new bedroom set. The mattress is nice, too."

The lovers talked for so long they did not realize how much time had passed until they heard a car horn beep. It was Lily, Amber's sister-in-law. She left her car and approached them saying, "I feel like a damned fool. Amber, please forgive me. I came to look for you. I wanted to be the first one to apologize."

Armand asked, "Why poke fun over what we have done after our marriage?"

"It was stupid, silly, strange, and senseless. Besides it was unkind and uncaring." Lily remarked. "Please forgive me. Some of the family have left. My husband told me he wants a few words with you, Armand."

"You know Lily, sometimes it is difficult to fit into a new family. I never thought they would poke fun at Amber's and my marriage," he remarked.

"Please come home with me," Lily asked. Armand helped Amber arise and they walked to the car.

In the seat Armand spoke, "Thanks for caring enough to come after us. You certainly are forgiven."

"The children came to me asking why you had left," Lily related.

Once in the house, Armand entered the kitchen. Dennis spoke first saying, "Please forgive me. I did not mean to laugh or poke fun at you and Amber."

Looking at his father-in-law he stated, "Believe me, we did far more than have sex with each other."

Dennis was taken aback and repeated, "Please forgive me." Amber and Lily heard what Dennis had said.

Her mother was reading in the living room as they entered. Meanwhile Wendell came to Armand and told him he was very regretful.

Stumbling for words Patricia then added, "I gave them all hell after you left."

Armand's arm was around Amber as he growled, "Mother, your comments are a little late. I never thought educated people, whom I admire, would speak like that. I am angry enough to call a cab and catch the next plane back home today, rather than on Monday."

Weeping, Patricia arose and went to Armand and embraced him saying, "Please don't do that."

Dennis and Wendell came in adding, "There is more family time tomorrow. We'll have some fun."

Wendell spoke to Amber, "It's pretty bad when your children notice or feel something has gone haywire."

Raymond and Sue were downstairs. When they heard Armand's voice they called, "Uncle Armand, Aunt Amber, please come play with us." They went to the basement and batted the table tennis ball, ladies against gents. As they played Armand thought, *these kids know, and are wiser than the adults.*

While the table tennis game was in progress, her parents prepared a light evening meal of leftovers and sandwich makings.

When they were called, the tennis players happily came up for some food. They sat at the table, prepared sandwiches and gobbled their food.

As soon as they were finished Dennis announced, "I have rented a movie, *Mrs. Doubtfire,* which I think we will enjoy."

Everyone helped to clear the table. Dennis prepared the TV for the movie. Armand sat with his arm around his nephew. Amber held hands with Sue. Even Wendell and Lily were cuddly.

During the movie Dennis served pop for everyone to enjoy. The delightful family-oriented movie made the adults forget what had happened.

Just before Wendell and his family departed, hugs and kisses were shared by everyone. Sue was asleep on her father's shoulder. Amber's parents hugged Armand and Amber and everyone went to bed. Armand held his love very closely, wondering, *why do families hurt each other?*

Amber knew her husband was still upset. His hands were cold. She talked with him a long time, saying, "We always hurt those we supposedly love. We all make mistakes. I know it's my family, so will not make excuses for them. Sweetheart, tomorrow at breakfast open up and let Mom and Dad know how you feel."

She kissed him with their bodies close.

After a good night's sleep, they were awakened by clatter in the kitchen and dressed quickly. They were greeted warmly by her parents. Dennis prepared crisp bacon. The eggs were superb. Patricia asked, "How did you sleep?"

Amber did not answer. She felt that question needed to be answered by Armand who responded, "I slept fine because I had Amber with me. I know apologies have been made. I accept them. However, I want to add, I don't want to encounter such a thing again. This action would cause me to never return. Amber could come if she wished."

"Sweetheart we are one. I would not come alone," she insisted, kissing him on the cheek.

Dennis spoke, "Armand, I would feel as you do if I were in your shoes. It was my fault for allowing that kind of conversation to continue. I know better. I am very sorry."

Patricia added, "Armand, I cannot express the feelings I have for you. I know you are a forthright person, honorable in all respects. I have become a better person, in your presence. I too, am sorry."

Amber had tears in her eyes as Armand hung on every word her mother spoke.

"Mom and Dad, Armand is very conscious of people and his clients' feelings and attitudes. That's why their name is respected and sought-after by business people who need their help. I have become part of this business. Therefore, I know how important it is to make people feel good about themselves, even though they have made a mess of their finances, have created errors in judgment, or made darned fools of themselves."

After breakfast, Amber insisted they go for a walk. Away from the house, she pointedly said, "My parents are sorry. You cannot blow their errors into something which would last until we die. Sweetheart, that's holding a grudge. It's forgiveness which you need to offer, or you will not be happy around them. When you make mistakes Armand, you expect to be forgiven, don't you?"

"Of course. As always, you are correct."

"Let's go back and help with the dinner," she suggested.

"All right, but I must have an embrace." He enfolded her in his arms, purring, "I miss you."

Kissing him she replied, "I'm happy you do."

"Man oh man! It's difficult for a new husband to be separated from his wife."

The grill was heating outside. Armand played catch with Sue and Raymond. Amber joined them later. When Grandma and Grandpa Breddgeforth arrived, Grandpa joined in the game. Once everyone had eaten, Armand and Amber played table tennis with their niece and nephew.

Later everyone gathered around the dining room table and played the game of spoons which delighted the children. Uncle Armand had such sharp eyesight and reflexes, he almost always won, unless he deliberately allowed one of the children to grab the last spoon.

When Armand and Amber were preparing for bed he questioned, "Wasn't that game of spoons fun?"

"Certainly if you win all the time!" she grumbled.

The next day Amber's parents took them to the airport. They parted with hugs and kisses. She invited her Mom and Dad to join them for the Thanksgiving weekend.

Back home, they made plans for work on Tuesday.

She made a gelatine salad for the next night. He helped her set the bar for breakfast.

When they were in bed, Armand embraced her saying, "I really miss your special touch."

"That's good, I'm glad you do. Please, not tonight, I'm tired."

Chapter 10.

The following day, Celeste told Armand that Francis was depressed. When Armand heard his father crying in his office, he went in and closed the door asking, "Dad, what's the matter?"

His father sobbed, "I can't explain here."

"Would you like me to take you home, Dad?" he asked. "It looks like you are in no condition to work or be here. Come on, let's go."

Amber did not know Armand had left until he called her from his parents' home. After that, he pressured his dad to let loose. "Something is eating you, Dad. Please tell me what it is," he insisted while obtaining a glass of water for his father. Armand sat on the ottoman declaring, "Dad let it out."

Clearing his throat and wiping his eyes, his dad began, "Son, this is something your mother does not know about."

"For goodness sake, Dad, you must get whatever it is off your chest or it will destroy you," Armand pressed.

"Armand, I'm telling you first. No one in the family knows."

"Knows what, Dad?"

"This may take some time but here goes. A few days after your birth, the time away from your mother was too much for me. I went to a bar, found a woman and made out with her. Armand, she was slick. She came to me later saying, 'I'm pregnant.' I took her by the arm saying, "Please come with me." We went to a health care clinic where she was 'taken care of".

"I thought time would heal the wound. It's only become worse. I feel

I've let your mother down because she believes I've always been faithful to her. I love your mother. I would do anything for you kids."

"Dad, how many times did this happen?" he asked, with tears in his eyes.

"Only once. Immediately after that, I had a vasectomy, but I never strayed again."

"Dad, let's go into the kitchen for something to eat."

He found frozen food to warm.

"Armand, now that you know, what do you think of me?"

"Dad, what you have told me changes nothing. I love you because of what you have done for me."

"I need to tell your mother, but how do I do it?" he asked.

"To start with, why don't you take Mom out to a nice place for dinner. Sit next to her. Hold her hand and embrace her. Then at a quiet time, declare what you told me. Knowing Mom, what you tell her will make her cry and love you more. You cannot spend as many years together as you two have and let something like this get the best of you. Both of you are too stable to let anything come between you."

Armand put food on the table remarking, "At this moment, our two women are at lunch. That's pretty good huh Dad? After you have told Mom, let Jennifer and Jeffory know. Coming clean will make you feel good. Ask for forgiveness and forgive yourself. I've already done that."

Armand's Dad held him in a long embrace. Both men were crying. Armand advised, "Dad, release that energy. You do not need it any more."

The men returned to work. Amber was wondering why Armand had left the building with his father without telling anyone where they were going. She went to Armand's office, asking, "What's up?"

"I'll fill you in once we are home."

At home, Armand cautioned her, "What I am about to tell you, please do not relate to anyone. This is a very private family matter."

"My goodness! Armand, is it that bad?"

"Yes." He continued as they changed their clothes, "Evidently this experience has been eating on Dad for some time. It came to a head when we were in San Diego, and he had his heart attack.

"A few days after I was born, Dad admitted that he had sex with a woman he picked up in a bar. They went to her house. Later she came to him saying she was pregnant. He took her to a health clinic where she was 'taken care of.' Dad told me only because I pressured him. Mom does not know.

"Amber, because of what he and Mom have done for me, this news of what he did behind Mom's back does not make me love him any less. We must forgive. We all have our weaknesses. You and I have a wonderful, caring relationship. In a few days my urges will be fulfilled again, for the first time since your accident."

Looking directly into his eyes she asked, "What makes you think your anticipations are any greater than mine?" He embraced her warmly promising, "On Friday evening after work, we need to eat out, come home, and then enjoy our coming together again."

"I'm looking forward very much to that evening," she agreed.

"Armand, what if your mother would ask for a divorce because of his unfaithfulness?"

"Mom works along with Dad. The business is just as much hers as it is his. Mom is very level-headed. She would not dump Dad. After all, he is our father. Can you imagine what kind of a mess would ensue? Jeffory would have his hands full."

"Armand, I have read that men really have a tough time when their wife is very pregnant. Then the baby arrives and he must continue to wait because she is still bleeding. Thank you, Sweetheart for telling me."

A few days later Francis told Armand, "I took your mother out for a nice dinner. When I told her, she looked straight into my eyes saying, 'Is that all?'"

Armand told Amber, "Mom and Dad were doing their thing, just as we were."

Armand and Amber shared as only they could. Later arm in arm, they talked over their experience. He sighed, "My love, you really let loose. Wow, when our women love us we certainly know it."

"How do you know?" she purred.

"I am embraced."

"Of course you are."

"I mean my penis is embraced. I feel your vaginal quivers, usually three or four times."

"That is wonderful," she agreed.

The next day at work Amber was helping Marshara when Jennifer and Jeffory came up the stairs. After they had been told, Jeffory called Armand asking, "Did Dad tell you why he was ticked off at himself? He wanted to know if the woman in question had given him anything. Fearful he may have contracted a disease he went to a doctor, who found nothing wrong with Dad. He did not want to pass on something to Mom."

Continuing, Jeffory asked, "Armand, how would you feel if Amber had relations with some other man?"

After taking a deep breath, he responded, "Dear brother, that will not happen. Believe me, I know how some women come on to men. If a man's emotions are not stable and his penis gets the best of them, things happen. It's quite simple, actually."

"Yep, Armand, we can become pretty hard up."

"Jeffory, Mom reacted the way I thought she would. While Dad had a heart attack and became all consumed, Mom just shrugged, 'Is that all?' Wasn't that a terrific statement?" Armand marveled.

"Her answer was great, which shows we have a terrific Mom and Dad."

Before their conversation ended, Armand asked, "Amber would like you and Eleanor to come over for dinner on Saturday night. Bring the kids, too."

"That sounds great."

The week passed rapidly. Armand and Amber shopped for groceries. Maraschino cherries were on their list. Amber planned to bake his favorite cake.

On Saturday night after they had eaten and played games with Gilbert and Gabrielle, Amber served the cake. Gilbert marveled, "This tastes just like Grandma's."

"It is very similar," Amber replied. "When you marry into a family, you must assume certain tasks like making your husband's favorite dessert." She later related how they talked of having this for the groom's cake.

After Jeffory's family left, Armand and Amber prepared for a short week. Work would cease after lunch on Wednesday to allow them time to prepare for her parents' visit on the next day.

Her parents planned to stay from Thanksgiving until the following Tuesday. Armand met them at the airport on Thursday morning. Amber had the holiday dinner ready when they arrived. This was the first time that Patricia and Dennis had visited Albuquerque. They were delighted with the townhouse and how Amber and Armand lived.

The table was set with translucent bone china, gold-rimmed goblets and sterling silver. Amber roasted a turkey with dressing, whipped potatoes, green beans, a gelatine salad, and home-made bread. Dessert was chocolate cherry cake and ice cream.

On Friday, Armand and Amber took her parents to visit the *Rambulet & Associates* building, which they found impressive. The yellow and orange colored carpet on the stairs and hallways was attractive. They admired Amber and Armand's official-looking offices with the new furniture, computers, and other related equipment.

Her parents realized their daughter had married into a family business, which was well-established in the city. Patricia thought, *It's no wonder Armand is so serious.*

Armand showed his in-laws his parents' offices saying, "My sister and brother-in-law's offices are on the other side of the building on this floor. My brother's legal office is on the first floor. My grandfather Rambulet started the business. Then Dad and Mom came aboard. Now we kids, with our spouses continue the operation. The business is growing as more people are added."

Back in the townhouse, Armand was feeling more comfortable with his in-laws. To them he related, "I learned about Amber's family during my visits to Oklahoma City. Now let me share some of my ancestors' history.

"My predecessors heard about Marquis de La Fayette's experiences in the new country of America, where he was assisting these new colonies in their fight to obtain their independence. Some of them left France and joined the Colonial army. They were paid by La Fayette himself, who was a personal friend of George Washington. Because financial help was sorely needed by the Colonial army, Lafayette used his own personal wealth to support the cause of freedom.

"Lafayette's influence was powerful enough that he arranged for the French navy to supply fresh troops and supplies, while blockading Atlantic seaports, preventing the British forces from being re-supplied.

"When the British surrendered in Yorktown, Virginia, in 1781, there were more French soldiers than Colonials in Washington's army.

"My ancestors were not seriously injured in the fighting. They stayed here, married American women and had children. That's how come I'm here."

Both Amber and her parents were very impressed with this history of Armand's background. She had no idea about early portions of her country's history.

Patricia and Dennis were very inspired by Armand's comments. "I knew a great bond had been forged between the Colonies and France, but I did not know of the sacrifices made by the French people and government," Patricia exclaimed.

Dennis remarked, "I am bothered by the fact that we have a glorious statue in New York harbor given to us by French citizens. Yet somehow, that's now forgotten. We hear negative statements about France. Armand, we need to remember."

"Indeed we do," he responded. "We do not have leaders with the qualities of Washington and La Fayette now. Our elected governmental officials are not statesmen, they are politicians on the public dole.

"Now let me change the subject. We have been so sedulously occupied at work we have not had a chance to look for a new car."

Amber interjected, "We have decided we need only one vehicle since we work at the same place."

Armand then noted, "I intend to purchase some exercise equipment, which we can put in the third bedroom."

They were invited to Celeste and Francis' home for dinner on Sunday noon. Celeste preferred a noon meal, allowing them to relax before work the next day. Francis related to Amber's parents, "Grandfather began the business. As Dad was growing up, he showed he was terrific with math. He was the first one in the family to graduate from the University. Dad began with his father after graduation. My mother helped when she could, but her primary job was raising my sister, older brother, and me."

Armand's parents had been quietly listening to the conversation.

His dad stated, "Celeste and I met at the University here, both studying business. When you marry and say 'I Do', you think you love that person. Heck, the love part is just the beginning. When we had our kids, thank goodness for the help of Celeste's mom. When our kids were grown and went to the U. here, Celeste was able to spend full time at work. Our children all joined the business to help it grow. Your daughter Amber, is a wonderful asset to *Rambulet and Associates*. The reason we have 'associates' in our name is because we are a number of people organized for a joint purpose, namely to assist other businesses with problems they may not know how to handle--insurance--to taxes--to legal assistance. Jeffory is the lawyer for all of us, as well as our customers when they need him.

"I believe it's unusual for a family to be as close-knit as we are. We buoy each other up if we are down. The saving grace has always been due to the women we have married." At this time Francis had tears in his eyes. He spoke saying, "It takes 'a heap a livin' to know what love is and what it all means."

Amber and Armand recognized intuitively how important his statements were and what they revealed about his father.

Armand hugged his dad and murmured, "Keep on lovin' Mom."

The conversation then turned to the annual balloon festival. Celeste stated, "This city is transformed to a major balloon ascension center. There isn't a hotel or motel room available within many miles of here." The foursome departed with embraces. Back at the townhouse, they all retired early.

After the noon meal the next day, Armand drove them around the city showing them the sights including University Boulevard. School was out which permitted them to 'gawk' more easily. Armand noted, "This school is not known for it's beautiful buildings and large campus areas. I have heard there are some beautiful campuses in other states where the architecture is blended from one building to another. Of the places we have seen, UTEP, in El Paso is the most architecturally coordinated around here."

After they returned to the townhouse, Amber and Armand prepared the evening meal. While they were eating, Amber's mother asked for more details on her accident, saying, "We were happy you called after you were checked over. Thank your lucky stars you are fine."

"Mom, I don't want to go over all the details again. But I will tell you, when one is traumatized, their brain does not work correctly. I did call 911 after I crawled out of the car, but I did not think to call Armand until they asked me where my husband was. My mind was zeroed on my car because it was hit so hard and burning. I was afraid it would explode. I sat on the ground behind a tree. That was a horrible experience. I was shaking so violently Armand could hardly understand what I was saying. A lady assisting me told Armand where to go. Once I saw him I broke down completely in uncontrolled weeping. I was a traumatic mess. Thank the *Great Energy* around me, I was not hurt, just traumatized."

Armand declared, "You cannot imagine what my thoughts were. I was praying she would be all right. However, from the sound of her voice she was so frightened she could barely speak. My love caused me such great concern that our neighbor drove me to the University hospital.

The next day, after they took Amber's parents to the airport, she and Armand drove to an auto dealership. Armand felt they needed a four-door sedan. Amber did not like the silver or black colors. She wanted a car which would give them good gas mileage. They purchased a vehicle which satisfied all their needs. Driving the new blue car home, they agreed that Amber would drive to work and he would drive home.

After work the following night, they purchased exercise equipment which was delivered on Thursday evening. Armand assembled his machine quickly. The next day when they had finished their evening meal, Amber cleaned the kitchen while he put on shorts and gym shoes to work out.

When she came to him he was sweaty. "Armand, you smell like male musk."

"Darling, I need to work out toxins," he explained. "Oh! I forgot to tell you, I invited Ralph and Lisa over for dinner tomorrow night."

"WHAT?" She instantly became very irritated. "Since I live here, too you could have asked me before you extended this invitation! I believe it's thoughtless and domineering for you to have done so and not asked me first. No special treatment for you tonight, Sir Armand!"

Very annoyed, she took her keys and went out the front door for a walk. She could mutter to herself and let off steam. He did not want her outside after dark. He climbed off his machine, threw on a jacket and ran to find her. He saw her at the corner and called, "Amber, please wait up."

She paid no attention and kept on walking, angry as hell at him. He ran to catch up with her asking, "Why didn't you wait for me?" He took her hand which was cold. They walked back to the house. Armand was not going to let her be angry this late in the evening. Once in the house she exploded. "Just who in hell do you think you are?" Her eyes flashed in anger. "I did not wait for you because I am not important enough in this house to be asked before guests are invited! If you do not respect me, why should I meet your commands?"

"Amber, I am extremely sorry I did not ask you first."

"Tomorrow night I am expected to be a kind, considerate, and hospitable hostess, when I wasn't asked," she repeated.

"Amber please forgive me," he begged.

He went to embrace her. With eyes blazing in fury, she yelled, "Don't touch me. You are an insensitive SOB."

"My mother is not a bitch. Please, we cannot continue this madness."

She did not answer him. Instead, Amber went to the bedroom and obtained her PJ's in order to sleep in the other bedroom.

"Oh no! That's not going to work," he growled, as he put his arm across the doorway preventing her from entering.

She looked at him ordering, "Then I leave the house."

"Amber my love, please think."

"Talk about think. I am not good enough to be thought of around here. You do as you damn please don't you?"

"My love, please take my hand."

She took it grudgingly and they went to the sofa where he seated her. Down on both knees, he pleaded for forgiveness. Tears rolled down his cheeks. Amber looked into his face. She was very upset herself.

She stated, "Armand, I am one-half of this household. I'm half of what goes on around here. I suppose it will be chocolate-cherry cake tomorrow night?"

"No, my love. We need to discuss your anger with me. I have the message. I heard it loud and clear. My bride is not to be ordered around. That is unkind and not loving."

"Armand, you could have come to my office. It's only a few steps from yours."

"Yes, you are correct my love." He arose to sit on the sofa beside her. Putting his arm around her, slowly bringing her toward him, he kissed her cheek asking, "May I be forgiven?"

After thinking for a moment she uttered, "Of course."

He kissed his wife very softly and tenderly. Then he asked, "Please sleep with me."

"I will, BUT THAT IS ALL."

"Of course. I could not perform if I had to."

With bedtime preparations in full swing, Amber saw that their disagreement had affected her husband, not only physically, but emotionally. When Armand was brushing his teeth, she went to him and rubbed his back. "My darling, that feels so good. Could you please rub the top of my shoulders and along both sides of my neck?"

"I'd love to."

She pressed her hands over his shoulders, rubbing firmly. Amber could feel the tenseness in his muscles. She continued as he flossed his teeth.

He muttered, "That feels so-o-o good."

Amber went to bed. Armand followed, cuddling close to her. His left arm went under her with his right on top. She was nestled in his arms. He caressed her until she went to sleep.

He did not disturb her as he gently pulled his arm from under her, then he turned on his side and pulled a little away from her. Just before sleep overcame him he thought, *Amber is not angry any more. She is with me. I must never be that thoughtless again--ever. Being beside her was all he thought about before he drifted off to sleep.*

After awakening Armand caressed his love and purred, "I love you."

"I love you too," she responded.

Both prepared breakfast. Sitting at the bar she thought, *what shall we have tonight?*

Knowing what she was thinking, he asked, "Could we have steak? I would be happy to make a large lettuce salad."

"That sounds good. Perhaps we could find a dessert at the store."

In the market they found what they needed for dinner, along with a good looking chocolate torte.

After they arrived home, while Amber set the dining room table Armand vacuumed the house. Amber appreciated his efforts. He was always helpful, assisting her whenever she needed him. Armand helped her prepare vegetables, then made the salad.

Happily, Ralph and Lisa arrived. Once they were seated, Armand brought champagne for a toast in goblets which had been a wedding gift. As their goblets clicked together, Ralph stated, "We have an announcement to make. We are pregnant."

Armand responded, "Congratulations."

Lisa stated, "I intend to work as long as I am able. We have saved enough so Ralph's salary should carry us through."

Armand added, "I am happy for you, if that is what you want. I have obtained a vasectomy. There will be no pregnancies in this house."

Ralph quizzed, "Don't you want any kids?"

Amber entered the living room. Sipping her champagne, she purred, "My sweetheart wants his intimacy and lots of it, without interruptions. We have agreed our children will be adopted. I hope to work for about five years. Now I'm needed in the business. When is your baby due?"

"Next May" Lisa answered.

"Oh, man! I can see Ralph changing, feeding and settling a crying baby. That is not for me. Good for you, if that's your desire." Armand suggested, then continued, "My love lets on as though I'm the only one enjoying intimacy, which is not true. Ralph, prepare yourself for weeks without that luxury."

Embarrassed, Amber's face was flushed as she retorted, "I have a story to relate about Armand and what he wanted in a grooms cake . . ."

He interrupted, "Please don't talk about me and that stupidity."

She related the story, but told in a manner which was funny, not putting him down. He ended up laughing with the others. He related, "I love chocolate, but instead of chocolate cherry cake, we'll enjoy a store-bought torte tonight."

After the meal, a card table, another wedding gift, was set up where the foursome attempted to play bridge. The evening was filled with banter, laughter, and chit chat.

Armand and Amber fell into bed about one a.m. When they awoke, the sun had risen over the mountains. He caressed his lady. Still irked over his insensitivity, Amber wanted no part of intimacy. She would not let him forget this incident soon.

As they ate, Armand's dad called inviting them to come over late in the afternoon.

"Sure, Dad. What time?"

"Around four."

"We'll be there."

Armand and Amber spent the day reading and relaxing. When they arrived at his parents' home, his sister, Jennifer and her husband, Ronald were there. His brother, Jeffory and Eleanor and family arrived soon after.

Francis had fixings for sandwiches, cut up fruit, and potato salad on the table. After the family had eaten, Celeste addressed their children and spouses. "I have forgiven your father. He's too terrific to let some other woman have him." Looking at Francis, she quickly added, "Only once!"

Jeffory answered, "Mom, you are great. My god! If you had wanted a divorce and wanted nothing more of Dad, I'd be devastated." Everyone agreed.

Armand asked, "Mom, did Dad do a good job in saying he was sorry?"

Celeste replied, "Oh, yes! I must admit, he could always turn me on. That is why you three are here in life form now. I hope you kids will learn that marriage is not always love, love, and more love. We make decisions, some very wise, others unfairly made because we are angry, frustrated, or in need of affection. This was what Francis needed. I was busy with a new baby. I had not recovered from the birth. I could not stay angry at your father. Forgiveness is necessary for us to continue the path we have selected. That was a small stone we pushed aside in our path.

Celeste and Francis were loved and shown great respect by their children and spouses. They left with fond embraces and kisses.

Once at home, Armand apologized for his unkindness. Amber was very affectionate. She led in their union. They enjoyed a prolonged and fulfilling experience. Armand whispered into her ear, "I love you."

"Good. I love you too."

They spent an extended time with arms entwined, savoring their powerful feelings before they prepared for sleep.

The whole family was at work the next day. Before Amber began, she thought about her husband's parents, especially his mother and her reaction. She thought, *Most women, including myself, would hold a grudge until the day they die. But Celeste and Francis have learned forgiveness. What's more, they understand what love really means. I don't think my Mom would be as forgiving. She would give Dad a kick in the crotch and say, 'Buddy Boy, that's just the beginning.'*

Amber was learning to understand the sensitivity which was needed in being a spouse. For harmony in marriage she realized, the other person must be considered first. However, she did not believe in subverting one's ideals or ideology just to keep peace. She understood that education should teach people to be able to talk and discuss their feelings without their spouses yelling or screaming at the top of their lungs because they were angry. So far Armand had proven himself to be a gentleman. *Now I must work.* She thought.

Armand came to her for lunch. Hand in hand, they walked to the cafeteria. While they were eating, Amber suggested they needed to begin Christmas shopping.

"Amber, are we going to spend some Christmas time with your mom and dad?"

"Certainly," she replied.

He then questioned, "Could we visit your family close to New Year's Day?"

"That sounds fine."

"I'll make plane reservations when we are back in the office."

After his parents returned from lunch, Francis went to Armand's office and informed him, "Your mother and I are going on vacation from December 28th for two weeks."

"Good for you, Dad."

"We'll probably be back here by January fourth," Armand replied.

When work was finished, they began Christmas shopping. Amber had prepared a list. She suggested to Armand, "Your mother does not have a mother's ring. Why don't we go together with your sister and brother and buy her one? We could have your Dad measure her finger size. She would think he would be getting her one."

Armand embraced his love, recognizing she had many good ideas. He had not realized how observant she was. He accepted all of her gift suggestions.

As Christmas approached, they both were occasionally able to spend time shopping during the day. Armand ordered a gold necklace with a pearl pendant as his gift for her. Amber had taken a couple of his suit jackets to have shirts ties and pink cuff links made in colors to blend with the jackets. She felt he would look good in a pink shirt with a pink tie with small blue and white stripes. She also obtained a blue shirt which could be worn with blue cuff links, which he already owned.

The days flew by. Armand gave his gift for Amber to his mother to put under their tree. They did not own a tree. The only look of Christmas in their home was poinsettias. This Christmas would be special--their first one together.

Amber took her wrapped gifts for Armand to Jennifer. One thing Armand had learned from her was that Amber did not want any love making in the morning. She told him she wanted her intimate moments in the dark, always with tenderness and loving. That was no problem for Armand, but he began thinking, *I would like to see if I could perform twice in one day again. It certainly worked on our honeymoon. Why not try again?*

Amber's reaction, "Forget it!"

On Christmas Day, Armand suggested she wear her Kelly green dress with a high neckline and long sleeves with no earrings.

His family was warm and hospitable. Each family brought something different for the meal. Francis and Celeste did not have responsibility for the whole meal, only turkey dressing and whipped potatoes.

The women talked in the living room while the men took over the kitchen. Armand had purchased champagne for a toast. Amber opened the bottle and poured the drink into beautiful butterfly-cut glasses.

Celeste had ordered a low floral centerpiece, permitting conversation to occur across the table. Instead of traditional colors, blue and white dominated the decorations.

Each person had a small package wrapped in white paper tied with a blue ribbon and a bow above their plate. Chairs were especially prepared for Gabrielle and Gilbert, allowing them to eat with the adults. The children's bubbly drinks were in goblets, just like the adults', but they contained no alcohol.

133

Celeste told of a memory when she was a child and was relegated to a card table in the kitchen with other children. In her memory, all the conversation was in the dining room. She did not want to put her grandchildren into such a situation.

Francis entered, pushing a cart loaded with turkey, dressing, potatoes, and other food. To his right, Gabrielle was attended by Jeffory. Amber served herself then passed the turkey to Ronald.

The children were delighted to be included at the *big table*. Gabrielle, a little chatterbox, was in kindergarten. She asked for an olive which was on her Aunt's plate. Amber gave it to her happily.

Francis told the family they were going to Cancun. He had never been there. Celeste had visited once before they were married. She remembered hearing of a devastating hurricane which raised havoc on that city a few years earlier. She was anxious to see what the area looked like now.

After their feast, Francis handed out gifts. The first one was for Celeste.

Amber was in shock and tears as she opened her box. Armand had purchased gold and pearl drop earrings and a necklace with a pearl pendent.

Through her tears she said, "Thank you so much. Where did you get this idea?"

"Oh! The jeweler helped me out."

Celeste was also in tears when her mother's ring box was opened.

When Armand saw his pink shirt and tie he was not quite certain how to feel. He loved the blue one. But the pink tourmaline cuff links caused him to question, "Are these for men?"

"Armand, you will look stunning in pink. That color will go well, especially with your gray or black suits. I know men are not used to wearing pink. Just because you are a male does not mean you cannot wear that color. It will not make you take on feminine characteristics," she flatly stated. "If I wore jeans, would I look more masculine?"

Armand did not answer. The rest of the family was so taken by their gifts, they did not meddle into this controversy. Before dessert was served, Jennifer and Ronald told the family they had started the adoption process. "We will not go for babies because I want to work part time," Jennifer stated. Francis and Celeste were happy to hear that news. At this time of the year they were not terribly assiduous in the business.

Jennifer and Ronald were going on vacation after Celeste and Francis returned. They were planning a Caribbean cruise.

Desserts were chocolate torte and pumpkin or pecan pie. Each person enjoyed his or her favorite. While the ladies were washing crystal, the men divided portions of the food to go home with each family. After all the dishes and small packages were removed, Francis put the dining room back together. By the time the turkey had been portioned out, not much of it remained. Celeste growled, "I'm not making any turkey soup out of that carcass." No one argued with her. The turkey remains were scrapped.

Amber and Armand left, followed by the others, all wishing their parents a good time on their vacation. At home Armand put the leftovers in the refrigerator along with the remains of Amber's salad.

In the bedroom, Amber had placed her shoes in the closet, then looked at herself in the bathroom mirror. "Armand this jewelry is beautiful. These earrings are wonderful. I love their feel," she emoted. He came to help her remove her dress after taking off his jacket. With more disrobing, their night of bliss began. She could not say no to her husband this evening. As she removed her earrings, he kissed her ears purring, "I am thrilled you like your jewelry. The jeweler told me they were something you could wear to work, giving a change from the amethyst."

"Thank you, my love. Only you could thrill me this much."

Armand slyly smiled, "Oh, it's jewelry along with our intimacy which will suit your needs."

"Armand Rambulet!" she exclaimed, as she tried to tickle him. Only when she reached his groin did he begin to squirm, uttering, "I am being attacked by a certain female who cannot get enough of me." She continued her tickling. He struggled so much he nearly fell out of bed. Both giggled and laughed with each other.

They awoke on the morning of December 26th. She accepted the adoring words Armand softly spoke to her. Looking into his adoring eyes, she murmured, "I know what you are thinking. I will make an exception today, because of your gifts. I'll keep my eyes closed because I do not want to be shocked out of my wits."

Armand fulfilled all of her desires. Afterward, he thought, *This is what I must do to gain extra love from her. This lady of mine does not submit easily.* "Boy, the poor sucker who would try to put the make on you would definitely have a hard-sell job," he announced.

Kissing him she agreed, "Sweetheart, you certainly have that right." These experiences proved to Armand that he could still love his lady twice in a twenty-four hour period. The rest of the day was spent eating and cleaning.

The 27th was a work day. On the way home, they stopped at his parents' to wish them a wonderful vacation.

At home after their evening meal, out of the blue, Amber posed this question, "Armand, when does life begin?"

Armand's answer began, "Life always was and always will be, whether in embodiment here, somewhere else, or at one with the *Eternal Energy*. Remember, we do not destroy energy, we merely change its form. We do not make babies. We think we do. That's what religions and culture teach, but they are not thinking about the real beginning. The life force of a baby always was and always will be. This life energy decides who will be its parents."

Amber permitted him to talk while he was projecting food for thought.

He continued, "The universe is still expanding. Therefore our thinking, as far as time goes, is not applicable. My love, why are you and me together now?

She picked up on his ideas. "We need experiences together this time around. We are to be happy, helpful, and honor each other and our fellow man. I am to love and cherish you and only you."

"Do I meet your expectations?"

"Without a question," she smiled.

On the 29th Amber and Armand flew to Oklahoma City, where they were welcomed by Amber's mother, who was delighted to see them in a wonderful, happy holiday mood.

Patricia announced, "We have not planned any special food. We felt everyone would be tired of turkey. Dennis will fix steak when he gets home."

In the house Patricia asked, "Are you wearing new jewelry from Armand?"

"Oh yes! Mom, isn't it beautiful?"

"Armand has excellent taste."

These words of praise inflated his ego. He was a well-loved man and had every reason to be on top of the world.

Her mother thanked Armand and Amber for her gold chain and earrings. Her father appreciated his globe, which fit on the desk in his den.

On New Year's Eve, her brother's family came for an evening meal. Patricia did not want them on the road, so she asked them to stay. "The children can be with us for as long as they can keep their eyes open."

Beds for Sue and Raymond were prepared. They were in their pajamas after seven. When Sue went to sleep, Wendell put her in bed. Her brother stayed up until nine.

The TV had been on for a time, but when the conversation became thought-provoking, it was turned off. Family talk was more important. Wendell said he enjoyed studying his Dad's globe very much. "I played a game with Raymond, asking if he could point to a continent or a country. That globe is a wonderful tool for this kind of education. I discovered where Lesotho is located."

"Where is it?" Patricia asked.

Wendell repeated the spelling, then indicated, "It is a small country completely surrounded by South Africa."

Just before midnight, Dennis opened a bottle of champagne. They toasted each other for a good and happy New Year, then all went to bed.

The next morning, the men made breakfast, after which Wendell's family left for home. When Dennis went to his desk, he found photographs of Amber and Armand's wedding. There was a complete album and individual pictures in frames for their desks. They all spent the morning admiring these photos.

The first look at her photos made Amber happy, especially the ones of her. She liked the way she appeared in her beautiful gown.

Armand became teary-eyed as he viewed the pictures. "This was our day. Thanks so much, Mom and Dad. Your daughter was so beautiful, my eyes about popped out. I had never seen that much of Amber's skin exposed before."

"I noticed how you looked at her. I was proud because she was a beautiful bride."

"Indeed, Mother."

Their time together was sweet and precious. It passed too swiftly. Two days later, her parents took them to the airport. They parted with embraces and loving words. Amber slept on the plane. She told Armand she was tired because her menses had come.

He was beginning to understand why women called this time of the month, *The Curse*. Amber certainly did not like it. To her, it was nonsense. She awoke and looked at him muttering, "Something went haywire in evolution here on earth. It's the female who bears so much responsibility in the reproductive process, while men are off to the side. In your case, you look at me with love and affection and think, *I'm sorry.*"

"I am sorry," he murmured.

"I'll have more to say when we are in the house. I don't want to talk any more, all right?" she snarled in disgust.

They arrived in Albuquerque. A cab took them home. Armand opened the door while Amber went directly to the sofa to lie down. *This is unusual for her,* he thought. After removing his jacket, he went to her. Kneeling, he asked, "What can I do for you?"

"Stay away from me!" she growled.

"Dear, why?"

"My period was a few days late. It comes with such regularity, I have it marked on a calendar in my purse. I'm having cramps and have passed some clots, which are one sure cause of cramps. Those clots make me wonder if I have sloughed off an early pregnancy. Armand are you certain you are harmless?"

"My love, I had my operation for that purpose."

"Sometimes these medical procedures fail, Armand." She spoke with assuredness.

"My love, you have seen my scars. We have been married such a short time, how could my operation fizzle so soon?"

Weeks passed, while Amber sedulously worked many long hours. When her next period was due, she only spotted. She was suspicious and purchased two pregnancy test kits. Both indicated positive for pregnancy.

"Armand, I am pregnant."

"You're what! Amber my love, please make an appointment."

Amber sat in the office of her Ob-Gyn on February 27th. She had dressed as she always did, in a suit, skirt, blouse or dress. She wore a blue and white rayon printed dress with ruffles at the end of the sleeves and skirt. She looked striking because her shoes matched the blue in her garment. Her hazel eyes were focused on a magazine article when her husband entered and kissed her cheek. He had been on an errand close by. "How much longer?" he asked.

"I don't believe very long. Why don't you ask at the desk."

He was told, "Perhaps ten more minutes."

"Thank you."

By this time, other women in the room had noticed the tall gentleman whose brown hair had been styled for him. His clothing also garnered their attention. He was attired in a lovely gray pin-striped suit with a pink shirt, pink tie with a small blue stripe, and cuff-links made from pink tourmaline. The women thought, *No doubt, this man was a father-to-be who wanted a girl.*

Returning to Amber, he extended his arm and helped her arise from the chair. With his arm around her, he ushered Amber into the hall where he proceeded to talk firmly saying, "My love, please allow me to speak to your doctor. You will have time to say what you want. Please, understand you are too important to me and to the business for a pregnancy now. I don't know what the hell happened, but it is obvious my vasectomy was no damn good. I've talked to my urologist and as soon as you feel better, I'll go back and make certain I am properly incised. Pregnancy would not be fair to us or to a baby. I don't want you to think I'm selfish, but we've been married only six months. We have just begun to know each other."

"Yes," she smiled, "Enough to be impregnated by a man who can't get enough of me." She continued, "I feel in my heart, something is the matter because I am spotting. I'm two weeks overdue, as far as my period is concerned. Tests show I am pregnant. Therefore, I'm with you, let's do something as soon as possible and not let this continue."

With her husband holding her hand, Mrs. Amber Rambulet was called into an inner room.

Armand had not been in a gynecologist's examination room before. "Amber, what are those metal things sticking up in the air on the end of the table?"

She was sitting between 'the two things'. "Armand, upon cervical examinations, we place our feet in them, spread our legs allowing the MD to have a feel or a look-see."

"My god! They look like part of an ancient torture machine, my love!" he expressed.

Dr. Steven Galsthrop entered the room. He greeted Amber first, then Armand. With supposed wit, he smiled, "Well, Amber, you've been married long enough to be pregnant. I read your wedding announcement in the paper."

"Doctor," Armand spoke. "My wife has taken two pregnancy tests. Both show she is pregnant, but I do not want her to be. I need her and so does the business. I've had a vasectomy. Evidently something happened. Our business needs both of us. That's why I had my operation. We talked with my urologist. As soon as Amber has that cluster of cells removed, I'll go back for more incising."

"Well Amber, how do you feel about your husbands attitude?" The doctor questioned.

"Doctor, we talked before we were married about adopting children, not having our own. I have an advanced business degree. That is why my husband's family hired me." Amber continued, "I personally feel that something is not right. I'm spotting. I hate wearing pads all the time."

"All right Amber, take off your panty-hose and panties. Let's have a look," the doctor said as he left.

Amber told her husband, "Do not be surprised if you are asked to leave the room."

"Why do I need to leave? I'm part of this process. I have loved you so much and so many times, I don't understand. Evidently my 'pistol' was loaded which I did not know. This makes me mad as hell. I need to hear what the doctor tells you while I am with you."

When the doctor returned, Armand asked, "Doctor, I hope I may be with her during the examination." A nurse was with the MD.

"If you feel more comfortable you are free to stay." The nurse carefully positioned herself between the doctor and Armand. With her legs in 'those gosh-awful things' the MD probed. When he finished Armand saw blood on the MD's latex glove.

The doctor questioned them, "Are you both certain you want to proceed?"

"Yes," they answered together.

"Amber, you may get dressed. Then we will talk more."

A few minutes later Dr. Galsthrop entered the room. He did not divulge he had reservations about Amber's pregnancy.

Armand spoke, "Doctor, we have talked about this many times. I am so angry that this happened. We plan to adopt children. I think that is our right. We have not concluded the number or when we will make that decision. I want to add, I love Amber so much I'd give anything to have her relieved of this worry and apprehension."

The doctor went to his appointment calendar. He found that ten a.m. the next day was available. To Amber he said, "Plan to eat nothing but juice or broth tonight. Only water tomorrow morning. Be here at nine a.m."

Armand thanked the doctor. He was more at ease, knowing his wife was being treated quickly.

On the way home Amber asked, "Will you stay with me?"

"Of course, my darling. I'll be as close as I'm allowed."

They both slept well.

The next morning, Amber dressed in pajamas, a house coat, and matching slippers. She sipped water while Armand ate a light breakfast. He did not feel like eating much. He had told his parents that Amber needed a medical procedure, which was true.

When the surgery was completed, the doctor went to Armand saying, "It's a good thing you did not plan on having your own children. For your wife, that would have been an impossibility. The lining of her uterus is too thin. That is why she was spotting. She would never be able to carry a baby to the point of viability."

Armand gave a big sigh and let his shoulders drop, then took a deep breath. "Thank you so much doctor," he uttered.

Coming out from the effect of the anesthetic, Amber felt 'woozy' and disoriented. Armand leaned over and gently kissed her lips pressing his right hand into her left. "My dear love, how do you feel?"

"Her eyes focused on a container of ice. "May I sip on an ice cube?" He quickly helped her. He continued showing affection until she was alert enough for him to repeat what the doctor had told him.

"What a relief! I knew something was not right with that situation."

"Before long I'll be able to take you home. The doctor said your bleeding may be worse than your normal periods but do not be alarmed. Your uterus was thoroughly scraped. My love, I feel terrible because you had to endure this. Isn't it strange, we don't want our own children, but there are people who have their own and abuse them?" he added.

Trying to take her mind off her pain, he continued, "Rain is predicted for this afternoon, which will be a blessing for the plants. The air will smell fresh again."

He then helped his wife into her nightwear, house coat, and slippers. He held her arm firmly. In the car, he fastened her seat belt asking Amber how she felt.

"I'm sore. My whole abdomen aches," she murmured. At home he helped remove her house coat. Putting her slippers by the night stand, he assisted her into bed.

"I'll eat a bite here. Keep your cell phone close. If you need me, I'll come home. Otherwise, I'll work until six tonight." Armand's mother, called at five saying she would bring food for them slightly after six.

Amber thanked her mother-in-law very much. Upon arising Amber found she had soaked her night clothing and left a lot of blood in the stool, which alarmed her. In her anxiety, she forgot to flush the commode. She found another pad and sought a tight fitting panty. Feeling faint, she leaned against the bathroom counter. After gaining some strength from within, she went to the kitchen and obtained a glass of ice cubes, then went back to bed and was dozing when she heard Armand and his mother talking.

Celeste raised her voice, calling, "I hope you feel better tomorrow, Amber."

Approaching, Armand bent and kissed his wife. He saw she was pale and told her, "Mom made some chicken broth for you." Still talking, he went into the bathroom and saw her bloody sleep wear, the blood-soaked pad and red stain in the stool, "My god! my love, this is not right." He called the doctor, asking, "Is it normal for so much blood to be lost?" He told the M.D. what he had seen.

The doctor responded, "Blood is cleansing the area where I worked. Tomorrow she should have less blood loss and feel better. I have given her medication for pain. This should enable her to sleep tonight."

Armand removed his jacket and tie, then asked, "My love, would you like me to bring you some broth?"

"No, Armand, I'll get up so I can talk with you."

He set the table with another glass of ice for her. He went to the bedroom to help her arise, feeling she might be a little *woozy*. She kissed him and they embraced very gently. He said, "I am so sorry you have to be this miserable."

"Somehow, *Karma* has a role here," she sighed.

He served her a ladle of broth with a few pieces of chicken and a cluster of noodles.

"Oh my! This is delicious," she exclaimed.

Armand was eating hungrily. He made toast with peanut butter for himself. He offered her a piece, with a little butter, "Enjoy, my love."

As they talked over their day, he went to the stove and served his mother's apple cinnamon dumplings. The kitchen smelled delightful. He served her a few slices of apples, smothered with the syrupy sauce.

"Sweetheart, please tell your mom thank you. If you don't mind I'll lie on the sofa. You enjoy those special dumplings."

When Armand finished cleaning the kitchen, he went to his love asking, "Are you ready to go to bed?"

"Yes I am. Please give me a hand."

He helped her arise. They both prepared for bed. In the bathroom he asked her, "Has your bleeding lessened?"

"I believe so," she replied, as she placed a new pad in her sleepwear.

After brushing his teeth furiously, Armand removed his clothes and was in his 'birthday-suit'. Sitting on the commode, Amber noticed how his penis wiggled. She washed her hands and brushed her teeth. She remarked, "Sweetheart, you are quite an intimidating man in your nakedness, even without an erection."

"My love, I'm all for you. However, I believe you have received too much of me lately," he remonstrated.

She went to their large bed. He followed, helping her recline. Armand then bent to kiss her. Because he was naked, she grabbed his *manliness* and tweaked it saying, "You have been too engorged recently."

He kissed her again saying, "If you need anything in the night, please awaken me.

"I will," she replied. He went to his side of the bed, obtained pajamas from under the pillow, and gently crawled beside her. He was soon asleep.

About four a.m. he was awakened by the flushing of the commode. He arose to meet his love in the bathroom, asking, "Is there something you need?"

"I'm hungry," she stated.

Turning on the lights, he held her arm walking into the kitchen. "Would you like some warm soup?"

"Yes indeed, and toast with peanut butter and jelly, please."

"Hot soup coming up." He put bread into the toaster thinking, A*s long as I'm awake, I might as well have something, too.*

While the soup warmed, the toast popped. He prepared it for her, then poured some apple juice (without Vitamin C), which she drank with gusto. She devoured her toast with fervor. She was hungry. Amber then tackled the warm soup with vigor. Helping himself to a bowl, he asked, "Have you been sleeping all right?"

"Oh, yes! I didn't know anything until a short time ago," she answered.

"I'm glad of that. How about cramps?"

"They're less. I'm ready to return to bed." He turned out the lights and they made their way back to the bedroom. He helped her slip under the covers, kissing her again, then crawled into his side of the bed.

As he fell asleep he realized how up-tight and upsetting the previous day had been. He determined he would sleep or doze as long as she did. She awoke about eight. Armand had been dozing. When she moved, he crawled toward her putting his arm over her body. "Good Morning, my darling." He then kissed her several times.

"My goodness you are love-struck," she uttered.

"Yes, for you. Are you ready to get up?"

"For a little while, anyway." He helped her don her house coat and slippers. Then she followed him into the bathroom. While washing her face, she expressed, "What a night! That medicine made me sleep so hard I think I snored."

"Right on!" he laughed. "But there was no way you could have obtained any sleep without it. I put my arm over my ear and slept well. We certainly do not want to become pregnant again, ever. That was a bad trip."

He took her hand and they went into the kitchen, finding leftovers still on the table. She put out clean silverware, bowls, and glasses as Armand prepared breakfast food, juice, and eggs. They discussed what needed to be done. As they ate, Amber related what food needed to be purchased. She expressed, "I certainly wish I felt good enough to shop with you, but I certainly don't."

He understood. Dresses and suits needed to be taken to the cleaners. He had to purchase stamps as well. (They had forgotten to order them from their mail-carrier, which Armand thought was a great new service).

He dressed, shaved, and went to the kitchen. Amber put the rinsed dishes in the dishwasher. She was cleaning the counter tops when he kissed her goodbye. After he left, she filled the washing machine with soiled clothes and lay down for a nap on the sofa.

During her nap, thoughts and memories of her single life and school days at Oklahoma State University passed through her mind. That is where she had obtained a full scholarship. Two of her sorority sisters served in her wedding party. She had graduated with excellent grades in business.

Thus began our courtship, she thought as she arose from the sofa, hearing the washing machine signaling that it was finished. Amber hung her husband's trousers rather than use the dryer. She put the rest of the clothes in the machine and started the cycle. She wiped the bathroom counter and washed the bloody plastic wastebasket. She was cleaning the sink when she heard sounds of the garage door opening.

She went to the kitchen door to open it for her husband, knowing he would have groceries. She was met by a weeping spouse, who uttered a 'thank you' through his tears. "Sweetheart, what happened?" she asked. Before he could answer, he handed her food for the freezer, which she promptly deposited. She finished storing the rest of the groceries, while he lay on the sofa.

She went to him asking, "Sweetheart, are you all right? What has you so upset? Amber wiped his tears and kneeled on the floor, putting her arms around him, kissing each eye.

Armand blew his nose with great energy. He took deep breaths and then arose. "Come and sit beside me," he asked.

Holding each other's hands, he began to relate his difficulty.

"Just before I paid the bill at the market, a strange feeling came over me. I felt cool and not in control of myself. I had to ask for help in putting the groceries into the trunk. I climbed into the car, sat behind the wheel for a time, when I felt energy from beyond myself and heard, *Carefully proceed home. You need to be at your house.*

"I then had a glimpse of a lifetime when I immigrated to this new country to grow grapes. When the plants did not have enough time to develop a good root system, torrential rains came and lasted a long time. Cascading water came creeping into the cabin. Amber, the lady who is now you, was very pregnant and was in the process of delivery, but you drowned. Your body was never found.

"This episode brought me a glimpse of another life when, again you were my wife, who died in childbirth," he blurted with more tears.

Amber held him tightly saying, "I am with you now. That's what is important. Remember, THE POINT OF POWER IS IN THE PRESENT. She placed kisses all over his face, finally embracing him and kissing his lips. "That was then. We are in the now, sweetheart."

He embraced her repeating 'thank you' many times. "We have lived through some trauma. That's why I was so taken with you at first sight. Thank goodness, you accepted my advances."

Later, Armand visited his urologist. His right vas deferens had regenerated. Raising his voice to his M.D. he growled, "Because of your ineptness, I have impregnated my wife, when we believed I was safe."

Dr. Blantz repeated his operation with no charge. Armand realized the doctor felt very badly about his problem.

Amber and Armand recovered from their procedures. On some days they worked all day, on others they stayed home to help hasten their healing.

As he recovered, Armand thought back to the day he met Amber, their courtship, marriage, honeymoon, and finally settling into work in the family business.

His family adored Amber. She loved Armand and was willing to follow established methods of the family business. They all realized she added a great deal to the business structure.

Amber was able to bank her entire salary, which eventually would be put into a new home for them. Armand was able to add additional funds.

They agreed she would work for at least five years before considering adoption. They had been told this process could be a nightmare. Jennifer had told her brother, "Every facet of your life is probed."

Armand and Amber found a great deal of special time as they used their exercise equipment. When they worked out, Amber shared her ideas of what she wanted in a home of their own.

He was utterly surprised when she stated, "We will have an enclosed swimming pool, a room for this exercise equipment, two bedrooms for children, a master bedroom with an attached bathroom, and a guest suite. Also, a living room, dining, kitchen and laundry--and of course, an attached garage."

"My god! Amber, that house will require a huge lot and will cost a million dollars!"

She ignored his comment continuing, "Some of the bedrooms could be upstairs. Because of the climate, the pool needs to be used all year long, otherwise, why have one?"

"I really had not thought of an indoor swimming pool, but that would be nice. However, Amber, we are talking about a lot of money here."

"I think it would be great to have some more exercise equipment in addition to what we have here."

Many nights before he fell asleep, Armand thought further about a house built to Amber's specifications.

As they worked out together, Armand tried to explain why he did not think they could afford the house she wanted.

Her flippant response, "Well, guess what? I'll just have work a little longer, won't I?"

Armand had lived with her long enough to realize she had a will of steel. What Amber wanted, she would eventually obtain. What could he do? Just go into debt a little more deeply; however, he realized that Amber was able to manifest what she wanted.

Chapter 11.

Amber and Armand's first wedding anniversary was approaching. He asked, "My love where would you like to go? Chicago, New York, San Francisco?"

"Sweetheart, those cities are hot humid or muggy and San Francisco is too cool. New Mexico is a beautiful state. Let's drive and see some of the special places here."

"If that's your wish, fine. We will be inside an exciting state. Where would you like to start?"

"How about Santa Fe? We could spend a day there. I have never been to the capital city." Armand thought that was a good idea. They discussed their plans in detail. Two weeks later they began their trip.

Once in Santa Fe, Amber feasted her eyes on artwork in the many galleries in the city square. They walked in the plaza, visiting a myriad of shops to satisfy her curiosity.

Once in their motel room she exclaimed, "What good are walls if you have nothing on them? I want something for our walls. I don't want any more jewelry."

"All right, we'll seek out something for our walls; however, let's also look in smaller towns."

As they traveled to smaller locations, Armand made certain they visited modest art shops and businesses. In one gallery, Armand spotted three paintings which went together. They attracted him and the price was suitable. Amber was thrilled.

"My love I like these. Do you?"

"Yes, Armand. They are beautiful. Let's buy them."

He asked the proprietor if they had other works by this artist.

"He lives on the *Jemez* Indian Reservation. I am sure he would have others for you. I can call him. He might bring some in for you today," the clerk suggested. The artist arrived later with more art. Armand and Amber studied the offerings. Independently, each one decided which pieces they preferred. When they consulted, they liked the same ones. The artist was happy to see two people who enjoyed his work. "I will give you seven for the price of six," he told them. Armand paid the artist.

The travelers continued their adventures, exploring Bandelier National Monument and Taos. Armand commented, "If we thought Santa Fe was crowded, these places are swarming with tourists too."

"Of course, my love. These tourists appreciate the American Indian peoples and their art," Amber observed.

They visited Angel Fire the Vietnam Veteran's Chapel and then went north around the mountains to Chama, Paragosa Springs, and Durango, Colorado.

They enjoyed this trip very much. Armand no longer needed to worry about treatment or his technique with his lady. However, he was finding when Amber had her heart set on something, (like the koala bear things on their honeymoon), she would be very upset if he objected. It would affect her loving him.

Next they visited Mesa Verde National Park, where both enjoyed spectacular walks near ancient Indian housing and culture.

At Shiprock, N.M. she admired paintings of this beautiful rock formation. She saw Navajo artwork and purchased a small rug which she planned to hang in their home. As they went into Bloomfield Armand told her, "By hook or crook, you are obtaining things to hang on the walls. Have you noticed, I have paid for all the purchases you wanted?"

"Sweetheart, whose money? I work too, but I believe you are hinting you would like something in return, other than just a kiss."

"Only if *Mademoiselle* would like me to be a part of her loving session tonight."

As Armand was removing his trousers in their motel room, Amber came from behind him and reached into his briefs for a feel of his precious skin uttering, "You were hoping for such a thing because you were preparing that 'bratwurst." Their evening was fulfilling for both. Each related to the other how much they were loved.

Back in Albuquerque before they went home, hand-in-hand, they explored the old town shops. She enjoyed being with him. He was a good shopper, patient, and always polite. They returned home with the car's trunk full and back seat stacked to the windows. The protective packing for the seven paintings took lots of room.

Armand was permitted no rest until the paintings had been carefully unpacked and hung. He made a quick run to his parents' home for a level. While he was gone she wiped the frames and protective glass of the art works. Then she arranged how they would appear on the wall.

After dinner as Armand hung the paintings, Amber hovered around him so closely he became upset. "If I have to be directed, 'an inch in this direction' or 'one half inch down', I'll let you do the hanging! I'm no infant. I do have some idea of how these should look!" he spat.

"Oh! I am sorry, sweetheart."

He was a little out of sorts, feeling they had spent a large amount of money. As he pounded nails he growled, "I'm sure as hell glad we did not go to New York. My god, this loot would have cost three times as much."

"Armand, you are forgetting these art pieces would not have been available there. Shoot fire, we could not even find these things in Oklahoma City."

Once the three related pictures were hung over the sofa, she asked, "Armand please come back here and take a look."

He was aghast at their beauty. Amber put her arms around him and kissed him purring, "Thank you Sweetheart."

Armand was pleased but thought, *Oh my, the money!*

Amber knew Armand was uptight. She asked him to please come to the sofa. Looking directly into his eyes, she stated, "Sweetheart, I know we spent a lot of money but think, we will have this beauty around us for the remainder of our lives."

With a shrug of his shoulders Armand sighed, "Oh what we don't do for the women we can't live without. This shows what I will do for my lady. Where do you want this hung?" he asked as he picked up another picture.

"Please put the two pictures one above another on the wall behind the loveseat." He stepped back and looked. He had to admit, once the art works were in place, they went well with the furniture. He hung two more pieces, one on each side of the vertical ones. Amber was pleased beyond words. "Sweetheart, I now have pictures on my walls."

"These are my walls too," he reminded her. Then, looking into her eyes, he added, "I won't be able to add any money to our savings account because of these purchases."

"Sweetheart, please think. We did not have to purchase plane tickets. We were not crammed on an airplane with foul air. We moved when we wished, determined our routes, and when we would return home. A value cannot be put on convenience unless you are a businessman, which you most certainly are. Therefore, you know time is money. There was wear and tear on the car plus depreciation. Or is that vehicle just for around here?" she smiled.

Saying nothing, Armand began mulling figures around in his head. He went to their bedroom and began to undress.

Amber cleaned the kitchen. She wanted to put a little more space and time between them.

He came into the bathroom in his pajamas. Amber could sense his strain. She dressed for bed. Before she laid down she took the koalas off the chair and was cuddling them when he entered the room. Seeing this action sent Armand into orbit.

"Amber, for god's sake, I'm here. Are you that deprived of love?" he growled. "May I have them, please?"

Giving him the toys, she sighed, "I feel guilty, I made you angry."

"I guess that makes us even-steven," he reiterated, as he went around his side of the bed.

"We won't be able to sleep because we are upset," she sighed. Please tell me what you are angry about."

Looking at her he stated, "For one thing, I have been manipulated; the second reason; I am overdrawn at the bank; thirdly, I do not tolerate being ordered around like a child."

"I'm very sorry, sweetheart. How much do you need to fill the gap? We can drop off the money on the way to work. Armand, I take full responsibility. You know I love to shop. I wanted something for our walls. We purchased all sorts of things which make me happy, not sad," she iterated. Leaning toward him, she gave him a gentle kiss. She continued to talk. "My sweetheart, it's only money. I will take care of the shortfall, or whatever you need because you take care of the house payment, food, and other expenses, while my money is all banked except for four-hundred dollars. What I do not spend, I put in a box behind the broom in the utility closet. Presently, I have three hundred in my purse. I believe there is nearly a thousand in the box."

"Amber, how in the world are you able to stash money away like that?"

"I do my hair to save money. I really don't shop except on occasions like I just did. Sweetheart, that outing was special to me," she answered.

"My love, stashing money away in a box does not make sense, nor is it something a successful businesswoman would do. That action is left over from a hundred years ago," he scolded.

"Armand, the money is here. We won't need to withdraw funds. This is my way of handling our 'Business Management Crisis.'" She climbed out of bed to obtain the box. She sat on the bedroom floor and dumped out the contents between her sprawled legs.

Seeing bill after bill, Armand sat down opposite her and began to count the funds. "One hundred, two hundred . . ." He was shocked to find more than two thousand dollars.

"My god! Amber, please don't squirrel money away like this. I could have looked at that box and thrown it away thinking it was waste," he growled.

"Armand, in this house, nothing is thrown away without checking its contents," she fired back.

"My darling, you're a professional. That kind of money belongs in the bank," he insisted.

'Yes Sir! Tomorrow that money will be banked, SIR! . . . Now, to get technical, that was my money. How I squirrel it away is my business!"

Armand sat on the floor beside her. Putting his left arm around Amber, with his right hand he turned her face toward him. "I believe some clarification is necessary. May I ask, when does my money cease to be yours?"

"Yes, my money is always yours, sweetheart. There is no need to answer your question. I feel like an idiot."

"My love, let's agree to disagree. To continue to make each other feel terrible is crazy," he spoke softly as he helped her arise. He tucked her into bed, then fell into his side. Turning to kiss her goodnight, he brought her body close to his. Her feel through the top of his pajamas was wonderful. They embraced.

The next morning, money was deposited to cover the art expenses.

Chapter 12.

At work Amber became immersed in helping a small private company out of too much debt. She picked Armand's brain as well as Jennifer and Ronald's. In handling the case she gained a great deal of valuable experience.

Amber and Armand spent Labor Day going to a movie and eating at his parents' home.

When Armand thought about Amber stashing money away, and when she was in the bathroom he checked the box in the closet. He found a $100 bill and put it back. Time passed quickly. They spent Thanksgiving with his family. Later they purchased Christmas gifts for each family member.

On December 13th, Amber's mother called saying that her Aunt Marion, who was two years younger than Patricia, had been injured in an auto accident as she drove home. Her aunt was in the operating room. Amber's mother needed someone to share her feelings. Because Amber had a client, she replied to mother, "I'll call you tonight at six o'clock your time."

Armand drove them home and began supper. Amber called her weeping mother. When Patricia finally gained enough composure, she reported, "Marion's and Greg's children have been called. We don't think she will survive her injuries."

Amber consoled, "Mom, you know very well we choose when we will take embodiment and when we will leave our husk behind. Was this a case of DWI?"

Her mother sobbed, "We believe so."

"Is Uncle Greg with her?"

"Yes. His brother is with him too."

"Mom, at eight o'clock tonight your time, gather everyone and pray. We will do the same. Call people who know Aunt Marion and have them pray too. Please call me tomorrow morning at eight thirty," Amber suggested.

"We will. Thank you dear. We love you."

"We love you too, Mom. Try to get some sleep. Prayer works."

At 7:00 p.m. Amber and Armand were in their bedroom sitting in lotus positions, meditating. She asked for healing energy. Armand asked that special energy be directed to the injured hip and pelvis of Aunt Marion. Each took their turn asking that rainbow colors be used for the good of the injured lady.

Amber finished with, "Aunt Marion, we love you. May you feel the energy of those praying for you. I thank the *Great Energy*. I thank you. I thank you."

They then prepared for bed.

The next morning Patricia called. From the sound of her voice, Amber knew her mother felt better. Patricia reported, "She made it. Marion is heavily sedated and hooked up to machines. The doctor spoke to Greg and the children, telling them, "Only two people can stay with her if they wish. We are keeping her heavily sedated because she suffered a broken pelvis, ribs, femur, and left humerus."

"My goodness Mom, she will have some tough hours, days, and weeks ahead."

"Indeed. It's tough on the family when they may be with her for only a short time every hour. Cynthia, Marion's and Greg's daughter, came from Atlanta. She is staying with Wendell and Lily. Her brother is staying with us," Patricia reported.

"Mom, I have a client tomorrow at eight. When I'm free I'll call you. If I catch you when you cannot talk I'll leave a message."

Dennis came to the phone. "I went to the police to find out the details of the wreck. Amber, Marion was hit by a character who was under the influence of a drug, speeding through a red light in a big burly pickup. He hit your aunt's car on the left side. The side air bag saved her life. She was wearing her seat belt, but the left door was caved in like cardboard. You know all about drunk drivers."

"Dad, I was very lucky. My car was hit in the back. I was in so much shock, I wasn't thinking straight. Dad I must run. I'll talk with you tomorrow. I love you. "After this conversation she went to Armand's office, telling him, "They think Aunt Marion will pull through. We can talk more at lunch."

When they were eating, Armand told her to suggest that her uncle obtain an attorney.

In her office she called her mother leaving a message to have Uncle Greg hire a lawyer.

That night after they had eaten, Armand quietly looked into her box. It now contained ten-ten dollar bills. This time she caught him scrounging in the closet. She asked, "Did you find what you were looking for?"

"Amber you're teasing me!"

"Sweetheart, you didn't answer my question."

With its contents intact he put the box back and closed the door. He went to her and complained, "You are squirreling money away which bothers me. Not only that, you are playing a game with me."

Still looking into his eyes she sighed, "If you are silly enough to check on that box, then please do. I felt that my one hundred dollar bill was becoming quite worn from your handling," she purred.

"Please, dear lady, I think we need to discuss how much money we should keep in the house. Amber, what is reasonable to you? I realize our views may differ."

"Could we sit in the living room and talk?"

"Certainly." Sitting beside her, holding her hand he asked, "How much?"

"I always keep four hundred dollars back when I deposit my check. Generally I have three hundred in my billfold. I put the remaining money in the box. If it's there when my next check comes, I add one or two hundred more.

"Now you have found my stash, I must find another place. I don't count the money in my box, I keep adding to it. I don't want to bother putting a hundred or two in the bank. Before I let you have your say, I will admit having two thousand dollars around is too much. How much do you think I should keep handy?"

"My love, I allow you to deposit your check. I pay the bills. Therefore, I think you need to respect my opinion, even if it differs from yours."

Realizing keeping money in the house was not a good idea, Amber asked, "Sweetheart, since my acting unprofessional bothers you, how much should I keep?"

"Amber, since you are in the habit of keeping four hundred dollars back, that's fine. But when you deposit your check, add the one hundred or whatever is left from your last check to your deposit. My love, you put in long hours and work hard for your money. Please put it in the bank. Don't keep more than four-hundred here. The house is not a safe place. A thief could watch our house and break in when we're gone. I have been thinking of procuring an alarm system, because of your jewelry. What do you think of that idea?"

"That's an excellent one. Because most of the expensive things are mine, except for your nice cuff links, I'll pay the bill for the alarm."

"Yes, it's time. I'll have one installed."

The next morning, after Amber worked with a client, she drove to his place of business to determine if there was any other assistance she could offer him. In examining his financial statements, she discovered some cost-cutting areas which he could incorporate into his procedures to save money.

She returned to the *Rambulet* building, parked in the shade and called her mother. Patricia reported, "Marion is holding her own. She has a damaged kidney and ribs and huge bruises on her arm. I squeezed her right hand and was elated when I felt her fingers move. We know she realizes we are around."

"Mom, is there anything we can do?"

"Both of you, just keep praying," Patricia answered.

"Mom, that we will do."

That evening, after the kitchen was in order, Amber and Armand prayed like they had done previously.

As they finished, Armand embraced her inviting, "Amber tomorrow is Friday. Would you like to eat out?"

"How nice, yes indeed."

He named a place and made reservations.

Amber kissed him, then began to undress. He followed.

When he had removed his clothes, she came to him. She was in her panties and bra. She placed her arms around him rubbing his back as he unfastened her bra. He softly spoke, "My dear lady, you have started something which leads to only one ending."

Her answer was to reach into his briefs to find his penis beginning to engorge. She exclaimed, "Oh, what I do to you!" as they removed each other's remaining clothing.

Pillows went to the floor. Covers were pulled down. "No my dear lady, don't climb into bed. Please put your arms around my neck." He gently lowered her into their bed. Her hands softly stroked his back.

As usual she was astounded to witness his arousal. She thought, *There is no question, I am always able to turn him on.*

After extensive foreplay, their subsequent experience thrilled them both. She was impressed with the energy required for his fulfillment.

They remained quietly in each other's arms for a long period reinforcing their love for each other.

The next morning, in a good mood Armand hummed as he shaved, while observing his love in her slip, hose, and shoes, putting on makeup. He began to apply after shave lotion which caused her to remark, "Yes, please use that. It makes you more sexy."

Naturally he complied.

Their day went well. Once they were home Amber took a bath while he showered. While he was in the shower, he made up a song about how he was being taken out to dinner tonight. "Am I certain she is the one?" he warbled. *She is my heart throb*, he thought. But he sang out, "My love, are you my heart throb?"

From the other bathroom, Amber's voice emitted, "I hope so. If there is some other woman I'll be mighty jealous." They finished dressing when Amber spoke, "Since you are my date tonight, I'll drive."

"All right. Since I am your date, then what would you like to be called?"

"I'm yours, of course. In case you do not know, I am a one man-woman."

They sat opposite each other in the restaurant. He always enjoyed holding her left hand across the table. They ordered a bottle of champagne. He told the waiter they were in no hurry.

They enjoyed a delicious meal. Amber told him she had called her mother during the day. Aunt Marion was still in critical condition, but was holding her own.

He pondered, "My love, that could have been you."

"Let's discuss something else," she quickly insisted.

"Christmas is approaching. Since your mother has her sister to worry about, suppose we stay here for the holiday?"

"I agree. I could not enjoy this holiday time over there with my aunt being so badly injured." She stated. "We could go over after Christmas. Why don't we wait until January?"

"That sounds good," he replied, as he looked across the table into her eyes. When they held hands he purred, "May I offer you some special loving tonight?"

"I have been anticipating that question all evening," she smiled, with a special twinkle in her eyes.

"Armand you are becoming quite adept at obtaining what you desire."

"I am making up for all those flying trips down to UTEP. That's not counting going over to Oklahoma City." They sat holding hands across the table repeating, 'I love you'. He added, "Those mere words really do not express our deepest love, which is constantly growing."

"Thank you sweetheart. I feel the same way," she tenderly replied.

After they finished their meal, they returned home. Then they slipped out of their clothes and tenderly loved each other.

Before they went to sleep, she murmured, "Sweetheart, you cannot say I do not fulfill your intimate needs."

"My love, I will never get enough of you. Goodnight and thank you."

On their way to the supermarket the next day, Amber's mother called reporting, "Marion is improving."

"That's great, Mom. Please don't expect us at Christmas. You have had too much on your plate. We'll come near the end of January."

Disappointed, Patricia asked, "Couldn't you come sooner than that? How about New Year's Day?"

"Let's see when we could catch a flight. Would that be all right? We are at the market now; I'll call you as soon as we can obtain tickets."

"Wonderful." her mother sighed, "We love you."

"We love you, too."

After shopping, they stopped at Armand's parents' home. As soon as they entered his father growled, "Did you take my level?"

"Yes Dad, I've forgotten to return your tool," he apologized.

"In order for me to use my damn level, I have to go get it!"

Hearing her husband's remarks, Celeste snarled, "Man, you certainly have a burr under your saddle."

"It makes me madder than hell when something I own isn't around when I want it. A damn kid took it!"

"Francis Rambulet! You should be ashamed," Celeste chided.

Trying to ease the tension Amber stated, "Dad, it's my fault Armand hasn't returned your tool. As soon as we are home again, I'll make certain your level is returned. Dad, your tool was important. I wanted to make sure our pictures were properly leveled. I take the blame for this difficulty."

Francis cooled down after Celeste poured some delicious apple juice.

Armand promised, "Dad, I'll bring the level back right away. I'm sorry I forgot."

As the lovers parted, Francis quietly murmured to Celeste, "He's your kid today." Celeste responded with a swat on his fanny. "For heaven's sake, they both apologized. Have you forgotten? I forgave you for a decision which was far worse--you old grump," she growled.

Seated in the car, Amber watched the swat on Francis' fanny.

On their way home Amber lamented, "I am sorry we neglected to take that tool to him. By the way, where is it?"

"I hung the Navajo rug in the second bedroom. I must have left it there."

When all the groceries were in the house, Armand located the priceless tool on the pillow in the second bedroom.

He returned to the car telling Amber, "I must return this to its rightful owner before he has another heart attack."

Celeste answered the door. "Mom, I am so sorry I caused a family disagreement. Let me take this level to the garage and put it exactly where I found it. Where's Dad? I'll tell him his level is replaced."

At the computer, Francis did not stop Armand from giving him a big hug. His father felt foolish making a totally inappropriate fuss. He arose and returned Armand's hug.

Kissing his mother on the cheek Armand related, "I must get back to the house and help Amber."

"Son, today your father will prepare our meal--or else. Goodbye and thanks."

Over their evening meal, Armand and Amber discussed the family feud. She laughed, "I saw your dad get a swat on the butt from your mom."

"I've not seen Mom that angry at Dad for a long time."

"Sweetheart, you did forget to return the level. Remember, he admitted he made a big blunder after you were born. Your mom forgave him then. Do you suppose that's why she was angry?"

"Sure. I'll bet you're correct, my love."

After the kitchen was cleaned and the floor scrubbed, Celeste called Amber's phone. "Is it all right if we come over tomorrow afternoon? I'd like to see your paintings."

"Of course. I'm sorry I didn't invite you. We'll fix a hot dish and a salad."

"The food does not matter, Amber. Thank you so much."

The next day, Amber and Armand worked outside after the house was clean. He did not like to see small tree branches and other debris strewn in their rock yard. Satisfied with their outdoor cleanup, Amber went to the kitchen and made a salad and began to prepare a hot dish.

When the doorbell rang, only Celeste greeted them saying, "I'm sorry, Francis is a party pooper."

Armand insisted, "Mom, we won't allow that."

Amber ordered, "Armand, please entertain your mother. I'll go and get your father."

"Amber, please use our car. Here are the keys. The door key is here, in case he will not answer."

Amber rang the door bell. After waiting a reasonable time without being admitted, she let herself into the house. She found her father-in-law at his computer.

"Please turn it off, Dad I have come for you. We are not going to allow you to sit in your den and sulk. I know you're uptight. We feel you need to get out of this house. If you are not willing to come freely, Armand is ready to come and physically carry you to our house."

"Oh all right, but first I need something to relax me!" He went to the refrigerator and poured himself a margarita with an extra long shot of tequila. Offering some to Amber, she took a few sips. After he had finished his drink he admitted, "Now I'm in a happy mood."

When they arrived home, Armand kissed Amber noticing she smelled like tequila. He knew why. He also noticed his father was in a 'happy mood' as he showed him their pictures.

"Dad, now you see why I needed the level."

His dad responded, "Your pictures are indeed nice, and they are level. Do you have margarita mix?"

Armand poured drinks for everyone.

His father soon blurted out, "I'm sorry I've been obnoxious about that darned level. I was swatted on the butt yesterday by this lady I'm married to and who bore my three children. I admitted to Celeste today, I claim you Armand."

Francis was loosening up. He began telling family jokes. For example, "When Jeffory was a small boy, he told a very pregnant lady, 'Whatever you do, don't eat any more or your belly will burst like my Mom's.' Then on the way home that day, Jeffory continued with 'Dad, didn't you say Mom was splagnant?' I laughed so hard I cried.

"We then gave Jeffory his first lesson about sex. Evidently it did him some good. Look at him now with his two kids. It's evident, he knows how."

With a slap on his leg, Celeste ordered, "Behave yourself." Then to Amber she asked, "What did you drink at our house?"

"Mom, I had a few sips of his margarita, which he made very strong. For himself, he had a belt of straight tequila before he added the mix. Sweetheart, let's put food on the table."

Armand put the hot dish in its rack in the middle of the table. Amber brought the salad in a large bowl. Armand had baked bread in their machine. Applesauce and yummy doughnuts completed the meal.

After his parents left, Amber and Armand shared a few chuckles over his father's antics. "I'll bet Mom took care of Dad once they were home."

"I'm certain you have something in mind which concerns me."

"Yes, my love. Please come with me." Their evening together began slowly but ended in a tremendous crescendo. Armand loved his lady. Amber loved her man.

Chapter 13.

Amber purchased poinsettias to add Christmas color for their house. Their gifts had been sent to her family in Oklahoma City. Armand bought plane tickets for mid-January.

The gifts for his family were on the other bed. They had spent a lot of time shopping for them. The whole family worked on December 23rd except Eleanor, who was home with their two children.

Armand helped Amber with a layered gelatine salad with Bing cherries. She baked a chocolate cherry cake and frosted it. It looked delicious after her final swipes with the frosting-covered knife.

Armand purchased new pajamas for Amber. She found two blue ties for him. One had yellow stripes, the other contained very narrow red and white lines. They had agreed to spend very little on themselves, but to spend more freely for their relatives.

Christmas Day was spent at Celeste's and Francis' home. A huge meal was served. All the Rambulets, ate too much, even the children.

Gifts were opened. The children received new robes and bedroom slippers, which looked like beagle dogs. Dressed in these garments, they played games on the floor with Uncle Armand.

Under the tree were small boxes for each of the adults and their spouses. Each box contained $1000. Celeste predicted, "I know where Armand's and Amber's money will go."

"Into our savings account," Amber declared.

The weather was pleasant. Everyone put on a sweater and went for a short walk. Gabrielle and Gilbert were allowed to run off their energy and act like kids until they became tired.

Returning to the house, Ronald and Francis carved the remainder of the turkey and wrapped portions for each family. Everyone went home with food and a sample of all the trimmings of the happy day.

On the day after Christmas, Armand and Amber visited Ralph and Lisa. She had suffered a miscarriage but did not tell their guests until Amber asked.

Ralph said, "Next time we'll say nothing in advance!"

Lisa added, "The doctor told me to wait at least six months before trying to become pregnant again."

Lisa had prepared a light meal. Afterward, they played cards but mostly talked.

Ralph had been a classmate of Armand's. They became friends when they were preparing for their master's degrees. During their visit, Amber said nothing about her pregnancy. Protecting her privacy, Armand did not mention it either. On the way home, Amber thanked him for remaining mum about their problems.

Armand responded, "After you have had a sterilization operation, then impregnate your wife, that's nothing to be proud of. I thank you for not yelling or screaming at me then."

"Sweetheart, I saw your scars. You believed you were harmless. In truth, you had remained quite virile."

The next four days they worked longer than usual, because Francis and Celeste were on vacation. On New Years Day, Jennifer and Ronald entertained her family for dinner.

In the afternoon a horrible snowstorm began. The freeway was soon shut down and the city streets were treacherous or closed. Armand and Amber took a long circuitous route to reach their home and called Jennifer to report their safe arrival.

They went to work on January 2nd but because of the storm, clients called postponing their appointments, permitting Amber and Armand to return home after lunch.

On Saturday before they were to leave to visit Amber's parents in Oklahoma City, Amber shopped for a gift of perfume to give her Aunt Marion. She then went to a health food store and purchased vitamins, minerals, pumpkin seeds, essential fatty acids, and saw palmetto for Armand to maintain a healthy prostate. She had noticed he had not been taking anything recently, so assumed he was out of these items. She thought *He certainly has no problem now. My gosh, the size of his penis when fully erect would scare the wits out of any woman, let alone a new bride.*

Armand had lunch ready when she returned. As she handed him the collection of health materials he remarked, "Oh good! I was out of most of those things."

"Armand, I don't think you realize how important food supplements are to you. Didn't your urologist direct you to use these materials?"

"Yes, but at the time I thought I'd purchase that stuff later. I certainly have no problem with erections my love. Just the sight of you walking at UTEP gave me a full blown one," he remembered.

"Armand, I don't think you are aware of what you would feel like if you wanted to become erect and could not. Please take these supplements. You men just can't be told anything."

As they ate, she asked him to sniff the perfume she purchased for Aunt Marion.

"That's nice my love, but not as lovely as what you wear. That's another thing that turned me on when we would embrace and I would hold you close. Your fragrance lighted my fire even more."

"I believe it would not matter what perfume or clothes I wore. You were attracted to me because of *Karmic* ties."

He quietly nodded.

Together they cleaned the kitchen. She then asked him to pull off sheets and pillowcases from their bed while she obtained clean bedding from the laundry cabinet. As he helped make their bed, he quietly asked, "Tomorrow we fly out of here. May we share some special closeness tonight?"

To tease him she purred, "Oh, I thought I would ask for someone else to come and entertain me tonight before I had to submit."

"That must mean I'm doing a poor job of being your one and only," he complained.

With dashing vibrant flashes from her lovely eyes, she murmured, "I don't get enough of you."

"My dear lady. I believe you are as enamored over me as I am over you," he murmured with a kiss.

"Of course. Now, please help me fold the sheets," she asked as she put another load into the washer.

They stopped for a rest and a margarita and began to laugh about his father's antics over his level.

"My love, I hope we never have fights like that," he stated quietly.

"Remember, different backgrounds are involved here. As long as love and respect are present, differences can be understood and worked through."

He remembered, "It's true, we've had differences of opinion once in a while. When I think back over our arguments, they seem small."

Amber's mother called, asking, "Do I pick you up at the same time? I hope you do not have a delay. Bad weather is forecast."

"All right Mom. I'll see what Armand can find out. You may not hear from us until we are ready to board unless there are major changes in our schedule. I love you."

Armand tried to find out about tomorrow's weather as his wife prepared a light meal. He called Malcom Wilcox, the executive secretary for *Abrams and Abrams*, whose corporate jet regularly flew from Albuquerque to Oklahoma City. Armand asked, "Will your plane be going to Oklahoma City tomorrow?"

"Yes."

"Will you have room for two more people from *Rambulet and Associates?*"

"We do, but because of the storm the plane will leave at five a.m. Is it your firm which Melroy Abrams speaks of?"

"I hope so," Armand answered.

"All right, there will be room for two."

"We'll be there."

"Tell the people at the desk who you are, that you talked with me. Each of you must have identification."

"Will my wife need two ID's?"

"Yes please. What is her middle name?"

"It's Cassandra."

"I will need your personal address, your business location, and both of your personal phone numbers."

Having given the necessary information, Armand replied, "We'll be there and thank you." He walked into the kitchen and stated, "Something smells sensually sensationally good."

"What did you find out?"

"There is a storm coming. We are going to leave here at five aboard the *Abrams and Abrams Inc*, jet."

"That sounds great."

After they finished their meal, he called the commercial airline canceling their morning flight.

Amber called her mother informing her, "We'll arrive at seven a.m. at the private jet terminal. We'll talk after we arrive."

In the kitchen they prepared for a very early breakfast.

They then readied themselves for bed. He set the alarm for three-thirty.

The next morning they found they had allowed plenty of time. They watched as the jet stopped at the gate. After ID's were shown, they were permitted to board the craft. Their seats were the rear two.

They belted themselves in as Armand commented, "I'm glad the plane will be full. The company will not lose money on this trip."

She asked, "Is this the company plane which was rented for our wedding?"

"Yes, Dad does work for Melroy Abrams."

When others came aboard, Armand and Amber introduced themselves. Finally Melroy Abrams senior, with his wife Sharon, boarded the plane. Mr. Abrams looked to see who was on board. He shook hands with Armand, saying, "I'm glad you're here. Is this your wife?"

Armand announced, "This is my wife, Amber."

"I am happy to meet you. Have you met my wife, Sharon?"

"No, it's not been my pleasure," Armand responded.

Taking charge, Melroy requested, "Armand, please come up and sit beside me so we may talk. I'll send my wife back to converse with Amber."

Time passed rapidly with questions and answers exchanged.

Coffee, juice, and donuts were served. The flight was smooth and progressed rapidly. Suddenly Melroy asked Armand, "Do you feel all right?"

"Yes, I feel fine."

"Please have my wife come up quickly!" Melroy directed.

Armand hurried to Sharon stating, "Melroy is not feeling well."

When Sharon reached her husband, he had his right hand on his chest. He mumbled something about pain. Sharon knocked on the pilot's door and told the pilots to radio for an ambulance to meet the plane. The jet began its descent. When Amber could see how everyone was acting she became concerned. She went to Sharon saying, "My mother is a nurse. If a heart doctor is needed I suggest you have the hospital contact Dr. Suantaz. I have written his name on this card. He is the best." Sharon told her to give the pilots this information. The radio message was sent.

The emergency at the front of the plane made Armand and Amber wait until the ambulance arrived. Amber gave her business card to Sharon as the medics opened the door and placed Melroy on a stretcher.

Watching the commotion from their car, Amber's parents became frightened. Once they were off the plane, Armand and Amber found her parents' vehicle and put their luggage in the trunk. They climbed into the car hearing, "It's wonderful to see you, but what happened!"

Armand answered, "Melroy Abrams, one of the owners of *Abrams and Abrams* asked me to sit beside him to talk business. Near the end of the flight he asked me if I felt all right, which I did. He directed me to get his wife who was talking with Amber. Apparently he had suffered a heart attack."

"Mom, I was concerned and gave them the name of the cardiologist you like so well. I told them you were a nurse."

They arrived at her parents' home. Dennis closed the garage door quickly because the wind was increasing and the temperature was dropping. Her parents were happy Amber and Armand had arrived safely.

Armand took their luggage into the bedroom. Amber noticed his hands were cold. "Sweetheart are you feeling well?"

"I feel fine, but I'm cold."

"Let's fill the bathtub so you can have a good soak until you perspire."

He followed her advice. He soaked as she talked with her parents about their work.

Dennis asked, "Amber, how do you feel about this man to whom you have been married for a year and a half?"

"Dad, like all people we have had our disagreements, but Armand does not shout or use profanity. He's extremely loving."

Dennis observed, "It's a good thing he had a vasectomy or you would have had one baby, with another one on the way by this time."

From across the room Patricia exploded, "Dennis Breddgeforth, that is inappropriate language!"

Amber then explained to her parents that she could not have children. She told them why. "Armand was completely willing to go through the procedure again. His second operation was free." She continued, "It's unusual for Armand to be cold. That's why I told him to soak in a warm bath. I hope he is not coming down with a cold or the flu."

"Dennis, why don't you find one of your sweaters for Armand?" Patricia asked.

Amber checked on her husband. "Sweetheart, would you like one of Dad's sweaters?"

"That sounds good. Perhaps the stress on the plane has caused this reaction," Armand remarked. As he toweled himself, she gave him a tweak on his derriere.

In the living room he put on Dennis' sweater. The two men went to the kitchen and prepared drinks. Since Armand and Amber had eaten so early, crackers, chips, and cheese were also served.

Patricia answered the phone. "Grandma, have Aunt Amber and Uncle Armand arrived yet?" Raymond inquired.

"Yes, they're here."

"Could we come over for lunch, Grandma?"

"Certainly."

"I'm helping Mom bake a cake," Raymond responded.

"Bring it along and come for lunch."

This conversation brought the foursome into the kitchen. Amber munched as she helped her mother prepare a green bean hot dish which Amber liked so well. After these preparations were finished they sat around the kitchen table and talked.

Hugs and kisses were shared as Lily, Raymond, and Sue arrived.

Lily had heard the weather forecast and announced they would return home about two. Snow began falling as they ate. Raymond asked, "Why did you come so early?"

Armand responded, "Because of the weather. We were told it was going to snow, with the possibility of blizzard conditions. We knew the flight would either be delayed or canceled unless we came early." He explained how he knew about the private jet and its owner, who was probably in the hospital right then.

Later Armand and Raymond enjoyed games of table tennis. Lily served her delicious cake before they left for home. Amber asked Lily to send the recipe to her by e-mail.

Snow was descending rapidly as Lily and her family left. Patricia asked them to call when they arrived home.

Amber directed her mother to call the hospital and ask about Melroy Abrams's condition. She learned a heart by-pass had been performed. He was recovering. She asked, "Is his wife with him?"

"Yes, she is."

Amber talked to Sharon, discussing Melroy's condition. Amber asked her, "Do you have a place to stay?"

"Yes we have lodging here. Amber, you told me your mother was a nurse."

"Yes."

"I know this is asking a lot, but would your mother be able to be with Melroy tomorrow?"

Amber gave the phone to her mom. "Mother, this is Sharon Abrams."

Her mother answered, "This is Patricia Breddgeforth. May I help you?"

"Mrs. Breddgeforth, could you be with Melroy tomorrow? Am I asking too much?"

"No, of course not. I'd be happy to help if the weather permits me to get over there," Patricia answered.

"Oh! I have been so consumed with Melroy, I have completely forgotten the weather."

Patricia explained the horrible wind and blustery conditions, with inches of snow. "I'll try to arrive about nine."

Giving a sigh of relief, Sharon said, "Thank you so much."

Wendell called saying his family had arrived home safely.

In the morning, Patricia and Dennis arose to watch the weather and road conditions. The TV reported that I-40 and I-35 were both snow-blocked.

In order for Patricia to reach the hospital, they had to zig-zag through many different streets before reaching the Southwest Medical Center. They arrived shortly after nine-thirty.

Plans for the day were scrapped. Dennis and Armand arrived back home after much delay. Armand said he had never seen so much snow.

By afternoon the freeways were opened. The trip to pick up Patricia was much easier. Dennis, Armand, and Amber went to the floor where Patricia was working and waited for her. As Armand entered Melroy's room, the patient greeted Armand with, "You and your wife have seats available on Wednesday. The jet leaves at ten a.m. The plane will be leaving late due to weather-related tie-ups."

Armand commented, "Melroy, it's no wonder your heart is giving you problems when you are concerned about how my wife and I will be getting home. I thank you very much."

"I so appreciate Patricia being here with me today. Sharon and my brother Andrew have gone to find something to eat."

Patricia and Armand wished him a good night's sleep. When Patricia was relieved by another nurse, they went to the hospital cafeteria where Sharon recognized them. Dennis and Andrew were introduced. Patricia assured Sharon and Andrew that her husband and his brother was on the road to recovery. "I'm sure Dr. Suantaz will prepare a diet plan for him."

They had a good chat which helped relax Sharon, before the four left the hospital. Sharon was going to spend the night in their townhouse. Andrew also had a dwelling with his wife Adelia.

Back home, Dennis fixed a drink while they relaxed before bed. Patricia stated, "I think Melroy's offer is too good to pass up."

Amber asked, "What offer is that?"

"There is room on the jet for us going home," Armand stated. "Tomorrow I must cancel our return airline tickets."

"Wow, that's wonderful," she exclaimed.

Patricia stated, "I told Melroy I did not need any stipend for today. In the back of my mind, I hoped there would be a benefit for you two. Perhaps in the future, there could be a benefit to us, also."

"Golly," Armand remembered, "I need to call my Dad and tell him about Melroy. Please excuse me." He went to the guest bedroom and called. "Dad, I thought you would appreciate knowing that Melroy Abrams is in the hospital here. Amber's mother was his private nurse today. He had a heart attack and a by-pass and is recovering."

"When did this happen?"

"On the flight coming over. Dad, do you know how much it costs to fly that jet?"

"I don't have that information in my head," his dad responded.

"Okay, Dad, we'll leave here on Wednesday at ten AM, local time. I love you."

After talking with his father, Armand joined the others in the living room.

On Monday night Armand and Amber enjoyed dinner with Wendell, Lily and their family. They played with the children until their bedtime. After the children were asleep, the adults shared wonderful conversation.

On Tuesday, Patricia allowed Amber to drive her car to the mall or wherever else she wished to shop. As they walked in the mall, Armand did not let her dwell too long looking in shop windows. Amber did not take time to shop for herself at home. Now she had time. In one store she gave Armand her purse while he found a chair. She tried on garments.

She found a dark blue suit which she thought looked stunning, but she wanted Armand's approval because his money was also involved.

When he saw her in the dress he expressed absolute delight in her selection. "My love, you need to wear colors like that more often. Please buy that garment."

Next she appeared in a dark brown dress which buttoned to the waistline. It had a small yellow stripe almost the color of her hair. He thought she looked terrific. "Buy that one too."

They ended their shopping spree at a men's store, where she went through the suits. He declared, "My love, I don't need a new suit."

"All right then, let's look for trousers which will go with some of your suit jackets. Sweetheart, you don't need to wear a suit every day," she suggested.

With the purchase of two pairs of trousers, a green shirt with a darker green tie, and a light violet shirt with a darker striped tie, she declared, "I think you will look handsome as the dickens in violet."

A delighted Amber drove to a shipping store to send their purchases home. When they returned to her parents' home, Patricia had the table set. Her mother could see that Amber was exhilarated.

With a kiss on her cheek, Armand greeted Patricia saying, "Thanks for the use of the car. In case you are wondering, Amber, please come in here and tell your mother what you bought. She gave Patricia the details of her purchases. Armand responded, "Mom, I was talked into buying slacks, shirts, and ties."

Her father stated, "When your daughter shops, man oh man, it's difficult for a guy to hold onto his wallet."

"Sweetheart," Amber rebutted, "We bought clothing we can wear to work. I did not go into crafty stores or linger in shoe places. I have enough shoes."

"Good. I'm glad you have enough of something to wear," he teased, "I thought you were going to buy out those stores and bankrupt us."

Kissing him on the cheek she said, "Mom, he has not had enough attention recently." Feeling his face begin to flush, Armand returned to the guest bedroom. To kill time, he went through his suitcase thinking, *Amber can certainly embarrass me.*

After dinner was finished, Wendell and his family came for dessert and to bid them goodbye.

With a gasp, Patricia announced, "My goodness! We have not gone to see Marion."

Amber retrieved the perfume for her aunt and bid her brother's family goodbye. Patricia drove them to the hospital.

Marion was delighted to see her niece, who dabbed a drop or two of perfume on her hand.

"Amber, it's wonderful to smell something that's not gauze or hospital stink!"

Kissing her cheek, Armand said, "Dear Aunt, you look good for the shape you're in."

Aunt Marion chuckled; Patricia laughed. They stayed a short time. Amber was devastated to see her aunt in such bad shape.

Patricia promised Marion, "I'll be on the floor tomorrow. I'll see you then."

After goodbyes Patricia drove them home. Dennis mixed margaritas and they chatted until their drinks were finished before they went to bed.

In the morning, Dennis went to work after bidding them goodbye. Patricia took the children to the jet terminal and bid them farewell.

In the terminal, Armand gave their names at the desk. They were told to use the back two seats. Armand was wondering what they should pay for their seats, when Andrew Abrams came to him and greeted Amber, saying, "Could you please give me your mother's address? I want to send her a thank you note." She complied with his request.

Armand asked Andrew, "We wish to pay for our seats."

"The plane was flying anyway," Andrew answered.

"That may be true, however, I know how my father feels. As a business, the seats must be filled or money is lost." He patted Andrew's arm. To Amber, Armand suggested, "We should pay what a commercial flight would charge. The luxury and comfort are completely opposite of anything commercial. What should we pay?"

Amber rolled some figures around in her head and gave him a number. He agreed.

"I'm glad we did not go to see Aunt Marion first. That would have spoiled the rest of our trip," Amber said with a yawn.

They both rested. When they arrived in Albuquerque they were refreshed and had a powerful drive for work the next day.

Once at home Amber washed clothes while Armand went for groceries.

Near the end of his shopping trip, Armand felt as if he was being bathed in a warm radiation. A voice spoke in his ear, directing, *You would be wise to purchase a lot before you seriously begin your building plans.*

Encourage your wife to go along with this idea. Real estate prices are escalating. Obtain your land first.

The voice faded before Armand could ask any questions. He thought, *Why do things like this happen to me in the supermarket?*

He greeted Amber at home with a kiss, as she began preparing a hot dish for their evening meal. Armand put the groceries away.

During their supper, Armand began, "While I was at the store, a voice in my ear told me that we should buy a lot for our home. It said real estate prices are rising."

"I think that would be a great idea," she exclaimed. "At work I sink my mind completely into what I am doing and think of nothing else. I must call Mom and tell her we arrived safely and will start work tomorrow."

He assisted her in clearing the kitchen. When she stood, their eyes met. His were filled with adulating glances. Amber purred, "I read those eyes of yours very well."

Amber went into the bedroom and pulled the pillows and blankets back. She then removed her slacks and sweater. She was folding clothes when he returned.

Approaching, he kissed and embraced her whispering, "Please put your arm around my neck." He carried his love to the bed and removed his clothes except for his briefs. Looking at her he exclaimed, "Oh my! there's my love waiting for me." He kissed her over her entire body. Removing her bra, he embraced her bosom. She whispered, "Why my bosom?"

"That's part of your very special feel he said as he left.

While he was gone, she removed her panties and went to him, pulled his briefs down ordering, "Please step out of these." He carried her to the bed and proceeded with more embraces. When their bodies met, their simultaneous movements increased. She stroked his back and returned his affection.

Armand purred, "I believe you are with me." She answered only with noticeably more energetic movements. Their enthusiastic fulfillment and gratification were complete.

He whispered, "My love, thank you for anticipating and accepting me."

"Mine was equally delightful," she purred.

"As always, you were terrific. I had my embrace," he tenderly murmured. "When men do not know how to successfully love their partner, they are not able to obtain their own response. No wonder some men have poor opinions of themselves."

He delicately moved her in his arms so her head was near his face. She could smell his after-shave lotion. "My love, I cannot express enough to you how important I think our purity was to us. I had good sexual training at home. Then, when you happened into my life, I read more about sexual intimacy and how important it is that couples experience each other and no one else. Amber, you have made me become more considerate."

Her response was to kiss his cheek, his jaws and finally his lips, while purring, "I thank you for being so loving toward me. Now, I'm tired and ready for my pajamas."

The next morning they were at work shortly after eight. The days, weeks, and months flew by. He purchased a laptop computer for home use. Amber helped him select a desk which would fit into their crowded third bedroom.

At another time he asked Amber where she would like to spend their second wedding anniversary. After some thought she suggested, "I really have not seen much of my new state. Why don't we just spend our vacation exploring New Mexico?"

"That sounds great to me," he responded, "Let's do it."

Another holiday, July 4th approached. They were home in the morning and spent the greater part of the day with his relatives. Each family brought food for the noon meal. Francis grilled steaks to the delight of everyone.

Chapter 14.

After the holiday, Amber called a real estate agent to look for a lot, as she continued to add money to their account. She carefully explained to the agent details of what they were looking for, and in what location. Amber explained that she did not have time to run all over town looking at property. She told the agent, Shelia Bartslaw, to take her time in her search.

When Shelia realized who her clients were, she took care not to burden them with unnecessary phone calls or e-mails. Occasionally Amber would call Shelia to determine what she was finding. One day Shelia replied, "If the price were reasonable, would you consider a property which has enough area for a swimming pool, but already has a house on it which needs updating?"

Amber replied, "I had my heart set on a new house. That's why I have been putting all my time into my husband's family business."

"With the help of an architect, this property could become very special. At your convenience, would you and your husband like to look at it? It has more area than most of the nearby houses. I'd like to show you some pictures."

When Shelia dropped off the photos, Amber was on the phone so the agent left with a wave, realizing that Amber's time was assiduously important to the business.

Over lunch Amber and Armand looked at the photos. Shelia had marked the location with street and house numbers. The house needed repairs and was much too small for them. But the location was excellent.

The lot was odd-shaped at the end of a short road North of Montgomery Blvd. Armand liked the location. Amber felt they needed to inspect the property.

Amber called Sheila asking to see the property on Saturday, one week before they were to begin their second anniversary explorations.

They viewed the house and lot with interest. Amber liked the back yard, "But Armand", she argued, "I wanted a new house. That's why I've been working so hard."

"My love, let's have an expert take a look. Perhaps the house could be altered in such a way that a pool could be included."

Thinking more deeply about the house she wanted and what would be required, Amber asked, "Armand, we will need to obtain a mortgage. I don't have enough saved for much more than a down payment."

"My love, the banker will be more than happy to help us."

On Monday, he called the architect who had designed the *Rambulet & Rambulet Inc.* professional building, and asked him to look at the property.

The next afternoon, the three spent a short time on the premises with Sheila. They were told the house could be expanded by adding a second story with a master suite, and a den, and more rooms.

Armand contracted with the architect to draw up beginning plans. Shelia suggested they put a few thousand down to hold the property.

To both Armand and Amber, the proposed area was great. They thought it was wise to place a deposit for a down payment.

On Sunday they stopped at his parents' home for a chat. His mother thought it was great that they were looking for something which would satisfy both of them.

His father shocked them by stating, "Your mother and I will provide one hundred thousand dollars for your new home."

His statement brought tears to both Armand and Amber. Armand spoke, "Dad, I did not know you were going to help us."

"I know you are surprised. We helped both your brother and sister this way. That's why I hover over my clients. By the way, Melroy Abrams said to say hello. He's at work and feeling well. If you determine this property is what you want, we'll help you. Celeste, let's drive by and take a look."

Later Celeste and Francis examined the property. Celeste did not like the house but could see there were possibilities. With a professional involved the area could be very special.

On Friday afternoon Ben Arthworth, the architect, came to the

Rambulet building. In the conference room, he spread elevation plans on the table for Armand and Amber. She exclaimed, "Oh my Ben, this is beautiful. The elevation is wonderful."

He then showed them floor plans which showed a kitchen with an island including a sink and eating area. On the wall behind the kitchen were cupboards with a sink, a laundry area, a commode, and a closet. A door went into the garage.

The other side of the kitchen wall was a large dining room, and a living area which overlooked the pool. The plans showed a broad entry with double doors. To the left were two bedrooms, each with a bath. Another bath served the pool area. On the far side of the pool was a mechanical room to house all the mechanisms for pool maintenance and storage.

A work-out area was on the opposite side of the pool; a guest suite was behind a two-car garage. Inside the entry, a stairway led to the second floor which had a master suite with lovely bath, a den, and another bedroom.

After Amber and Armand saw the layout, Ben suggested an adobe wall be built to enclose the property. For the house he suggested an open area with a sliding glass door for easy entrance to the patio.

Amber's eyes and mind were filled with wonderment. She thought what Ben had planned was great. She was so pleased she began to weep.

Ben knew they had a place to live until the work was finished. He continued, "The existing house will be taken apart. Plan on the whole process taking more than a year."

Armand asked, "I can understand the time and labor involved, but to secure privacy, do you plan to build the wall first?"

"Yes. Because of the easement requirements, we will build the wall three feet inside your property line."

They all shook hands with thanks. With tears in her eyes, Amber managed a quiet "Thank you." She and Armand went home, thrilled. Amber said she would write the check for the down payment.

Armand talked with his banker, Anthony Petell, who asked how much they would need. "We don't know for sure. Why don't you take a look at the property. We believe we obtained a buy. The house is going to be torn down. I suggest you talk with Ben Arthworth." Armand gave Anthony the home's location.

He continued, "We were quoted a million dollars for the complete makeover, which will include an indoor swimming pool. Amber plans to work another three years before we adopt. We both feel that, down the road, we need to be parents. Our goal is to have that property half paid for before Amber quits work. We'll sell the townhouse in which we now live.

Speaking with authority, Anthony expressed, "You and your family have good minds for money."

"We've taken the education to understand how good-sized businesses, as well as smaller ones work. We have been fortunate enough to marry spouses who had the same interests. Amber has a Masters Degree in Business Crisis Management. We need to use our training for our own benefit."

Frances and Celeste called Ben Arthworth inquiring what the projected cost would be on a final contract. "Ben, I feel that our son's efforts in this matter need to be checked because Armand is still love-struck. He's now on his second anniversary trip."

After their conversation with Ben, they recognized the architect did careful work. He was honest and sincere. They later made an appointment to talk to the banker to discuss funding.

Francis asked Anthony, "Do you think our children are making a wise decision?"

The banker responded, "By the time they finish that home it will be worth nearly two million dollars, because of its location. I know you are conservative, and that's an excellent approach to any purchase. Their work ethic is like yours. How can they fail?"

Celeste asked, "I am sure they are not thinking about any serious health problems or something which would prevent them from working."

"Aren't they well insured?"

Francis answered, "They are, but there could be problems with that house."

Anthony's abrupt answer, "Then they could sell, if it became too much for them. I have spoken to Armand. His wife banks her entire salary."

Celeste expressed, "I know she is not much for shopping except on special occasions. Anthony, please do not let Armand or Amber know we talked with you!"

"Of course I will not reveal any of our conversation," he replied.

Francis gathered up their plans stating, "We'll return these to Ben. Thank you for your help."

This conversation was never revealed to Armand and Amber.

Chapter 15.

Armand and Amber left Albuquerque on I-40 after breakfast, heading west to Grants. They had purchased a cooler and food for lunch, then ate picnic style at Bandera Ice caves.

At El Morro National Monument they admired the numerous names inscribed on the soft stone. They were impressed with the engraved names which early explorers had carved into the monument. Their next stop was the Zuni Indian Reservation.

Armand had made reservations at a lodge outside of Silver City. It was late when they arrived. Hot soup and sandwiches awaited them.

When they fell into bed, Amber admitted she had not realized how large this state was. Before they went to sleep, the two talked about what they had seen on their first day.

The lodge representative told them to stop at Deming and see the wonderful refurbished historical museum which surpassed what many larger cities have to offer. They admired the carefully preserved old objects which had been used in bygone times. This museum was outstanding, in their opinion.

The next day they were in Las Cruces, where they visited numerous art museums and galleries. The following morning Amber showed Armand the cash in her billfold. "My dear lady, you should not carry that much money," he insisted to his love.

"This way, we won't have credit card bills," she reasoned.

"My love, how did you manage to keep this money? We just bought some real property and will soon sign papers making that land ours."

"Sweetheart, this outing is not going to be expensive, like a trip out east. We are not spending a great deal of money, except, perhaps here. Don't worry. I know we're going to have to pay for that property," she commented, "If my carrying this money is a problem, please take half of it yourself," she stated, handing him a hand full of bills.

"Thank you, my love. I don't like having this much cash in my billfold," he muttered.

"Don't worry. Some will soon be spent. Let's be on our way and enjoy ourselves. I am happy you're with me. Our time together is very special, particularly on trips like this. You know, I normally do not spend money wildly," Amber declared.

She explored galleries, taking a long time before she decided, "They have nothing which turns me on." In other places she found small paintings she could not live without. In Mesilla, she admired craft stores and galleries which intrigued her. She bought a few things. She was remembering she was going to own a very special home. They put her purchases into the car trunk before they returned to their room for the night.

The next day they were in El Paso where Amber visited her former professors. She admired some newer buildings and a parking ramp near the Sun Bowl which had been desperately needed during her year there.

From El Paso they went to the Guadalupe National Park on a very hot day. One of Amber's professors had told them to take food and plenty of water. They purchased materials for lunch. Hiking and walking in the park made them thirsty.

In the car again, Amber laughingly remembered their wedding day and her requiring his assistance in a restroom and their later discussion of the wisdom of using ground facilities rather than an aircraft's toilet. They giggled remembering their lack of experience with restrooms reserved for the other sex.

"Now I'm a married man who knows what it is like to impregnate his spouse, and a man who has gone through two incisions. Tonight my love, may we have some special stimulating, satisfying time together?"

"Of course. You are such a sweetheart. I appreciate your being cool and laid back while I shop," she lovingly answered.

They enjoyed each other especially, being away from the pressures of work and family. Just the two of them thoroughly enjoying each other.

Carlsbad Caverns National Park was their next stop for the night. They were thrilled to watch millions of bats emerging into the night for their hunting. This was a new and exciting experience for them.

Amber did not like the smell as they explored the underground crystalline cavernous rooms the next day. "This smells too much like Oklahoma," she growled.

As they drove north she remarked, "Just think, when we get back home we will purchase that property. Work will begin on our house. Armand, isn't that exciting?"

"I suppose for a woman, a home is as important as a car is to a man."

"Yes, doggone it, you insist on driving all the time, which disgusts me," she chided.

"I suppose I still see myself as courting you. Remember, I had a terrible time winning you my love, but tomorrow you drive."

As they neared Roswell, Armand asked, "What are flying saucers?"

"We are being visited by beings from other systems or universes. The reason we see different shapes is because they are from different galaxies."

"Do you believe in abductions?"

"Of course."

"Do you think something fell from the skies at Roswell?"

"Yes, I do. I don't know why our government is hiding this information. When it comes to things like this, we need to let our minds be free. To heck with the government and its attempts to save us from fear. Baah." She then began to discuss her feelings and anger with politicians and politics. He was surprised at her fury with government attempting to keep information from people.

"Armand, there is no such thing as honesty in our government. Everyone is on the public dole. Not one of our political electees would be worth a damn in the private sector. In fact, in government it takes three people to do a job which could be done by one person in private business. "I hate voting, It's a waste of time. I don't know about you, but I believe my time is too important to bother with such an ineffective activity."

With a twinkle in his eye, Armand remarked, "Oh, your time is very important, especially in an experience like last night."

"I knew you would say something like that," she spat. "I'll just have to become less available."

"My love, absence makes the heart grow fonder."

They stopped at a motel in Roswell. She shopped more. He was happy to be with her, thinking, *She's doing more looking than buying. She must have the expenses of our house in mind.*

In an art gallery she found two small paintings which would blend with the art in the bathroom. She found a pottery container which she thought would look good on the dining room table. Her next discovery was a fabric weaving in colors which would fit in the living room. She realized the texture would add softness to that room. He stood nearby watching her every move. He loved it when she would ask him if he liked something, which she always did. He liked everything she had purchased so far.

He then suggested, "Isn't the money becoming a little tight?"

"Yes, sweetheart. I've looked enough here."

The next day Amber drove, heading west to Ruidoso and then to Alamogordo. The next morning they purchased food so they could spend time at the White Sands National Monument. Amber was ecstatic as they drove past the gypsum dunes. "Sweetheart, this is a special place." They took off their shoes and stockings and pleasantly walked on the warm white hills. "Armand, it sticks to your skin," she exclaimed. As the heat became worse, they stopped at a table under a cover for their luncheon. Each picnic area had a different colored sunshade.

Back in their hotel room, they realized they were both sunburned. Armand drove to a drug store for sunburn cream. She rubbed some onto his red face. Amber was lying in bed as he applied the wonderful soothing cream to her overheated skin.

The next day, after purchasing hats, they drove to Carrizozo to see the Valley of Fires National Recreational Area, where they ate lunch, again from their cooler.

After a little more exploring, Amber drove home. They were both tired as they retrieved the packages from the car, piling them on the dining room table.

They dropped their suitcases in the laundry area. While Armand emptied the cooler, she loaded the washer. When the car was empty, Armand made margaritas. They sat talking about their trip experiences and what they had seen.

Amber related, "I didn't realize how big this state was. One can certainly become tired from traveling long distances and also from the heat. Sweetheart, that was wonderful cream you purchased for our sunburn. It really cooled my skin. I don't believe either of us is going to peel."

When the washer was finished, she put clothes in the dryer and returned to sit with him. Finishing their drinks, he tenderly murmured, "My love, didn't we have a wonderful time?"

"Oh my, yes!" I intend to stay home tomorrow. If you want to work, that's fine. However, I'd like our purchases hung on the walls first," she asked.

"I'll be damned if I'll take Dad's level again," he growled.

"What we have here are small pieces. We can probably 'eyeball' them. We need to make arrangements for the property too."

Armand agreed, "The more I've thought about the property, the more I realize we obtained a good buy. Do you remember what Shelia said when I asked her if she would accept an offer of twenty thousand less?"

"No, what did she say?"

I quote, "*This property has been on the market for sometime. It's time to let it go, because the heirs could use the money.* I told her the offer would be in cash."

"Oh, yes! I remember hearing you say that."

"My love, we can take time before closing. I'll want Jeffory there."

The next morning Amber called her parents reporting they were home.

Her mother's response was, "We never see you!"

"Could you come over here for labor Day?" Amber asked.

"It's probably too late to obtain tickets."

"Mother, we would like you to come over here. We are negotiating for property which we would like to show you. I'll see what Armand can do about tickets."

Armand made arrangements for closing on Friday at four. Next he called Melroy. "My friend, I am ashamed for not checking on you more often."

"Heck I'm fit, I'm losing weight and feel good," Melroy answered.

"By chance will your plane happen to be in Oklahoma City on Friday before Labor day?"

"What a coincidence. Yes, it will be. I was going to call you to ask if your wife's parents would be interested in flying over to see you for the holiday."

"That's great. I'll call them. If you do not hear from me, you will know the seats are taken. They understand two forms of ID are required."

"That's correct," Melroy answered, "How are you and your wife doing?"

"We've just returned from our second anniversary vacation trip."

"My, I didn't realize you had been married that long."

"That's true, and what's more we are both very happy," Armand related as he told Melroy goodbye. He then called Amber's mother. "Patricia, plan to be at the Abrams plane at six p.m. on the Friday before Labor Day." He then handed the phone to Amber.

She stood with her mouth agape before beginning to chat with her mother, who was also very surprised.

They worked diligently the rest of the week. On Friday afternoon they both were in high spirits. At the bank, with Jeffory present, they closed on the property. Anthony praised them for their foresightedness in obtaining the house and land.

Amber commented to Jeffory, "Now I must work for three more years."

Jeffory replied, "You will find out what trials and tribulations are really like, after you have kids," he chuckled.

Anthony asked, "Isn't your sister Jennifer, planning an adoption, too?"

"Oh yes!" Jeffory answered, "She and Ronald are obtaining a four year old boy."

"Really?" Armand asked, rather shocked.

"Oh! you've been so love-struck these past two years you hardly know what is going on," Jeffory responded with a laugh. "Maybe this home will bring you down to earth. Amber, he's in your grip."

"Really!" she smiled, "If that's the case, then I'm completely possessing him? I don't believe that's true."

"I'm just kidding. My brother is happy. It's a good thing he married you, Amber."

Jeffory ended the meeting by placing papers in his briefcase, shaking hands, and telling everyone goodnight. They all responded with thanks to him for his help. In the car Armand growled, "I don't know why in hell I said thank you to Anthony. We are in debt up to our eyeballs."

"Sweetheart, we'll be paying for our house for several years. Remember, I'll work another three years."

"I know. We should be fine unless something unusual occurs."

Patricia and Dennis arrived on Friday night. On Saturday the four looked at the house and lot. Patricia peeked here and there as Amber explained, "The kitchen will be enlarged. The garage will be widened." She showed her mother where the dining and living rooms would be, the wide front door and hall, beyond which would be a bedroom. Further away in the back yard, a swimming pool would be located with the house surrounding it.

"You have made a good decision," Dennis praised.

"Thanks, Dad," Armand replied.

They spent an enjoyable weekend together before Dennis and Patricia returned to Oklahoma City on the Abrams jet.

On Monday, Ben stopped to see Amber and Armand at work. They gave him money to begin the new house. Amber instructed him to reuse studs. They wanted to remove the old nails from the wood thinking that would be something interesting to do.

The adobe walls were underway when Amber and Armand stopped on their lunch break. Amber was upset about the people constructing the walls not speaking English. She called Ben later complaining. He listened, then responded, "Amber, no American worker could perform like these people, at the wages they earn. If they were Americans, you would be paying three times as much. Please take them iced tea and perhaps a treat sometimes. Let the workers know you appreciate what they are doing."

"All right, Ben. I'll do what you suggest. Thank you."

As she put her phone down, Armand suggested, "I'll bet you did not think of the money angle did you?"

"Oh! you men. You think you are so damned smart," she spat. Then went to her office and focused on her work. She was an individual who could concentrate and compartmentalize her thinking.

Taking a break, she walked around inside the building. Both her husband and father-in-law had clients. She went back to her desk and became so caught up in her work she did not realize how late the time was until her husband stood in the doorway, saying, "My love, it's time to wind down your work."

"Of course," she replied, gathering her papers, shutting down her computer, and wiping her desk. Armand offered her his arm.

In the car they discussed work. At home they talked about the new wall. "Armand," she related, "I made an error in judgment today. Ben told me to take iced tea and goodies to the wall workers. He really put me in my place. Yet, I have my own thoughts, because my background is not here. It's where the language is always English. Our constitution, legal systems, and language is always English. I hope this does not change."

She began preparing their meal. He set the table, poured water, and was making a lettuce salad when she began to weep. "On second thought, I don't know what to think."

"Please tell me why you are upset."

"Oh! I don't know," she muttered as she wiped her eyes and returned to the meal.

"My love, may I express what I think some of your frustration is?" he asked, "I believe you want to save money while on the other hand, you are upset because the people working on our property speak another language."

With big tears in her eyes, she went to him. He fondly embraced her saying, "My love, whatever is best is best. Do you know the poem by Ella Wheeler Wilcox?"

"No. I was never into poetry. What they call poetry today is garbage. Don't say any more. I've heard enough," she spat.

When Armand finished the salad, he kissed her cheek, saying, "Now, please forget what Ben said. Let's talk about specific plans for the house, may we?"

As they ate, he listened to more of her house ideas.

Wiping a tear she began, "The only wall-to-wall carpet will be in the bedrooms, unless you want it in your den."

With eyes twinkling, he remarked, "Oh will I have a den?"

"Of course, and the wall color will be whatever you desire."

"What color does Ben suggest for the outer adobe stone?" he asked.

"We'll need to ask him next week."

When the meal was finished and the kitchen cleaned, they retired to their bedroom.

In the bathroom Amber noticed her menses had begun. She thought, *this is why I'm out of sorts.* In his pajamas, he watched her put on a panty and place a pad in it.

Still grouchy, she asked, "Did you get your eyes full?"

"I'm sorry if you felt I was intruding on your privacy."

After she donned her pajamas, he asked her to lie down in the bed beside him. He had removed the pillows and pulled the comforter down. With outstretched arms, he reached for her. Amber needed to be embraced. He knew she felt down-in-the-dumps, in spite of the fantastic things which were happening in their lives.

He began, "My love, we had a wonderful trip and purchased some things for the house. We saw outstanding places. On top of that we bought a house and property so you will have something which will reflect your input."

"Sweetheart, thank you for understanding. Please bear with me," she asked.

He embraced her, rubbed her back, and gently touched her lips, savoring their feel. He pulled her more closely to him, quietly murmuring, "I love you."

"Thank you for your loving touch sweetheart. I love you too."

"I am sorry you're having problems."

"I'll feel better tomorrow."

The next morning Jennifer called asking them to come over late in the afternoon. On the way, they talked about becoming an aunt and uncle again.

When they arrived, Ronald made margaritas while the others sat at the kitchen table.

Jennifer was so happy. She showed a picture of their Floyd Christopher and described the process of adopting him.

Ronald suggested, "We have cleared a path for you to follow. "

Armand agreed, "It may seem terribly selfish of us, but Amber wants to work three more years."

Amber added, "This was part of our game plan when we became engaged. I told Armand I needed to work full time to satisfy the effort I had put forth in my schooling."

"I can understand how you feel, Amber," Jennifer stated, "Ronald's mother will baby-sit for us twice a week. I hope to work two or three days when I can. I'll use the computer at home and work when Floyd naps. We have been told to have relatives come here to visit. At first Floyd may be afraid we will leave him. We are entering a new phase of our lives."

Amber answered, "Of course. I had not thought of parenthood like that. But indeed, it is another phase in people's lives."

The two women prepared food while the men discussed fatherhood. Armand pondered: We *want more time to think this through. Because we just purchased a house, Amber insists the place be made larger. Bigger, it shall be. Anything to please my love will be done. I fell head over heels in love with her. Now I'm up to my eyeballs in debt.*"

Hearing this, Amber stated, "I believe it's my debt too."

The evening ended on a high note of congratulations. "Call us, we'll be over."

On the Friday before Labor Day, they met her parents at the Albuquerque airport. They would return on a commercial flight.

Each time Amber's parents met Armand, he appeared to be happy with their Amber, and exhibited a solid footing in his life.

The next day after breakfast, they visited the property. Patricia was impressed when Amber described the house being almost torn down and greatly modified.

At home on the dining room table, Armand laid out the elevations, then the floor plan. Amber's parents began to realize their daughter was going to live in a lovely, expensive home. Armand pledged, "You will see what our family life is like, because every one of us, spouses and children, will be at Mom and Dad's tomorrow. My sister and her husband have just adopted a four-year old boy. We have not seen him. She believes he is a special lad. We hope with all the family around or nearby, he will grow to know us and begin calling us Aunt and Uncle."

Patricia assisted Amber in preparing lunch. On the patio, after they had eaten, Armand served margaritas. Many hours were spent discussing the new home.

They all enjoyed their Sunday with fun, games, and hilarity, with adult participation. The time passed quickly.

They spent Labor Day with her parents at their home. They chatted about relatives especially Aunt Marion who was improving very gradually from her auto accident. Patricia stated, "Your cousins are coming for Christmas. We would like you to be with us too."

Amber responded, "Mom, you will have guests. We'll come later."

"Why not for Christmas?"

"Mom, I'm the daughter. I don't like playing second fiddle."

"Amber, my dear, we have not invited your cousins to our house. I feel I'm doing enough for my sister and her family. Her children will stay at her house. Armand, would you like to come for Christmas?"

"I'll do whatever Amber wishes. My love, we were here last year. I think it's fair to your parents for us to take turns."

Amber responded, "That's fine, as long as it is our family and no one else. We see each other so infrequently, our time together is precious."

"It's not too early to make reservations. I'll call for December 21st"

Patricia elatedly went to Armand, giving him a big hug and a kiss on his cheek, saying, "We really would like to see you more often."

Amber responded, "Mom, you and Dad both work. We do too. You knew I needed the satisfaction of working after we were married. That's why I spent those college years wasn't it?"

Her father responded. "Of course. Since your Aunt Marion was injured, your mother is high strung. I can't get her to take a vacation. Amber, I think she wants to feel important, as far as your Aunt Marion is concerned. I'm glad you will be with us."

The next day they took Amber's parents to the airport, then drove to work. Ben called Armand suggesting they hire laborers to take nails out of the boards. "I'm certain Amber does not realize how tedious and difficult that job is. Besides the boards will be needed faster than you could keep up. Try it briefly for the experience."

"Ben, what tools would we need?"

"Just a claw hammer and a screw driver. I suggest you do a little, just for the fun of it. Remember you both are working full time. Armand, I must tear the house down because large equipment will be needed for the pool and beams. Starting anew would be easier."

"That sounds smart to me," Armand replied.

That night at home Armand reported to Amber what Ben had suggested.

"I guess he knows what he is doing," she agreed.

At the house on Saturday, they found it had been completely taken down. Boards were lying in piles with nails still in place. Armand questioned, "My love are you certain you want to tackle nail removal?"

"No, you're right. But I want to look at the concrete after it has been swept clean."

The only 2 x 6's left standing were at the back of the garage.

As the two roamed around the property, a neighbor came to them saying, "I'm Bruce Malver. I live across the street. I came to see what was taking place here. My wife said she saw trucks coming and going."

Amber and Armand introduced themselves. He told Bruce, "We were going to rebuild but it was easier to tear down and start nearly from scratch." They found that Bruce was an Aeronautical Engineer. They told him their thoughts for the new house before he left.

At home they talked about the house plans, Armand emoted, "It certainly will be exciting when they finish the hole for the swimming pool."

"I did not realize how much easier it would be with the old house completely gone. Equipment can be brought in so much more simply. The pool will take a long time to construct."

Early Monday morning, Ben called. "Amber, have you tackled the nail removal?"

"No, Ben, those piles of boards were too ominous looking," she observed.

"Please don't. You'll scratch yourself. Here's the name of a man you can contact who has the proper tools to do that job. Give him a call.

Equipment is on the site for beginning the excavation for the pool. The soil will be piled on your lot. It's too expensive to move. I have instructed the workmen to dump some next to the foundation on the north side of the house and tamp it down well. Once the hole is completed, we'll add more concrete for extra foundation. Please go to the spa and pool store, and select tile for the lining.

"I've ordered steel beams which will go over the pool, and some steel framing. I use steel because it's stronger. The price is competitive with wood."

"How soon do you need the tile pattern?"

"Please select it before Thursday. I'll have the pool people pick it up," he stated.

Amber thanked him and found the location of the pool business. She made an appointment to be there in the afternoon. She walked to Armand's office. He was on the phone. She left a note for him concerning her appointment at four.

She spent the rest of the morning working with a client, sorting through a file of information. At noon she stopped at her husband's office. He closed down, whispering, "Whew, what a morning! My love, I'm delighted to have lunch with you."

As they ate, he had plenty to talk about. He was in a situation where he felt there was little he could do. She rose to the challenge offering to help him.

"This afternoon we need to leave at three-thirty to look for pool tile, no matter what happens at work."

At the pool business they selected a soft light blue tile with darker flecks. They told the assistant the size of the pool, permitting him to calculate the number of tile needed, and the cost.

She phoned the tile pattern number to Ben's office.

Back home for the evening meal, both changed to lounging clothing. She could see that her husband was uneasy.

"Sweetheart, what's the matter?"

"My day was very stressful."

"In what way?"

"One of my accounts is not doing well."

"What's the matter?"

"Poor management decisions were made."

"'What have you advised them?"

"To downsize, sell a building, and consolidate raw materials wherever space is available."

"Is there room on their property for a steel building which would fit their space? How much is the building worth, that you recommend they sell?"

"I'd say a million dollars."

"To ease their immediate burden, could the building be sold for less than appraised value to move it?"

"I have that in mind, my love. I think your idea of a smaller building which could be erected in a short time is a good one."

"Do they have any special assets such as extra product which could be reduced for sale, allowing them to sell their warehouse?"

"Yes, I have suggested that. Do you know when a product is made, many of the company's top management do not realize how important production equipment can be. Instead they involve themselves in totally unimportant dealings, such as buying foreign currency, rather than investing in more efficient production equipment. The currency value went down and they lost the company's funds. The treasurer was against this asinine idea. He called me about it. He had said no, but his superiors went ahead with their crazy notion."

As they ate supper, Amber expressed her concern for her husband's tension, saying, "Sweetheart, you cannot let block-headed people bother you. I'll have to relax you tonight."

He kissed her, happily accepting her offer saying, "My love, you know exactly how to activate my switch."

After the kitchen was cleaned, he went into the bedroom, removed his clothing and showered. She undressed, put on a shower cap and joined her husband. This was a special thrill for Armand. He was able to stroke her lovely body which assisted his erection. She knew it would.

When he was toweling himself, she went to him and reached for his special 'goody part', purring, "I'm demanding a good performance, regardless of how the mental part works." She removed the pillows. He helped her pull down the covers. She placed her arm around his neck and he gently lowered her into the bed.

As he approached on the other side, she covered her eyes murmuring, "My dear man, you would frighten any woman. Mama, I'm scared."

He pulled her toward him and kissed her neck and lips, saying, "My love, I need your feel badly."

"Yes, I see.

Amber realized her husband needed her very deep affection. He had all he could do to last long enough to satisfy her excitement, knowing if he did not she would be very unhappy. Both of their intimate needs were fulfilled intensely.

Afterward, she made decussate marks on his chest and thanked him for a wonderful performance. "It was I who desired your affection my love. Thank you for your suggestion I'm going to prepare for bed and ask you to be my bed partner, not only tonight but always."

In the bathroom, he thought, "*No wonder why I flew to El Paso to take her out. My dear Guardians, you certainly helped me win her.*"

She came into the bathroom and 'tweaked' his manliness, then brushed her teeth. Admiring her body, he watched the curvaceous contours of her bosom shake, which made his heart go pitter-patter.

Holding her in a warm embrace they talked about the pool and what a thrill it would be to swim whenever they wished.

The next morning, his brother-in-law Ronald called inviting them to their house for dinner. She accepted, then called Ben to ask about the next operation. She told him she had contacted the two men he had suggested to begin work on the pool on Thursday.

Ben continued, "I have ordered skylights and a sand-colored metal roofing material and solar panels. The plumbers are now working. The next operation will be pouring concrete where it's needed. Tile for the pool will be laid when the base hole is completed. Now please select the colors of the bathroom fixtures and floors. I suggest you write your colors on your copy of the floor plans. We will get together and convey that information to the workers. That's it for now."

After thanking Ben, she began her workday and did not stop until lunchtime. She and Armand ate their largest meal at noon because it was more convenient.

On Saturday they selected a white commode and a sink for the laundry area, light yellow sinks for the kitchen, and sand colored fixtures for the first bath. For the second bath, they chose light blue fixtures. For their bedroom, they selected beige units. The other upstairs bathroom colors were light brown. She wrote the colors on her copy of the floor plans.

Saturday they ate only a salad for lunch, knowing that Jennifer would prepare a full meal. After showers, they discussed their new nephew as they drove to his sister's home. Ronald greeted them, holding Floyd's hand. She kneeled to embrace her nephew. "Floyd, you remember this guy. He's your uncle Armand who you played horse with." Armand bent to greet his nephew and handed him a new toy. Floyd's eyes sparkled. He thanked his uncle and aunt while he removed the toy from its box.

Floyd sat in a highchair for the meal. He ate well. In Amber's eyes, he was a perfect little gentleman. After the meal, Armand played horse. Ronald laughed as he watched thinking, *I'm glad to get a break from being the horse tonight.*

Playtime was over and dessert was served. Jennifer made her mother's chocolate cherry cake. This family favorite delighted Armand.

After a restful Sunday, their work-week began.

Amber's first phone call was from Ben.

"Amber, the plumbers are still working. The steel beams will be delivered next week. The longest pieces will go over the pool. If you go out during the week, you must wear a hard hat. I'd prefer you not be on the site unless I'm there. The tile installers are working on the pool. I'll have the gates installed next week after the beams are delivered."

"Ben, I agree, we need to visit our spot when you're around. Since I'm not into plans for a house, I couldn't tell one area from another. I do have the kitchen and laundry figured out however," she offered.

Ben continued, "I would prefer that you be with me. The workmen could become distracted. Also, there's a possibility of you getting hurt. Don't go out unless you are wearing flat shoes. It won't be long until you see some real development."

"Thank you so much, Ben." Amber settled in her chair and began work. She finished a little before noon and began to write notes regarding Christmas purchases before Armand arrived.

While they ate, Armand noted the firm was happy to have Marshara aboard. He could help out because Jennifer was now at home with Floyd and couldn't handle her full load. He then questioned, "When we become parents, then what?"

"If our child is not a baby, I'll be able to help some. Personally, I would not want a child that young, would you?" she asked.

"Since I have not been around babies or very small children, I would feel uncomfortable. One of Floyd's age would be acceptable," he answered. "If I had to be the horse to a boy that age, I would certainly wear out the knees of my trousers," he laughed.

They discussed a desirable age and sex of children they might adopt. "The boy must be older. Girls naturally mother their younger siblings. How I hated my sister hovering over me. She was bossy," he remembered.

Amber kissed him on his cheek then put her hands to his face and kissed him on his lips. She did not care if people were watching. She remembered her parent's telling her, *Let your love show. Be affectionate in public. If people watch, what the heck! If they thought this couple were newlyweds, so what? That's fine.*

Their week passed quickly. On Saturday, with Amber wearing flat shoes, while they visited their lot, they became excited to see the work progressing on the pool.

They then went Christmas shopping. In a woman's store she purchased lounging gowns with matching slippers for each of their mothers. After the purchase of another toy for Floyd, they shopped for groceries.

Arriving home hungry, both helped prepare lunch. They worked on household chores in the afternoon. Amber planned to purchase a hammer, a level, and three or four kinds of screwdrivers for Armand.

"What kind of tools do Jeffory and Ronald have?"

"I don't think they have many. They use Dad's tools."

"All right, tools for them, so your father can't accuse them of taking tools and not bringing them back," she chuckled.

"Does that mean I get some too?"

She flicked some water from her glass at him in answer.

"My love, what would you like?" he asked.

"Oh, lounge wear, something like we purchased for our mothers," she responded.

"Armand," she continued, "We need to cut back on Christmas buying. Please don't buy any jewelry for me. I want money spent on the house. When the time comes for our anniversary, let's spend it here. We want to keep close tabs on the house construction."

"Whatever is your desire. You rule the roost around here."

"Who rules the roost at work? What say, you, Sir Armand?"

He kissed her on the cheek saying, "As always, you win."

Chapter 16.

Their plane tickets for Oklahoma City were purchased. Wrapped gifts for family members were sent to her parent's home.

Celeste planned a meal for everyone before Armand and Amber left Albuquerque. She wanted the family together so their gifts could be opened at the same time. Jennifer planned to be with Ronald's parents on Christmas. Jeffory and children would be with Eleanor's family.

On December 26th, Armand and Amber flew to her family's home. Her parents were very happy to see them. Two good sized boxes from Albuquerque were in their bedroom. After they opened them, Amber positioned the wrapped gifts around the tree.

At meals, the conversation centered around Amber's and Armand's projects and the house. Patricia wanted to stay away from her sister's problems. She mentioned that Marion was home with her children and she was undergoing extensive therapy and was learning to walk again. Patricia planned to bring food and visit them on the 28th.

Amber made special place cards. The table looked lovely with red place mats and special Christmas dishes. Everyone ate too much, including Sue, who was a little chatter box. Now nine, Raymond was being taught how to be a gentleman. He talked to his aunt about school. He was pleased to be doing well in math. He told her he liked school and was hoping that during the vacation, he could invite a friend over to his house for an overnight.

His mother agreed insisting, "Just one friend not more." Wendell felt as a father he must give his child good direction. "One good friend is better than half-dozen sorta friends," he suggested.

Armand sat next to Sue, who was elevated in a chair with books and a pillow. Her uncle helped her with food. Her parents had enrolled Sue in a first-grade. They felt being with other children would help her develop social skills.

During their wonderful, entertaining conversation, Sue confided to her uncle, "I remember when you married Aunt Amber."

"That's good, Sue. Did you enjoy that day?"

"Yes, but how come you don't have a baby?"

Everyone sat quietly embarrassed, wondering how he would reply.

"Sweetheart, some married people agree not to have babies. Instead they plan to adopt older children. We will do that in about three years. Sue, would you like to join us at our home next Fourth of July? You could visit places in my hometown. You could see where your aunt and I work, and the house which is being built for us. It will have a bedroom for children we will adopt."

Her mother answered, "Armand, that would be a joy which is something to look forward to for us, but now it's Christmas gift-opening time."

Sue was asleep when Wendell, Lily, and Raymond left for their home.

Everyone went to bed and slept late the next morning. Armand enjoyed the late sleep and held Amber in his arms before her parents began kitchen work. Dennis made a substantial breakfast, one which would hold them until late afternoon.

They spent time discussing the new house, catching up on each other's work, and making plans to visit Aunt Marion on the twenty-eighth.

Armand and Amber obtained a dozen red roses for Aunt Marion whose house was full of people. Four more only added to the bedlam created by so much conversation.

Armand presented the roses to Aunt Marion as he kissed her right cheek. Elated, she asked if Armand and Amber would help her stand up. To her it was great to stand, instead of being seated or lying in bed. She stood with her walker. Her children insisted that was enough exercise for her.

Amber enjoyed conversation with her cousins, while Armand talked business with her cousin Gregory, who had recently started a business with a friend. Gregory and his associate had disagreements over some management areas. Armand helped Greg understand the importance of keeping careful records and the need for the company's department heads to maintain a visible chain of command in order to forge co-operation and not become a dysfunctional company.

Continuing, Armand related to Amber's cousin, "Often when problems occur, each person will point a finger at someone else and diatribes begin. A resolute management plan must be developed and followed."

Greg was elated to receive this free information.

They left Aunt Marion and Uncle Gregory's home at midnight.

Armand and Amber spent most of their vacation time with her parents. Dennis had baked before they arrived, while Patricia worked. Dennis would not allow Patricia to work while the children visited.

At midnight, they enjoyed a margarita toast.

When politics was mentioned, Armand growled, "Politicians are corrupt people who could not lay straight in a round house. Politics is absolutely rotten. These people have brought us into the mess we're in now. For example, why haven't the auto makers, on their own, developed a car which could get 40 or 50 miles per gallon.

"Because, the company management officers were milking the company and receiving huge salaries, by thinking only on the short term, they have allowed foreign auto makers into this country to produce vehicles with higher quality, which obtain better gas mileage, to outsell their products."

After the New Year's celebrations, they turned in late.

The Wednesday after New Years, Amber and Armand returned to Albuquerque. They pitched into household chores and grocery shopping. After their evening meal, they went to bed early, preparing for work the next day.

Celeste and Francis were going on vacation. Jeffory and his family would return on Monday. Armand, Amber, Ronald, and Marshara held down the fort. Grandfather Rambulet came in to help. He felt good to be working at his son's desk. He had worked his way through college while his wife, Alma, raised their two boys. Frank always liked business. He had started *Rambulet and Associates* when he realized he wanted to direct a firm rather than work for someone else. He steered his eldest son, Grant, into business partnership while his second son, Francis, was at the University.

The business was moving along well, when suddenly Grant suffered a fatal heart attack. This was a severe shock to the family and his wife, Vanessa. Francis joined his father in the business as soon as he graduated. Celeste who had graduated from the University of New Mexico where she had met Francis, joined the company and helped as often as she was able in the early years of the business, even when she was pregnant. After Jeffory was a year old, she returned to work while grandmother Alma took care of little Jeffory.

As he grew, Jeffory would often go to his Aunt Vanessa's home after school.

When Celeste found she was pregnant again, she worked part-time to help the firm grow. A year after Jennifer was born, Celeste again returned to work part-time. Vanessa and Grandma Alma assisted, as before.

Celeste was much more comfortable working than being a mother, although she and Francis showed their children how they loved each other with outward signs of affection, which they shared generously with their children. Celeste counseled her young ones in honesty and accepting responsibility for their actions.

Francis and Celeste found Jeffory the hardest to guide. He was very inquisitive, questioning, and definitive. He wanted exact answers. They both had to give logical answers to him. He would not accept any vague or capricious responses.

When Jennifer was born, three years after Jeffory, Francis made certain their boy was given plenty of attention. Jennifer was much easier to guide and was not as willful as her older brother. She was gentle and doll-like.

In another three years, Armand came into their lives. Most of Celeste's time was occupied in rearing her three children, who were fortunate to have two devoted grandparents to assist their development and help stabilize them. The three children were taught high values which helped them as they grew into adulthood.

Francis and Celeste were financially challenged while Jeffory was in law school. Before he finished, Jennifer entered college, then married Ronald after they both graduated from UNM. Armand began college when Jennifer was in her last year. He spent five years at the University, earning his master's degree in business.

Because all their children and their spouses helped at the family business, the firm grew rapidly.

Armand had worked for two years before he attended the seminar in El Paso and quickly fell head-over-heels in love with Amber.

Now Amber and Armand were working full time and Jennifer worked whenever she could.

Eleanor helped Jeffory as much as she was able until it was time for Gilbert and Gabrielle to arrive home from school. Eleanor attended daytime school functions, while Jeffory went to evening educational activities with her.

Amber added backup help to *Rambulet and Associates*. She knew her father-in-law understood the world of business. She saw how the whole family worked sedulously together. A wonderful part of the family attitude was forgiveness. They did not hold grudges.

Jeffory's law practice was very important to the business. Eleanor needed to stay at home during the summer. When his secretary, Brenda, became ill, Jeffory called Amber, who went directly to his office to answer the phone and take messages. He directed Amber to tell his callers he would return their queries in the order they were received.

Amber was amazed. Jeffory was assiduously driven by clients needing help. She assisted him the entire day. She went to lunch with Armand and Jeffory. Over lunch the discussion was about children and the time they take as they grow older.

Jeffory had hired Brenda after she had obtained her paralegal degree. He told her she was appreciated and missed when she was ill. "However, I told Brenda to stay home until she was completely well. I said I didn't need her cold."

He then related what a health-freak Eleanor was. "I kid you not, we drink only bottled water. I believe you need to do so too. Heavy metals are not totally filtered out of our drinking water. We certainly do not need them in our bodies. Don't drink out of aluminum cans either or eat food wrapped in that metal. Aluminum is another metal our bodies tend to retain."

Jeffory talked the entire lunch hour while Armand and Amber listened. The attorney continued, "We should purchase food in glass containers rather than metal. Don't eat too much tuna and salmon, especially the fresh products. These fish retain mercury which some people's bodies cannot remove. Tetanus injections and flu shots are preserved with a mercury compound."

He then switched to food products. "Farming procedures have destroyed much of the minerals in the soil. Multi-vitamins are a must. Also use zinc, vitamins A and C, but don't overdo the C. An excess of this vitamin can interfere with the ingesting of vitamin B-12 which is necessary for the immune system."

Armand asked, "You make your own bread, too, don't you?"

"Heavens yes! That is the first place we started in eliminating preservatives. We purchased a bread machine. We use unbleached flour and try to find foods which contain fewer preservatives. Amber, please use unbleached flour when you make your delicious chocolate cherry cake. Sea salt, which contains natural iodine, is better for us than regular table salt."

As they parted to return to work, Armand asked Amber, "Can you remember all that?"

She kissed him without an answer. She wrote a note to herself: *Get out the bread machine which we received as a wedding gift,* as she thought, *I'll get it out and see if I can make a decent loaf of bread.*

Jeffory called her asking for more help that afternoon. She spent the rest of the day assisting him. Amber began recording food advice he had given them. He shut down his office at five-thirty. She realized his day had been a grueling one. She had obtained a first-hand view of how difficult his days could be.

After their evening meal Amber located the bread machine. She brought it out and placed it on the counter. She called Armand who had been working on his treadmill. "Sweetheart, here is the bread machine that my friend Delores gave us. It's so large, do you think we could keep it on the counter?"

"There's really is no space, is there?" He went to the broom closet. "Perhaps we could put a shelf for it here."

"That would be a good idea. For now I'll put it on the dining room table. On Saturday afternoon, after we have shopped, we can start some bread."

Armand pulled papers away and found a book of bread recipes. He gave the papers to her for her recipe file.

Remembering the machine had come from her St. Paul friend, Delores, Amber decided to call her while Armand returned to his workout.

Chapter 17.

Delores was happy to hear Amber's voice. She was excited because she had received an engagement ring. "The man I'm going to marry is a PhD research scientist in chemistry," she excitedly reported.

"Wow, that's pretty fantastic," Amber responded.

"We've planned our wedding for the second Saturday in June, a year from now. I would like to have you as my matron of honor."

"That would be wonderful. I'd be happy to assist you," Amber promised.

"We want to be married when the weather is nice and not so cold. With our luck, it will probably rain," she laughed.

Amber explained their work, their building, and the new house under construction. "My sister and brother-in-law have adopted a four-year-old boy. The business is doing well. We are living in the townhouse Armand purchased before we were married, until our home is finished."

Delores asked, "How is your family?"

"They're doing well. They'll spend some time with us over the Fourth of July. My brother and family are coming too. We'll have a full house. We have three bedrooms, with two bathrooms. We should be fine," Amber related.

Delores asked, "Mom wants me to come home and be married in Oklahoma. What do you think?"

"Delores, that's up to you."

"Now my friends are up here in Minnesota. However, it would be easier to have a place to dress, other than my house," Delores reasoned. "I thought that day and a half before your wedding was so great. We had a ball. You married quite a gentleman."

"Oh yes! He is very considerate. Perhaps you did not know, he had a vasectomy before we were married. He still chuckles about what a time he had chasing me down or I should say, courting me. He does not like my use of disgusting language," Amber laughed. "Please stay well. Goodbye."

"Goodbye. Enjoy yourself."

Armand was in the shower. She took pillows from the bed, picked up the koala bears and carried them around talking to them. Seeing her with these toys, Armand muttered, "Are those bears so special they take my place?"

"Armand, are you jealous of me holding these toys? They should not threaten you. My word, you receive plenty of love from me," she answered disgustedly. Putting the bears down, she embraced and kissed him. "My goodness sweetheart, don't think for one second they can replace my affection for you. Please tell me why you are threatened by my holding these toys?"

He was stepping into his pajamas when she reached for his penis. "My dear, sweet man, there is no love like yours, whether it's your kiss, embrace or your intimate touch. Nothing can outdo you, sweetheart. Please answer my question," she urged.

"I suppose I see you paying attention to those toys instead of me."

"My love, there will come a time when we have children. You cannot feel that way. Girls like stuffed toys. I guess I've not grown out of that part of my youth. Those toys are sweet. They are a remembrance of our continuing honeymoon. Armand, you are very special to me and always will be," she insisted.

She donned her pajamas and placed a new pad into her panties. Armand hated the time he had to be away from her.

In bed, he held his love in his arms and embraced her as she rubbed his chest. She kissed his neck, his cheek, and finally his lips. He pulled her close and returned her embrace.

The next day Amber helped Jeffory again. During the day he told her, "Tomorrow, Mom said she could help me. You may be relieved. Eleanor will be able to help me on Thursday.

During the week, Ben called Amber saying, "I will meet you at your house on Saturday and show you what we've accomplished. Wear flat shoes and dress warmly.

"We'll see you at ten a.m.

On Saturday, Ben walked them through the pool area where the material around the pool was being poured. The steel 2 x 6's were in place for the front wall. "It'll take another week to finish the framing in the house. The rooms outside the pool area will be framed later. The pool tiling was finished and was covered with two layers of heavy durable material to protect the tiles from anything dropped onto them. Ben told them, "It's easier to put tile into the pool first because of the time required for its placement. The grouting will be finished and sealed soon. The final job at the pool will be floor finishing. For this I use a plastic material rather than concrete. It will be easier to maintain. Any cracks which would occur between the floor and the house wall will be easier to seal."

They laughed to see their bathtubs beside studs. Armand commented, "I can see why they have to be in place before the 2 x 6 walls are erected. You would not get them in later."

Ben asked about stairway details. "Open sides or closed? If open, the holes will have to be small. Because of our climate, I suggest windows which have a darkening sunshade built into them."

They then discussed window sizes and locations of glass blocks for light into the bathrooms by the tub and shower areas, and determined how soon they should be ordered.

Ben showed them where the furnaces were being installed.

"Ben, the front gates are lovely," Amber marveled.

"Do you like the iron work?" he asked.

"Of course, they are classy looking," she answered.

Armand wrote a check for Ben to cover the windows, growling, "Any foul-ups come out of your pocket."

"Armand, that's why you hired me. If I goof, it's my fault," Ben agreed. "Before framing of the utility area for the pool, the machinery will be installed. Do you have any questions?"

Amber asked, "Will we be able to open the windows above the pool?"

"Of course. The windows in the ceiling will be electrically powered for opening and closing."

Valentine's Day was approaching. Armand decided he would take his love out to dinner and purchase flowers for her. But that would be the only extravagance. Their money was being applied to their home. He instructed Amber not to purchase anything for him.

However, she paid no heed to his order and purchased hand tools.

She put a heart-shaped 'sticky note' saying, *Happy Valentine's Day* in each package.

On this special day, after work they dressed for their dinner at a nice restaurant. Amber left her flowers on her desk, not wanting them to be left in a warm car. She was feeling 'fuzzy' and warm. They sat across the table from each other. His eyes were twinkling tender timely thoughts. When their eyes met, hers were filled with tears.

Handing her his handkerchief, he asked, "My love, why the tears?"

"These are tears of happiness. I could not be happier," she emoted.

They discussed their new home as they sipped champagne. They ate their food slowly and carefully, listening to each other's conversation. One time Armand was momentarily rendered tearful.

"Imagine my sweetheart, feelings are growing deeper as the years go by," she murmured.

"I cannot visualize that. It's a good thing we cannot foresee the future," he pondered.

After they returned home, Amber went to the trunk and brought out two sacks with heart-shaped 'sticky notes' attached. "What's this?" he asked.

Armand opened them on the kitchen counter. "Oh, my! These are tools I don't have!" he exclaimed.

Amber smiled, "Now your dad won't be able to complain about a 'damned kid' taking tools and not returning them."

"Down the road, I'm certain they will come in handy. Yes, this 'damned kid' now has his own tools, thanks to his wonderful wife," he chuckled.

"It was too bad we forgot. It was partly my fault," she remembered.

Amber put pillows on the floor and pulled down the covers. She was taking off her shoes when he approached. Folding her in his arms, planting many kisses on her lips she muttered, "Sweetheart, I have the message."

He was nude when he approached her again. She put her hands over her eyes purring, "I can't believe what I am seeing!" Then put her hands around his neck and was gently placed on the bed. He crawled in beside her.

Amber was loved the way she wanted him to love her. He was tender and gentle, but the effort of love making required on his part, made her realize it would tire any man. *No wonder it takes time to recover from such an event,* she thought. Amber lay in his arms for some time as they quietly discussed their future.

The days passed. By the end of February electricians were at work.

Lumber for the sub-siding arrived. Huge piles of wood were positioned to allow the workman only a short distance to carry them.

The lower floor of the house was framed by the end of March. Holes for the windows and outside doors were cut. The four-foot wide stairway leading to the second floor was started. A few rafters were installed on the north and south ends of the house. The garage was well underway. Upstairs plumbing was finished. Second floor rafters were installed by the middle of March.

In April, holes for windows in the pool area were framed. Electricians and plumbers were hard at work. Roofers were progressing with the sand-colored metal roof.

Duct work, insulation, final electrical work, and windows over the pool were installed. Before the end of May, the last framing was finished.

Early in June the windows arrived. The small ones for the mechanical room were placed first, followed by the larger ones. One noontime, Armand and Amber were fascinated to watch the window installers at work. Ben and the owners-to-be realized the men were experts in their field.

Back at work, Armand and Amber stayed later than usual having spent extra time watching the house construction.

The week before July Fourth, Armand and Amber shopped. They filled the refrigerator. She baked his favorite cake and two batches of cookies.

Before their guests were due to arrive, Armand accepted delivery of packages from Oklahoma. Their visitors had sent their clothing ahead to eliminate baggage problems at the airport.

The next day, they carefully cleaned the house and swept the patio. Amber baked two loaves of bread. Because of the number of people arriving, Francis had agreed to help with taxi service. Two cars were at the airport when the plane arrived.

At times like this the inter-family cooperation showed clearly. Francis was very proud of his children. He often told them of his pride in the fact that Celeste was his solid 'rock'.

At the airport, Armand called to attract their attention. Francis helped Patricia and Sue carry their small bags. Hugs were shared generously.

Both cars drove to what Sue called, 'Amber's house'. They all thanked Francis for his kind taxi service. After Sue entered her aunt's house, she asked, "Aunt Amber, where does Uncle Armand sleep?"

Lily took her hand and led her to the workout room where the fold-out sofa was ready for them. Sue again asked about Armand's sleeping location. Hearing this, Armand picked her up, held her lovingly, kissed her cheek, and took her to the master suite. "Sue, do you remember when you carried flowers and tossed them in front of your aunt when she was all dressed up? You walked to where I was standing?"

Sue nodded.

"Remember, we ate a nice meal and we cut a pretty cake and you ate some? Later you danced with me."

"Yes, Uncle Armand, I remember that."

"That was your Aunt's and my wedding day. Your Aunt Amber and I were married. We made promises to each other. We became man and wife, so we could live together, and sleep together too. He went to the closet and showed her both his clothes and Amber's dresses. "This is your aunt's and my closet. This is our bedroom and we sleep together here. Does this answer your question?"

"Yes, thank you Uncle Armand."

"Now you go and play. There are toys for you," he said giving her a pat.

She ran to the kitchen where her aunt had the oven door open taking out food. Sue came very close to the hot oven. The women all shouted, "be careful."

Wendell was annoyed by his daughter's actions. He carried her to their bedroom and swatted her commanding, "Sue, no more of this obstreperous behavior or you will receive another 'womp.'" Sue began crying,

"You know you cannot be near the hot oven when food is being removed. Please, my dear daughter, act like a lady."

Armand placed books and a pillow on a chair for Sue beside him. He then went to help Amber.

The table was filled with food. Armand lifted Sue onto her chair and helped her get started eating. Then Sue looked at him and said, "I have to piss." Armand was shocked.

Her mother blurted, "Sue, what did you say?"

Wendell grabbed her from her chair. Lily marched Sue to the bathroom. After she had used the facilities, her mother furiously swatted her smartly on her bare fanny, growling, "Where did you hear that word?"

In between sobs, Sue answered, "A-t s-c-h-o-o-l."

"Who said that word?"

"I-t w-a-s ROBERT," Sue sniffled. Lily hugged her crying daughter, kissed her and asked, " Honey, what do we say when we need to go? What do I say to Daddy?"

"I ask-to go-to the-bathroom," she sniffled.

"That is correct. Always ask. All right now, let's go back and eat."

At the table, an embarrassed Wendell was quiet. Nine-year old, Raymond just looked at his plate. Finally Wendell exclaimed, "I sure don't know where in the world she heard that word."

Raymond answered, "I'll bet it was school. At home we always ask to go to the bathroom."

Wendell questioned his son, "Why don't we use that other word?"

"Dad, it's vulgar, gutter language."

Wendell turned to Amber and Armand saying, "When you have children, you can expect some unforeseen words to be uttered by them, despite what they have been taught."

Lily brought a still sniffling Sue to her chair. The child meekly held her head down while her uncle loved her. Lily asked, "Honey, what do we say when we make a mistake?"

With her head still down, Sue quietly answered, "I'm sorry."

Armand kissed her on the cheek as the other adults said, "You are forgiven."

Armand helped her eat, making a sandwich from their bread, with butter and jam. A hungry Sue quietly ate a good meal.

When the meal was finished, Armand played with Raymond while Wendell and Sue watched TV. When the kitchen duties were finished, the women came into the living room, and conversation reigned.

Sue soon began to tire. Lily took her to their bedroom. In the pajamas which Armand and Amber had given her for Christmas, she was put to bed gently, with both parents talking to her kindly and lovingly until her eyes closed.

Raymond played with his challenging toys. He could make cars, buildings and anything which came to his mind. When he became tired his father put him in his grandparents bed.

The adults talked until late. Then Armand inflated a mattress. Amber brought bedding for Raymond. Sue was put onto the sofa for her bed. When she awoke in the morning, she crawled into bed with her parents. Wendell wrapped her in his arms. This attention was what she needed to return to sleep for a short time.

Raymond awoke and came into Armand and Amber's bedroom asking, "Uncle Armand, for Christmas would you buy me more of those toys?"

"Certainly. Jump in and we'll talk a bit before we get up," Armand suggested as he put his arm around his nephew. They discussed in detail what the boy had in mind.

After breakfast, Francis came to provide transportation to the new abode which was under construction. Dennis was astonished at the size of the new house. Meanwhile, in the car with Amber, her mother's eyes widened as she exclaimed, "My god! Amber, you are going to spend a terrible lot of time cleaning."

Walking through the house, Lily exclaimed, "It is going to be beautiful." Everyone gathered around Armand who lifted a corner of a cover for a view of the pool. Raymond exclaimed, "Uncle Armand, every summer vacation I'll come over and visit."

Armand explained how the ceiling windows would work. Dennis remarked, "Amber has certainly planned enough bathrooms."

"Yes, the next time you visit, everyone will have their own space."

Because the stair railings had not been installed, Wendell carried Sue. They looked at the eastern view. The room was large, with an area like a closet, but no details were finished. A large bathroom and a smaller room with a bath, and a good-sized bedroom completed the upper floor plan.

Lily stood transfixed over the view, thinking, *To look out toward these mountains with their own special features, which have been worn by the ages, will give a restful feeling for the beginning of a new day.* She studied the mountains and noticed the tramway. She thought again, *There are full grown trees up there, I suppose pine mostly.* Her thoughts continued, *Down here it's sand. The only trees I see have been planted by man.*

She continued viewing the rest of the house. Amber approached her asking, "We have made the stairway four feet wide. Do you have any ideas for a pattern for the railing?"

"Goodness, no!" Lily exclaimed.

"I want an open feeling. I'll need to get some ideas from Ben."

They all left and Armand locked the gates.

Back in the townhouse, Wendell took his children outside. He asked Raymond to go in and tell his aunt, "Dad and I will eat on the patio."

While the women prepared lunch, Armand called for reservations for the *High Finance* Restaurant at the top of Sandia Peak for seven p.m. on Sunday, asking for window seats. He knew Raymond would enjoy the tramway ride.

After lunch they used both cars. Armand took the men in his father's car while Amber took the women. They visited the Museum of Anthropology. On the way back to the townhouse, they stopped at a burger place to satisfy the 'kid' in everyone.

Immediately after breakfast on Sunday, they drove tramway loop drive, ending at the tramway terminal. Everyone piled into a cable car. As they ascended, Wendell and Armand took turns holding a frightened Sue. Raymond could not believe what he was seeing, and how high they were, almost two miles above the city. Amber, who had not been on the ride, was very impressed.

Out of the car at the top, everyone walked the trails, which gave the children a chance to stretch their legs. The adults kept a close watch over the children. A few low-lying clouds added to their spectacular view. After running on the trails, the children became quite breathless. Armand explained the effect of altitude.

Their supper meal was very good, and the view was excellent, especially when the city lights began to appear. Amber's parents picked up the restaurant's bill.

The last tram car of the evening returned them to their vehicles. Everyone enjoyed the city lights.

In the coming days, the family visited more museums and the botanical gardens. On the fourth, Armand's parents offered a holiday 'bash' at their home. Francis manned the grill. This was another opportunity for the children from both towns, to become better acquainted with their extended family, and to play in a moderately warm outdoor tub. Floyd was happy to splash around with his new cousins.

Celeste sat in a comfortable chair with a margarita, watching her brood and the relatives of her daughter-in-law enjoy themselves. Celeste had grown to like Patricia. Patricia had ordered a red, white, and blue cake, to help celebrate the holiday. The ladies enjoyed watching the children; who were well behaved- because Wendell had made a rule, *If you quarrel, you will not be able to play in the water.*

Amber had told Lily to pack swimming suits for the children. The women sat on the wonderfully soft outdoor furniture under a veranda.

Celeste marveled, "I'm sorry we did not think of adding a swimming pool. I think Armand and Amber are smart to put theirs indoors. Have you seen it?"

"Yes, we have. Both Dennis and I are impressed. I must also commend you as a mother. You have taught your children some wonderful values. I see Armand is so loving toward Amber."

"Thank you," Celeste replied.

The day was joyous for everyone. Fun, games, jokes, and banter were mixed with lots of food choices. Amber's relatives did not leave for the townhouse until after ten p.m. using Francis' car.

The following afternoon Amber took her family to the airport.

Armand put his father's car into the garage and Amber drove to work with Armand beside her.

At the end of the day, before Celeste and Francis left, they stopped at Armand's door. Celeste requested, "It's time to leave. If you two take us home, you're invited to have supper with us. There's all kinds of food left. You might as well help us enjoy it again."

At his parents' table, Armand told of the great dinner the visitors had enjoyed at the top of Sandia peak.

His father related, "The night I spilled my guts to this lady, I took her up there."

"It's hard to accept an apology when the one you love admits to a terrible loss in judgment. Armand, you better not do that to Amber," Celeste ordered.

Before Amber could answer Armand burst out, "Amber would emasculate me to the point I would not know whether I was an 'it' or still a male in name only."

Francis spoke, "With you two, that should not happen. I kid you not. The time waiting for a child to be born is terrible. Then the baby receives all the attention. The result of not loving my mate was more than I could take. But, what a damned fool I was. Before I was intimate with Celeste again, I went to the doctor. He is the one who recommended a vasectomy for me. Now my problem is I need medicine. Before, I was erect too much of the time."

"So that is where Armand's passion comes from," Amber smiled.

"AMBER!" Armand fumed.

Francis ended all comments by stating, "Thank god vasectomy was introduced."

"Yes, Dad, but sometimes they do not work."

"It appears yours is working now," Francis smiled, as the women laughed so hard tears rolled down their cheeks. The fellows chuckled. What else could Armand do?

Amber thanked Francis for the use of his car. "To answer any thoughts or questions, I will satisfy your son's intimate needs tonight."

"Goodnight, Amber. Do your thing," Celeste responded. Francis closed the door laughing.

In the car Armand growled, "You didn't need to announce to the whole world what we will be doing in a few hours."

"I spoke before your parents, not the whole world," she muttered.

As Amber stripped the beds for washing, she found an envelope where her parents had slept. She called Armand to be with her when she opened it. A note stated, *We helped Lily and Wendell. Now it is your turn.* Enclosed was a substantial check which caused Amber to weep. Armand thought her parents' gesture was wonderful. The money would be very helpful.

Amber continued with laundry duties. Armand had other plans and prepared their bed. He was in his underwear when she entered. Amber probed into his briefs--exactly the stroke he wanted. Shortly, they satisfied each other's needs warmly.

The next night, Armand forgot some of his tenderness. Amber was not satisfied. She yelled. "You are as bad as the animals!" She went to the other bedroom. Even though she did not like the furniture, she would sleep on the mattress which Armand had used. She was still livid.

Since she was ready for bed she was mulling ideas over in her mind. She thought of calling a cab and finding another place to stay. On second thought, the other bedroom was a better answer to show her displeasure over his love-making that night. In her mind she felt he had not considered her at all. Yes, she was what he wanted, but his self-centered behavior showed he was interested only in his own satisfaction.

Amber turned on her side to try to sleep. He came to the bed begging, "Amber, please forgive me. I know you loathe what I just did, but, please forgive me. I was letting my penis rule my mind. Please move over. I will not be able to sleep until you have told me how you feel and what I must do to be forgiven."

She was silent--thinking. He bent to kiss her cheek. She shrieked, "Don't touch me. You are nothing but a sex fiend!"

"My actions speak louder than my words. I am so very sorry. Will you please come out in the living room with me?"

She crawled out the other side of the bed, stormed out of the room, went to the living room, and turned on a lamp.

He came, wanting to embrace her.

"Your embrace is a little late," she spat. "Just what the hell do you want?"

"Nothing. Will you please talk about what happened?"

"Just what in damnation is there to talk about? You used me. I am not a woman you, or anyone uses," she snarled, vehemently angry with him.

"Please, Amber," He tried to touch her hand. She pulled away.

She stood up, looked at him, then snapped, "If you know what is good

213

for you, I am not to be touched. I have a good notion to put on my clothes, call a cab, and look for a place to stay."

"Amber, you would hurt yourself as much as me. Would you like me to leave?"

Bursting into tears, she spat, "Don't touch me. You're a monster."

"Yes my love! I am a monster. Let's talk about monsters." She continued to weep.

He agreed, "You are married to a monster. Correct?"

With beet-red eyes, she blew her nose and wept, with her voice breaking, "Yes. I satisfied your intimate needs. What about mine? I'd like to take that penis of yours and do some trimming."

He answered, "I'm certain you feel that way now; but look toward the future."

With tears streaming she cried, "A happy marriage cannot continue when a man acts like you just did, I am not any woman. I do not lay with just any man. Do you get the message?"

"Yes, my love, I certainly do."

"Because of what happened this night, how in hell do you expect me to be 'lovey dovey' with you in the future?"

"I don't know."

She sat on the sofa wiping her eyes. He was angry over his actions and was in agony because she was so distraught. He knew she had every reason to dislike him, but he could not stay away from her. In his mind there was no valid reason for him to remain away. He sat beside her and put his right arm around her. His left covered her left hand. He then asked, "Do we throw away what we are working to build because of one horrible error?"

She leaned toward him finally, with her chest heaving huge sobs. Her muffled answer was, "No".

"Tell me, my love, what do we do?"

"Let me sleep in the other bed."

"No, I will not allow you to prolong this misery and agony," he insisted.

He went down on both knees in front of her, as she sat on the sofa. He begged, "Please forgive me."

"Yes, I forgive you, but it's tough," she replied.

"Thank you," he said as he arose. "Please think of all the happiness we have created for each other. I goofed terribly. I know I have created a huge hill for myself to climb in order for you to accept my intimate advances again. Amber, I was a fool to have created such a problem. We always hurt the ones we love the most."

Weeping, she answered, "That's correct."

"Now, please tell me what I need to do to help me get back in your good graces."

"The damage is done. I guess we go forward from here."

That was exactly what he wanted to hear. When she looked at him he was crying. He directed, "Please put your arm around my neck."

He carried Amber gently to her side of the bed, but did not kiss her. In bed he put his arm under her with his right hand and drew her close to him, murmuring, "My love, I need you. I could not stand to have you sleep in the other bed. You need to be here."

He kissed her cheek, still tenderly expressing his love. "Amber, I have failed once. Let's dwell on all the happiness we have created together."

She turned to put her arms around him. She found him still weeping. Their faces were together, their tears were washing away a situation neither one wanted to happen--ever again.

Finally, they slept. Armand awakened first. As she stirred, he embraced her as tenderly as he knew how. This was what he had not done last night.

She quietly spoke, "Without affection and tenderness beforehand, I will not allow you to go forward."

"I know better and you know better. The next time my love, I must be aware of you and your feelings. I broke that bond. I'm very sorry. I understand your anger. How do you feel this morning?"

"Much better," she answered.

They began their day later than usual. Together they made breakfast.   She drove to work with him beside her. He was thinking, *I hope she always will be with me.*

Days and weeks passed. The next important day for them would be their third wedding anniversary.

They had not eaten a good steak for awhile. He took her to one of Albuquerque's finest restaurants. He sat beside her showing tenderness as though this was their first honeymoon. In a sense it was. They ordered steaks and champagne.

He marveled as she responded to his attention. He wanted and needed her full affection. In his mind he thought, *I have allowed this length of time go by, I hope she will desire my full devotion tonight. She is my love. Life without her would not be worth living.*

Their conversations covered their two years together, her being pregnant, her accident, his mistake, and the progress on their new home.

In a thoughtful moment, he asked, her, "Why are we together now?"

She answered, "Evidently when our consciousness was in the *Ethers,* we had no bodies, only thoughts and memories of deeds, or misdeeds to study. We choose where to spend our next embodiment, our parents, and with whom we would live while here. Mistakes are made which, during the next life, will need to be considered. Everything which happens to you or me has been predetermined before we ever arrived here.

"As for others, they too, determine their parents, life experiences, style, and location. Remember, there are other inhabited places beyond this earth. Our minds tend to be boxed in. We do not see what is beyond our thinking during this life.

"When you consider all the sordidness here, wars, killings, incest, rape, and the rest: Sweetheart, the reason is *Karma.* It's complex, yet simple. We reap what we sow. What happens to us, is due to what we need to work out in this earth's dimensions. In esoteric thought, this planet is the cesspool of all thoughts and creations, mostly nefarious, because of damage done to our *Spirits.* We may think we are hurting others, but when spirituality comes into play, we hurt ourselves more. That injury is retained in our personal *Karmic* diary."

Continuing, "Sweetheart, I have forgiven you. Evidentially, we both needed that difficulty. In greater thought is it really an error? No, was an experience which was necessary for us to grow together."

Armand sighed, "I'm so happy to hear I am forgiven. It's a good thing your period came along as you struggled with plans for the house, or I'd have gone bonkers. Have you thought about house upkeep? You will not be able to handle all that home, even when you are there all the time. Just ask Jennifer. She'll tell you how much time Floyd takes."

"Yes, the more I see of the house development, the more I realize I will be the mistress who makes many decisions within those walls."

After their last sips of champagne, they left the restaurant. He was still courting her. It was nearly midnight when they arrived home. He took time to caress her lovingly, leading them both to a blissful event which only they could share.

Driving to work the next day, Armand's father called him saying a client wanted to talk to him.

"Where is he?"

"He's in your office."

"Tell him to have any questions, facts, and figures laid out. I'll be there in ten minutes." The call meant Armand would probably work with this client the rest of the morning.

He went to his office. Amber retrieved their mail. There was a card from her parents. Her mother wrote lovingly to both of them. Another check was included. Her mom and dad wrote, "We've spent money to educate Wendell. Amber, here's your share. Because of your scholarships, we did not need to educate you, except in your last school year."

With tears in her eyes, Amber climbed the stairs to her office. She noticed Armand had closed his office door. As she read her parents' note again, Ben called her. "Hi Amber, did you have a good evening?"

"How did you know?"

"Armand told me when I called him suggesting a walk-thru this weekend."

"Would Friday about five-thirty work?" she suggested.

"That's fine. Please go to the tile store and select floor tiles for around the tubs and individual showers. Next, will be wall color selections. Carpet and cabinet styles may be chosen later.

Amber realized that Ben was sedulously detailed. She thought, *he has to be. That's his line of business.*

She continued thinking of house details, writing notes to herself. Amber then worked at the computer until her husband invited her to lunch.

As they were leaving the building, the clouds let loose. Lightning and thunder were the worst Amber had seen. Armand returned to his office for an umbrella.

He ran to the car and drove as close to her as possible. Sheltering her from the rain, her purse protected most of her hair.

They drove to a different restaurant. He helped her out at the door. Once they were seated, she offered, "I know you've had a tough morning, but in our mail today, Mom and Dad sent another large check. They are sweethearts. Their note is touching and sweet.

"Ben called me this morning. We'll meet him at the house on Friday. We'll need to select tile colors before we see him. How did your morning go?"

He answered, "Some people who establish their own businesses really do not have the capability to make good business decisions. In this case, Ashbery and Brown are having management problems. Dean Ashbery does not agree with Lowell Brown. The situation is now at the point where Dean needs to part the ways. It's either he buy out Lowell, or vice versa, which I don't believe either can manage now. Lowell is coming tomorrow. I'll see then what his prospects are.

"It's a shame when two good friends have a business disagreement over management decisions.

"Further, my friend Ralph has asked for time tomorrow. I have no idea what his questions will be about," he added.

The rain had diminished when they returned to work. Amber's friend Miranda called from Dallas, weeping. She had broken up with a guy who wanted her to move in with him. She said, "I told him no way until I know what I would gain from such an adventure."

"Good for you," Amber praised.

Miranda continued, "Amber, he called me a gold digger and said that I was out of touch with the real world. Today kids live together before they are married. I told him that's rubbish. What he wanted was service, at the cost of my very personhood. I told him to get out of my life. That was difficult."

"I'm certain it was, Miranda. Remember dear friend, any man with an ounce of moral character would not demean himself. Really you are better off. He would put you down every chance he could."

"Amber, he was doing that already. I would like to talk more. May I call tonight?"

"Of course. Goodbye for now."

This conversation made Amber realize she had a very fine partner to share her life. *What would I do without him?*

After work, she prepared for a call from Miranda. On the way home she discussed her friend's problem with her husband. He agreed Miranda had made the correct decision.

Armand was working out when her call came. "Amber, did Armand ever talk with you about sex before you were married?"

"Yes, we talked over each other's views and ideas. Miranda, he discussed his thoughts very gently."

"He went to some pretty strong measures to woo you didn't he?"

"My dear friend, this is why we are both very happy. Stick to your guns. Do not give in. There are some men who are not worth their salt. Just be patient, the right one will come along. Are you invited to Delores's wedding?"

"Yes, I'll be in the wedding party."

"Perhaps you could come up here, spend a day, then fly to Minneapolis with me. Have you ever been up that way?"

"No, Amber, I have not. I'm looking forward to the wedding. I'd enjoy going with you," Miranda answered.

The conversation lasted until Armand appeared in this 'birthday suit'.

Amber told her friend "I must prepare for a full day tomorrow. I love you. Thank you for calling." A shower with her loved one began a happy evening interlude.

The next day, Armand was busy. Lowell Brown tried to undo what his partner had described yesterday. Being a bottom line guy, Armand saw through the charade after listening and looking at figures. Armand knew Lowell was not correct.

Cutting directly to the chase, Armand asked him, "Why don't you buy out Dean's share?"

"I can't do that."

"Why?"

"I need Dean's input."

"If that's the case, then listen carefully to what he tells you."

By lunch time, Armand suggested a conference be arranged with both men. Other members of Armand's firm would be present at their meeting.

On Friday morning, Amber and Marshara waited in the conference room when Armand, Lowell, and Dean came in. After introductions, Armand led the meeting. Detailed discussions between Lowell and Dean enabled the three to develop a plan to help them.

Amber began, "Your assets are co-owned by you both. I suggest we assist you in management. The two of you must be involved, but don't concern yourselves with your partner's details."

Marshara then gave them some pointers to help their immediate concerns. Armand offered, "We're here to point the way. Please use our concepts and together continue your business. We've discussed your problems. You are good business people. Take our suggestions and you will succeed."

After their clients left, the three discussed their morning work over lunch. Back at her desk, Amber realized she had seen the professional side of her husband. She thought, *It's no wonder he gives firm directives and is so serious.*

At five they left to visit their home construction site. Ben was present when they arrived. They noticed hardware cloth was being attached to the sides of the house which would be the foundation for the outside walls. Ben had samples of the stucco colors. Amber chose a color which was darker than the sand-colored soil and roofing.

The front doors were manufactured by the same company which made the windows. Each door had a frosted glass window to allow light to enter. Ben pointed out that the insulation was finished. He reported mechanical equipment would be brought in next week.

The pool was covered with a heavy material. Ben explained that it would protect the pool from any damage from the insulation and wallboard installers, who would be working in this area soon. Amber told Ben they would select a tile pattern tomorrow.

Ben suggested, "Choose one which is textured and does not permit wet feet or shoes to slip. Next week we'll begin wallboard installation. This is one real messy job. Let's plan to meet again at the same time next Friday night."

The following day, they selected non-skid tile for the floor in the hallway, kitchen and utility rooms. She chose light yellow with browns and beiges, flecked with white to make very attractive floors. It was expensive, but both agreed it was exactly what they wished. The tile color for the first bathroom would be darker. The walls in the tub and shower area of this room would be light brown with darker brown trim. She felt their selections were very attractive. Armand then suggested a light blue tile for the three-quarter bath in the pool area because this bath was away from the others. Amber agreed.

Amber had marked the copy of her house plans with tile colors for each room.

Before they finished, they stopped at a carpet store and selected color and patterns. On the way home they both laughed, saying they were spending money like drunken sailors. Armand muttered, *What the hey, We'll be living there the rest of our lives.*

In the car Armand asked about her ideas for the stairway.

"I wonder if a brown enameled metal could be used?"

"That sounds good to me," he stated.

Amber removed prepared meals from the freezer. They both were tired and hungry. He poured apple juice and placed peanut butter and jam out for their bread.

As soon as the supper cleanup was finished, they donned their sleepwear and crawled into bed. Amber lay in his arms talking about the house. "Sweetheart, I've not really looked at the roof, have you?"

"I did as we were driving in. The roof line would look better, viewed from the south and east."

"What about the stairway?" she asked.

"The idea you suggested in the car sounds good to me. Why don't you call Ben tomorrow? Did I tell you Ralph had an appointment with me today?"

"What did he say?"

"He and Lisa are getting a divorce. He told me they were growing apart, rather than together. Lisa is seeing someone else. Ralph wants no part of two-timing women."

"I don't blame him," Amber growled.

"Amber, could we invite him over on Saturday night? I'll make a meat loaf. We could have baked potatoes and your delicious green bean casserole."

"That would be fine."

"He has rented an apartment. They are going to divide their possessions. She has the furniture and is living in the house. He has the car. He was down in the dumps. I tried to explain, sometimes our lessons are hard to deal with, but we have designed them in our life plans. He felt better when he left. I told him to call me on Monday. I also told him to do something over the weekend, even suggested he go over to the campus and look around a little.

Chapter 18.

The next Friday evening they met Ben at the house. The wall boarding was complete in the back portion. What a mess!

On Saturday night, they entertained Ralph. They noticed he no longer wore his wedding ring. His conversation was bitter. They both assured him 'What goes around comes around.' Armand offered, "Sometimes it just takes time."

Amber suggested, "Be aware."

"Yes," he answered, "I would not be surprised that this guy staying with her will get the boot. She would say I was the father. Armand, how would you feel if some other man was using your bed?"

"That, I would not tolerate! Be careful. If she calls or comes crying and knocking on your door some night, don't talk to her, Call 911. Don't let her near you unless your lawyer is present."

After Amber tidied the kitchen she joined the men while they talked. Ralph could see that Armand was extremely happy, remembering all the weekends he had spent in El Paso with Amber.

It was late before Ralph left. The lovers quickly slipped into bed.

The weeks passed quickly. They spent Labor Day with his parents. Everyone went to see the house. It was apparent the heavy cover on the pool was very much needed. Armand told the family the cover would remain until painting and window washing were finished. Someone asked if the pool would be done before Christmas. Armand answered, "No, but I'll bet we'll have relatives asking to come over as soon as it is completed."

Amber smiled, "We'll have to keep the gates locked."

Someone else asked, "When will the house be finished?"

"We're really not certain. The railing for the stairway may be a hold up. We would not want children here until that railing is installed."

Jeffory's and Eleanor's family were visiting. In the excitement of exploring the new, unfinished building, Jeffory's children ran ahead of their parents. He growled, "If you run, fall, and bang-up your knees, don't come crying to your mother or me."

As they ascended the unfinished stairs, each child's hand was held firmly by a parent. Floyd was carried by his father the entire time they were upstairs.

The next morning a little before eight, Celeste called saying, "I wanted to catch you before you left for work. I warn you, be careful who and when you allow as guests into your home. Sometimes kith and kin can be a pain in the---you know where."

"Thank you, Mother." Amber answered.

As she dressed, Armand asked, "Who was that?"

"Your mother, alerting us to be careful who and when we allow guests into the house. The pool will be an attraction. We must control who comes in very carefully, she stated."

"Indeed," he answered. "Liability insurance is hefty. Supervision by an adult is needed at all times.

At work, Amber stopped in to thank her mother-in-law for calling.

Later Ben reported that the wall board was finished. He asked them to come out with him to check on the number and positioning of electrical outlets, including one in the floor which would serve the kitchen island. "As strange as it may seem, you may want to whip potatoes there."

While they were in the house, Ben asked Armand to help him lift a heavy ladder, which they carried to the pool area. In the middle of the pool cover, Ben climbed the tall ladder to check the outlets at the top for the fans.

Outside, he climbed onto the roof to check bathroom flues. As he walked on the roof, he realized this was a huge house. He checked the furnace chimneys. With the official inspection over, they left locking the gates.

After shopping and errands, Amber and Armand were hungry when they arrived home. After a light lunch, they napped before beginning housework.

They were interrupted by a call from Ronald. "I must take Jennifer to the hospital. Could you come over and stay with Floyd?"

"We'll be there," then to Amber, Armand announced, "We must go and take care of Floyd. Ronald is taking Jennifer to the hospital."

"Oh, my goodness! What's her problem?"

"I don't know. A neighbor is there now."

When they arrived, Floyd was crying, "Mommy is sick. Daddy took her to the hospital." Armand picked him up and quieted him while Amber talked with the neighbor lady.

When night came, they put Floyd in bed. After many hours of waiting, Ronald called reporting, "Jennifer has been having a tough time with her periods. She will have a hysterectomy in the morning. I'm on my way home now. My mother will stay with Floyd tomorrow."

When Ronald arrived he was very tired, but felt he would sleep better if he had a nightcap. They chatted briefly before Ronald yawned, signaling it was time for them to leave.

The next morning, Armand called his parents with the news of Jennifer's scheduled surgery. "We stayed with Floyd until his dad came home. Ronald's mother will be with Floyd today."

As they drove to work Armand observed, "I know Mom will go to the hospital to be with Ronald. Neither he nor Amber had appointments that morning. He went to her office where she was writing.

"I couldn't concentrate on what I was doing. I decided to come here." Soon Francis came in growling, "I can't look at that computer screen any more."

They all took an early lunch break. After returning to work, Celeste called Francis reporting, "Jennifer is out of surgery and is recovering. I saw her for a few moments. I'm on my way back there. Tell Jeffory his sister should be fine."

They were with Francis when Celeste returned, reporting, "Ronald will stay until four today. Jennifer will be given a sleep medication tonight. She told her husband to go home to be with Floyd. Ronald's mother will stay until Jennifer can come home."

"Francis, the doctor told us she should be fine. However, once at home she will not be able to lift Floyd."

Work stopped at five. As they changed their clothes at home, he sighed, "Amber, I certainly hope you remain healthy."

"If you were Ronald, you'd be a basket case by now. Do you know why?"

"No, why?"

"Because your romantic interludes would be interrupted."

"Amber, that remark was unkind," he answered. "My love, I would be very concerned if you were in that situation and bleeding."

"That's the case with fibroids. No doubt Ronald has been kept away from her by them. Now that I think back, she looked a little pale when we saw her on the Fourth."

Ben called and suggested Amber contact an interior decorator to help her with the window treatments and furniture selection. He knew she wanted a top-notch showcase home.

Ben was disappointed to learn the manufacturer had not begun the steel stair railing project. However, the company promised it would be done in a month. Ben did not have the heart to give Amber and Armand this disappointing news.

As the house finishing progressed, Ben announced a completion date by Memorial Day next year. Tape and texturing of the house continued until Christmas week. After wall texturing, floors were vacuumed, the windows were protected, enabling the painters to begin. The tile laying was begun while cabinet installers worked in the closets and dressing areas.

On Friday Ben told Amber there would be no work done on their house for two weeks. "Happy Holiday." Before leaving their property this time, Armand and Amber drove south to see how their house looked between the neighbor's existing homes. They were favorably impressed.

With a twinkle in his eye, Armand asked, "What do you think, my love? Do you wonder if we will be able to love each other more because the house is certainly larger than what we now have?"

Putting her hand on Armand's leg, she answered, "I believe so. Remember the ball is in your court!"

"Yes, madam. I hear you loud and clear." Driving past their house again, they observed the eight-foot high stucco wall, the color of the north-south roof line above the pool and the large bedroom and bath with a fitness room which opened into the laundry area.

She asked, "Sweetheart, look at the upper level windows. Don't you think they are in good proportion for that part of the house?"

"My love, we have an outstanding home already. Now to pay for it and manage the darned thing."

"Sweetheart, I've another two years of work before any family additions," she assured him. "That's two more years to be profoundly tender and passionate toward me."

"Touché," he agreed.

The holiday was to be celebrated at Armand's parents' home.

On the Tuesday of the week before Christmas, Melroy Abrams called Armand stating, "There will be two seats on the company plane on the Tuesday before Christmas. It will return on Sunday. Are you interested?"

"We'd be delighted to be aboard," Armand answered. "What time on Tuesday?"

"We aren't certain now, weather will be a factor. I'll have my secretary notify you."

"Thank you so much for calling," Armand responded.

"What's up?" Amber asked.

"We'll be aboard the Abrams plane on Tuesday. They'll give us the time later this week. I know you did not have any input in this decision, but I thought the offer was too good to pass up."

"How will we get the gifts to my family?" she questioned.

"I'll call Abrams and ask." He was told, 'You may take two medium pieces of luggage weighing no more than twenty pounds each. All your bags will be weighed and inspected.'

This meant that gifts for Amber's family would be sent by ground shipping the next day.

Armand called Amber's mother, saying, "We will be there for Christmas on Abrams plane. We're not sure of arrival time. We'll return on Sunday."

Amber's mother asked. "What do we prepare?"

"Mother, we'll all pitch in. It'll be fun creating a nice meal at the last minute. We'll need a special toast for this one."

Later Patricia called her daughter again. "I'm thrilled you will be coming, honey. What would you like to eat?"

"Mom, turkey, dressing, whipped potatoes, green bean casserole, and gelatine salad with a chocolate cherry cake for desert."

"All right, I won't worry about food."

"Goodness sake, we aren't coming to eat. You know Armand is a good help, and so is Dad."

On Monday, Melroy's secretary called. "Departure time would be at nine a.m."

When they ate, they discussed how long it would take to finish the house. They marveled about the eternity it took to tape and texture the walls.

Ben was a no-nonsense, professional person around them. They were impressed that on final checks, Ben made the inspections himself. Armand observed, "He has not told us when the solar panels will be installed or the furnaces will be running. Having the air cleaned will help. We won't have to dust as often. Have you thought about what will happen when our condo is put on the market?"

Armand was developing an idea. "Do you suppose Marshara would be interested in this place?"

"Sweetheart, that's a wonderful idea. Ask him," she exclaimed.

Ben had given her some interior decorating ideas. Seated next to her, Armand watched as she flipped pages of her notebook of house concepts. Together they discussed what would be preferable for coverings.

After some time, Armand drew her close to him. Looking into her beautiful hazel eyes, he requested, "My love, may we?"

"I knew that was why you were so affectionate, sweetheart. Just for you, of course."

That night she teased him. He loved to be the center of her attention. They both realized their loving resulted in helping to stabilize each other and their marriage. Their love for each other was deeply and profoundly shared that evening.

Saturday was errand day as usual. Since his sister was feeling better, they invited Jennifer, Ronald, and Floyd for Sunday dinner. Armand put on blue jeans knowing he would be asked to be Floyd's *horsey*. The idea of having a horse to ride gave Floyd a good appetite. Ronald was happy to be released from his *horsey* duties for a change. On the carpeted floor, Floyd mounted his steed. On all fours, his horse became frightened and began to buck and neigh. Raising his left leg and buttocks, the rider had a difficult time hanging on. Armand grabbed him or he would have fallen out of his make-believe saddle. Then the horse began to gallop with more neighing. Floyd screeched and held tightly to his uncle's clothing. "Uncle Armand, the ride is too rough," as the horse held him tightly in the saddle again.

Amber, Jennifer, and Ronald laughed at the antics taking place.

"Floyd, that gallop made the horse tired," Armand admitted, breathing heavily. The adults talked as Ronald played with Floyd and his toys. The time passed quickly. Soon the boy yawned, alerting Amber to prepare dessert. Then Floyd was dressed for bed with pajamas and slippers. Jennifer and his father watched over Floyd until he slept.

Ronald marveled, "Armand you are quite the horse. At times like this I am relieved. Goodness, your knees must be red. When rough-housing like that, jeans certainly are a must."

They talked about Jennifer's recovery. She still was not able to lift Floyd. Her final checkup was due after Christmas.

When time came to leave, Armand helped Jennifer into their car, and opened the rear door to place a sleeping Floyd on the back seat. He kissed his sister's cheek, then said, "Goodnight and Merry Christmas."

Chapter 19.

On Tuesday, Armand and Amber were at the airport counter at eight a.m. with IDs, and small bags. They went aboard the plane and seated themselves.

Andrew Abrams came aboard before his brother. Melroy then arrived and gave them special holiday greetings. Soon the plane was airborne. Armand told Melroy he looked good. "I've cut back my hours a lot. Would you like to come forward and chat with me?"

Armand joined him as Melroy asked, "What's new with you?"

He told him about their new home and described it. "Hey, that must be the house we see at the end of Morocco St. Isn't it the one with a metal roof the color of the mountains, with a high wall around it?"

"Yes, that's the one. The building process is taking forever."

"And there are just the two of you?"

"That's correct. We plan to adopt children after Amber has worked five years. We have a swimming pool which will certainly be attractive to children."

In the back of the plane Sharon Abrams talked with Amber. She noticed the house decorating magazine in Amber's lap. Amber told her about the house and Sharon observed, "We know where you are building. Your house certainly puts up a majestic appearance."

"The main attraction will be an enclosed swimming pool."

"Wow! No wonder it appears to be so large."

"It is. I'll need help. I want to work for another year and a half before we begin the adoption process."

"Why don't you call a professional maid service? When your home is finished I'd love to see it. I'm sure Melroy would be interested too."

"We'd be happy to offer you a swim and show you around," Amber offered.

"Amber, that would be great. Now I must work out in the gym. A swim is a luxury. Are you visiting your parents?"

"Yes, I came from Oklahoma City."

The pilot announced, "Please fasten your seat belts. We'll be landing soon."

Armand and Sharon exchanged seats. They were overwhelmed over the convenience of this form of travel. After landing, they obtained their baggage and walked to her parents' waiting car. Patricia jumped out to greet her daughter and Armand. Dennis's eyes were tear-filled as he embraced Amber.

Her parents were delighted that Amber and Armand could join them for the Christmas Holiday. In the car, conversation overflowed. Amber reminded them she planned a whoop-de-do party over Memorial Day week end next year. "You must make arrangements to fly over. The house will be finished."

The next morning they purchased their needs for Christmas dinner. Turkey and all the trimmings, including green beans for Amber's casserole, and ingredients for a gelatine salad. Armand found a chocolate torte which looked good. Dennis purchased champagne.

At home Amber made salad. She had also purchased ingredients for pumpkin pie. She searched in the back of the cupboard and found a glass pie plate where her mother's most useless objects were hidden. Amber was happy to be home. She was away from sedulously demanding work and was releasing tension.

Amber was determined to make a pumpkin pie.

Armand's startled look announced, Amber you have never made a pie.

"Just you never mind!" she grumbled. "I am going to make a pie."

She claimed one end of the counter for her work. It was true, she had never made a pie. However, she realized how important it was to use the correct amount of moisture in the crust mixture. She carefully forked and forked the ingredients before adding water. She worked the dough energetically pressing her mixture onto a flour-dusted, opened paper bag.

Using a rolling pin, which she had also found hidden in the cupboard, she began to roll her creation. It was thin in places, thick in others, but she was determined. Armand watched wordlessly, eating an apple.

The pie-chef took a piece of thick dough and pressed it into a thin spot and repeated the procedure so often that the crust began to look like a patch-work quilt. "Never mind," she crowed. "I am making a pie!"

It took most of Armand's energy to keep from laughing as she began to thumb-print a scalloped edge in her creation. Having problems, she finally asked Armand to help. After washing his hands, he proceeded to create a thumb-print scallop, asking, "Is this what you want?"

"Of course, sweetheart," she answered with a cheek kiss.

The pie filling recipe was a cinch. She put the filled pie shell into the oven. As the pie baked, Armand set the table while Amber's father prepared lunch.

During their meal, Amber checked her creation. She turned down the heat when the crust began to brown. Her mother laughed, "I'll bet that's your first pie." The three began to snicker.

"Of course. You three can stop your doggoned snide snorting and snickering remarks," she muttered. "I'll eat the pie myself. I've not had any pumpkin in years and I'm hungry for one. SO THERE!"

Amber left for the bathroom and her mother smiled to Armand. "When she has an idea, steer clear. Come hell or high water, she will see her project through. I'll bet the filling sneaks through those crust patches. "

Amber returned to the kitchen confident and self-assured. Her husband knew she was on top of the situation. He thought, *let the pie be. Its taste will please her; therefore we should all be pleased.*

Armand asked, "Mother, do you have any whipped cream?"

"No we don't", Patricia answered. Dennis and Armand went to the store for topping to go with Amber's creation.

Back from the store, they smelled deliciously aromatic aromas in the kitchen. Armand and Amber chatted as they washed dishes.

The washing was completed just as the pie was finished. Amber tested it with a knife. Confident over her efforts, she placed the hot pie on the stove and turned off the oven. She then grabbed her creation and triumphantly raised it up between two hot mitts, not noticing that one of the mitts was smoking. In a very flirtatious manner, she deflagrated around the kitchen purring, "Armand, doesn't this smell good?"

She showed her best yang actions, some resembling dancing. She teased her husband with green emitting from her hazel eyes, saying over and over. "I have baked my first pie, I've baked my first pie!"

She ended her brisk dance, flitting, titillating, and tantalizing her husband as proud as could be. She placed her treasure on the stove and kissed her husband.

He responded in kind, then reminded her, "My love, your mitt is on fire." She quickly doused the mitt in the sink.

He thought, *This display of enthusiasm is one reason why she is so good at what she does. One does not tell Amber NO. She was not satisfied with the townhouse. She demanded a beautiful home of her own. She would work for five years before leaving full time work.*

She sat down to relax while Armand's mind returned to the first time he flew to El Paso to meet her.

He remembered: *After the rental car fuss, she answered my knock with, Oh, hello. You arrived safely. She responded to my invitation to eat by saying, That would be nice; but it took all my charm to finally be able to kiss her. That kiss made me recognize that she was the lady I was searching for.*

Looking at her I feel how terrific she was then, but now she is far more fantastic and extra ordinary. I now know that our experiences together were what make our marriage work.

"Sweetheart, you look pensive. What were you thinking?"

"I was remembering my first experience in El Paso, taking you out to dinner. I finally got to kiss you. Man oh, man, you really sent thrills through me!"

"I suppose that caused your *manliness* to sit up and take notice."

"Of course. What other reason would I go through all those machinations and efforts? I've told you before, you were not an easy woman to win. But when I gave you the ring with your favorite color, I found you were very lovable, and you have been that way every since."

"Thank you."

He thought, *That answer is typical of Amber.*

"Sweetheart, we need to wrap our presents. I'll ask Mom for some paper." Patricia gave her everything she needed. The two went to their bedroom and spent some time covering their gifts. The one for Lily and Wendell had been sent to them. Raymond's box required a lot of paper. Her mother had told her not to bother with ribbons and bows. "Our being together is the best gift of all."

The four ate a light meal on Christmas Eve. Dennis offered a toast and became choked up because his precious daughter was with them.

They retired early. The Christmas meal would take lots of effort.

On the big day, Armand helped Patricia set the expanded table. A chair for Sue had a thick pillow to enable her to be even with the adults. Amber made her green bean casserole. The turkey was in the oven. Her father would act as chef for the carving.

Lily called asking if the celery could be skipped. Patricia directed, "Tell her to forget that. She knows it is only good in dressing or soup."

To Armand and Amber, Patricia reported, "Lily and Wendell were bringing an appetizer dish." That news reminded Dennis to put champagne and a bottle of bubbly into the refrigerator.

The meal was nearly ready when Wendell, Lily, and the children arrived. Everyone knew Uncle Armand would be required to play table tennis with Raymond. Amber finished work in the kitchen, then read to Sue.

When the call came to come and eat, Armand and Raymond freshened up in the bathroom. As Armand used the toilet, his seven-year old nephew joined him. "Uncle Armand, you are bigger than I am."

"Raymond, you are growing. Your body will continue to grow."

As they washed their hands, the boy noticed his uncle's wedding ring. "Uncle Armand, will I wear something like that?"

"I'm certain you will. We'll come to your wedding," he promised.

Dennis poured the proper bubbly into each goblet, even though at that moment everyone was munching on the tidbits brought by Wendell and Lily. Sue ate many olives. Pickles were not present, because they are processed with aluminum, something which is not good for the human body. The family enjoyed a wonderful avocado dip and fresh vegetables.

Amber was seated next to Sue, while Armand sat beside Raymond. Patricia was seated near the window. Dennis, who was closest to the kitchen, asked everyone to hold their neighbor's hand as he offered a Holiday prayer.

"With chaos around us in this strife-torn world, let us, at this table, offer forgiveness to those who do others harm. They have not reached the point in their lives when they realize they harm themselves gravely.

"To my family here, I am thrilled beyond words to have us all together. For this I thank Armand. May we understand that the world still turns, the sun is still out there, for which we are eternally grateful. We ask the Great Power to be with us and send our love wherever it is needed. AMEN."

Observing the table Patricia complained, "This is segregation. The men on one side and the women on the other."

"Mom, I believe that happened due to the children, Amber observed.

During the meal Patricia suggested, "Wendell and Lily be sure you take food home. Tomorrow I'll work to fill in for someone on vacation, but only tomorrow. We should plan to see Aunt Marion."

Lily added, "Aunt Marion is doing quite well. The insurance company is coming through for her."

After they finished eating, Armand and Amber cleared the table. Food portions were packed for Lily and Wendell to take home. Everyone relaxed in the living room.

"Mama I'm thirsty," Sue asked.

"It's no wonder my dear. You ate so many olives."

Sue answered, "I dreamed about working in an olive orchard the other night."

"You did?" Armand recognized what the child was saying.

"How old were you, Sue?"

"I was bigger than I am now."

"Were you a girl?"

"Yes. I was with my brother."

"Is your brother here in the house?"

"Yes."

Her father interrupted. "Sue don't answer any more questions."

Armand apologized for being so probing. "Having lived before is a subject which intrigues me."

They returned to the table. More *bubbly* was poured. A dessert dish was at each place. Amber had cut her pumpkin pie into small pieces, allowing everyone to have a taste of her first work, and to appreciate the theatrics she had exhibited while creating it.

As her mother ate her first bite, she exclaimed, "Amber, this is very good. The pieces came out of the pan well without any leaking."

Armand stated, "Amber, you must make this for us at holiday time when we are home."

"Grandpa, may we open our presents," Raymond asked.

"As soon as we finish here."

Wendell ordered the children to sit quietly until the adults had finished their dessert.

They then went to the living room. The children pushed gifts aside until they found their own. Their gifts kept them occupied while the adults opened their packages.

Amber opened a billfold-sized box. It contained a check. Thrilled, she went to her mother and kissed her saying, "Thank you so much."

"That's one reason I need to keep working."

Admiring a lovely pull-over sweater, Armand did not see what she had received. "What is it, my love?"

Patricia apologized, "I am sorry Armand, I did not realize how my comment sounded. I know you are supporting Amber in a very lavish life style, but as her mother, I still want to help my daughter realize her dreams, even in some small way."

Armand was on the floor helping Raymond build something with his new toys. Amber and Lily took the dishes to the kitchen to rinse them. They began washing the bone china while Patricia and Dennis put the food away.

Wendell cleared the dining room table, taking goblets and champagne glasses to the kitchen. He asked if Patricia wanted the leaves removed and the table returned to its original shape. With her nod, Armand helped him with that chore. Then Wendell vacuumed the floor.

The next morning, Armand's mother called, reporting that Armand's grandfather had passed away. "Don't hurry home. His body has been cremated."

" How is Grandma holding up?" Armand inquired.

"She's devastated."

"I guess we're never ready to answer the call from yonder space," Armand pondered.

"Call us when you're on your way. We'll meet you."

"Thanks, Mom."

Amber did not hear the conversation. Patricia had already left for work. Armand sat, emoting to his father-in-law what his grandfather had done for him.

"My goodness, your family has done well," Dennis marveled.

"Some of that is because the whole family married spouses who helped in the business. Amber has added a great deal since she came aboard. Her entire salary is used for our house."

"That's good," Dennis replied.

"Isn't it interesting how we keep trying to satisfy our women but they always want more," he smiled.

Amber went to her father, kissed him on the cheek murmuring, "That's part of our nature. Remember, we think differently than men do."

Dennis suggested, "Amber, we need to get serious."

"Why?"

"Your husband has just lost his grandfather."

"Oh, my goodness! I'm sorry sweetheart. What can I do for you?"

"Just let me weep, he answered.

She kissed him on the cheek and began to rub his back asking, "Sweetheart, what would you say to your grandfather? You know he can hear you."

With tears running down his face, he murmured, "Granddad, look out for Grandma. I thank you for all you have done for my parents and me. There's no way I would have been able to enjoy my worldly possessions without your courage and foresight to establish the business of which we are now a part."

Armand then called his mother who told him, "Your Dad is at the mortuary with Grandma and Jeffory."

"Mom, is there anything I can do from here? What happened?"

"He expired in his sleep. What a way to exit."

"Where are you now, Mom?"

"I'm home. I thought I'd let the men do the honors for him."

"I'll call when I know what time we'll be leaving."

"Please greet Amber and her parents for us," she asked

"I certainly will, Mom. Remember, Grandpa just traded his husk for a shining, shimmering *Eternal* garment."

"I know," Celeste replied, beginning to weep.

"Mom, I love you. Tell Dad I love him too. Goodbye."

On Saturday they visited Aunt Marion and her family. She had improved a great deal, and was learning to walk again.

She bluntly asked Amber, "When are you going to become a mom?"

"Aunt Marion, give me about two more years. You know we plan to adopt."

"Why adopt?"

"One reason is, before I married Armand I told him I wanted to work. He agreed. The second reason is I am not able to carry a child to viability."

"Oh! I'm so sorry I asked. No wonder Patricia would never discuss this."

Amber answered, "You know, Aunt Marion, Mom is a professional. She knows how to keep something confidential."

A call interrupted this conversation. Armand was told when the plane would leave.

"Amber, we leave tomorrow morning at nine."

Many thoughts passed through Armand's mind. He remembered the times his grandfather played with him. He still had toys to help keep his grandfather's memory alive.

Chapter 20.

Armand kept his *shades* on because he was heart-broken. However, He was able to sleep because of Amber's spiritual statements.

Over breakfast he related to Amber's parents more about his grandfather. Then as he thought about his grandma, again, tears began anew. He called his mother giving her the time they would arrive.

His parents met them. Francis greeted Armand warmly. They clung to each other for some time. Francis gave the car keys to Celeste saying, "Here, you drive." The women sat in the front, the men, in the back seat talked about funeral arrangements. Armand suggested, "Dad and Mom, why don't you have Grandma stay with you, at least until the funeral on Tuesday?"

"That's a good idea. Dad's death has caused her to shake."

Amber suggested, "I know that's trauma. She must be feeling terrible."

Francis answered his daughter-in-law suggesting, "Can you stay with us tonight?"

Amber responded, "I think you need Armand more than me."

"No, Amber. You're a part of this family. Where your husband sleeps, you do too."

"All right. Please drop us off at our house. We'll pick up a few things and then come over. Please get Grandma," Amber urged.

"Come for lunch. I'll get Mother," Francis agreed.

At home, Amber began washing clothes. Armand gathered ingredients for bread, put it into bags, and put the machine in the car while Amber filled an overnight case. Francis had returned with his mother.

On the drive to his parents' home, Armand said little. Amber continued talking about life. Again she stated, "We make our own reality."

At Francis's and Celeste's home, Amber immediately went to Alma who was seated and trembling. Amber put her arm around the elderly lady and held her hand, stating, "I am not you, but Grandma, life goes on. That may sound heart-breaking and cruel, but it's true. The problem dear lady is you were not prepared. No one was. Just think, he passed over at his own choosing and he was with you. Grandma, it does not get any better than that. Your husband was not in a hospital, a nursing home or an Alzheimer's clinic. He was with you in your home, in bed with you."

Sitting on the sofa, Armand and Francis listened to Amber's loving message. It was good for them too. "Grandmother, are you satisfied with the arrangements which are being made?" Amber asked.

With tear-filled eyes, Alma responded, "I would like candles lighted at the service representing myself, Frank, the grandchildren and great grandchildren.

Amber answered, "That can be done. Armand would you please call?"

He made the call and then started the bread machine.

Celeste loaded the kitchen table with food. Armand helped seat his grandmother. The feeling in the room was somber and dirge-like until Armand began searching his memories. "Grandma, do you remember how I opened a bag of flour and dumped it on myself? I coughed and cried, because some got into my eyes. You picked me up and took me to the bathroom, removed my floured garments and proceeded to give me a bath. First my hair was all pasty. You scolded me saying I should leave your things alone. I have thought later, if you were really angry, my bare butt was before you. Why didn't you swat me?"

Grandma Rambulet began to chuckle, saying, "That situation was funny. I had this precious child before me all covered with flour, because he was curious. I think you were frightened enough, you would not get into Grandma's cupboards after that."

At the table Celeste suggested, "Jeffory and Jennifer should be invited for supper tonight. However, do not invite the children. Just the adults."

Celeste made the calls and explained the need for the adults to cry, laugh, or have any emotion which might arise. They would be together.

Neighbors brought food. The newly-baked bread was a welcome

addition to their meal. The family members discussed plans which needed to be made. Amber and Celeste worked in the kitchen while the grandchildren with Francis and Alma discussed a fitting tribute.

Francis announced, "This is as good a time as any to establish an endowment at the UNM Business School."

Armand quickly spoke, "Dad, I've assumed debt up to my eyeballs. I could not contribute much."

Jeffory stated, "I could contribute a little, but I've started a family."

Francis answered the children by saying, "The business will assume the responsibility."

Alma added, "We have saved some money. If each one contributes a little for remembrances, Francis's idea will work.

Francis continued, "I'll call the University tomorrow, but now I'll contact the mortuary and ask them to include that information on their leaflets. Perhaps a special notice could be put in the *Albuquerque Journal* too."

Jeffory took his sister home, while those at the house prepared for bed, feeling warm and fuzzy with memories of Grandfather.

The next day, the President of the University told Francis he would attend the services and would handle the funds for an endowment.

When Francis heard Amber say she had no black clothing, he stated, "Forget about black. You would not look good in that color. Instead of buying something, put that money into the endowment. As Mom says, 'it all adds up.'"

Before the service on Tuesday, Francis gave the University President a large sum.

Mortuary personnel distributed pamphlets announcing the endowment to the attendees. After everyone had been seated, Francis lighted the large candle saying, "I had a loved one by my side who bore these three beautiful children who, with their spouses, are now involved in the business full-and part-time. I ask each of them to speak as they light their memorial candles. I introduce our first-born. "

Jeffory announced, "I am an attorney and am deeply committed and involved with the Rambulet business. My wife, Eleanor helps out when she is able. We have two children, Gilbert and Gabrielle. I have many fond memories of our grandfather, Frank Charles Rambulet." He then had his children light their small candles.

Jennifer offered, "I have just left the business to care for our five-year old adopted child. I remember Grandfather well and think of him often.

I would like to introduce my husband, Ronald." He stood, holding Floyd who lit his small candle.

Finally Armand spoke, "I work full time. My wife, Amber, works full time as well. We are committed to the business which Grandfather started." He then lighted his candle.

Dr. Worth, the University President, then commented, "The University Business School is honored to receive the Rambulet endowment. This contribution reveals the intensity which this family has toward the school itself and to assist in educating our citizens. Private business is very important to New Mexico. On behalf of the University, I accept these funds in remembrance of Frank C. Rambulet."

At the end of the service Francis stood beside his mother, with their children in order of their births.

Melroy Abrams and Sharon and others handed Francis condolence cards.

Alma was given her husband's ashes as her children, grand-children, and great grandchildren surrounded her. They all placed their hands on the urn, which had been lowered to permit the youngsters to participate. Each one silently remembered Frank with his or her own prayers.

In Francis's and Celeste's home, conversations included the children. Ronald held Floyd. The ceremony and proceedings had been explained to the youngsters. Floyd was a little gentleman. He quietly told his father, "I no understand."

Gilbert was nearly a teen-ager. This experience made him fully realize that his great-grandpa ceased to be.

At eight years of age, Gabrielle realized she would miss her great-dad, as she called him. He had taken her on shopping trips to her favorite store in the mall.

The family had a late meal as they discussed the Rambulet business. Alma was able to sleep because her husband was fondly remembered. Eventually each family returned to their own homes.

As he entered their dwelling, Armand collapsed onto their bed after removing his jacket, tie, and shoes. His cell phone was still attached to his belt. Amber placed a blanket on top of her exhausted husband. She slept in the other bedroom, not wanting to disturb him.

He removed his trousers when he awakened during the night. He placed them on the side of the bed usually occupied by his wife. In the morning Amber did not arise until she heard him in the bathroom.

When he saw her, Armand spread his arms to embrace her. His kisses were generous. "My love, we have been though a tough trip. We now know Granddad was a tremendous businessman. He started us on a business adventure, which continues. This time around my dear Amber, you have decided to join me. We'll have a great journey together, you and me, working to improve each other's personalities and grow more deeply in love.

His father called. "Are you going to work this morning?"

"Yes, Dad, we'll both be there in an hour. We have determined we'll ease back into work because it's a slack time. Why don't you stay home with Mom and Grandma?"

"Will do," his father replied.

They both helped with breakfast. While they prepared for work, Amber put on eye makeup and Armand selected a special shirt and tie. Amber drove. At her desk she caller her mother who told her, "Francis will receive a check---just a little to help with the endowment."

On New Year's Eve, Armand and Amber went to bed early. The next day the family gathered at Francis and Celeste's home. The conversation was light, with thoughts of the future. Armand told his family that work on their home would resume soon. The next job will be painting the walls. "The floor tile which Amber selected is beautiful."

Conversation then turned to Grandma and what she needed to do. She already had decided to sell her house and purchase a condo. She had decided that she did not need to worry about keeping up the big house where they had lived for so many years. Alma reminded Francis of the years she took care of Armand, before he entered kindergarten, permitting Celeste to work.

Amber remembered the wedding gifts from Frank and Alma---their beautiful limited edition plates.

Everyone in the business slowly settled back into their routines.

Chapter 21.

Amber and Armand worked on President's Day. They became more excited about the house. She spent time with an interior decorator to help with window coverings, and deciding what new furniture should be added to the pieces they already owned.

After the tile was laid in the bathrooms and mechanical room by the pool, a final protective coating was applied to the floor around the pool. The heavy covering was removed to reveal the beauty of this part of their home.

Grouting of the bathroom and shower area took forever. Ben explained to them that the house bathrooms would take a while longer, but the dressing area cabinets in the two large bedrooms were finished, only awaiting carpet.

In February, all the inside trim was completed. Cabinets were installed in the laundry and kitchen. The kitchen counter tops were made of a sealed non-porous natural material. Cement for the driveway and parking area was poured.

Outside, patio stones were placed by the sliding door to the kitchen-dining area. Even though the house was very nearly completed, Ben would not turn over the keys to Amber and Armand until the windows were washed, inside and out. The pool was being filled.

The third day of March, the stairway railing was installed. Their front entry had become beautiful. The day Ben turned the keys over to them after a final inspection, the new owners invited Francis, Celeste, and Alma to see their new homestead. Francis wrote a check for Ben.

Part of Amber's paycheck for March was used for window coverings and furniture for the two downstairs bedrooms. Armand gave Marshara a good deal on their townhouse. His move-in day would be April first. Therefore, each night after work, Armand and Amber filled their car with things which they could move. Amber found that cleaning the refrigerator took much more time than she had anticipated.

They moved their clothing, dining room chairs, and bathroom supplies. Amber hand-carried her bone china, protected with towels, in laundry baskets. Francis assisted them by taking kitchen pots and pans. Their car was used for many trips.

On a Monday, movers came to haul furniture and exercise equipment. After the house was emptied, Armand vacuumed the entire place. He went to their new home finding Amber in full control. He was impressed. The new furniture looked splendid. She was ecstatic as she removed food from the refrigerator for lunch. Amber was quickly becoming used to her modern kitchen. They delighted in looking out onto the patio and drive, thinking *We really need some shrubbery to spruce up our view.*

Movers brought the hutch for the dining room and later their bed and dresser.

After lunch they worked together to remove the china from Amber's careful wrappings and place pieces into the hutch. After it was arranged to her taste, Armand put his arm around her saying, "My love, we need a rest."

They went to the sofa where he extolled her with many kind, loving words. She knew what he was hinting. Looking at him, she smiled with hazel eyes dancing and purred, "I'd be most happy to love you tonight, sweetheart. You are my dearest of dears."

In the kitchen, many boxes needed emptying. Together they put all the dishes away including the plastic koala ones.

A pass-through led from the kitchen to the work-out room, a short distance from the pool. Now those honeymoon dishes would be utilized. As they continued to un-clutter the kitchen, men with furniture for the pool arrived.

Armand placed lounge chairs where Amber directed. He opened the ceiling and east windows. The pool water temperature now approached the proper setting. Ben came to check the pool equipment and solar heating units. He told Armand there was an automatic switch to maintain proper water temperature.

Once the pool furniture was in place, they realized this area was beautiful as well as functional. In the kitchen, Amber continued to unpack pots and pans. A special place on the counter held the bread machine. The canister set helped to make the kitchen look like home. Armand came to her saying, "My love, we need towels for the sink in the laundry area." She entered this need into her kitchen notebook.

She had him fold towels, wash cloths, which had protected the stem ware and china during their move. The movers then brought a fold-away bed to be put in the upstairs den.

Next they prepared their bed with the covers and sheets pulled down. He inserted the dresser drawers which had been moved by car. Their bedroom was now finished.

Workmen had hung the drapes and special window treatments last week. In the downstairs children's bedrooms, desks, dressers, and beds had been delivered. Armand had permitted no computer outlets in these rooms. He would monitor the computer installations, which would be in the den.

For the evening meal, Armand made meat loaf and baked potatoes.

Amber asked Armand to hang some pictures. He smiled to himself remembering he now had his own tools hanging in the garage. He would not need to borrow any from his dad. As he hung the pictures, Amber did not hover over his shoulder. She told him where a picture was to be hung, and he carefully measured the space. As each picture was placed, the house looked more homey and lived-in. While he worked, he was becoming more thrilled over their new home. He was proud to have it look professional. Armand realized his wife had excellent taste. True, she did not care for the bedroom set he had purchased when he was alone, but she did not cast it aside. His old furniture was put in the guest bedroom. Amber said it looked nicer there than in the townhouse. It was big, bold, and heavy. The large bedroom made it look like it belonged. She said it was proportioned well for the space it occupied.

There would be nothing added to the children's rooms until children arrived. The upstairs bedroom needed furniture which would be purchased before Memorial Day weekend. Otherwise the house was complete.

Both were hungry. They ate, looking out at the patio. With a twinkle in his eye Armand told Amber, "If you keep me working like I did today, I'll surely lose weight."

"That was just today and the past few week nights," Amber responded. "But don't we have a lot to be proud of?"

"Of course, my love. Why don't we swim?"

They donned their suits. He swam to the far end while she admired the whole pool area. To her, it was beautiful.

They had not heard the forecast of rain. While they swam, the skies let loose with a barrage of lightning, thunder, and rain. Amber closed the side windows. With the electric switch, Armand closed those on the roof. (A manual device could be used to close the windows in case of electric failure.) Armand opened the window in the mechanical room for ventilation.

After their swim, they showered together. Then, with tenderness, they loved each other.

The next day, Amber stayed home to make lunch for Armand and his parents, who had been invited to inspect the finished project.

Afterward they went to the bank and met Marshara to sign papers for the townhouse. He told them he was seeing a lady from India whom he met at a University meeting.

"That's good," Armand echoed. "Keep us informed."

They urgently needed groceries. Amber had let their stock run down. They restocked their larder enthusiastically. The next day she drove him to the furniture store to purchase bedroom furniture for the upstairs bedroom, an end-table for the sofa bed in the den, and more patio furniture. She paid for these from funds she had set aside.

His parents had been invited to swim on Saturday night. The next day, Jennifer's and Jeffory's families were invited to see the house and swim. Amber planned easy food. She used the plastic dishes. People could eat at tables around the pool area. Jennifer baked a chocolate cherry cake for her brother. Eleanor made a cabbage salad. Floyd enjoyed splashing in the water while his father began to teach him the essentials of swimming. Quite naturally the pool was a big hit with the children.

Armand and Amber put in a full week at work. On the next Saturday, Melroy and Sharon Abrams were invited for dinner and a swim. After they arrived, Armand made margaritas, then pressed the electronic system to shut the gate and turn on lights to illuminate the drive. A tour of the house ended at poolside.

The dining room table was set with their china. The hutch was illuminated, which made the room look lovely. The new grill in the kitchen was used for steaks. Armand had ordered especially fine ones for this occasion. The food was well presented. Amber had put thought and care into the meal. The conversation included discussion of Grandfather Rambulet's passing.

Melroy informed Armand there would be four extra seats on the company plane which would be bringing Amber's parents from Oklahoma City on Memorial Day weekend. "Amber, will you ask your mother if she knows anyone else who would be able to use them?"

"Melroy, I'll call Mom tomorrow. Thanks for letting us know."

Amber put the food away while Armand and their guests changed into swimwear. Melroy swam with fervor. After his swim, he worked out for a time while the other three chatted in the pool area. Then Amber served a dessert which she had ordered especially for this occasion. Afterward, the guests parted with many thanks.

The next day, Amber called her mother, informing her that four seats were available. Later, her mother responded, announcing, "The plane will be full. Wendell and Lily and the children were very happy to hear this. Does Melroy want us to write checks to *Abrams and Abrams, Inc?*"

"Yes, Mom, please do. We are looking forward to your visit. We love the house and find the pool wonderful. It won't be long until we see you. Goodbye. "

The weeks passed. The new furniture was in place, ready for company.

On the Friday before Memorial Day weekend, Amber stayed home to prepare for company. Armand hired a housekeeper to come when their guests left. In the meantime, fun was on the agenda.

Francis and Armand met Amber's family at the airport and took them to the new house. Francis left for home after dropping off his passengers.

Amber's mother was overjoyed at the sight of the completed house. Inside, she was aghast at the rooms. The pool was very special. Armand showed Sue and Raymond their rooms. Lily and Wendell would occupy the guest bedroom upstairs. Ambers parents were put in the large guest bedroom downstairs.

The family ate a good meal in the dining room, prepared by Amber. Children's laughter and adult conversations mixed comfortably. Amber's mother helped her clean the kitchen while Armand went upstairs to put on swim trunks.

Wendell told the children they could not be in the pool area until their uncle came downstairs to be with them, while he and Lily changed into their swimsuits. Jubilant children delighted in the water. They seldom had been able to swim. Armand realized they needed practice but thought, *What difference does it make?*

While in the pool, the children joyfully recalled the plane ride. Wendell was delighted at the ease of that kind of flying. Amber's parents enjoyed the water, too. They felt the temperature was just right.

After a great deal of splashing and some swimming, everyone was encouraged to let their swimwear drip while they sat in the lounge chairs poolside, talking. Wendell held his tired daughter. Amber encouraged them to shower. Lily went upstairs to obtain Sue's sleep wear. She brought Wendell's pajamas. He had not packed a robe; Armand loaned him one of his. Dessert was served and Sue was put to bed in the girl's bedroom. Raymond watched TV in the den upstairs for a time before he slept.

On Sunday noon, Dennis asked everyone to sit at the dining room table while he discussed their ancestors and what they had done to make the family secure this day. His conversation revealed Amber's Swedish background to Armand, who thought, *No wonder her hair is blonde, but her eyes are hazel, not blue. That must be from Dennis's blood line.*

He asked Dennis, "Where did you and Patricia meet?"

"At Oklahoma State University. We met at a get-acquainted dance. Why is it when a guy sees the right girl, he moves heaven and earth to obtain her?"

"Dad, that's a feeling I have not overcome at this time. I don't believe you have either."

"You are absolutely correct."

Wendell broke in with, "I think it is my turn to talk about my lady. Yes, once you see a gal who turns you on, you never forget her."

Speaking to Raymond, Armand began, "Look at what you are up against."

"Girls suck," was his response.

Lily raised her voice, almost yelling, "RAYMOND A. BREDDGEFORTH you're terrible!"

Patricia defended her grandson. As she rubbed his shoulders, she remarked, "He was expressing an opinion, for which he has a right. He is going through that time when boys hate girls and vice versa."

A ringing doorbell announced Eleanor, Jeffory, Gabrielle and Gilbert. As they were greeting each other, Jennifer, Ronald and Floyd arrived.

The men stayed with the boys while the women changed into swimsuits. Armand watched for Amber to join them. She was waiting for his parents who chose not to enter the water because Grandma Alma was with them.

The pool area was a mad-house. Amber felt they needed more sound-absorbing material on the walls, as the children shouted and shrieked, having a wonderful time. Ronald carefully kept an eye on Floyd. Francis and Armand brought drinks for the adults who were sitting as far as possible from the noisy children. Francis commented, "They have quite a party going."

Armand finally brought out a whistle and gave it a long blow. When he had everyone's attention, he ordered, "Kids, I will not tolerate any more high pitched squeals. You can play, but don't scream. The next screamer will be out of the water. You will then find out if it is more fun to watch, or to be in the water." His whistle brought an end to the deafening noise, allowing the adults to talk almost normally. He ordered, "Any child wandering away will have to shower or dress for bed." The children continued to have a quieter rip-roaring, rousing, romping good time.

Later, Amber suggested that her parents, Francis, Celeste, and Alma retire to the living room for some peace. Later, she and Armand showered together, enjoying a few moments of body-to-body contact, then put on sport clothes and began to prepare something to eat. The *zoo* dishes were used for lunch. Jeffory, Ronald and Wendell continued watching the children.

After everyone had showered and was eating, Armand began to mop up the water left from wet bathers and their swimming gear. He returned the furniture into place.

Food and dishes were handed through the pass-thru to those near the pool. In the dining room, Amber sat next to Grandma Alma. "I think it's so nice you could have both families share this wonderful time," Alma praised.

"I'm finding it much easier to handle adults than rambunctious children. Alma, why do girls scream so much?" Amber asked.

Alma smiled, "I don't know. I just had boys. I am glad that Armand called a halt to most of the noise."

"For awhile I thought the house did not have enough sound-absorbing materials in the walls and ceiling, Amber admitted.

It was nearly nine p.m. when Armand's siblings and families left. Sue was asleep when Wendell put her in bed. Raymond accompanied his uncle as he closed the lower windows. He left the ceiling ones open and the fans running at a low speed.

Raymond went to bed. The adults talked in the living room. Amber remembered the washed towels and put them in the dryer.

Everyone sat back, relaxed, and savored the quiet time until a yawn from Amber suggested it was bedtime. Tomorrow the plane would leave at ten a.m. Francis would assist in taking family to the airport.

Amber stayed at home to clean. She had lunch prepared when Armand returned. The maid came and dusted, cleaned, and vacuumed while Armand and Amber ate.

"Our holiday was wonderful," he whispered. "My love, tonight I need you." Amber looked at him dressed in his pink shirt, pink and white striped tie, and pink cuff links and answered, "After such a commotion, we both need to relax. I hope the house took the company all right. For awhile, the noise level was terrible."

"I should have ended that screaming before I did. Now my love, I must return to work."

Amber was at work on Wednesday. Their maid came every weekday at nine and left at five. This service was a great help for Amber. She could then shop with Armand.

On Saturday evening, after a workout and swim, they showered together in the pool shower. Nude, they went upstairs. Armand placed his lady in bed and they loved each other.

Later, he discussed the holiday and how well she had planned the food and hospitality. The following Monday, the maid left a note for Amber along with two sealed envelopes she found on the pillows in the guest bedrooms. One envelope contained a note and a check for Amber. Dennis had written a check for Armand and placed it on the pillow.

Amber's parents realized that no amount of money would repay them for their efforts on such a wonderful holiday. These notes and money were thanks because the time they enjoyed was priceless. An added benefit was that Amber's brother's family had also enjoyed a wonderful time. They would have had to spend a great deal more money if they had stayed at a resort. That money would be added to Amber's June deposit.

Chapter 22.

The weeks passed. The Rambulet family would spend the Fourth of July with Armand and Amber. Each family would contribute food.

Celeste talked to Jennifer, Eleanor, Vanessa, and Alma. All would fix food ahead of time. Alma would bring pies and her special kind of chocolate cake. Their time together would not be as noisy because only three children would be present. Jeffory told Gabrielle if she screamed she would be taken out of the pool.

On the holiday, everyone swam. The children spent so much time in the water their fingers wrinkled. That did not stop them from antics galore. After the families left, Armand and Amber dried the area around the pool. She wiped down the shower, because the tile was so beautiful, she did not want any scum buildup. Tired from this chore, they went upstairs and laid out tomorrow's work clothes.

Their fourth anniversary was approaching. Ralph called, saying he had found a lady friend, "She really turns me on. I'd like to take you out for your anniversary. Then you could meet Marlene."

"Where is she from?" Armand asked.

"The City of the Crosses. I went back to school as you suggested. Marlene obtained her Masters in Business Management in June from NMSU in Las Cruces. I met her there," he replied.

"Fine, the women will have something in common. We accept your offer," Armand stated. "Let me know what time. I must run now, my client is here. I'll talk to you later."

On the way home Armand told Amber about Ralph's invitation. The conversation turned to their upcoming anniversary. "Goodness, my love, four years with you. It doesn't seem possible."

"Without me, sweetheart, you would be a basket case---a frustrated bachelor," she teased.

"You have that correct," he admitted as the gates opened.

The next day Armand suggested, "Let's go home and make lunch." This was something they normally did not do. The house was new and they enjoyed being in it. Arriving home, they discovered the maid had guests. Before they entered the house, Armand called the police. They waited a few minutes before going in. They found the maid, who had been highly recommended, had invited two grandchildren over to swim in the pool. Amber was speechless.

Armand welcomed the policeman. With her hand over her mouth, the maid had a strange expression on her face. Amber was shaken and angry.

The policeman asked the maid many questions. "Do you realize this will cease any further employment for you in this capacity?"

Armand immediately called her employment agency and related to them what she had done. The police officer had the kids sit in the kitchen, as he asked Amber to check all the rooms for losses of jewelry or any purses in the house. He asked the maid, "What have you taken from this home?"

Through tears, she mumbled, "Nothing, officer."

"How about identity theft?"

"Officer, I don't know what that means."

Armand told the officer, "We keep no checkbooks or money in the house.

"Who, besides these two youngsters know about this house and what is here?"

"I told my sister," she admitted.

"Now you have breached your contract with these people and your service agency as well, " the officer growled.

Armand had called Jeffory, who walked in very officiously--enough to intimidate anyone.

With two men grilling her, the maid could do nothing but weep.

Jeffory spoke menacingly, "Armand, do not pay this woman. Cease her employment. "To the youngsters he asked, "How long have you been here?"

"We came with Grandma."

"What have you been doing all this time?"

"Playing in the water."

"All the time?" Jeffory looked at their fingers. They were very shriveled.

"Mister, we don't have a chance to play in a pool."

"That may be so kids, but you were not invited by the homeowners. Your grandma does not have that authority. This is not her home," Jeffory intoned.

The officer looked at Jeffory, with a look of, *What do I do with this woman?*

"Anything missing in the house will cause you to be put in jail. Now you may leave," the officer ordered.

Weeping, the maid left, followed by the officer. She quickly put her children's toys, which were on the hood of her car, into the trunk.

Being nervous and somewhat anxious over these children, Amber sat while Armand finished making sandwiches, which the maid had started.

Jeffory stated, "I hope we instilled the fear of god in her and the kids. If there's anything missing, it will be jail or a fine or both. How stupid can a person be?"

Armand suggested to an upset Amber, "My love, why don't you go to the children's bedrooms and make certain all the toys are where they should be."

She returned saying, "I guess it was the water that interested them."

She then opened some applesauce and chips, apologizing to her brother-in-law, "This is not much of a lunch, Jeffory."

"If I had been home, it would have been peanut butter and jelly sandwiches, and I mean no affront to Eleanor either. Kids keep you going at full speed from the time they awake until they sleep."

They left the house, anxious to return to work. Amber had a client scheduled for two, which relieved her. She could forget about this unpleasant incident.

When Jeffory told Francis what had happened, Francis called the employment agency, *The House Guards*, and put the threat of the universe on that organization.

Armand and Amber prepared for their fourth anniversary celebration. When Ralph came with his friend, Armand asked them to come in and see the house. Ralph introduced Amber to Marlene, who was enchanted over the home. She had never been in a place with an enclosed pool. She could not believe how large the home was. She thought, *Goodness, it would cost a fortune to keep up this place.*

As they chatted, Ralph asked, "How did your week go?"

"Fine until we discovered that the maid had invited youthful guests over to swim. We happened to go home. I caught two kids in our pool. There were toys on the hood of her car. Thankfully, I saw them and called the police before we went in."

"Good grief, Armand, that's enough to give anyone a heart attack or certainly at least a creepy feeling."

Amber related, "I did feel crawly while I checked to determine if any of our toys were missing. We found everything in order. The kids were mostly interested in the pool."

Marlene observed, "It would be a thrill for me to swim in a private pool where I would not be teased or glared at by bratty kids."

"Armand and I would be delighted to entertain you for a swim."

"That sounds wonderful to me," Marlene responded.

"Had the maid asked," Amber suggested, "We would likely have allowed her to bring the children, with a deadline of how long they could be in the water. No wonder insurance is so expensive, with a pool in the house."

Ralph stated, "You two work very hard for what you have."

"All of Amber's salary is put into the house," Armand told him.

I want to work another year at least," Amber indicated, while they entered the car to share dinner together.

Each gentleman held his lady's hand as they approached the green canopy of the restaurant. Ralph held the door. When the two men were shoulder to shoulder, Ralph told Armand he had received an increase in wages.

In the booth after drinks were ordered, Armand asked, "Ralph, you look terrific, but what has happened? You look like you're on top of the world."

Jeffory has seen to it that I am free of Lisa. She did nothing for me except give me freedom."

Marlene added, "I am divorced, too. Sometimes it takes a wake-up call to get one on the right track. After my divorce and settlement, I went back to school. I'll see how life goes. I may go back for my PhD. I enjoyed my studies."

They toasted each other. Ralph asked Armand to talk about his life with Amber, saying, "It must be pretty good!"

"Yes, without Amber, I'd be a terribly frustrated man. But what is wonderful, we talk over and sort out any misunderstandings. We have agreed never to go to sleep angry. We talk long enough to finally say, 'I am sorry', 'I apologize', or 'please forgive me.' We have a pact that when one may be angry as hell, the other one listens quietly. When Amber is angry, her eyes spit fire. I must listen."

Looking lovingly at Armand, Amber revealed, "This man is always a gentleman. He helps me in and out of the car. At home he assists me whenever I need help."

"Marriage is a two-way street," Armand added.

Ralph agreed, "But Lisa did not see it that way."

After a delightful evening, back at home, Armand and Amber loved each other.

Labor Day came soon after their anniversary. Amber decided rather than family, she would invite Ralph and Marlene over for a noon meal and a swim, because Ralph was such a good friend of Armand.

At noon on Labor Day, Ralph and Marlene arrived. As always with good friends, the time passed quickly. Marlene insisted the dishes be done before they swam. She told Amber her china, stemware, and silverware were lovely. Only when the kitchen was spic and span, did the foursome dress in swim attire.

Armand noticed Marlene's well filled breasts. He thought, *They would be something great to feel. Good for Ralph.* His thoughts continued as he looked at Marlene. *Yes, the haptic sense of a woman's bosom is, indeed, special.*

When their day ended, before they went to sleep, Amber asked, "Did you get enough looking at Marlene? I saw you admiring her boobs. Your eyes about popped out of their sockets. I'm somewhat lacking in that department."

"Not for me," he exclaimed, reaching under her pajamas to caress her left bosom. After goodnight kisses, they slept.

The next day was quiet at work. Amber hired another maid. After much scrutinizing, Jessica Arnolds was hired. Jessica met them at eight the next day. Amber, impressed with her professional manner, related the basics of what she expected. Jessica told Amber she would leave a note explaining what she had done each day. Amber related she could eat anything in the house unless a note was left on a food item. Jessica loved to cook. She often had the table set and something in the oven when they arrived home.

One day, the new maid baked a chocolate cherry cake which Armand loved so much. This meant she had probed every inch of Amber's recipes.

They were late arriving home that evening due to early Christmas shopping. Naturally they were thrilled to have food prepared.

Thanksgiving was spent with Armand's family. After dessert was served, everyone enjoyed swimming. As night approached, children were asleep. Fathers carried their kids to their cars.

The day after, which is called *Black Friday* in department stores, Armand and Amber relaxed. It was the first day they had been able to enjoy their home together alone. They were surprised when Jessica came. "I know you were not expecting me, but I thought I would prepare lunch for you, and then leave."

"Jessica, that's wonderful. We were swimming," Amber praised.

"You go ahead and swim. I'll be in the kitchen for an hour or so. Then I'll go if you have nothing for me to do."

"Thank you so much. Leave whenever you desire."

They swam, then sat and talked, observing the room. Armand turned on the fans saying, "We do not use these enough."

Jessica announced she was leaving and was thanked sincerely. Even though the house was large, the odors of food were tantalizing. Realizing they were hungry, they went to the kitchen without showering. Swimming resumed after lunch.

Armand wanted to tease his wife, but he could not muss her hair. He knew she spent a lot of time taking care of it. Instead, he permitted her to tease him. All he could do was to tenderly love her. He adored the attention she gave him.

Following an afternoon swim, they showered, then went shopping for a Christmas tree. She insisted on one because they would be hosting a large family get-together. They now had space to store it, upright and decorated.

Ben had directed that all inside doors would be four feet wide, to accommodate any large packages, or wheel chairs. He may have had Christmas in mind.

Armand set the Christmas tree up in the living room where Amber directed. After supper they decorated it in yellow and white.

On Monday, Celeste asked Amber to come to her office. She wanted to discuss plans for Christmas and wished to know when Amber's family would be coming. Amber told her they would arrive on the twenty-third and would leave on the twenty-ninth. Celeste suggested that the Rambulets have their gathering on the twenty-fourth. Amber realized that her mother-in-law was a little upset because Amber's family would cause some disruption with Celeste's holiday plans.

As she talked with her mother-in-law, Amber stated, "Mother, plan your gathering. My family will enjoy their time in our home by themselves. Don't worry. We will be at your place. At what time?" she asked.

Celeste replied, "About four o'clock."

"I'll talk with Armand. I think that would work well."

Driving home, Amber related to him his mother's concern over a Rambulet Christmas dinner.

"What did you decide?"

"I told your mom we would spend Christmas Eve with them. We are to be there at four p.m. My family can stay in our home. We'll have our Christmas meal well prepared before we leave."

"I'll have a talk with Mom. She has her chicks and spouses around whenever she wishes. This Christmas your family will be here. Mom needs to learn to share. She has called the shots for many years. My love, you have had the nerve to intrude on her time."

In the house, Amber noticed Jessica had the table set. Amber took food from the oven while Armand stated, "My love, I want our Christmas to be very nice."

"It will be. I do not think your mother would want our Christmas to be harmed. Hey! I have an idea, why don't we invite your parents to be with us on Christmas Day?"

"That's the ticket, my love. We could eat late in the afternoon. That would work."

"Of course," she replied. "Please invite them."

The next day Armand dutifully followed her instructions. He knocked at his mother's door. Seeing her son's stance, Celeste knew he was going to give her a directive. In the back of her mind, she wondered if she had been too obtuse with Amber. She would find she had raised her son's ire a little.

"Mom, you and Dad are invited to spend Christmas Day with us. Please stop being so plutocratic around Amber and me. Remember, there is now another family to consider. Come whenever you would like. Bring swimwear, but no food," he directed.

Later, Celeste did not mention to Francis that Armand had been somewhat uptight. She only told her husband, "We're invited over for Amber's shindig on Christmas day. Armand mentioned bring swimsuits and no food."

"Does this mean Christmas Eve with us?"

"Yes," Celeste replied.

Armand and Amber prepared for their big holiday by shopping and wrapping gifts which were placed under the tree. Poinsettias decorated the tables. Jessica cleaned part of the house before Amber suggested, "I would prefer for you to bake. I'll ask you to clean after our guests leave. You will be excused at five on the twenty-second." Jessica was happy to hear this. She was told she would not be needed until January second.

When they returned home on the twenty-first, they were happily surprised to find a large container filled with several kinds of cookies. Armand sampled one, finding it excellent.

He put a package of Amber's favorite perfume under the tree. Amber put food on the table while he admired her, bedecked in an apron. When she began to sit down, he arose and seated her with a peck on the cheek.

During the meal as they chatted about the holiday plans, he told her that his dad had agreed to pick up her family at the airport. She kissed him delightedly.

On the evening of the twenty-second, a delivery truck brought gift packages from Oklahoma City. Soon, another truck arrived. Amber knew what this delivery was. She had ordered a workbench for the garage. Armand would have a place to store the tools which he had been collecting. It was the beginning of a wonderful Christmas.

Armand and his father delivered a happy group of loved ones. Her family was greeted with hugs and kisses and many happy *Merry Christmas* greetings. Lily produced a loaf of home-made banana bread. Patricia handed Amber a loaf of maraschino cherry bread. With a gleam in her eye she smiled, "I was thinking of Armand."

Amber chuckled as she placed the well-wrapped bread in the cool garage.

She and Armand assumed the pool would be of interest to Sue and Raymond. Both, had a short swim before everyone ate lunch at poolside. Armand directed the youngsters, "You must not make a lot of noise, particularly if the adults are not in the water, they'll want to talk."

It was late when everyone had enjoyed a swim. Amber asked the guests to use the pool shower to save time. She wanted the shower to be dried after it was used. With Wendell's help, Armand completed the shower cleaning and rearranging of the pool furniture. Dennis helped in the kitchen drying the zoo dishes. Sue was asleep and Raymond was playing with construction toys at bedtime.

Because Armand and Wendell were not needed in the kitchen, they sat talking in the living room. Wendell revealed how exciting his particular work had become because of new technology. Instead of digging up a street or road; pipes or wires could be pulled through an area of soil using an air compressor, which was more powerful and efficient than older equipment.

The people from the kitchen soon joined them.

Armand had been so immersed in the conversation he had forgotten his wife had been working in the kitchen. Her last chore was setting the table for breakfast.

In the morning, as the men prepared breakfast, Amber worked at the island making a gelatine salad. Armand then prepared another loaf of bread which would be a gift for his parents.

When the children peeked under the tree, Raymond became interested in a gift labeled with his name. It was not the size or shape of boxes in which toys would normally be packed. His father discouraged him from handling the box.

After breakfast, the pool became the main attraction for the whole family. They swam, paddled, and enjoyed fun with each other. The women showered first. Then it was the men's turn, after which they cleaned the shower.

Lunch was simple, again on the zoo dishes. After lunch, Wendell insisted that Raymond play with the construction toys in the bedroom. Lily went upstairs with Sue to work on the computer. Armand and Amber set the dining room table for tomorrow's late afternoon dinner. Their wedding china, stemware, and sterling silver were used.

Raymond asked, "Aunt Amber, may we have pizza tonight?"

"Certainly," she replied. "There are two in the freezer. Tell your mother to bake both of them."

When Armand and Amber arrived at the Rambulet gathering with food and gifts, the air was festive and lively. The grandchildren added to the excitement. Floyd wanted to play horsey, but Ronald explained that on this day the horse could not play because he was dressed in a suit, tie, and shiny shoes.

Celeste made certain enough books and pillows were placed on Floyd's chair. Because they knew their children were going to be served turkey tomorrow, Armand's parents prepared a loin roast.

Jeffory whipped potatoes, Ronald made gravy, while Francis sliced the roast, and put it on a pretty platter, with cut radish garnish. Almond-flavored green beans were the vegetable, along with Amber's gelatine salad.

As they were seated, all held hands and closed their eyes when Francis spoke, "We thank the *Great Energy* for this family gathering. We thank each one individually, because of the special person each one is. We give thanks to the *Great All*, for allowing us to obtain our earthly possessions and the means to acquire what we have this day. I thank my spouse, Celeste, for helping in my family's endeavors. Finally, to you Mom, thank you for what you've done for me and my family, and to you Dad, flying in the Ethers, help make this a better place for those who follow. I thank you, I thank you, I thank you."

Francis passed the food to his mother, who was the *Guest of Honor*. Everyone received plenty of food from the feast. Ronald cut the meat for Floyd, the youngest grandchild.

After everyone had eaten, the children demanded to open their gifts. The adults yielded to their request. A wastebasket was made available for wrappings.

When Armand opened his gift, it was a certificate for a Business Management Seminar for both himself and Amber, to be held in Chicago on July 30th for both himself and Amber.

Amber's gift was plane fare, reservation, and hotel accommodations in Chicago. She hugged her mother and father-in-law. "How wonderful," she exclaimed, "We'll be able to celebrate our fifth wedding anniversary there."

After all the gifts were opened, the children continued to enjoy their new toys. The adults cleared the table while Amber washed the dishes, which the others brought to her. The kitchen was buzzing with activity when Gabrielle shouted, "Uncle Ronald, Floyd swallowed something. He's choking!"

Ronald grabbed his son and held him upside down and gave the child a firm swat on the middle of his back. Out popped a piece of the toy with which he had been playing.

Everyone watched, horrified. Alma exclaimed, "My god! I could have had a dead great-grandchild." She hugged Ronald. Francis praised his son-in-law for being so alert and knowing exactly what to do. Ronald stayed with Floyd, while the others returned to kitchen work. It took Floyd and Ronald some time to recover from their mutual traumas. His father's last admonition was "Floyd, food is the only thing we put into our mouths. Do you understand?"

He nodded 'yes' with his big hazel eyes looking sad and frightened.

Celeste served a six-layer chocolate torte, which was presented on small beautiful, gold rimmed bone china plates with a blue floral pattern, which had come from France. Gold rimmed water goblets were filled with bubbly drinks, which complimented the dessert. Once the dishes had been washed and dried, they were carefully returned to the hutch.

Food for each family was stored in the refrigerator. A great deal of good conversation was exchanged before Amber and Armand left to return to their house guests. They left early with many thanks and Merry Christmas wishes.

Once at home, they quickly changed into swimsuits. The Breddgeforth family was relaxing in the pool area. Sue was practicing being a fish. Raymond was trying to see how long he could hold his breath under water. Sue soon tired. Her mother helped her shower. Once in her pajamas, her father tucked Sue in bed. Raymond soon followed. Wendell was in his pajamas, wearing one of Armand's robes. He had mopped one side of the pool earlier. Armand finished the other half, set the alarm, and went upstairs to his bedroom, feeling tired. Amber finished brushing her teeth remarking, "I'm bushed. How about you?"

"I sure am too, my love," he agreed, dropping into bed beside her with a kiss. They were both quickly asleep.

The next morning everyone slept late. The breakfast was wonderful with scrambled eggs, bacon, hash brown potatoes, and home-made bread. There would be no more food eaten until late afternoon. Lily made a chocolate cake in the morning.

Amber cleared an area of the cupboard, preparing to make a pumpkin pie. While she flaked the crust, she asked her mother to prepare the filling. This day in her own home, she did not need to put on a display. She carefully rolled the crust, again on a floured paper bag. This time she was able to scallop the edge of the crust properly with her thumb and finger. She filled the pie crust and placed it into the oven with a shriek, "I did it AGAIN!"

Armand hurried to the kitchen to see what the fuss was about. Patricia informed him, "We have a pumpkin pie in the oven, as well as a chocolate cake."

"May we open our gifts now?" Armand asked. He was anxious to present his gift to Amber. The women quickly cleaned the kitchen and everyone went to the living room. Armand asked Dennis to distribute the gifts, while he went to retrieve Amber's present, which he had stored in the guest bedroom. Armand came rattling down the hall with a modern tea cart which had a large red bow on the handle. He knew this gift would be needed today.

"Sweetheart it's lovely," she purred with a kiss, thanking him.

Dennis handed Armand a gift from Patricia and himself. It was a carving set which would be utilized today.

Raymond opened his gift with an exclamation, "Uncle Armand, how did you know I wanted something like this?" Uncle Armand was given a hug. Aunt Amber received a kiss on her cheek.

Everyone took their gifts to their rooms except Raymond. He wanted Uncle Armand to play with him. This meant Amber would tend the turkey alone.

The cake had cooled. Six hands, holding turners, lifted the cake from its baking pan and lowered it onto a plate. When it was cool, Lily cut it in half. Placing filling between the halves, she then frosted the whole cake. Patricia peeled potatoes. Amber worked on her green bean casserole.

The turkey looked and smelled more 'yummy' by the minute.

The men played with Raymond's remote controlled car in the driveway. As the ladies watched, Patricia laughed, "They all act like kids." The men made exclamations of joy as the car performed special maneuvers. Raymond was learning from his grandfather how this special toy could perform.

Armand's dad called asking, "What time?"

"Any time is fine, Dad. We're outside playing with Raymond's car. The women are preparing food."

A rising wind forced the car operators to return to the house. His parents and grandmother arrived. Alma had baked a pecan pie. She was all smiles as hugs and kisses were exchanged. Francis thanked Patricia for the money they had sent for his father's endowment. Alma and Celeste sat at the kitchen table and talked with the other women.

Alma related that Vanessa, the widow of her deceased son Grant, was helping her throw or give away things which she and Frank had not used.

Addressing Amber, Alma questioned, "I hope you won't mind, but I have told Jeffory to come and take his grandfather's desk for Gilbert."

"Of course not Grandma. Gilbert is the logical one to receive that part of the family legacy."

Alma continued, "I am going to put my house on the market and purchase a condo. I have been discouraged from buying anything else because of upkeep problems."

The dinner was ready. A small pillow was placed on a chair for Sue. The tea cart was placed near the kitchen. Armand carved the delicious-smelling turkey. He put cut slices on a china platter.

After everyone was seated, Armand offered a prayer. *"Dear Great Energy, we ask for your continued love. We further ask for your Great Protection, especially for Grandma Alma. Oh, Energy of Light, continue to be with all of us in both families. Amen. We thank you. We thank you. We thank you."* Serving his grandmother first, everyone filled their plates. Armand had to return to the kitchen for more potatoes, gravy, and turkey. Finally, he was able to eat.

Sue asked for more olives, while many different conversations filled the large table. Armand thought, *How could I be happier? I have the one I chose to go through life with me and all of our loved ones gathered here.*

After everyone had gorged themselves, they moved to other rooms, while plates were returned to the kitchen and cleaned. Only left-over white meat of the turkey was saved to be used in sandwiches the next day. Wendell went with Raymond to play with the toys in his room. Sue played games on the computer.

In the kitchen, Armand helped put food away. Amber cleaned the residue from her green bean casserole, enjoying every last bite. Patricia, Lily, and Celeste washed and dried the beautiful china dishes. As each piece was dried, Grandma Alma placed a doily between each one. Armand took his Dad upstairs to change into swimsuits.

Downstairs again, Armand assisted placing the goblets back into the hutch. When this job was finished, he put the cart against a wall and went to the pool. Everyone enjoyed splashing quietly as their dinner digested. For several hours, the pool was the center of family activities.

It was late when people began to leave the water and shower. Armand suggested that his Dad and Mom use the shower in their upstairs bathroom. Amber and Armand finished cleaning and drying the pool area. After a quick shower, they prepared desserts which their guests relished.

His parents and grandmother left with many thanks for a delightful day. Alone in the kitchen, Armand warmly embraced Amber whispering, "I love you. Thank *the great energy* you came along. Thank you for this wonderful day."

Tears welled in her eyes as she thanked him for being who he was. They cleared the dessert dishes and the kitchen, turned out the lights and secured the house. They were happy to fall into bed. Before they went to sleep he predicted, "This place will rock tomorrow when Jennifer's and Jeffory's families arrive."

The next morning, Celeste phoned saying, "Amber, the food was delicious. I enjoyed your pumpkin pie, too."

"Thanks so much," she responded.

Amber called Eleanor and Jennifer asking them to allow their children to stay overnight. Her requests were happily granted. The children arrived wearing swimsuits under their street clothes. Armand's prediction came true. The house 'rocked', but there were no shrieks or shrill noises in the pool. Ronald stayed close to Floyd as he dog-paddled.

Patricia was happy for the exercise. At lunch time, a call came from *Abrams and Abrams* announcing: "The plane will leave at eleven tomorrow morning." Armand conveyed the message to the Oklahoma guests.

Patricia helped Amber and Armand place lunch on the kitchen table. Amber enjoyed her lunch hearing the sound of happy voices. Her mother sat beside her proud daughter. Patricia regarded her daughter and Armand as two people with terrific self-esteem and was happy they were so willing to share their beautiful new home. She thought, *I may be prejudiced, but I claim that right.* She leaned over and kissed her daughter lovingly on the cheek.

Understanding her mother's thoughts, Amber asked, "Well, Mom, we have quite a house-full. Everyone is having a wonderful time don't you think?"

"Amber, we've had a great get together, thanks to you and Armand. We won't forget this Christmas."

"Thank you, Mom."

When Armand returned to the table, he bent and gave Amber a kiss on her cheek. The adults enjoyed listening to the children and their loquacious talk as they ate.

Amber and her mother put cookies and bars on a large platter. Patricia offered the goodies to the men first. The children then received their portions. When Floyd began to act up, Ronald cuddled him on his lap until the boy quieted down. He still wanted Uncle Armand to play horsey, but the horse was busy with his guests. Floyd was getting tired.

Jennifer took him to the bedroom and put him in his pajamas. Floyd wanted to sleep in the same room as Raymond and Gilbert. Armand prepared a blow-up mattress for him and tucked him into bed with a kiss.

Sue, Gilbert, Gabrielle and Raymond quickly followed for their sleep.

The adults talked until late, before departing for their beds.

After breakfast the next morning, Jennifer and Ronald returned to Amber's house to help her and to retrieve Floyd. Francis again acted as taxi driver, taking the Breddgeforths to the airport before he went to work.

Floyd sat beside Amber as she ate breakfast. His mother made up the beds freshly in the girl's room. Ronald did the same for the boys sleeping quarters.

When Jeffory and Eleanor came, they pushed tables and chairs aside in the pool room allowing them to mop the floor before they left. Jessica came at ten and changed the sheets in the large bedroom, then cleaned the room.

Now alone with a cup of hot chocolate, Amber put her feet up in the living room and relaxed, daydreaming about the holiday. In her mind she relived what had gone on. Forgetting her chocolate, she remembered children's laughter, lots of adult conversations, and seeing again how wonderfully Armand treated their guests.

She was brought to the present when Jessica took laundry out of the washer and restarted the machine. Jessica gave Amber two envelopes which had been left on pillows. Hers contained money and a sweet note thanking her for the wonderful holiday, It ended with 'I love you'. The note to Armand was similar ending with, 'You are a special person. We love you'. It also contained money.

Unable to control her emotions, Amber sipped her cool cocoa as tears of joy welled in her eyes--a joy which would stay with her from this time forward. When her cocoa was finished she went to the kitchen as Jessica asked, "What time do you want to eat?"

Before she answered, Armand called asking, "Would you like company for lunch?"

"Certainly, come on."

"I'm on my way."

The three ate lunch together. When they were nearly finished, Armand asked, "Amber, please come to work. I'm lonely down there."

"Aren't your parents there?"

"Yes, but you're not with me my love." He leaned to kiss her.

Jessica cleaned the table while Amber went upstairs to put on a slack suit. Armand checked the pool area. The tables were clean and the floor had been mopped. He dumped a remaining pail of water outside.

On the way to work he explained how all the commotion was up-lifting but when it ended, he had a sagging feeling. "I need you nearby my love." He opened the car door and planted a kiss on her cheek. Hand in hand, they entered the building. Once in her office, she closed the door to give her sweetheart a warm kiss and embrace. He did not want to let go and break this happy moment. He held her firmly saying, "I've missed you."

"I'll take care of your loneliness tonight," she promised. Armand thanked her and went into his office. He felt better having her in the building. Celeste stopped to thank Amber for the good pie and for asking them to be with her family. "Mother, my husband's family is important to me. I could not leave you and Grandma Alma alone."

Francis opened her office door and blew her a kiss saying, "I have an appointment; but thank you for the holiday."

She and Armand worked late. Back in the house Jessica had set the table and left a note saying, *Please check the linen cabinet. The sheets are mixed up. I'm not certain how you want them placed.*

Dressed comfortably, Armand began to scramble eggs. Amber found left-over food in the refrigerator. Noticing the pie pan, she thought, *I need to return that dish to Grandma Alma.*

Armand seated her. As they ate he held her left hand. When his eyes met hers she purred, "I read you, sweetheart. We could finish eating later..."

"My love, I can wait."

While they discussed work, Patricia called, thanking her for a wonderful holiday. Amber thanked her mother for the money and the carving set. Patricia finished the conversation saying, "We love you. We have ended this year on a very high note. Thank you again."

"We love you, too, Mom."

After they finished eating, Amber cleaned the kitchen then went to check the linen closet. She found bedding sizes were mixed. She was thrilled that Ben had included a pull-out shelf enabling her to sort sheets and blankets. When she finished, she went upstairs while Armand set the alarm.

In the bedroom he found Amber clad only in a shower cap. He quickly began removing his clothing. She reached for his precious body part saying, "Just like I thought. You're preparing your bratwurst."

He was soon nude and responded, "My dear lady, around you that piece of meat does not need much preparation." In the shower she soaped him. He did more loving than soaping. After they toweled each other he requested, "Please put your arm around my neck."

Armand gently placed his love in their bed. The moments which followed were ones which both needed to satisfy their intimate touches, to obtain their desires. Amber laid in his arms, finding herself being embraced and kissed. She returned his affection, which was so pleasing for him. Amber never let him feel lonely or unloved. He admitted that he was one loved man. Armand spoke many kind, loving, true words to his lady.

They arose and prepared for sleep. She lay in his arms. He continued to kiss and caress her until she fell asleep. His sleep followed quickly. During the night, he awakened to gently pull his arm from under her.

He awoke first, but lay quietly until she arose. He asked, "My love, how about a repeat this morning?"

Her response was to sing the words from an old song, *"Never on a Sunday, a Sunday. . .that's my day of rest. . ,"* with a snicker. "But you may do your thing. I'll keep my eyes closed. Your manliness would frighten me."

He repeated his loving touches to generate another very fulfilling experience.

They arose, showered, and donned swim wear and robes. Then they went downstairs for breakfast. After they ate, Amber checked the bedrooms to make sure all beds were freshly made and determined which of the bathrooms needed Jessica's attention.

They went to the pool and swam using lots of energy. As they swam, Armand's cell phone rang. He let it ring. He was quite certain it was one of his parents. "Why would they call on a Sunday? I'd think they would want to give us some time to rest, wouldn't you?" He quietly muttered, "I'll call them as soon as we finish swimming."

Amber's phone was upstairs. As they continued swimming, his phone rang again. "All right, I'll shower and return their call. Where's the fire?"

They toweled each other, put on their robes and went upstairs. Armand called the number shown on his caller ID. It was not a number he recognized. The call was from his father at the hospital. "Your mother fainted this morning and hit her head. No one has come to be with me. I am worried sick," Francis stated.

"What hospital, Dad?"

"University Hospital, fourth floor."

"We'll be there as soon as we can. We were swimming."

When Armand and Amber arrived, Jeffory and Jennifer were seated, waiting for a medical report.

Francis reported, "She said she had a headache, which is unusual for her. She took a pill and then fell."

Amber asked, "Have you noticed any difference in her speech, walk, or stance? Has she complained of blurred vision? Has she had any tremors? How about pain?"

"After breakfast, she complained of a headache. Her speech was fine. We talked over the fun we had at Christmas."

Amber then asked, "Please, let's all of us join hands and offer our personal prayer for this special person in our lives."

They held hands, bowed their heads and remained silent for many minutes. Jeffory began weeping saying, "Mom spoke to me, telling me she was very ill. She said she had a blood clot."

Francis moaned, "Oh god! No. I feel guilty. Since you kids were grown, I depended on her to help me too much. This is my fault."

"Dad," Jennifer spoke, "We know you help Mom whenever possible. You are not a man who forgets his wife." She rubbed his back. He began to weep.

"Oh! That feels so good. Please keep it up."

Armand and Amber continued to pray, focusing on the positive.

Hours passed. Jeffory took his father and Jennifer to eat. While they were gone a nurse came to Armand and Amber telling them, "Mrs. Rambulet is in surgery. She had a blood clot in her brain which is being treated. Keep praying."

Armand spoke, "I think this is a wake-up call for Dad. He expects too much from Mom. As we were growing up, I have never heard her yell or argue with Dad. I'm certain she wanted to tell him off more than once. She probably did that in their bedroom away from us."

Amber smiled remembering the day he had said, *Today he's your kid.* and she swatted him on the fanny. "I still think that was funny."

When the three returned from eating, Armand told them that the nurse had said, keep praying.

Amber and Armand went to the cafeteria. He held her hand tightly. As they ate, she stated, "Please listen. Someone will be needed to help your dad. Your mother will survive but she will need a nurse and help at home. For a time, a hospital bed may be required. I personally believe your mother would recover faster at home. She would be more comfortable in her own surroundings. Women need their homes, Armand."

He smiled, "Yes, I have found that out. My place would not do. You wanted your own dwelling. From time to time, I will remind you of our debt."

"And I will remind you, every month that debt is being reduced by what I earn. I must add of course, you help too, but my dear sweetheart, it is your intimate feel that I need." Her eyes emitted a greenish glow of special love which almost always made him feel better.

Back in the waiting room, faces were serious with a feeling of doom and gloom. Armand spoke. "Dad, I remember the story when Jeffory was small, and Mom was pregnant with me, Jeffory made the statement, Mom was 'plangent'. With quick laughs, the family opened up. They talked, remembering childhood problems and humor. Jennifer could not pronounce words which began with 'D' when she was young. They remembered special Christmases. Armand stated, "The Christmas just past will be a memorable one for me, but I'll always remember my first holiday with Amber."

The surgeon approached them. "I am Doctor Barniski. I successfully removed a blood clot from the left temporal lobe of Mrs. Rambulet's brain. Her blood vessel was repaired as well. Mr. Rambulet, your wife is going to need special care. She may not remember or be as quick to answer at times. We will watch her carefully for five days. If she improves, she will be released to a special care unit."

Amber asked, "Doctor, could that care unit be utilized in her home?"

"I suppose so, but it would be easier for the therapist to work where his equipment is in place."

"Oh! I am sorry. I was thinking of help further down the road," she apologized.

"Mr. Rambulet, your wife is in intensive care. I suggest the family split up your time to see her.

Dr. Barniski asked, "Are you her children?"

Amber replied, "I am Armand's wife," as she stood holding his hand.

The doctor instructed, "Sleep in your homes. We have Mr. Rambulet's phone number. However, I don't want any of you to think the worst. Mrs. Rambulet is on a number of medications. She is under quite heavy sedation. I further suggest when you see her, get close to her ear and speak softly. We shaved the left part of her head. Later Mrs. Rambulet can determine if she wants her whole head shaved. She is starting a new hairstyle in your family," he quipped.

Later a nurse took Francis to see Celeste, who was hooked up to all kinds of equipment. The nurse assured Francis that what he was seeing was temporary. "Your wife is in good health except for this episode."

Francis spoke softly to Celeste, saying, "You are my one and only. I hope you can hear me. The kids are in the waiting room. Tonight I'll leave at ten, and Jeffory will be here after that."

At nine o'clock, Armand went in. He was shocked to see his mother lying flat and still, with her head bandaged, except for some hair remaining below her right ear. The magnitude of machines with their numbers and lights made him close his eyes and concentrate on what he needed to tell her. First he quietly said, "Mom, I love you. I hope you had a good Christmas. Someone will be with you when we are allowed to come in."

After Armand had seen his mother, he and Amber drove home and quickly went to bed. The next morning, they left for work feeling the need to put in a long day.

Jennifer spent the afternoon at the hospital. Eleanor took care of Floyd. Grandma Alma answered Celeste's phone. Armand took his turn to see his mother after supper.

Armand was home at nine. After setting the alarm he went directly upstairs. Amber heard his 'hello' and went to him. She was in her pajamas awaiting his return. She took the pillows off their bed while he undressed. "Sweetheart, please lie down. She rubbed his back asking, "How is your Mom doing?"

"I really can't tell but I believe she will be lying flat a lot longer than five days. Dad was briefed and said, 'So far so good.'"

Amber turned to esoteric thinking, saying, "Your mother has chosen this problem. She has done so much for you my love, now it's pay-back time. Do what you can for her because she deserves all the tributes and time each one of you can put in seeing her. Your mother is aware of your thoughts, such as--*I'll be with you whenever you need me, I am here.*"

"I talked with your grandmother tonight. She told me she took the names and phone numbers of people who called about your mother. I was happy she came to your mom's office. She was delighted to help."

As she rubbed his back and neck up into his hair, Armand stated, "Dad and Jeffory are going to the hospital tomorrow at nine. Dad arranged for a security car to take Jeffory to work after he sees Mom. His morning appointment is so critical, he cannot take time to struggle with traffic. A client had a legal foul-up which he must handle quickly.

"Eleanor will take care of Floyd while Jennifer is at the hospital in the afternoon. Dad said he had slept well with the help of pills."

Amber continued, "I called my Mom and told her we will call her about Celeste's condition but she shouldn't call us. Marshara was so upset he called the University to find if there was a grad student who would like to help out and learn about business at the same time."

"Wow! That's a terrific idea. I'll not call Dad this late tonight. He's probably in bed."

"And you're just about asleep yourself," she observed.

"I'm really tired my love." He put his arms around her and kissed her all over her face, finishing with her lips. "Goodnight, my love. I love you."

Chapter 23.

The new year saw the Rambulet family handling their problem as best they could. Celeste gradually improved. Her family was ecstatic when she was able to squeeze their hands. The next day she wanted her hand held. Spouses supported their mates. Eleanor continued to baby-sit Floyd while she did some of Jeffory's work at home.

New Year's Day was a quiet one because everyone's mind was on the recovery of one of their own. Jeffory, Jennifer, Armand and Francis took turns visiting the hospital.

The weekend after the new year, Amber invited the Rambulet family including Grandmother Alma, over for swimming. Everyone had a good time except Alma. Jessica prepared an egg salad for sandwiches, waiting until just before the salad was served to add the dressing. Other salads were included in the light lunch. They also enjoyed left-over Christmas cookies.

Francis was the last to join the group. He reported, "Celeste can talk now after the mechanism was removed. She's getting better. She's bitching about the breathing tubes in her nose." Everyone laughed understandingly. Francis swam with vigor.

Jennifer's and Jeffory's families left. Francis finished eating and Amber put the left-over food away suggesting, "Dad, you really need to have someone help out at the office."

"That's right, Amber. Do you have any suggestions?"

"Marshara has been very concerned. He called Professor Cox asking if there were any people working on advanced business degrees who would like to work and learn at the same time. It's up to you to follow up his lead."

Francis was speaking when Armand entered the kitchen. He growled, "I'll be damned. The firm made the commitment for that endowment. Now Celeste gets sick and more help is needed. Don't either of you expect any raises. If anything, no doubt you both will need to work longer hours."

"Dad, do you want us to cancel our trip to Chicago?"

"No. What you are going for is a seminar. That's a business expense."

Amber added, "Dad, I'll do what I can. Once Celeste is home, you will need a housekeeper. We have Jessica who is a wonderful help."

"I know. I have been thinking about that. All the money going out."

"Look." Amber spoke, "You have good insurance. I believe she will recover to be of some help. However Dad, you cannot think of business twenty-four hours a day, seven days a week. You need to start kicking back."

Armand added, "Dad, new ideas are needed for a firm to stay on top. If you can realize that all experiences are good and necessary, the business will benefit."

Amber turned to esoteric thinking saying, "Dad, you asked for this experience, just as Celeste did. We think it's a wake-up call for you both."

"All right, you two win. I'm exhausted."

Amber directed, "Dad, please go upstairs to bed. Armand will rub your back."

Francis did not argue. Armand gave him a pair of pajamas. Once Francis was ready for bed Armand rubbed his dad's back. That was just what Francis needed.

When Amber and Armand were in bed, they discussed the business. Armand decided he would be the one to call Professor Cox, permitting his dad to spend time with Celeste.

The next morning Francis left after breakfast to go home and then to the hospital. Armand and Amber went to work. Armand called Professor Cox who had two people he thought might be useful. Armand could determine which, or both could suit their needs.

He went to his dad's office, turned on his computer and noted recent e-mails. He replied to all the messages which had come in, acting as his Dad's representative.

Jennifer came in saying she would help Jeffory, while Grandma answered Celeste's phone. Jennifer also spent two hours in the afternoon at the hospital. Jeffory went whenever he had a break between clients. Armand went at night.

Talking to Amber, Marshara asked about Celeste observing, "She's the glue which holds this business together."

"Marshara, that's about to change. I feel that Celeste's working days will be fewer. Even though she is now able to speak, her wording is not correct according to Armand."

Celeste was moved to a therapy center. She enjoyed seeing loved ones. Vanessa, (Grant's widow) and Alma visited her in the afternoons. Alma was excited because she had an offer for her house. She was hoping to purchase a condo close to her family.

Celeste was an only child. Her other relatives lived away from Albuquerque. Vanessa had two girls. Karen was a research scientist in Denver. Cynthia was a veterinarian, living in Omaha. Vanessa was pretty much alone. She approached her mother-in-law, wondering if she and Alma might buy a dwelling jointly. Alma's first reaction was, *This is a repugnant idea.* However, with the turn of events, Alma felt the need to help her son and family with that endowment which was uppermost in her thoughts. This meant Vanessa would sell her house. Francis was not privy to these ideas.

Before his demise, Grant had worked in the business. Vanessa felt she needed to contribute something in Grant's name. She had educated her two daughters, but their interests were obviously not in the business.

Vanessa and Alma planned a method to help everyone. Amber found out about the plan when she returned the pie dish. She spent her noon hour enjoying a sandwich with Alma. She promised that their idea would be kept secret until Alma broke the news.

The day Celeste came home from the care center was a red letter day. Francis had purchased a wheel chair. She would enjoy sitting more and being in her own home. Francis hired a housekeeper, who was working in the kitchen when Francis brought his wife home.

Jeffory had taken time out over lunch to see his mother. Naturally she cried. That night Amber and Armand stopped on their way home. Jennifer and Ronald were leaving as they arrived.

Celeste requested a family gathering on the last weekend in April. Francis set the hot tub temperature at 100 degrees. He did not want the tub any warmer than that. The boys agreed to assist their mother in and out of the tub, allowing her to exercise her leg muscles. Celeste was delighted to have her boys lift her into the swirling water.

Armand interviewed one of Professor Cox's students, Barbara Bentley. He found her very studious and conscientious. With Barbara's help, Jennifer could be home more of the time. Eleanor helped Jeffory when the children were in school. She attended school functions and did errands for their household. She was able to fill in a few hours each day at his office, but the need for another lawyer to assist Jeffory was paramount. He was dead tired when he came home. He also spent some Saturdays with clients. He was always delighted to have some swimming time in his brother's pool. He left a swimsuit at poolside so his children would not know he had relaxed in this manner. He would swim after work, before returning home.

Chapter 24.

The Wednesday before Delores's wedding, Miranda flew to be with Armand and Amber. On Thursday they flew to Minneapolis for the ceremony.

Amber had sent her measurements and money for her dress. She and Armand had purchased a set of glass baking dishes and stainless steel pots and pans which they mailed before they left.

Rain was pouring in Minneapolis when they arrived. The group had brought no umbrellas. Amber called Delores from the airport and mentioned the rain. Delores responded, "Don't worry about your hair. Tomorrow we'll have everyone's hair done by my beautician, which will be on my bill."

"That sounds wonderful." Amber replied. They were picked up at the upper level of the terminal and were taken to Delores's home, where her mother had prepared a simple meal. Armand, Amber, and Miranda were invited to stay at Delores's home for the night, where they met the rest of the bride's family. Amber had not seen Delores's parents since college days.

The next day the ladies all had their hair done. The rain had subsided.

The ceremony on Saturday was beautiful. When Armand observed the frantic activities, he became teary-eyed. He knew what the groom was feeling.

The day after the wedding, Armand rented a car. Taking Miranda with them, Amber guided them through the downtown area and to Mounds

Park to see the mighty Mississippi and St. Paul. They marveled at the beautiful green color of the grass.

Delores had told them to drive the I-94 corridor to Wisconsin, to see the St. Croix River, a National Scenic Waterway, which formed the state border with Wisconsin. Along the way they saw the campus of a large company where Delores's new husband worked. Armand enjoyed being with Amber and Miranda. As he drove, she thought, *My husband is a ladies man.*

They returned to Minneapolis, and crossed the 'Father of Waters' again. From the freeway, they were able to see the Metrodome stadium. Delores had told them to find a place to eat near the Minneapolis branch of the University of Minnesota. They drove past the campus on University Avenue, then down Washington Avenue and then back across the river to the western part of the University.

Armand marveled, "The University of New Mexico would fit in one small corner of this place." Amber responded, "There's another campus in St. Paul."

They ate in a trendy campus restaurant then drove to downtown Minneapolis, where Armand parked the car. The threesome walked the Nicollet Mall. After their stroll, they drove the freeway loop around an area much larger than where they came from. They ate dinner near their motel, a short distance from the airport.

The next day Armand returned the rental car. They flew back to Albuquerque. Miranda returned with them, spent the evening with her hosts, who took her to the airport the next day. Armand and Amber spent the rest of the day at work.

A few days later, the *Abrams & Abrams* secretary called telling Armand there would be one seat available, both ways from Oklahoma City over the weekend. He immediately called Lily asking if Raymond would like to take that seat to help them celebrate the Memorial Day weekend.

Gilbert would be invited for overnights, giving the boys a chance to enjoy each other's company. After talking with Wendell and Raymond, Lily replied, "Of course."

Celeste was improving and using a walker. Armand and Amber made plans for a rousing holiday time. Francis suggested grilling hamburgers, hot dogs, and sausages. Instead of cleaning, Jessica baked cookies and made two pumpkin pies. Amber made the crusts.

Amber had come to the realization that Jessica was a very special, helpful person. The Friday night of the holiday weekend, she stayed late to help prepare for Amber's family affair which meant she would not need to come at nine the next morning. Amber allowed her to choose her hours. Amber was more interested in results. She wanted her house and contents well cared for. Jessica did that.

Armand and Amber met the *Abrams* plane. Raymond was delighted to be able to travel by himself. "Golly Aunt Amber, the owner of the airplane talked to me." Their nephew spoke of little else as they drove home.

While Amber prepared the meal, Armand went to pick up Gilbert. The next day the boys played with the model car all morning. After lunch they were allowed into the pool. Armand did some work upstairs while Amber spent time with her nephews. When their uncle appeared in his swimsuit, the boys shouted, knowing there would be dunking and all sorts of fun-filled games in the water.

After supper, Gilbert's family came to swim. Gilbert was invited to spend the night.

The next day while the boys were playing with the car in the driveway, squealing and yelling over what they could make the vehicle do, a neighbor from across the street came over. Peeking through the gate, he asked them if he could be let inside. "What's your name?" Raymond asked.

"It's Bruce Malver."

"Wait a minute. I'll call my uncle."

Armand opened the gate to meet his neighbor again. Bruce stated, "I noticed someone was home and thought I would stop by and say 'hello'. We don't see much of you."

Armand related, "My wife and I work full time. Lately it's been overtime because my mother, who also worked in the business, suffered a stroke. We've not had time to meet our neighbors."

The men chatted for a few minutes. Bruce asked Armand how the solar panels worked. Armand knew he wanted to see the inside of the house, but he did not invite him in. He said, "We are preparing for a family get-together. My wife is hard at work. Please excuse me, I must help her," he stated as he locked the gate.

On Memorial Day, Celeste was helped into the pool. The men held her up while she used her feet to paddle. Amber explained to Raymond what had happened to Gilbert's grandmother. As the water games continued, Celeste asked the men to stand by her. She wanted to try and stand at the edge of the pool. When she succeeded, a broad smile crossed her face. She thought, *perhaps I am depending on my walker too much.* She stood several times before she was helped out. With her husband's help she walked to a poolside chair.

In the kitchen Ronald and Amber talked, commenting on Celeste's improvement. The food was served like an indoor picnic. After the lunch, Amber played in the water with Gabrielle. Everyone stayed in the pool until their skin shriveled.

Celeste always had a wonderful time with her family. July was a time of rapid development for her. She gave up her walker and used only a cane most of the time.

Late in July, determined to once again become a part of the family business, Celeste called a cab and went to the building. Francis was startled to see his wife at his office door. He embraced her asking, "What are you doing here?"

"I belong here," she answered gruffly. He pulled up a chair next to his desk and explained some of his recent business transactions. In his mind he was amazed at her reactions and the knowledge she had remembered. How wonderful!

Thinking he heard his mother's voice, Armand went to his dad's office. Sure enough, there she was, in a dress and low shoes, with her head covered in a pretty scarf. He hugged his mom saying, "You look great, Mom, how did you get here?"

"By cab. I don't believe I flew," she snapped.

"My, you are full of vim and vigor. I'll not argue with someone who has that kind of spunk. Carry on."

As they drove home that night, Armand and Amber discussed his mother's willpower. He commented, "Once her mind is made up, that's it. I believe I live with someone who also has that kind of a will. My love, it's your way or else."

Armand and Amber talked about the need to send luggage to Chicago for their seminar and upcoming anniversary.

Chapter 25.

Armand and Amber flew to Chicago four days before the seminar was to start. They visited the Shedd Aquarium, the Adler planetarium, the Field Museum, and enjoyed the sights of the city. On the day before the seminar they walked down Michigan Avenue. Armand made certain she did not spend too much time in any of those exotic shops.

On their fifth anniversary, they ate in a swank downtown restaurant.

Seated opposite Amber, Armand took both her hands, especially rubbing her ring hand. Looking into her eyes, he spoke succinctly, sweetly, softly, and slowly to her.

"My dearest love, there are no words in any language which could express my love for you because of all the work you do in the business and in our home. Your energy gives me help when I need it. I appreciate your unconditional love. It goes without saying how much my male character is admired when we find our bliss. My love, your touch is so special for me. It could only be found with you, Amber. I love you as completely as I know how. I admire you, I adore you, and realize you were meant for me to love, which I certainly do."

He moved to sit beside her and embraced her while the server quietly stood, waiting to take their order.

With tears in her eyes, Amber replied, "Sweetheart, I love you too. We've had all this time to get to know each other. Hopefully, we understand each other well enough that we will be comfortable accepting the challenges of parenting. This may well cause us to love each other even more deeply."

When their meal was finished, they took a cab to their downtown hotel.

They spent the next two days listening and taking notes at the lectures. They returned home on Friday. Both worked on Saturday. Francis asked for a report by Tuesday morning. They were late getting home from work. The phone was ringing as they entered. Amber's mother was calling, "Honey, we have not heard from you for so long. We would like you to come over here. . . ."Amber began weeping.

Having a good idea of who was on the line, Armand took the phone and began, "This is Armand. We have been assiduously persevering over here. If you would like to see us, we'd love to see you. But please, don't make Amber feel guilty."

As he continued, Amber answered his cell phone. It was the secretary from *Abrams & Abrams* informing them, "The company plane will have two seats from Oklahoma City to Albuquerque leaving on Thursday and returning Wednesday after Labor Day. Can you use them?"

Armand was still on the phone. "Mom, did you hear my phone ring just now? Amber tells me there are two seats on the Abrams plane leaving for here on Thursday and returning on the Wednesday after Labor Day. We've just returned home. Since Mom became ill we have put in long hours. We have not opened our mail for days. I'm not kidding. Do you want these seats? "

Her mom answered, "Of course." Amber gave her the schedule and then yawned. Her mother heard the sound and asked, "Have you received the letter from us?"

"Mom, our mail has not been opened since we returned from the seminar. Please don't think that what goes on here is more important than you. However, now it is. Please give us a break. Mom, I'm extremely tired and stressed. We'll pick you up. Goodnight. I'll call you when it's more convenient. We love you. Bye bye."

Armand put the toaster on the table, prepared to scramble eggs, and was thawing French fries. Amber found some of Jessica's cookies in the freezer.

Sitting at the table, she sighed, "Sweetheart, I don't think Mom and Dad understand what it's like to work in a private business when one of the leaders has been extremely ill."

"I know you are correct. I don't want to hurt your feelings, but I believe you need to set them straight."

"I have an idea. Let's have your parents pick them up. That way they'll see your mother's head. Mom is a nurse. She should realize we have been doing our best to handle a difficult and serious situation here."

Amber answered her mother's call the next morning at eight. "Mom, we were still sleeping. You woke Armand. I want you to understand, we have had rough going over here. You're a nurse. You know how serious an embolism is, especially one in the brain. We're extremely tired. Please let us sleep. I'll call you. Please be patient. Love me."

The next morning Amber took time away from breakfast to call her mother. "I love you. Armand loves you; but Mom you do not understand what it's like to be part of a company and a family where each member makes important decisions. You are not part of the overall management where you work, nor is Dad. When the number two person in this family company became so ill less than six months after the founder died, each one of us had to work overtime. We are still doing that. We've hired new help, but there is training required. Mom, when was the last time you trained someone and how long did that take?"

Patricia remained silent, knowing her daughter was very stressed. She apologized, "I should know better than to call on Saturday morning. I am sorry."

"Mom, last night we slept well and stayed in bed late which felt good for both of us. As a spouse, I did not feel the pressure as much as Armand or his bother or sister. Please listen Mom, as I continue to explain. Jeffory hired another lawyer to help him because he was so sedulously occupied with clients. He was even working on Saturdays. All of this has taken its toll on us. We eat and sleep here, that's all.

"Mother Rambulet is doing far better than I expected. She wears pretty scarves which Jennifer purchased to cover her shaved head. She has a tremendous will. I think it's interesting she did not have her entire head shaved. She has hair on the right. When we are able to read our mail and become a little more relaxed, I'll call you again. The more sleep we get, the better we feel. I'll be more at ease the next time I call. Please come over. You'll see for yourselves what life is like around here." Almost as an after thought, she asked, "How are you two?"

"We are fine. Everyone over here is doing well."

"That's great. I must leave to grocery shop. I love you."

Amber and Armand proceeded on their Saturday errands. After lunch they both napped. For the first time on an August Saturday, they were able to swim. Wearing her tightly fitting swim cap meant he could tease her in the water.

Night was falling when they finished their showers, then they dressed in their sleepwear. After eating, they began going through their mail. He told her, "The bills have been taken care of. These are personal letters."

In sorting through the mail, Amber found one from her parents. With tear-filled eyes, she asked him to read it. A check was included. After quietly reading the letter he suggested, "Amber, please call your parents."

"Sweetheart, are you in a better mood?" her mother asked.

"Yes, Mom. Thanks for your precious remembrances. This is the first Saturday this month that we have been able to nap and swim. Jessica has complained she does not have enough to do. She has prepared our evening meals and baked. We want you to come over and enjoy the house. By the end of the month, new people will be in place at work."

"We are looking forward to seeing you. Please try to limit your long hours. That is not good for you over a long period of time."

"Today, we came home and ate then went to bed. We have had plenty of rest recently. The killer was the stress of the sadness in the family when so much was at stake. On Wednesday, Armand goes for his annual checkup. I hope he is fine. My physical will be on Thursday."

"Sweetheart, get plenty of rest. Try to release the stress. We'll see you soon. We love you, bye bye."

Except for their physical examinations, they worked the full week. The doctor directed both of them to limit their intake of Vitamin C. Too much of this interferes with the adsorption of Vitamin B12 which is needed by the immune system. The physician directed them to eat at least one egg every day. The sulfur found in them builds precious antibodies which the immune system requires.

Amber asked him, "Armand, did the doctor tell you not to eat low-melt soft cheese? During its processing, aluminum enters this product."

"Yes. Not only that, but he said, don't drink from aluminum soda cans. This metal collects in the body. Further, he urged us to eat foods preserved in glass rather than metal cans for the same reason."

"Yes, he told me that too," Amber replied. What did he say about your prostate?"

"That part of me works quite well, don't you think?"

"Of course, sweetheart. However I believe the state of mind and one's overall view of himself plays a great role in that performance, too."

"Certainly, my love, but you help a great deal because your attitude is wonderful."

"Thank you sweetheart."

Time passed quickly. Frances and Celeste met Amber's parents at the airport. Amber had given them the code number to open the gate because they both had late afternoon appointments.

At Amber's home, Patricia had prepared an evening meal for them. They were delighted to see Amber and Armand come into the house. Dennis greeted his daughter warmly. Patricia told Amber she became lonesome for her.

Amber asked, "Mom, how do you think Celeste looks?"

"She appears to be doing well. I do not work with brain-injured patients though. I can only judge by the first observation. Other than her head being covered with a scarf, she walks and converses well."

Armand noted, "Mom speaks fine. Once in awhile she mixes up words. We are grateful she is doing so well."

The foursome enjoyed a lot of conversation as they enjoyed Patricia's meal. Amber thanked her mother for the food preparation. After the kitchen was cleaned, they sat in the living room, sharing more exciting conversation. That changed when Patricia complained, "We miss you so much."

"Mom, we try to see you as often as we can. We deserve vacations once in awhile too, don't you think?"

Armand stated, "Our lives have become complicated, due to our trip. Dad allows each family a week off when possible. We took the week of our wedding anniversary. Back home we had to play catch-up by working long days. We are up to speed now, as long as Mom doesn't have any more problems. She is part of the business. We missed her.

Armand and Amber invited his parents for Sunday dinner and a swim. The conversations between the two families, were warm and wonderful. Patricia was able to see Celeste's scar and observed her hair beginning to return. His mother continued to wear her scarf in public.

The next afternoon, the house rocked with children after Jennifer and Ronald came. Floyd wanted to swim, which meant Uncle Armand would help him paddle in the water. Armand thought, *This is much easier than being a horse.*

Jeffory and Eleanor then arrived with their children. Each visiting family brought food, which was a great help to Amber. Celeste played with her grandchildren. The observers could see she felt well and was enjoying her time with the children.

The koala dishes were used in the pool area. Food was brought to pool side on the wheeled cart. Jeffory told Armand, "Grandmother Alma is nearly ready to be moved. I have obtained Grandfather's desk, his desktop computer, and a few other accessories for Gilbert."

"That's fine. Does she need any help with good dishes, or special glassware?"

"She gave Jennifer her bone china and stemware," Jeffory reported.

"Is there anything for me?" Armand questioned.

"I'm certain Grandma will give you something."

After a long swim, the children were put into bed. Their parents would pick them up after breakfast tomorrow.

The next day, Amber spent some quality time with her parents. Armand went to work. Their day was delightful. The threesome swam after which Patricia prepared their evening meal. Armand returned late. After the meal they had a long pool side chat while Armand swam. Patricia mentioned Christmas. Armand said they would try to work out something. The next day, Armand and Amber took her parents to the airport. Back at work, she asked Francis about Christmas plans.

"I see no reason why you can't take some time for yourselves. We plan to go back to Cancun in late February. However, we would like the family to be together for Christmas. Why not have Thanksgiving with your family?" Francis asked.

"That sounds great. Mom will be pleased." Her mother was delighted to hear the news. Armand called *Abrams and Abrams* about their plane's availability over Thanksgiving. He reported, "There will be room for us on Thanksgiving, but it will be filled at Christmas time." Her mother was delighted to hear this news.

Chapter 26.

Amber called her mother with their arrival time. The two boarded the private jet after seven o'clock on the Tuesday before Thanksgiving.

Amber's parents greeted them warmly. The plane ride was wonderfully relaxing. Armand told Amber's parents that Melroy and Sharon Abrams were aboard along with other employees of the company. He and Amber filled two seats which would have otherwise been empty.

Armand related, "We'll work between the holidays; but it's a slack time for us. Clients' thoughts are only on Christmas and New Years."

Patricia asked, "How is your grandmother progressing?"

"She has now moved to a smaller place. We helped her with some family heirlooms. She gave us a *Picasso* painting which Amber loves. Grandma enjoys walking around our house looking at the artworks we've collected."

For Thanksgiving Lily was to bring dessert. Amber made preparations to bake a pumpkin pie. Armand watched as she forked the ingredients thinking, *Goodness, isn't that enough?* She persisted until the correct time to add the few tablespoons of water.

On Thanksgiving day, Amber's family had a wonderful gathering. Dennis was delighted to have his family with them. When he gave his blessing, Patricia became teary-eyed.

Armand sat beside Sue. He thought she was a delightfully sweet child, until she piped up asking, "How come you and Aunt Amber don't have a baby?"

Armand thoughtfully replied, "In about two years we will adopt a child who will be perhaps five or six years old. Your Aunt Amber spends her days and sometimes Saturdays at our business. Neither she nor I have the time to spend with a baby."

Wendell cautioned, "Sue, if your aunt and uncle wanted you to know when they wanted a child, I am certain we would know what their plans were."

"Yeah! Aunt Amber would have a big stomach."

Grandma asked, "What would that make me?"

"I don't know," Sue replied.

"That would make me a Grandma again," Patricia smiled, "When that happens, you will be ten or twelve years old."

The family finished their meal and played table tennis before desserts were served. The adults then played card games.

Raymond asked, "Uncle Armand, when can I come over again and play with my car?"

"Whenever you have a break at school."

"Do you let Floyd play with it?"

"No, Raymond. It's stored in our bedroom closet. Could you come during one of your school vacations?"

"Dad, would that be possible?"

Wendell stated, "I would have no problem if he could fly in the private plane. Otherwise, I would say 'no'."

Gilbert added, "Kids fly by themselves. A boy in my class flew to Chicago to see his mom. His parents are divorced. He was spending some time with his mother."

Wendell suggested, "With the airlines, sometimes you need to change planes. If a plane is late, a real mess can ensue. People are running and pushing to get aboard."

"I agree," his mother stated.

The next day the family went to a good children's movie. After the show, Wendell's family left for home while the four went to see Aunt Marion. They did not stay long. Her complaining and grumbling soon drove them away in disgust.

In the car, Amber angrily recommended that Patricia set her sister straight. "She had you as her nurse for all this time, for goodness sake."

On Sunday, the family had dinner at Wendell and Lily's home. Raymond pestered Armand so badly, wanting to come to Albuquerque, Armand called the airport. He was told that all flights were filled until after Christmas. Armand assured Raymond that he would try to find a way for him to visit them.

On their flight home, Armand talked with Melroy about Raymond's request. "The plane likely will be flying from Oklahoma City to Albuquerque just before Christmas."

"How many empty spaces would you expect to have?" Armand asked.

"As many as six seats should be available."

"I would certainly like to have you save them for Amber's relatives."

"That should work. The plane will return on the Wednesday after Christmas," Melroy advised.

"Please reserve those seats. I'll get the information to Amber's family."

"Fine. We may just as well fly that plane. Costs continue even when it's in the hanger."

Amber took Celeste dress shopping on Saturday. The next day, she went with Armand to purchase a new suit. Globes were purchased for Jeffory and Ronald, while the ladies would receive lovely expensive perfume. Gabrielle and Gilbert would be given money. Floyd's toys were selected based on his parent's request.

Jessica cleaned the house, permitting Armand and Amber to be ready for company. She also baked sweet breads, a cake, and other desserts. She was excused on Tuesday.

The Wednesday before Christmas the Oklahoma City relatives arrived. Francis transported some of the visitors to Amber's and Armand's home, before returning to work. Armand followed with the rest of their guests in his car.

Amber and her mother prepared their evening meal. Raymond pestered his Aunt to play with the car. Amber said she did not know where it was stored. This action made Lily and Wendell angry at their son. "You have two choices, play with toys in your room or swim."

Sue's swimming had improved. In her cap and swim suit, Amber swam and played with her in the water. When Armand arrived, he was warmly greeted, especially by Raymond, who asked, "Uncle Armand, may I play with the car tomorrow?" His answer was, "If you are good for the rest of this day."

Amber called Eleanor, "Please bring the children over tomorrow. This will allow you some free time." She invited Floyd over as well. The next afternoon, the model car was put through its maneuvers in the driveway. Amber did not allow them on the street.

After work, Armand came home to find delighted youngsters having a chivaree of squeals and laughter in the pool. He blew his whistle. "You may continue to play in the water, but keep the noise down. No more screaming." Dripping wet, Amber climbed out of the water to kiss him. She then showered. Armand helped towel her dry. Amber dressed while Armand removed his jacket and tie.

Amber announced, "Food will be served at pool side. We do not need any help." In the kitchen Armand embraced his love. Together, they put the food on the cart, with the zoo dishes and silverware.

Armand quieted everyone before he would allow anyone to eat. Amber knew he was not in a good mood. Later, she would find out why.

After they finished eating, Dennis and Patricia cleaned the kitchen. The owners excused themselves. Upstairs in their bedroom, Armand exploded, "I have an account and I cannot make the figures work. Could you help me for a while tomorrow morning?"

"Armand, tomorrow is Christmas Eve day."

"I know. I'm uptight and uneasy because I've been looking at a computer too long," he growled.

"Before we go any further, your parents are invited here for our Christmas meal. Can't we bring up what you want on the computer here, tomorrow? Mom and Lily can prepare the noon meal."

Jeffory came after his children who wanted to stay over. Jeffory insisted, "That was not part of the agreement."

The next morning after breakfast, Amber assisted Armand with his problem. She helped him clarify his thinking and calculations. In two hours they were finished. He became mellow and wanted to relax after he had thanked her.

The men went outside to put the toy car through its maneuvers. They played until it was time to eat. Amber had made her traditional gelatine salad for Christmas Eve with his parents. Her family enjoyed the Rambulet household, filled with the energy of youth.

In his parents' home, the women helped in the kitchen. Celeste watched. She did not trust herself near a hot stove. Her movements were still erratic. Francis prepared steaks. He knew everyone would have turkey the next day. Great Grandma Alma and Aunt Vanessa came to add conversation in a home already filled with laughter, jokes, and good humor.

After they had eaten, their gifts were opened. Francis's gift to Celeste was a brown leather purse with shoulder straps, for daily use. Celeste had made arrangements to go to a seminar in San Diego. All the tickets were in boxes under the tree. Francis's mouth was agape in surprise, as he opened his box. Celeste announced, "I am taking you on a business outing." Francis embraced her bringing tears to her eyes. "Our trip will begin the middle of January."

Armand laughed, "You must bring us back a report."

"Yes, Armand, we'll do that. However, we will enjoy each other, even if I have to take something. By god! I'll make myself work!" The house resounded with laughter.

After the gifts were opened, both Vanessa and Alma handed Francis large checks for the endowment. Francis broke into tears saying, "My god! What women won't do to thrill us to our very core."

The base of the business was money of course. His whole family understood the importance of this commodity. His mother, Alma, helped in the early years as she could. Before his death, Grant worked with his dad and brother. Vanessa promoted the business. She found firms which could use financial help and guidance until she became pregnant. After that she helped when she was able.

Francis was so thrilled, he kissed his mother and sister-in-law. He asked his sons, "How can we deliver this money?"

Jeffory suggested, "We need to deposit the money now. Then, after school resumes, contact the Dean and Professor Cox and arrange a grand, formal presentation." On Christmas Eve, Jeffory took his dad to the bank, because of the large sum of money which had been presented to Francis.

After this excitement, they all ate dessert. Then the children were dressed for bed. The adults talked until midnight, after which the Rambulet families headed for home.

The Breddgeforth children were kept up late so the adults could sleep the next morning. Amber and Armand slept later than usual.

As soon as he arose, Armand put the thawed turkey on a spit. Amber planned to eat at four o'clock. The children were antsy to open their gifts, but Lily insisted they play with toys they had there.

Gilbert growled, "I don't want my sister in my room."

"Why?" Lily asked.

"Because she is a nerd," he snarled.

"Well then, I guess it takes a nerd to know another one. Do we need to start calling you a nerd?" his mother asked. "I am going to leave now.

You two get along, OR ELSE!" She directed, as she went to the kitchen to make dressing.

Amber's pumpkin pie was placed in the oven with cheers. Then the children were permitted to open their gifts, creating a mess. Wendell directed the children to pick up the papers when Armand brought a waste basket.

Celeste and Francis arrived; the kitchen timer soon rang indicating the turkey was done. Amber put cranberries and the other food on the table. Using the carving set he had received last Christmas, Armand sliced the bird. He filled two platters to prevent him from needing to carve more meat a second time.

Lily made gravy. They put food on the cart, which the men carefully moved to the table. Armand offered a special blessing, bringing tears to the guests's eyes as he ended with, "Grandpa, please watch over us."

Everyone thoroughly enjoyed the feast.

After the meal, Wendell insisted the children play or read until an hour had passed before they could swim.

After water fun, they all showered and dressed before enjoying a late dessert.

Francis and Celeste stayed longer than usual to help clean up; however most of the mess was left for the next day. Everyone was tired after swimming and conversation.

In their bedroom, Armand pulled an envelope out of his jacket pocket. It was airline tickets for Key West. He and Amber would use them after his parents returned from their trip to San Diego. Amber pulled a small box from her purse. In it were citrine-yellow cuff links. She stated, "You have yellow shirts. Why not yellow cuff links, sweetheart?"

He embraced his love with "thank you", then purred, "Please, my love, will you give me your special attention tonight?" In response, she turned on the TV quietly, then pulled down the bed covers. As he hung his trousers, she came to him and experienced a feel before he stepped out of his briefs. Both had their longings fulfilled as a final Christmas gift to each other.

The children had been told that the adults would sleep late and if they made any noise their swimming rights would be revoked. Armand and Amber slept late. Having family around, while necessary, required more expenditure of energy. Therefore more rest was important.

In the afternoon Floyd, Gilbert, and Gabrielle were brought for swimming and an overnight; which meant Jeffory, Eleanor, Jennifer and Ronald would have some time to themselves.

When the parents came the next day, all the males were outside playing with the remote-controlled car, which Raymond would receive when he became thirteen. This was an expensive, slick, highly colored model.

Amber had purchased lots of cuddle toys for the girls. Some toys slept in a small hammock which was stretched between two walls near the corner of the bedroom. Amber also found a place for her koalas there. They were no longer appropriate in their bedroom. The people in the Rambulet household went to bed early.

Tomorrow was the departure day for the Breddgeforth family. "What a way to travel," they marveled, as hugs and embraces abounded when they parted at the private terminal, thanking Francis for his chauffeuring.

Armand went to work. Amber cleaned the dining room, dusted, vacuumed, filled the dishwasher, and wiped the counter tops. With water left in the sink, she scrubbed the kitchen floor.

As she worked, her husband drove into the garage and entered the house happy as a lark. He returned earlier than usual. They ate leftovers from the Christmas dinner. He held her left hand during the meal. "Company is wonderful, but I find they distract me from you," he commented. "Ralph called me saying he was thinking of 'tying the knot' again. I told him, make certain you have made a good choice. I asked is it Marlene?" He indicated it was. I wished him good luck."

On New Years Day they stopped to wish Francis and Celeste a Happy New Year. Armand told them, "I am going to turn off my cell phone. I want peace and quiet in our house. All I want is Amber's soft statements about how much she loves me and her delightful feel."

"Armand RAMBULET!" she shrieked. "How embarrassing."

His mother growled, "A statement like that is far better left unsaid. Armand, you'll be sorry for making that personal remark," she decreed.

Francis told his son, "Let this be a lesson about comments which are best left unspoken."

In the car Amber castigated him up one side and down the other. "I suppose I will be living with a sex-fiend all weekend," she snapped.

"I've had a family fun-filled, frolicking weekend. Now I need to kick back and enjoy some of your sex appeal," he announced.

In the garage, Amber dragged her hands through his hair, mussing it terribly, allowing some of it to fall over his face. She lowered her voice to a growl, snarling, "How sex-appealing do I sound and look now?" Helping her from the car, he drew her very close and firmly kissed her with a lusty passion, which she hated. She slapped him, uttering, "Dammit; I hate that!"

He kissed her on the cheek. No way was he going to become upset.

"I hope you got a face full of hair," she spat.

"I did. My love, but it's your hair which I've always admired and thought so beautiful."

"Think again!"

Amber pulled the car keys from her purse and was striding to the car when Armand stood by the driver's side door. "Where are you going?"

Weeping, she uttered "I'm going to the drug store to buy some hair dye."

"Oh god! Please Amber don't do that," he pled as he stretched his arms to cover the car door.

Instead of arguing with him she turned, ran into the house, and quickly ascended the stairs. He was right behind her so she could not lock their bedroom door. She flung herself on the bed with her face buried in pillows.

I certainly will not do that again, he thought. *I've forgotten how she rejects forceful kissing and lusty language. I should know better. Besides she is, and always was, a liberated woman. No way could anyone force her to do something she did not want to do unless she was drugged. Yes, I wanted full loving, but I've made that impossible because I am a damned fool.*

He hung his jacket and removed his tie. Sitting beside her, he begged, "My love, I'm so sorry." Lifting her body closer to him, he continued, "I'm the biggest asshole alive." He gently held her close. Her face came to lie against his. He held her for a time kissing her softly on the cheek. Then he carefully placed her on the bed, where she continued to recline. He thought, *I hope I made my point.*

She arose and opened a drawer looking for barrettes. Instead she saw her precious jewelry pieces. Watching, he asked her, "Do you think the asshole who gave you those things loves you?"

With weary, dulled eyes, she looked at him and fell into his arms.

"Amber my love. We need to eat," he suggested as he released her. She splashed water on her face. He brought her a pair of slippers. While she wiped her face, he kneeled to remove her shoes and put on the slippers. Going ahead of her downstairs, he gently kissed her lips when they reached the hall.

"That was better," she stated flatly.

"Good," he replied.

He warmed food for her, then took some for himself. He placed his left hand over hers asking, "Please, my love, forgive me. I am so sorry."

She reached across the table and kissed him saying, "You are forgiven."

After they ate, they changed into swimsuits. She removed barrettes from her hair, quickly grabbed her shampoo and towel, and raced Armand down the stairs to the pool.

She made a dash for the water, wetting her hair. They teased each other. Once Armand swam under her and lifted her completely out of the water, kissing her before lowering her back into the pool.

Armand knew he had a lot of loving to make-up. He pondered, *I pity the poor sucker who would try to put the make on you. He'd have a hard-sell job for certain.* Now it was Armand who had a full scale sell-job on his hands.

Amber climbed out of the water to wash her hair. He followed, wanting to run his hands over her body. She permitted his action. Amber closed her eyes as she shampooed. Armand soaped her down using soft, gentle touches. His actions were affectionate and tender. She knew he was usually very sensitive to her emotions.

When her hair was finished, she stepped out of the shower to towel herself. He shut off the water and wiped down the shower tile before he dried himself. She noticed the effect this set-to had on him. He looked at her and growled, "You might as well have thrown ice in my crotch."

She ran away from him, her bosom bouncing beautifully before his eyes. He caught up with her. Tenderly bringing their bodies together, they shared a long tender kiss with skin-to-skin caress. They smoothed each other's bodies with lotion. She gave his penis a tweak smiling, "Oh, what I do to you."

"Yes indeed. I cannot blame you. It's my own damned fault."

"Now who around here is the crude one?"

"I am," Armand quickly answered. The pillows were put on the floor. Both donned their sleep wear. "I need to go down and wipe up the water and set the alarm." She followed, and went to clean the kitchen and finish drying her hair. Tired, she went to bed.

Armand went to the bathroom. When he finished he found her asleep. He gently kissed her on her cheek before turning onto his side for his rest.

In the morning, Amber awoke first and snuggled close to him. He awoke and turned to face her. With their arms entwined, many embraces followed.

They arose late that morning. He began breakfast. She boiled eggs for a lunch of egg salad sandwiches.

She had not been into the guest bedroom since their company left. On the pillow were two envelopes. She brought them to the kitchen. They read the dear, sweet thoughts in the notes to each of them. Armand suggested, "Perhaps you should call your parents."

"I want to wait awhile, I want to think about us. My family must realize how necessary private time is for you and me," she stated.

In the evening, Amber called Lily, wishing her family a Happy New Year. "Lily, if you talk to Mom, would you please not permit her to become so hot under the collar because I don't call when she thinks I should."

She then called her parents. Her father answered. "Happy New Year, Amber."

"Thanks, Dad, Happy New Year to you. What's Mom doing?"

"Oh, she is sitting over in her chair sniffling."

"Why Dad? Because I did not call her when she thinks I should?"

"I guess that's correct."

"It's time Mom comes to grips with what I do. I have my life, my time, and a husband. I do not march to her drum. I'm not some flunky she can push around. Thank you for the money. Because Mom is so ticked, maybe we should send it back."

"Please don't do that," Dennis insisted. "Here, talk to your pissed-off mother."

When Patricia took the phone she acted as if she did not know who was calling.

"Happy New Year, Mom and thank you for the money."

Gaining some composure, her mom answered, "Why did you wait so long to call?"

"Oh! to upset you and piss you off! Why aren't you happy that I called? What difference does it make what time it is? Please understand we were taking time for ourselves."

Her mother hung up.

Amber yelled into her phone, "Fine, stay pissed off! You're only making yourself miserable."

Armand smiled, "See, I thought your mother would be angry. Let her sulk. Is she still trying to control you? No wonder she's frustrated."

Amber turned off her phone and they went to swim.

After their swim she set her hair before going to bed. The next day Armand went to work while she relaxed at home. Her phone was still off.

Patricia called Armand at work. They had a pleasant conversation. She asked, "Is Amber all right?"

"Mother, she had a house full of company. She works very hard. Please do not be upset because she does not call when you want her to. You of all people should know Amber. She does something when she wants to. I don't think you understand the demands our jobs place upon us. Would you like your money returned?"

She broke down weeping and hung up. He had heard enough of weeping women. He thought, *I guess Amber is like her mother, but she doesn't control people--or does she?*

Armand had returned to work when his phone rang again. It was Dennis who said, "Please don't return the money. We had a wonderful time. I'm at work, away from my grumpy wife."

Armand pleaded with his father-in-law. "Please don't allow Patricia to become so upset over what Amber does, or does not do. Amber has a mind of her own. She did call, maybe not when her mother wanted, but she did call and thank you for the money."

"You are most welcome," Dennis replied.

"Please Dennis, don't be upset. Amber is at home with her cell phone turned off. She is out-of-sorts. I think it's a good thing for her to be home to enjoy what she has worked so hard for. She will be at work tomorrow if Patricia wishes to call her then."

Amber had their evening meal prepared when Armand arrived. She admitted she enjoyed being home. She had put fresh linens on their bed, dusted, vacuumed their bedroom, and enjoyed a swim. She was warm and loving toward him. He hoped she had overcome her anger. He did not tell her he had talked to her parents. Together they cleaned the kitchen and worked out before a swim and shower.

Amber was in bed first. When Armand came to her, he was not quite certain what to expect. As he crawled into bed, she snuggled toward him. Her arms went around his neck. She was very loving. He quietly requested, "May we?"

"Of course." Their evening ended with extensive euphoric feelings for each other.

Days passed. Armand's parents left for their trip to San Diego. Both Amber and Armand worked long hours on some days. Their weekends were spent at home.

Chapter 27.

Armand's and Amber's luggage was shipped to Key West, scheduled to arrive before they did. They flew to Florida on a commercial flight. Both were delighted to be away from work. When Amber stepped into their suite, she became excited.

"Hey! We're on the top floor with large windows to view the ocean." Amber noticed a window was open about two inches which caused the window treatment to rustle in the carefree breeze on gentle air currents. Amber watched at the window. Armand put his arm around her. Together they observed the waves catching the sunlight as though the water was playing a game with light. They listened to the sound of the surf cascading on the beach. People's voices mingled with the characteristic sounds of the water caressing the shoreline.

Armand suggested, "My love, let's eat. We can unpack later."

At dinner, sipping champagne, they continued to watch the water and wave action. Armand became very affectionate. She knew what to expect. After their seafood dinner and champagne, Armand felt very relaxed. In their room, he finished unpacking his suitcase, then went to her. She had partially undressed. Her actions stirred the growing fires within him. He tenderly embraced her and led her to the bed for more tender, loving moments. With characteristic charm, he led them into a shared bliss fully enjoyed by both.

The next morning they ate breakfast at the hotel's café. He put all their services on their hotel bill except for tips. Amber handled these costs. Their first purchases were wide-brimmed sun hats. She was like a child, as each store window caught her attention.

In a store window, Amber spotted a blue-green bikini swimsuit she thought was attractive and pulled Armand into the store to see it. When she held up the skimpy top, he imagined the green being pulled from her dancing emerald eyes. "Sweetheart, I'll wear this at home when no one but you is around."

"My love, you win." he smiled as he produced his credit card.

She found some pretty blue short trunks for him in a different shop. Their time away from home went quickly. They snorkeled, visited museums, enjoyed the Dolphin Research Center, and the Everglades National Park. In Key Largo she found some shoes for pool wear and another swimsuit which was suitable for family fun times.

On their flight home, they both day-dreamed about their wonderful outing. Armand held Amber's hand the whole flight, except when they changed planes. They had shipped all their purchases and luggage home. She carried her beach bag and purse, while he had an overnight case. After they changed planes, they discussed their Valentine's Day meal at the hotel. Armand's eyes twinkled brightly when he looked at her. Other people wondered if they were on their honeymoon.

Five months later they would celebrate another wedding anniversary. Armand asked her where she would like to go.

Thinking, Amber said, "Could we spend a few days and visit Denver? I've never been there."

"That's a wonderful idea. We'll drive. After that trip we can purchase a new car."

Arriving in Albuquerque, a cab to took them home. Jessica had prepared a meal and left a note telling Amber what she had done. They quickly fell into the work routine. The months flew by quickly.

One day Amber called her parents. Her mother invited them over for Memorial Day. "Can you come?" she asked.

"Mom, I'll talk it over with Armand and call you back." When she mentioned it to Armand he said, "I'll see what I can do." The *Abrams* jet was not available. Armand purchased regular airline tickets.

He told Amber, "I purchased our tickets. We leave on Thursday and return on the Tuesday following the holiday. This means we won't have to entertain here."

Work days were filled. They shipped a large suitcase to Oklahoma City. She was hoping that the weather there would not be threatening.

On their arrival, her parents were thrilled to see their daughter and son-in-law. Amber told her parents about the wonderful time they had in Florida. After their first greetings, Armand spoke to Patricia. "Mother, I don't see how you can show such a lack of understanding because Amber does not call when you think she should. She becomes very upset when you are angry at her. Mom, she's a grown woman, who has a mind of her own--thanks to you two. She is assiduously engaged in her work."

Patricia changed the subject, questioning sarcastically, "Amber, when are you going to settle down and become a mom?"

She answered her mother directly. "I believe I've told you I wanted to work at least five years."

Armand entered the conversation. "At the time of our engagement, Amber expressed this is what she wanted. I thought you understood that."

Patricia muttered, "You don't have to comply with her every wish."

He responded, "Mother marriage is an important step in a person's life. One's life is changed forever." He was witnessing Patricia's forceful personality.

Dennis had remained quiet during the exchange. He was embarrassed by the harsh statements from his wife. He crossed his arms and uncrossed them. He shuffled his feet. Finally, running his hands through his hair to help reduce tension; he entered the deteriorating conversation.

"Armand, thank you for bringing up this subject. I have not been able to make Patricia understand that Amber is away and has her own life. I have tried to tell her: *Your children are not your children. They come through you, but do not belong to you . . .* She does not understand that. She is like a mother hen, cluck, cluck, clucking over a chick that must pursue life as she demands."

Armand replied, "As one who lives with Amber, I know her strong viewpoints. I don't always agree, but if you love someone, you love them regardless. Mother, don't you love Amber for who she is?"

Patricia began to weep. Dennis felt he now had some backing, so pointed out, "Oh, don't start your sniffling, Patricia. You use that as a mechanism to obtain what you want."

Amber and Armand realized Dennis was correct. She asked, "Mom, do you try to manipulate Lily and Wendell?" Before she could respond, Dennis answered, "Of course she does. Did you know after the school year, they are moving to the Denver area?"

"Goodness no! When was that decision made?" Amber asked.

Dennis answered, "I have known about their plans for some time. That is why they do not let their children come and stay with us."

Arising from her chair, Patricia went to their bedroom while the other three continued talking. Dennis explained, "Wendell became furious at his mother several times. At least they won't be living in tornado country."

Amber emoted, "Wonderful. They'll be in Denver where we have made plans for our anniversary outing."

Armand thoughtfully asked, "Dad, what has made Patricia become so domineering?"

"Perhaps she has not told you. She has been given some added responsibilities at work. I pity her poor supervisors, co-workers, or patients if she pushes them around like she tries to do her family," Dennis revealed.

Amber went to her father saying, "Dad, I'll bet you've had a hard time trying to make Mom see the light. She is breaking up the family with her demands."

Dennis responded, "You know she has said, 'When we retire we are moving to be closer to Amber.'"

"Oh! goodness," Amber exclaimed, "Two strong-willed women in the same town. That would never work."

Armand added, "I believe your wife needs some counseling. What is she trying to do?"

"I don't know except she has been difficult to live with," Dennis agreed.

"This is terrible. We can't let this go on," Amber insisted, "I'm going to talk with her."

She breezed toward her parents' bedroom. When in the room, Amber asked, "Mom, what's your problem?"

With tear-filled eyes, and a tissue in her hand, she replied, "I'm very stressed. My family does not understand. I've rocked the boat at work so badly that there is talk of firing me, because I have been too aggressive in my authoritative actions. Evidently I stepped on some toes recently."

"That is still no reason to push your family around. There's no way I'll be prodded. I have a wonderful job, a very loving husband, and a beautiful home. I will not allow you to cause problems like you have with Lily and Wendell. Cut the cow-shit. Seek a new job--perhaps you need a change. Whatever you do, for gods sake, stop bossing your family to death! Mom, would you go for a few sessions of therapy?"

Patricia realized Amber was correct. She was sitting on the bed. Putting her arms around her, Amber kissed her on the cheek. "Mom," she pleaded,

"We love you too much to let work interfere with our lives. You're a workaholic. You and Dad take no vacations except to see us. I am certain that won't change once we adopt our children."

The two women embraced for a long hug. Amber assured her mother that she did not need to work under conditions in which she was stressed. She directed, "Please talk to your boss as soon as possible and resign. You do not need to work day after day. Have you thought about going to work for a health-care facility rather than a hospital?"

"Your father has encouraged me to do just that. But old ways die hard."

The men were walking outside, when sirens began to sound.

Dennis looked at the sky and shouted, "Oh my god!, run to the shelter." The women were ahead of them. Dennis closed the door. Patricia lighted a kerosene lamp. Dennis asked, "Did you see that cloud, Armand?"

"My gosh, is that what a tornado looks like? I have seen pictures, but not the real thing." Patricia turned on the battery-powered radio. The funnel was on the ground north and west of them. The announcer was telling people to seek shelter. He was carefully describing the area, close to Piedmont.

Dennis told the women when he saw the cloud, it had not touched the ground. There was no noise and it was white. "Thank god, there was only one I could see!"

Armand asked, "Why do you live here, where the weather is such a problem many times during the year?"

"We grew up with this sort of thing, because our family was here. We have good *Doppler* radar and excellent reporting. The firm where I work has its own emergency generators and a sturdy building. Nothing short of a direct hit would stop the assembly line," Dennis replied.

After the 'all clear' sounded, they returned upstairs with Amber leading the conversation reporting, "Mom and I talked and she agreed to resign, rather than being dismissed."

Patricia agreed, "I'll let the *powers that be* do their thing. I'm certain, you and Armand would say *THE POWERS* are running our hospital very inefficiently."

Upstairs, Dennis turned on the TV and learned that electricity was out north of them. Dennis laughed, "This town is a good one for electrical repairmen."

Armand observed, "Amber enjoys our drier climate very much. However, we can't all live in a risk-free area."

"Do I ever enjoy our home town," Amber exclaimed. "I do not like to be scared out of my wits by tornadoes."

Wendell called asking, "Is Armand there?"

Armand answered, "Certainly, we would be happy to come over but we don't have a car."

Dennis offered, "Use my car." A time was arranged and Amber drove because she knew the area.

Lily had prepared a meal over which conversation concerned their move. Wendell asked his sister, "Have you talked to Mom? She has been acting like a commanding general, which I will not put up with."

"She started telling me what I had to do. I told her to lay off," Lily reported.

Raymond spoke, "Grandma has changed. Grandpa is the same, but she orders everybody around, like we were under her control."

Lily responded, "We cannot allow that. Wendell found an advertisement in a professional journal. He flew to Denver. He liked the company. I flew up with him two weeks later. My mother took care of the kids. Five weeks from now we'll make the change. The company will pay for our move. I plan to take our special treasures with us in the car."

During the conversation, Amber realized that Sue wanted attention. The rest of the evening she played with Sue while Armand entertained Raymond until Lily called, "Dessert is served." The visitors left soon afterward.

When they arrived, they found Amber's parents had gone to bed. On the table was a note from her mother saying she would resign her job tomorrow.

In the morning at breakfast, Amber and Armand assured Patricia she was doing the right thing. In the living room an hour later, Patricia arrived back home saying, "I had a talk with the personnel director, then resigned. I feel very relieved."

Later, Aunt Marion called, demanding that Amber and Armand come to see her. "Let me talk this over with them, "Patricia answered.

"No, I want to talk to Amber now," she insisted.

Patricia hung up and turned off her phone.

"Who was that?" Dennis asked.

"It was Marion, demanding to talk to Amber. She wanted them to come over and see her immediately."

"Hell no! These kids will determine when and if they go to see her. Enough all ready," Dennis grumbled.

Patricia reported, "She has asked for your phone number, Amber. I have refused to give it to her. I've told her, 'I don't want you taking Amber's precious time.'"

Amber observed, "It sounds as though Aunt Marion has become very dictatorial. I'll deal with her." Later, Amber called her aunt and made arrangements for a visit.

On the way to her aunt's house Amber surmised to Armand, "I wonder if my aunt could be a part of Mom's problems? Mom took care of her for a long time. I'll bet Marion doesn't recognize what Mom did for her. Please don't chide me if I become blunt with her. It seems there are some people in my family who have forgotten that others are important."

At her aunt's home, Marion immediately became dictatorial. This made Amber livid. She declared, "You are self-centered. You do not realize what my mother did for you. I'm going to instruct my mother not to talk to you. Aunt Marion, you are not bossing a child around. You are talking about my mother. I'll be darned if I'll let you make her feel inferior. I am not staying here to listen to any more down-grading of anyone."

Armand took her hand and they left.

Her parents had the table set and were somewhat surprised to see the young people back so soon.

"Mom, Aunt Marion is part of your problem. I told her you were not going to talk with her. Please don't listen to her. Hang up if she becomes abusive."

Since Patricia was not answering her phone, Marion called Dennis. He snarled, "Marion, you are a son-of-a-bitch. Leave Patricia alone or I'll serve you with harassment papers." He slammed his phone down and turned it off.

When their meal was finished, the four were playing cards when the front door bell rang. Dennis and Amber went to answer. The door was not completely open before there was a shout. "I WANT TO TALK TO PATRICIA." Marion used her cane to try to push Dennis aside. Amber called 911, telling the responder "We have an harasser at our front door."

Dennis would not let her get past him. Amber pleaded, "Aunt Marion, please sit on the step." Marion was shrieking and causing such a commotion, the next-door neighbor came over. He suggested a chair for her. Dennis kept her cane. She pounded him with her hands everywhere she could. When that wasn't enough she tried to *knee* him. She retrieved her cane when Dennis tried to protect himself. In back of her, the neighbor made certain her aim was off. Aunt Marion was angry, furious, agitated, obnoxious, and was causing a scene.

Amber realized that this behavior required treatment. It was not her mother, it was her aunt who needed mental health care.

When an officer arrived, Marion assaulted him with her cane. With the help of Dennis, he hand-cuffed her and had the neighbor and Dennis help him get her into the squad car. He then returned and talked with Dennis and Amber.

Amber pleaded, "Officer, please do not release her until someone in authority has talked with her. She is very angry at my mother for some reason. Mother, who is a nurse, helped her when she was hospitalized. My Aunt is belligerent and hostile. I believe she is transferring that anger toward my mother."

Dennis stated, "Officer, we need her car keys to move her car out of our driveway." The officer demanded the car keys, then gave them to Dennis, and left saying, "We will get back to you, if necessary." He left with Marion shrieking in the back seat.

In the house Dennis held Patricia's hand when the play-by-play was related. Armand talked with Patricia about her sister to help her relieve stress.

Dennis drove Marion's car back to her house; Amber followed in his car. At Marion's house, the lights were out. Uncle Greg was not around. Dennis deposited the car keys under the front door mat. As he went home with Amber, she wondered out loud if Uncle Greg might be having a *fling*. Dennis remarked, "If that's the case, we're staying away."

Arriving home, Amber related, "Mom, I wonder if Uncle Greg may be having an affair."

Dennis reported. "The house was dark and he was not there."

"Mom, please stay away from your sister until she has received counseling."

They talked long enough so they could all relax for sleep.

The next morning, an officer came to Dennis and Patricia. The policeman said they had not found Greg. He asked, "Does Marion Janier have children here?"

Dennis answered, "No. Have you called where Greg works?"

"Yes. He is not there. No one could tell us where he might be. I need someone to guide us as to where we go from here." Patricia gave the officer the name of their daughter in Atlanta. Aunt Marion had refused to tell the officer about her children.

Dennis told the policeman, "We don't want anything more to do with what has happened. She intruded on a family gathering. Officer, she was harassing us."

Amber then added, "My aunt has caused all kinds of problems. My parents do not need to be placed under duress in their own home. Marion Janier needs mental therapy."

As they were talking Dennis's phone rang. Greg asked, "Do you know where Marion is?" Dennis snarled, "Where the hell have you been?"

"I received my annual medical checkup. Then I had a meeting over in Weatherford. I stayed there overnight. Marion's car is here. Do you know where she is?"

"Yes, she created a problem. To answer your question, she's in jail. An officer is here talking to us. I'll put him on."

Greg's call came at a opportune time to permit Patricia and Dennis to back away. The officer thanked Dennis when his call was completed. With tears in her eyes, Amber said, "That was a *serendipitous* experience. Mom, please advise Uncle Greg about someone he can contact to get help for Aunt Marion."

"Honey, here is you uncle's phone number. Tell him to ask Dr. Alvadar to be her therapist."

Amber called her uncle, who had not reached police headquarters. "Uncle Greg, Aunt Marion really needs some good therapy. Mom recommends Dr. Alexander Alvadar as a therapist. Mom is upset now. I have to hang up, but I wish you the best. Bye bye."

Armand suggested, "Let's go to a movie, or a museum, to get our minds off this problem."

Dennis drove them to the 45th Infantry Division Military Museum. Armand particularly enjoyed World War II cartoons by Oklahoman, Bill Mauldin, which are housed in a special room. The lovers held hands as they explored this part of American history.

After a late meal, they watched a movie which Dennis had rented. They laughed at the antics in the movie *Bird Cage*. Armand thought the last few scenes were hilarious. The next day Amber's parents took them to the airport. Before leaving, Amber suggested, "Mom, be professional regarding Aunt Marion."

On the plane, Armand talked freely. He felt in her parents' home he needed to listen, but he wished to talk with Amber privately. "I may not have agreed with everything that was done, but I felt I was not really in a position to offer any new ideas."

Amber kissed him for his support and being the gentleman he was. "If that were your aunt, would you have done anything differently?"

"Goodness, no. Your family did very well. I believe mental health is something we take for granted. When mental problems hit us or someone close we are devastated," he answered.

Chapter 28.

At the airport they found their car and returned home. Armand appreciated that his family did not call as soon as they knew they were back. Armand needed no bad news.

Armand had once vowed to swim in the nude. Amber agreed this was the time. He undressed her. They both needed a good swim to cleanse themselves of the agony of the past two days. Once out of the water, they showered, and returned to their bedroom where Amber called her mother who reported, "I spent the day on the phone job-searching."

Armand called his father saying they would be at work the next day. Armand and Amber needed relaxation and happiness that night to settle into their routines again.

The next morning Celeste came to Amber's office for a short chat. The ladies embraced. "Amber," she spoke, "I had another check-up and am doing quite well. I am concerned about the business name. We are having to hire extra people."

"Mother, others would need to buy the business. For many people, that would not be possible." She reassured her mother-in-law, with a kiss on her cheek. "Remember, I have another year of full employment. Armand and I agreed upon this before we were married. This permits me six years of work before we begin the adoption process."

"All right. Thank you. Did you know that Jennifer and Ronald are going to adopt a little girl? Her pictures are just darling. Jennifer has said she's a little doll. Now I have to run."

In the meantime, Wendell's family had made their move to Denver. Raymond had found a new friend. They all liked the area very much.

Amber's mother became depressed after Wendell's family moved away. She had no contact with her sister, except through Greg. Marion spent time under twenty-four hour observation and treatment. She was being helped a great deal.

Patricia found a new job which she liked very much. She had asked for the week of Christmas off.

The weeks passed normally. Soon the Fourth of July was upon them.

The Rambulet shindig was held at Francis's and Celeste's home. Jennifer and Ronald introduced their newly adopted daughter, four and a half year old Desiree. Jennifer had dressed her in a sundress with little white sandals. This blue-eyed blonde resembled her mother.

The older kids played in the hot tub. Desiree did not want to get her hair wet. Her brother Floyd squirted her with a water gun. That ended that play. Ronald took the gun away from him, declaring, "No more guns for you."

Later in the afternoon, the party moved to Aunt Amber's and Uncle Armand's home. The kids were allowed to play in the pool. Jennifer and Ronald took turns helping Desiree paddle.

Armand grilled chickens while Amber, Eleanor, and Celeste worked in the kitchen. Amber and Eleanor made brownies. Jennifer brought a huge bowl of potato salad. Celeste cut freshly baked bread.

While the meat grilled, Armand prepared a three-bean salad. He checked the pool area occasionally. The children were behaving well. Jennifer Ronald and Jeffory were in the water playing with the kids.

At seven o'clock food was wheeled to pool-side on the cart. Dishes, silver, and glasses were put on the pass-through. Everyone ate well. Before the brownies were all eaten, Armand tucked a few away for another day.

Desiree was dressed in her pajamas and slippers. She went to sleep on Sue's bed, while her brother played in the water with Gabrielle and Gilbert. At nine, Floyd was happy to shower and put on his sleep wear.

Those not requiring a shower were given the task of mopping the floor, straightening the furniture, and returning the dinnerware to the kitchen, where Amber and Celeste were doing dishes. Jennifer's family were the last to leave. Armand and Amber quickly collapsed into bed.

The next morning Armand showered. He came to bed naked, asking for Amber's special loving. He was affectionately embraced and deeply loved, but only after she had placed decussate marks on his chest, mussed his hair, which he hated, and tweaked his manliness. Armand then spent a lengthy time telling Amber how much he loved her. She responded in kind.

Armand had made hotel reservations in Denver for their sixth wedding anniversary celebration before they learned that Wendell and his family would be living near Denver.

They called Wendell telling him they were driving up. They left two days before their anniversary. They both agreed they lived in a beautiful state. Amber was impressed with the mountainous beauty at Raton Pass.

When they approached Denver, they exited I-25 and drove west to Wildcat Reserve Parkway. They found Wendell and Lily's home, beautifully built into what Amber called the hillside. Armand corrected her saying, "My love, it's built into the mountain." Raymond and Sue ran to greet them warmly. Lily was happy as a lark. "We love it here," she emoted.

Amber asked, "Please show us your house." As the tour progressed, she praised, "Lily, this is beautiful," as Lily took them upstairs to see the balcony which served as a den for Wendell, who was then at work. Beyond the den were two bedrooms and a bath-and-a-half. Amber loved the interior wood which gave the house a very warm feeling.

Sue was taking voice lessons, which Amber knew she loved.

On Amber's and Armand's anniversary, Wendell's family went out to dinner with them. Wendell insisted on picking up the check. The following day, Armand and Amber went sight-seeing. She saw many golf courses and remarked, "Man, oh man, there's money here. It's expensive to play golf."

"Yes, my love. That is something we've never found time to do."

They spent the evening with Wendell and his family. The next day was a long one. Amber had a breathing problem with the altitude in the Rocky Mountain National Park. Her ears also bothered her. She asked Armand take her back down to Denver. She was glad to return to their hotel room. They spent a few more days exploring the city and surrounding areas and visiting with her brother's family again.

On their return they admired the *Garden of the Gods* in Colorado Springs. "They are beautiful. What colors!" she marveled.

Back home after a very pleasant week, they returned to work.

On Labor Day they ate with the family at his parents' home.

Amber's mother called, reporting her sister was much better, but was on daily medication. She admitted she missed Wendell and his family. "I am so sorry I got caught up with Marion's problems. I let my own family down," she admitted.

"Mom, you need to phone that apology to Wendell. We'll see you here for Christmas." The two ended the call with loving goodbyes.

Amber sat in her chair, closed her eyes and meditated over the last six years. *My love is at work twelve feet down the hall. I love and admire my office. The comfort of my surroundings is exceptional. The atmosphere in my office is wonderful, while the outside air is very hot. Yet I work in air-conditioned ease and ride to and from work in pleasant comfort. My home is something out of a fairy tale. So is my marriage. My husband dotes on me. He's always very kind, loving, and generous. My life is good.*

Her ponderings then turned to her home. *My beautiful place contains what we both wanted, but I chose the interior components. The window treatments, the carpets and tile, the cabinets, and the many drawers in the kitchen all meet my needs.*

Her meditation was interrupted by her husband at her door asking, "My love, may I take you to lunch?"

"Of course," she answered, shutting down her computer.

Their work kept them thoughtful at times.

The weekend of Labor Day, Amber took Armand shopping. As always, she had ideas for Christmas gifts. At breakfast before they left home, Amber offered her thoughts of gifts to Armand. If he disapproved, she asked for another idea. On their shopping spree, Armand was happy Amber had written down her ideas in her small note pad. She recorded all their purchases in her book.

They were tired when they returned home. As usual, Armand helped her in the kitchen. After they ate, they swam for relaxation. Both were now receiving plenty of rest so they could be fully engaged in their work

As Thanksgiving neared, they decided to stay at home. Celeste planned for a late afternoon meal at their house. A swim at Amber's and Armand's home concluded the festivities. Everyone played like a fish. It was late when all the families left for their homes. Armand carried a sleeping Floyd to his parents' car and put him in the back seat while Jennifer held Desiree.

Gilbert and Gabrielle had brought their sleepwear, robes and slippers which they wore home. Their parents put their regular clothing into small suitcases.

Armand had an idea. After the Thanksgiving weekend, Armand called an entertainment center, then Ben Artworth. With family around them and visitors over the holidays, they needed more to offer guests. He then proposed the idea to Amber. "My love, I have been thinking and doing some research. Since we have land space, I've talked with Ben. He has said we could add an entertainment room onto the house.

"Before you say anything, please hear me out. We could add on to the east side of the garage. What I have in mind is a room where we could have a screen and projector with seats for--say twenty people, watching a film like at a theater. We could have our own movies."

Amber's response, "I suppose you've looked into the cost. Equipment like that is expensive."

"Yes, I ran through the cost with Ben. He thinks it's a good idea."

"Of course he would. He has something to gain."

"We can handle the expense and costs," Armand replied.

"Are you certain? I'll do some of my own research."

Armand related, "Mom and Dad have told me that we kids are going to receive a nice sum of money for Christmas. The reason is that Aunt Vanessa and Grandma have contributed to the endowment more than Dad expected. He and Mom are giving each of us extra money. I know Jeffory is talking about adding a small pool in his back yard."

"Oh! It's his yard only?"

"I did not mean my statement the way it sounded," he apologized.

On Monday, Amber did her own research. In between her business calls, she received one from Ben. "Amber, let me give you some perspectives of what can be done."

"All right. Please continue."

"The window on the east side of the second bedroom could be changed to a door going to an attached media room. Projection would be from above, toward a screen at the opposite side."

"OK, Ben, but the architectural and building costs would be as expensive as the equipment," she stated. "I don't understand why Armand talked to you when he had not confided in me what he was thinking."

Ben answered, "I'm sorry, I don't want to interfere in a difference of opinion between you two. Please talk it over and let me know."

After her conversation with Ben, Amber became upset and very irate. Armand had not shared any details with her. She was fuming inside from her husband's actions. *Dammit,* she thought, *I wanted the house to be half paid for by next year. Now he comes up with this hare-brained idea.*

Very un-ladylike thoughts were streaming through her mind when Armand stepped into her office. Still wrapped in anger she did not shut down her computer until he asked. "My Love, may I take you to lunch?"

Amber did not answer when he came to help her out of her chair.

"How was your morning?" he asked.

She did not answer. She did not take his arm or hand. In the car, once he was in the seat, she screamed, "JUST WHERE THE HELL DO I LIVE?"

"With me," he answered.

"Leave the car here. I have a few choice words for you, Sir," she sternly growled. "Since I live in that house with you, would it not have been a good idea to ask me what I thought of your concepts before you talked to Ben? I find your actions repugnant. Because of the investment involved, I repudiate your concept. We are in a marriage in which each one of us is important. Going behind your spouse's back, I find repulsive. Why didn't you run more of your ideas past me before you made any calls? The one to Ben, I find deceitful and frustrating. You know I wanted to have the house half-paid for by next August. Now you come up with this idea of adding on."

Finally Armand was able to speak and console her by saying, "My love, I was only questioning when I called Ben. Did he call you?"

"Yes, I am so angry with you I don't know what to do. Take me home!" she commanded.

"All right, but Jessica will not be expecting us."

"That's fine. I'll make myself a sandwich. You go to lunch and enjoy yourself. While you are there, fuck yourself," she growled, weeping.

Armand was livid over Amber's vulgarity. He was beginning to understand why she was so upset. He drove home and opened the door. Jessica was eating at the kitchen table. While Amber ran upstairs, Armand spoke to Jessica, then went to their bedroom.

Amber was lying face down, surrounded by pillows, sobbing. Her hair fell over her face. He remembered, *When both people are angry at each other in an argument, one must take a deep breath and listen.* He allowed Amber to express herself.

He sat on the edge of the bed. She made her move. With her left arm she hit him in the side. He caught her arm as she attempted to hit him again. He bent over her, pressing her left arm close to his body. He brought her toward him, calmly asking, "Now, my love, please calm down. All I did was make some phone calls. One certainly was to the wrong person."

With tears falling on his jacket, a furious Amber slapped his face. "Get away from me!" she screamed.

"Amber, please stop being so emotional," he begged. She tried to slap him again but he caught her hand, saying, "Please calm down. I'm angry too."

She screamed again, "Get away from me!"

"I will. I'm going downstairs to find something to eat. I have a meeting at three o'clock"

"Armand, when you return I won't be here." He did some serious thinking as he descended the stairs.

Hearing that a full scale battle appeared to be going on in the house, Jessica began to make sandwiches. She had soup cooking when Armand entered.

Jessica saw the red spot on Armand's face and grabbed an ice cube and a fresh dish cloth urging, "Hold this on your face."

"I certainly made Amber angry," he stated. Over soup he told Jessica what he had done.

"Armand, never go behind your spouse's back. Talk your ideas over before you act," Jessica advised.

After eating, Armand left for his appointment. Amber came to the kitchen for something to eat. "Thank you so much, Jessica," she said when she found soup and a sandwich awaiting her.

Jessica knew it was none of her business, but she could not stand seeing her employers angry at each other. When Amber finished relating why she was so angry, Jessica spoke to her as a much more experienced woman in marriage. She advised, "Amber, it's true, Armand made an error by not discussing his ideas before he acted, but that's no reason to slap your husband so hard he had a big red spot on his face."

Amber rebutted, "I'll not be here when he comes home."

"What good is running away when you need to face each other and talk? Forget about slapping. Amber you've assaulted him."

"Dammit! He deserved everything I did," she aggressively snarled.

"Amber, please think instead of being so angry. If you are not in this house when he comes home, will you not be at work tomorrow?"

After she had eaten, Amber felt better. She slipped into a more pensive mood. Jessica's statements made her think. While Amber was in thought Jessica suggested, "Please call him. Tell him you're sorry and you'll be waiting for him when he arrives."

Armand answered her call, with his voice breaking, "What is it, my love?"

"I am very sorry I hit you, sweetheart. Let's talk over our anger when you get home. I'll be here."

That statement was music to his ears. "Thank you my love. I'll be home at five-thirty." Amber worked at home until it was time to prepare their meal.

Because she was still in the house, Jessica helped Amber prepare their supper, including a chocolate-cherry cake. When Jessica left, Amber was in better spirits. She hoped Armand would forgive her.

Armand's meeting with his client was not an easy one for him. He was tied in knots inside. He hoped the redness on his face had diminished somewhat. He was still angry at Amber, but he realized her feelings needed to be expressed. Only he could help ameliorate her attitude.

When his meeting was finished, he quietly sat in his chair and thought, *I must listen to what she has to say.*

In the car driving home, he sang love songs to himself. One of his favorites was, *Love Makes the World Go Round.* His thinking turned to everything they had accomplished in their six-plus years together. He had too much to lose if he did not forgive her after she had apologized.

Amber heard him come into the garage. Once he entered, he put his briefcase on a kitchen chair and went to an apron-clad Amber. Her arms were outstretched. He returned her embrace, both wept. Through her tears, Amber repeated, "Please forgive me."

"You are completely forgiven my love. Shall we talk now, or wait?"

"Let's talk some now. That will make us both feel better."

Being a gentleman, he asked, "Amber, please relate what I did that made you so angry."

"I believe I told you. Do you understand how important it is to relate what you plan to do? You would not be happy if I went behind your back and did something which you did not know about, but which affected both of us."

"I now understand, my love. This matter was made worse by Ben calling you," he stated. "I'll speak to him, but that's a side issue. What do I do now?"

"Come and eat with me," she smiled. They continued their dialogue as they ate.

After their meal, he invited her to sit beside him on the sofa. He had his brief case with him; but Amber's embrace was foremost in his thoughts and feelings at that moment.

He began, "Amber, I love you. I cannot allow this hurtful situation to continue. I will not do that again. My love I have a treat for you. I did not know until this afternoon I would receive this check. That's why I had to keep the appointment, even though I was so very uptight. I did not put these funds into our account because I was coming directly home."

"Amber's eyes gleamed over the large amount. "My god! Armand, how long have you been working for this company?"

"It's been since before we were married. I truly did not know for certain I would receive a check until this afternoon. In the back of my mind I recognized if this did happen, we certainly would be able to add a media center to the house. That is the reason I did some checking."

"Sweetheart, I needed to know."

"Yes, of course. I hope this check helps mitigate my insensitivity toward you my love."

He arose to removed his jacket. She stood and embraced him. Their affection for each other was made apparent by their loving actions. Their arms enfolded each other. Their embrace lasted for some time before he released her.

Armand took his jacket, briefcase, and check; then secured the house. Amber went upstairs to their bedroom.

Armand placed the clothes he would wear tomorrow on his valet chair. Amber determined what she would wear, then undressed. She turned to see Armand naked. She embraced her husband wearing only panties and bra, which he quickly removed.

Amber asked him to get into bed first. She rubbed his back, made decussate marks wherever she wished, and massaged his back. When she finished she asked him to turn over.

My, Armand thought, *this will be the interesting part. I get to caress her bosom,* but there was no such luck. He pulled her toward his chest and emoted, "My love, I receive a feel by hook or crook."

Amber kissed him everywhere but his lips, which made him pull her head toward him. After his hard day he needed affection. Like the tease she could be, Amber finally submitted to the caresses Armand desired.

Over breakfast, he brought up his thinking again. "Now, my love, does my idea make sense?"

"I suppose so," she relented, "but I do not understand how the addition could be made with ease."

"That's where Ben comes in. However, I need to talk with him."

After they arrived at work Armand called Ben, asking, "Why did you call Amber, Ben? You must be in a slack period."

Somewhat taken aback, Ben replied, "Do you have time? I'll be over as soon as I can get there." Armand went to Amber's office. He left a note for her, because she was on the phone.

Later when she heard Ben's voice in Armand's office, she went in and chided Ben for calling her. He apologized, admitting, "I was not acting professionally."

She responded, "I understand Armand's idea, but I am concerned as to how an addition would work visually, as well as be made so the entry would be outside of the house and garage. I will not allow entry to the projection room through the upstairs bedroom. That's poor planning."

Armand began, "I think an area for entertainment needs to be built separately. We have the space. Could it be arranged close to the house, but not attached?"

Ben replied, "Let me come over so I can measure the area with Armand helping me."

At four o'clock, they met Ben at the house. He asked, "May I first have a walk through?"

Armand led him on a house tour, while Amber set the table for supper. The three then walked around the house. Both Ben and Amber took notes and made visual observations.

Amber suggested, "Because of the concrete driveway, large cement trucks would not be able to run on the drive. Therefore, any addition to the property must be placed close to the front of the house, Ben." Amber asked, "Would that be close enough for concrete to be poured?"

"No," Ben replied, "I will need to come up with an idea."

"We would want heat in the floor and in a half-bath. This will be a building with no windows, but we will need another furnace and cooling equipment," Armand directed.

Hearing her husband's remark, Amber suggested, "We really don't need this. We could pay off the house instead."

"My love, we need this. Remember, when we have a family, this will be another reason for our kids to stay home," Armand replied.

"Yeah! All we will be is glorified baby-sitters," she growled.

Ben asked Armand to hold his flexible tape. "Amber," he asked. "Would you consider placing the building at a slight angle?"

"That would be fine."

"If you would like that, we would not need to grade any land. I could use a tractor with a blade to smooth the surface," Ben added as he pounded in stakes. Amber noticed that in late summer afternoons there would be a shadow on the West bedroom.

Ben left after the stakes were placed. Armand and Amber went to the kitchen to eat where she asked, "Sweetheart, are you really determined to carry through with your idea?"

"Indeed. When something comes to you in a dream it's important to follow through," he replied.

In the morning before leaving for work, they examined the stakes again. She asked, "Can we live with the building at an angle?"

"I think that's reasonable."

Ben came over on Friday. At the dining room table he revealed different plans for elevation, floor layout, details for duct work, electrical, plumbing and positioning of the projector. Amber and Armand made their selections from these plans. Ben stated, "I think you chose the best ones."

To save space, Ben planned for a spiral staircase to reach the second floor projection area. One-by-one, further details were revealed, including a half-bath which would be connected to the onsite plumbing. Amber had no further suggestions.

The front elevation appealed to Amber's sense of beauty. She was exceedingly pleased to find it blended perfectly with the house design. Armand was very happy to hear she was satisfied.

The forms were finished before Christmas. Armand met Amber's parents and her brother's family at the airport. Patricia was happy and mellow. She told Amber she had seen her sister twice; but Dennis had visited her quite often. Greg was supportive as usual.

Christmas Eve and Day were a repeat of previous year. Armand's parents and Grandma Alma all enjoyed a wonderful Christmas dinner. On Wednesday after the holiday, Armand took Amber's parents to the airport. Wendell's family left on Thursday morning.

Amber and Armand were home on New Year's Day. Ralph and Marlene spent the afternoon and early evening with them. Marlene was wearing a commitment ring. Ralph appeared to be extremely happy. To make their money work, they were going to live in his apartment until they could buy a house. Armand suggested, "Purchase a new one if possible."

That discussion encouraged Ralph to begin looking for a home.

Ralph asked Armand if he would stand up with him. Because his family did not accept divorce, they wanted no part of this wedding. Marlene asked Amber to be in her wedding party, to which Amber agreed. As soon as blood tests were completed, Ralph and Marlene would procure their license.

Armand and Amber worked overtime in January while his parents vacationed.

On the third Saturday in February they served as witnesses at Ralph's and Marlene's wedding. Armand and Amber hosted a wedding reception at their home for the newlyweds to help them save money. The next time they saw Ralph, he reported, "I am very happy. I have found marital happiness at last."

The entertainment building was well under way. The two were working late nearly every day and did not have time to inspect the new building until Saturdays. Armand suggested a vacation for them when his parents returned. Amber said she wanted to wait until August.

They entertained Amber's family again over the Fourth of July. The entertainment building was completed on the outside, which blended beautifully with the house.

Armand promised Raymond he would ship his car to him after his family arrived back home. Raymond loved his uncle, who spent lots of time with him when the families were together.

Sue's voice lessons were helping her develop a very lovely singing voice. Amber sent money for a lesson every month to help her parents.

For their 7th wedding anniversary, Armand purchased tickets to New York City. He planned for a week in downtown Manhattan. As usual, they sent their luggage ahead to the hotel.

Once in the 'Big Apple' they could not believe the congestion. Not only were the streets filled with traffic, but so were the sidewalks. They visited museums and walked a lot in spite of the hot, humid weather, which Amber did not like. Armand delighted her by going to Greenwich Village. Amber went crazy there, purchasing artworks which were shipped home. In Amber's opinion, that alone made the trip worthwhile.

Back home they continued working.

One evening they discussed their love and marriage. Amber mentioned she felt their love had grown so much, and they deeply loved each other so strongly, she recommended, "Armand, I think it is time for us to begin the procedures for adopting a child. I have an ambition I have not mentioned to you. I want to be a mom. Since our financial situation is stable and the house is more than three-quarters paid for, I think it is time to follow Jennifer and Ronald's idea."

Armand thoughtfully added, "I believe your idea is a good one, but no baby. The child must be a boy and be younger than our marriage."

"Sweetheart, you're correct. I agree with all your suggestions."

Conversations on this subject took place on many evenings as they ate, picked up the kitchen, and swam.

The second Thursday of September, Amber made an appointment through the adoption section of *Family and Youth Services Inc*, following the advice of Jennifer. Armand was somewhat aloof about the whole proceedings. His hand was cold, as hand-in-hand, they walked together into the building.

They met Roslind Frichie, the adoption coordinator. They were not as intimidated as they expected to be. Jennifer's advice helped them a lot. In the car going home, Armand admitted, "I'm glad we waited these years. I can see we are going to be making a tremendous change in our lives."

Melroy Abrams called Armand saying, "There will be room for four on the plane from Oklahoma City on Tuesday before Thanksgiving. It will return on the Tuesday after the holiday."

Armand left a message with Patricia and Dennis that there would be room for four. They made appropriate reservations for two of the seats.

The media room was finished, but had not been used. Ben had asked to be included for the first viewing, and purchased a movie to be shown the day after Thanksgiving.

With a full house, Armand operated the equipment. Jessica prepared a reception after the film was finished. The initial movie was a huge success.

Lily called inviting Armand and Amber up for Christmas. As they discussed Lily's offer, Armand said he wanted to spend Christmas Eve with his parents.

Chapter 29.

On Christmas day Amber and Armand drove to Denver to be with Wendell and his family. Patricia and Dennis had flown in earlier. Amber had a wonderful time with her relatives. Patricia was more laid-back and happy. She thoroughly enjoyed her new job.

Armand discussed their pre-adoption sessions. He was gradually getting used to the idea of becoming a father. Patricia asked him, "Do you have any indication of when the adoption day will come?"

"Heavens no, we haven't a clue. Don't worry, when we know, we certainly will call you. They ask us so many questions, I thought Roslind would ask when the last time I was intimate with Amber." He laughed along with the men.

Patricia stated, "Your intimate desires better be with Amber and no one else or you'll be sorry."

He smiled, "I guess that would be emasculating time."

Hearing him, Amber expressed, "Sweetheart, please be a gentleman, if that's possible!"

"I am, but this adoption process is getting to be too much."

"All right, we'll forget our meeting this week," Amber directed.

She then told her mother about evening parenting meetings which they had been attending. "I think the information we are receiving will be helpful."

Patricia questioned, "Have you asked about age and sex?"

"Oh my yes, Mom!"

Armand insisted, "We want a boy for the oldest. My older sister always mothered me, which I hated. No girl will be older than a boy in our family."

The adoption conversation continued, led by Armand. "We do not care about skin color or national origin, but we do want a child who wants to learn and is capable of doing so. I would accept some physical disabilities, if necessary."

Amber demurred, "No. I believe there will be enough problems in being a parent without adding a child with a disability. Mom and Dad, I would hope you will come and see us after we receive the child."

"We certainly will," Patricia responded.

The holiday with her family passed rapidly. When the time came to return home, the weather report was for snow. Amber and Armand left for the long drive in very early morning darkness. It was still dark when they reached Raton Pass. They stopped in Raton for an omelet breakfast. They sat at the lunch counter to save time.

Back in the car, snowflakes began to fall. Armand slowed the car. Snow was falling heavily before they reached Santa Fe. The roads were wet, but not slippery. Armand drove carefully while Amber watched road conditions for him. They were happy to arrive home safely. Amber called Wendell to report they had arrived.

"I thank you and Lily so much for your Christmas hospitality. Please tell Lily we're tired and will relax the rest of the day. The next winter trip we make up your way, we'll take more time for the drive."

Upstairs, they removed their clothes and worked out for a short time. They then showered and slept. The next morning, as Armand checked the house, he was shocked to find the window in the door to the mechanical area was broken. Someone had gained entry into the house. Without touching anything, he rushed to the kitchen and shouted to Amber, "Call the police. Someone has gained entry. Somehow the alarm was not tripped!"

Amber called the police and then Jeffory. Armand continued to search. Nothing appeared to be gone. Amber's jewelry was untouched. The police found the loss was in the media building. Equipment was stolen or vandalized. Armand asked, "How did they gain entry? I locked that door and set the alarm." The policeman told him, "Someone in your area is watching you come and go, and knows how to disarm your alarm system."

Armand questioned, "They would need a ladder to get over the wall."

The detective suggested, "We'll look for marks, but my guess is they came through the front at a gate."

Armand was very upset. Amber did not know what to think. She sat at the kitchen table with her head in her arms. Jeffory helped his brother a great deal by knowing how to answer the detective's questions.

One detective suggested, "In the future, come and go from your property at different times. Do not establish a regular pattern."

Armand came to the kitchen saying, "My love, whatever you do, avoid the media room." He did not mention the vandalism there. Amber looked at Armand, then hurried to the kitchen sink and vomited.

A detective came into the room while she was at the sink and directed Armand, "Hold on to her, she's in shock."

"My love, would you like to lie down?"

"Yes, please."

"Put your arm around my neck." He carried her to the sofa, found a pillow and blanket to cover her. The police carefully checked the upstairs rooms. One officer reported, "They did their dastardly deeds elsewhere. They had a swim and left." Amber thanked the officer and felt better knowing the culprits had not been upstairs.

A lady from the Crisis Center was called and spent some time soothing Amber. She reasoned, "The personal part of your home was not disturbed. Your workout room, guest bedrooms and baths were untouched."

Armand talked to an insurance company representative. Jeffory returned to his office. The officers examined all the property, especially the outside, observing the neighborhood to determine which neighboring properties had a good view of their home. One officer told Armand, "Someone knows how to by-pass your alarm system and gain entry through locked doors."

"Do we need to put razor wire on top of the wall?" Armand asked.

"No. That probably would not deter these individuals. The entry was gained at the gate."

Armand taped cardboard over the broken window to keep out rain and snow.

A final suggestion by another officer was to have someone they trusted come in and out at unusual times. Once the officers left, Armand and Amber went upstairs and tried to sleep.

The next morning, Amber prepared breakfast. In another room Armand called the company which had sold the entertainment equipment to order a new screen, chairs, and a projector. All these items had been stolen or destroyed.

Their insurance agent came to record an inventory of the damage, because of the high value of the losses. Armand would not allow Amber into the media building which was his pride and joy. It had been so severely violated that he developed a headache. The insurance agent suggested Armand put in an unbreakable window in the mechanical room door.

Armand responded, "We use this window for ventilation."

The agent suggested, "Put a window higher on the wall."

Soon after the agent left, the entry gate was buzzed. Armand opened the gate to meet the neighbor, Bruce Malver, who said, "I felt I needed to come and tell you, I saw two people go around the back of your house the night before last. I did not think anything about that until I saw all the police activity here. Did you have a burglary? Did they do any damage or steal anything, Mr. Rambulet? Because of the new building, I cannot see the front of your house any more."

Armand closed the gate and invited him in. As they walked toward the media building Armand asked, "Is there anyone around here who is a knowledgeable locksmith?"

Bruce reported, "I believe the people further down the street on the right side own several locksmith stores. My god! Why would someone do something like this?"

"Probably jealousy. We are fully insured," Armand replied.

"I hope what I told you may help find these culprits."

Being cautious, Armand did not invite Bruce into the house. He related, "Bruce, my wife is suffering from shock. I have a headache and need to take something. But I thank you for your help. I presume you will tell the police what you told me."

"Of course. I thank you for permitting me to offer some help," Bruce offered, as he walked to the gate. Armand quickly returned to the house. He called the detective who had given him his business card, and repeated what Bruce had told him. Finishing the call, Armand collapsed grabbing a living room chair. Amber laid him on the floor with a pillow under his head. "A drink of water and something for my headache please," he mumbled.

She brought him what he needed, asking, "Can you sit up enough to lie on the sofa? You will be more comfortable there than on the floor."

After a nap, he felt better. They both worked out and had a swim to help them relax. She prepared a light supper, after which they both enjoyed a long sleep.

The next day, Armand installed more lights around the house until something more professional could be added. Jeffory had told his parents of their plight. Celeste and Francis came over to offer them comfort.

During this hubbub, Amber realized they needed groceries and vitamins and went to purchase them.

Armand remained at home adding lights to their house. When Amber arrived, he was in the kitchen preparing their noon meal. She put the groceries away while he finished with their food.

After eating they both *crashed* for a nap. They were feeling the effects of this traumatic event. Armand was very uneasy because his locked house had been no match for some thief.

Armand then talked at length with his brother who suggested, "The people who entered your home when you were away are *chickens*. They would not want to meet you face to face in your dwelling."

"I'm not certain about that," he demurred.

Jeffory suggested, "Talk with your neighbors. Give them your phone number. Ask them to call you if your back motion-sensing light goes on. Get to know your neighbors. They have to be professional people. You may learn something you need to know."

Armand understood his brother's advice was important. He told Amber, "I'm going to talk with the neighbors who have a view of our property. I'll give them a business card and have them call us if our back lights go on."

His final stop was at Bruce's home. Armand was surprised to find a detective had talked with Bruce. His wife, Beverly was out-going and very conversant. He was impressed when Beverly said, "Please do not think we are snooping. We just want to be good neighbors. We see a portion of your house. I work part time and am home some days. I think it's important to know our neighbors. Sometimes when help is needed they are the first to respond to a distress call, especially at night."

"Thank you so much. We'll have you come over when we have time. I believe I explained to Bruce that my grandfather passed away, then my mother had a stroke. We have had lots of stress lately."

"Thanks for the added information," Bruce answered.

Armand bid them goodbye and went into the house. He found Amber working out. While he was gone she had made a hot dish. Amber said she planned to go swimming before they ate. She noted that her husband was in better spirits. He joined her in the workout room dressed in his swim trunks. Armand was doing hand-presses when Amber arose from her stationary bike and kissed him on the cheek suggesting, "Sweetheart, we need to get back into our routine. We cannot let this incident in our lives totally disrupt us."

"You're correct my love."

They spent New Year's Eve at home. At midnight, they shared a warm embrace before going to bed.

The next day, Amber called his parents and families to come over about two o'clock. That afternoon the house was alive with happy children and adults laughing and enjoying the water. Jeffory worked out before entering the pool. He was even feeling romantic. When he came into the pool, where Eleanor was at the water's edge, he gave her cheek a kiss.

Seeing that, Francis gave Celeste a kiss. All were thoroughly enjoying the water.

As the family sat at the table for dinner, Francis asked everyone to please hold hands and bow their heads. He offered a blessing. "We ask that the love energy be directed to all of us. We also ask protective love to be with us, especially Armand and Amber and this house. May we accept our daily occurrences with grace, dignity, and understanding. Amen."

After eating, the children played games at the tables until their parents permitted them to return to the water. They played until quite late.

Desiree was first to shower with her mother. In her night clothes she was tucked into bed. Floyd soon followed. Gilbert and Gabrielle stayed in the water after their parents had showered. Finally, they went to bed. Then adult conversation briefly turned to the break-in. However, the joking soon returned. The atmosphere again became festive.

After the family left, Amber and Armand dropped into bed. The following morning Armand worked, while Amber stayed home. She made lunch for them. When he returned to eat, Amber was dressed for work. He told her his morning had been easy.

In the days that followed, a detective came to the business to ask Armand more questions. Armand told him, "Our architect has contracted with an electrician to install lights and motion-sensing cameras on the house."

"Mr. Rambulet, that's a very good idea."

Celeste and Francis took their vacation. The rest of the family went about their normal work.

Jessica returned from her holiday, very refreshed.

Finally, the insurance company directed Armand to purchase new media equipment, which was delivered in mid-January. A different lock was put on the media room door, which was now more secure with added lights, cameras, and a heavier door.

They worked the month of January. Armand then made special plans for Valentine's Day. Jessica accepted a delivery of flowers from Armand for Amber that afternoon. That night Armand and Amber ate out.

Amber purchased a new shirt and tie for her love. Their evening was special, concluding with another loving experience.

On February fifteenth they were in another session with the *Adoption Department of Family Services*. This organization had inspected their home while they were at work. Roslind Frichie had personally made the tour. She wanted to make certain there was a locked door guarding the pool area preventing a four or five year old from entering alone.

Jennifer and Ronald had given Roslind family details; but the adoption agency director wished to know Amber better. The next day, she visited her at work. Amber patiently answered the questions.

Going home Amber asked, "What would she have done if I had been consulting with a client? By the way, how did your afternoon go?"

"I am sure she was wanting to see how you would react. My afternoon went well. Dad was with me. Mom was with a client."

"I know. I didn't see your parents all day."

Armand and Amber invited their neighbors, Bruce and Beverly Malver over on a Saturday evening in March. Jessica prepared food before she left. Jessica did not normally work on Saturdays but helped when she was needed to assist for entertaining.

Roslind called and asked them to come to her office the following Tuesday. Armand and Amber were introduced to a nearly five year old boy named Lyle Allen. The boy had hazel eyes, light brown hair and wore a wide smile. Amber and Armand were able to take him out for a hamburger and french fries with lots of catsup. Lyle ate hungrily while Armand and Amber looked at each other, knowing that was not healthy food.

Lyle told them his favorite color was blue.

Chapter 30.

Many months of conversation, interchange of ideas, and plans occurred before Lyle Allen's adoption was completed. On the happy day he went home with them, Armand helped Amber into the car while he held Lyle. Then he belted the boy into a new, blue child's seat, and gave him a cuddle toy.

Jessica had made food for them. The table was set. In the house, Amber and Armand showed Lyle his room. The bedspread was decorated with different colored cars on a blue background. The curtains matched the spread.

He and his father urinated together. With hands washed, they walked hand in hand to the kitchen where Amber was placing food on the table. Armand helped Lyle into his booster chair. Then with heads bowed and holding hands, Armand asked, "Great loving Energy, please surround us as a family and unite us in a special bond of love. We thank you, we thank you, we thank you."

Lyle was so excited, he asked question after question. He could not believe this was his house and kitchen. Jessica had made hamburgers using buffalo meat, their homemade bread, and french fries. Lyle's favorite vegetable, green beans, were in a bowl.

Amber cleaned the kitchen while Armand took Lyle to his bedroom to change into blue swim trunks matching his dad's. Hand in hand they went to the locked pool door. Roslind had insisted this door always be locked unless they were swimming together.

At the shallow end, Armand let Lyle paddle, take a deep breath, then duck under the water and come up. He was so happy to have his father's attention. He squealed when he saw his mother approaching the pool. She was carrying her swim cap. Lyle asked, "What is that funny thing?"

Amber explained while Lyle closely watched as she tucked her hair under the cap. She told her men that she would swim first while Armand played with Lyle in the shallow water.

When she finished her swim, she helped Lyle with swimming fundamentals. She assured her little guy she would be by his side. As they splashed, Amber told Lyle that on Friday they would go to the courthouse. Roslind would be there and that he would see her from time to time.

Armand finished his swim and played with Lyle while Amber showered. She dressed in her sleepwear and went to the pool area. Armand showered with Lyle, then helped his son towel himself. Together they wiped down the shower. Armand wrapped the towel around his torso, then went to Lyle's room for his pajamas. With his father's help, the boy was dressed in blue printed pajamas with matching slippers.

Amber met them carrying a children's book. Lyle sat on his father's lap as Armand read to him. Lyle soon began rubbing his eyes. Amber kissed him on his cheek and put him into bed, as Armand rubbed his back and sat with him until fatigue closed his eyes. Armand left a night-light on.

In the morning when he awoke, Lyle tiptoed to their bedroom and gently asked to have a snuggle between them. With smiles and tears, they both welcomed him warmly.

The next day Armand left for work, dressed as normal in a suit and tie. He worked a full day.

Lyle enjoyed being home with Amber and Jessica. His mother worked at her lap-top for two hours. She was playing with Lyle in his room when her cell phone rang.

"What's that?" Lyle questioned, "A phone? Mom, it's so small. How can you talk?" The call was from the car dealership. Her new car was ready to be picked up. She called Armand who decided to come home for lunch. Then he could take her to pick up the new wheels.

When Armand arrived, Lyle marveled, "Dad, you're in a suit." He picked up Lyle; but embraced Amber before he kissed his son on the cheek.

Jessica sat at the table with them. Armand stated, "Jessica is a lady who helps us. Your mother has so much to do, she can't take care of the house without help. If you have a favorite food and use the word *please*, and if Jessica has time, she'll make what you want."

Lyle quickly looked at her and announced, "I like green beans, but my favorite is chocolate brownies. Will you please make me some?"

"I'll see what I can do," Jessica responded, with a smile. Lyle then observed, "These sandwiches are good. The bread is different."

Armand explained, "We make our own bread. Store-bought bread contains preservatives, which we try to avoid. Do you like our bread?"

"Yes, but it tastes different," Lyle observed, while he moved his legs exuberantly as they dangled from his chair.

After they ate, with Lyle in his car seat, they went to the dealership for Amber's new car. Lyle's questions were numerous. He had never seen so many new, shiny, clean cars; but the yellow one out front was the one his mom was buying.

Lyle said he wanted to ride in the new car with his mother. Armand transferred his car seat and strapped his son into it. Armand had a difficult time unfastening the seat from his car and concluded that he would purchase a new seat for his vehicle.

In the new car Lyle rambled on and on about the wonderful smell and the lights on the dashboard. He finally observed, "Mom, your hair is pretty."

On Friday afternoon, dressed in new clothes, Lyle and his parents went to the courthouse. His uncle Jeffory joined his parents before the judge came into the room. Jeffory was there to make certain that no previous encounters with Lyle could ever separate him from his new parents. Roslind was there, too. She had been informed that Lyle had a very high IQ. The judge asked Lyle, "Do you like math?"

Lyle responded, "Mister, my Dad works with numbers. If you have four things and add four more, that's eight. But if you say you have four things and times them by three, that's twelve. Four times four is sixteen."

"You handle your numbers well, young man," the judge observed.

After the legal portion was finished, the judge asked Lyle what else he liked to do.

"I like to read, too," Lyle answered.

The judge dismissed them, asking Roslind to come to his chambers. His honor asked, "Can that child be privately educated?"

"I believe so your honor," she responded.

"If possible, try to direct those parents into obtaining a good education for him."

A short time after his adoption was finalized, Lyle told his mother that his head hurt. Amber arranged a doctor's appointment.

When the doctor examined his head, he quietly asked Lyle some questions. The MD was shocked to find that in one of his foster care homes, the lady had hit him so hard, he fell into a door frame. "Sometimes my head hurts."

Amber and Armand were stunned. Armand stepped out of the doctor's office and called Roslind, telling her what they had discovered. "Please check this out to see if it is true."

The MD made phone arrangements for a brain scan at the University Hospital. Dr. Schultz indicated, I'll be here most of the day tomorrow. I can see Lyle at ten for a scan."

In his car seat, Lyle recognized that his parents were very upset. Amber and Armand were numb and weak-in-the-knees. They were worried that their little guy had a medical problem. At home, out of Lyle's hearing, a very nervous Amber called Roslind, insisting that any children which that foster care woman had, must be removed immediately, "And ask any other children who have been in that home about abuse they may have received."

Jessica's food awaited them when they arrived home. After eating they went into the living room. With Lyle watching, Armand and Amber sat on the floor in a lotus position, holding hands, with Lyle between them and meditated. Armand received assurance: Dr. Schultz suggested, with an operation, Lyle's growth could be safely removed and he would be fine.

After they released hands, Armand sat on the sofa. He ran his hand gently over Lyle's head. He could feel a bump. Amber felt it, too. She grabbed her little guy, hugged him, trying hard to be brave and not cry. Armand took him to his bedroom and prepared him for sleep, then brought him back to the living room.

Amber read poetry, then she made up a story in which she changed her voice. She held him very tightly at times. He put his arms out to embrace his mom, which made her voice quiver. She continued her story, then permitted Armand to add to it.

Lyle grew weary. His dad carried him on his back. When Armand walked, he bounced his son around a bit, but Lyle had his arms tightly around his dad's neck. He was tucked into bed, with a light left on.

Armand set the house alarm and heard Amber sobbing as he entered their bedroom. He could not stand to hear his wife weeping. What could he do? Kissing her cheek he asked, "My love, what can I do to make you feel better?"

"Love me," she answered.

"I do love you."

"Please my love. You know what I mean. We must be strong. We need to give our son lots of love and strength; but we have to keep up our own strength too."

Armand removed his clothes while Amber did the same. Wiping tears, Amber went to her husband. Reaching into his briefs, she found the precious part of him for which she longed.

"My love, I am not certain I can perform."

She pulled down his briefs. He stepped out and carried her to their bed. Amber led her sweetheart into an experience which was very endearing for them. Their loving moments enabled them both to sleep.

The next day they were in the hospital at ten. Lyle was wheeled away, being a brave little lad. After the scan Dr. Schultz explained, "There appears to be an object like a splinter around which an abscess has formed. No wonder Lyle says his head hurts. If I find there is an operating room and an assistant available, I would like to take him to surgery right away so the pressure can be removed."

"That sounds wonderful," Armand answered. "We're here. I for one, would love to have this load off my mind."

"I completely agree, please do it," Amber said, thankfully.

Before Lyle was wheeled into the operating room, his parents assured him they would be by his side when he awoke. Being nervous and upset, Armand called his mother and told them where they were. "We'll be right there. Tell me exactly where you are," his mother responded.

Francis and Celeste arrived, each carrying a small cuddle toy. They came to support Amber and Armand and to be nearby. Their conversation concerned Lyle. His grandfather realized, "He must have had severe headaches--and he's so young . . ."

Weeping, Armand answered, "He is one sweet youngster. He is adjusting well to us."

Amber offered, "My Mom and Dad are coming over for Memorial Day weekend. I know they will be upset when I tell them this news."

While they waited, Armand remembered, "I need to bring Lyle some low vitamin C apple juice and some of our bread."

After the surgery was finished, Dr. Schultz briefed them on what he had found. "Your son will be fine. That mass was pressing on nerves. There was a piece of wood in the center. Infection had formed around that thing. Your little lad has a story to tell."

Armand and Amber were at Lyle's side when he began to awaken. Lyle started to cry, but quieted when his mom and dad began talking about his ordeal and telling him he was a brave little boy. Armand explained why he was connected to all those machines, saying, "You must lie quietly for awhile. Your head is shaved and bandaged."

Amber kissed him, but he still cried. He needed to vomit. Amber and a nurse helped him empty his stomach, both feeling very sorry he had to go through this trauma.

Afterward, he felt better. Armand had big tears in his eyes when he told Lyle, "Son, you are very courageous."

Dr. Schultz came to examine his patient. Lyle asked, "Why did I throw up?"

"Probably the medicine upset your body. People often react the way you did."

Lyle's grandparents arrived with cuddle toys. Lyle cried. He had never had so much attention. A toy was placed in the cradle of each arm. He could love and kiss each one separately. He would name them when he felt better.

In the afternoon, Uncle Jeffory arrived to see his nephew. He was determined that the *Adoption Department of Family Services* would check out the family where Lyle lived when he was injured.

While Lyle was hospitalized, Amber stayed with him. Armand worked, shopped for groceries, and went to see his son and wife daily. He missed having Amber with him. He found the empty house upsetting.

Before Lyle left the hospital, his head was re-bandaged. Armand came for them in the late afternoon. Lyle was crying, happy to be going home. His father strapped him into his seat and kissed him on the cheek. He had his cuddle toys from Grandma and Grandpa. On the way home, he asked, "May I have a peanut butter and jelly sandwich when we get home?"

"Of course. What would you like to drink?"

"Oh, whatever . . ."

Both Armand and Amber chuckled over this remark.

At home, Armand helped Amber out of the car. She carried bags of toys and other belongings. Lyle carried the cuddle toys from his grandparents. Jessica had prepared food for them and left a note with a happy face she had drawn for Lyle.

A peanut butter and jelly sandwich was the first order of business. He also had part of a veggie burger and green beans. Three people were very happy to be home and settled.

Amber was especially tired. She had not slept well on hospital cots.

Kissing Lyle and Armand she went upstairs to bed early. Armand read him a story while Lyle was drifting into sleep. As usual, a light was left on.

Armand set the alarm and hurried upstairs. Quickly removing his clothes, he snuggled gently into bed to kiss his love, whom he had missed so much during this ordeal. He stroked her neck and cheek and gave her an extended kiss, saying, "I love you. Goodnight, my love."

Chapter 31.

A week passed. It was time to take Lyle back to the doctor. Their son seemed to be feeling good. "No headaches," he proclaimed to Dr. Schultz. The doctor directed, "The bandage may be removed. I suggest Lyle wear a cap for awhile to protect his head."

Later in a children's store, he and Amber looked for a cap with a dolphin or a fish pattern. Lyle was not into sports. She selected a blue one with a fish decoration. Putting it on he asked his mother, "How did you know blue is my favorite color?"

"Lyle, you told us when we first met you. That's why you sleep under a blue bedspread."

"It is a color of the rainbow. Angels gather to make the rainbow. I've seen a *Blue Angel,*" he revealed. My angel wears beautiful blue garments.

"That's wonderful, Lyle," his mom exclaimed. When Amber belted him into his seat she asked, "Please tell me something about the *Blue Angel.*"

"In one house, they prayed a lot and taught me to pray so I could see an Angel, and they told me other angels wear other beautiful colors."

After they were home Amber asked him what went on in some of the places he stayed. "I'm with you now. I don't want to talk about other places," and he began to weep. Amber hugged and kissed him, telling him they would not talk about anything but the *Blue Angel.*

Amber's mother called, "I am very concerned about Lyle." Amber put Lyle on the phone. He listened as his other grandmother spoke. He smiled when she told him she loved him and that they were coming to see him. "What would you like for us to bring you?"

"Ruff is my favorite toy. Buff, from my grandpa is my second favorite." I want another Ruff," he said, returning the phone to his mom.

"What's a Ruff?" her mother asked.

Amber replied, "It's a dog cuddle toy." She described the toy in detail, giving her mom the manufacturer's name. "Lyle named his dog 'Ruff'. He carries it with him a great deal of the time."

After she hung up, she gave Lyle two kisses, one on each cheek. "This one is from your other grandma and that one is from grandpa number two. They are my parents."

Days passed into weeks. Armand worked and Amber took care of their son. Memorial Day approached. Amber planned food for a party. Jessica did the household chores. She told Amber how amazed she was over Lyle's neatness. He kept all his cuddle toys on top of his pillow. Each had been named. A larger toy dog was Ruggles. There was Snuggle, Beetle, and Bang, besides Ruff and Buff. Floyd gave him a small car named Speed. It was placed on his night stand.

Lyle loved to see his dad come home. He thought a suit and tie was super special dress. Armand and Amber learned that in homes where he lived before, he had never seen the man in a suit. Lyle was accepting love from a new grandma and grandpa, plus uncles and aunts. Beside that he had a cousin to play with. Floyd was only two years older. Lyle could see and feel the love between uncles, aunts, and cousins.

The day his Breddgeforth grandparents were coming, Lyle rode in his seat while his dad drove to the airport. Lyle was surprised to see his grandparents so tall. He remained in his seat while baggage was put into the car. Grandpa Breddgeforth bent and gave Lyle a kiss on the cheek. His grandmother gave him a cuddle toy just like Ruff. He thanked his grandmother for a second Ruff. "This one will be named Ruff-Ruff," he decided immediately

At night grandpa slept in the other bed in Lyle's room. Grandpa dressed him in pajamas and put him in bed. Then he told Lyle stories about when his mom was a little girl.

In the middle of the night Lyle awoke screaming, which awakened his grandpa, and brought his parents running to him. Lyle had a nightmare. He said he dreamed he was in a car which was on fire. He was having a difficult time getting out.

His mom cuddled him first, then his dad, and finally Grandpa tucked him back into bed. The next morning at breakfast, Armand explained to him that his nightmare was a memory from another lifetime. This explanation satisfied Lyle. He and Grandpa spent time in his bedroom playing with his toys. Then they enjoyed water games. Grandpa and Lyle showered together. Grandpa helped Lyle into his pajamas.

Dennis shared with Patricia the fact that Lyle was not circumcised. She discussed this with Amber. Patricia was distraught about this fact. Amber was not particularly upset over the idea that Lyle would need this surgery performed.

"Mom, after what we have been through, this is a small thing. To obtain proper schooling for him is a larger issue." Patricia admitted Amber was correct. Amber related to her mother that an appointment had been made for the following Tuesday with Dr. Peterson for Lyle's physical.

Hearing this Patricia felt better. She praised Amber for being a good mom. Armand rented a children's movie. Armand's whole family was invited to come and see it. He knew Floyd and Desiree would enjoy the film. If Gilbert and Gabrielle did not, they could return to the house and swim.

The time with Amber's parents passed too quickly. Armand took them to the airport, with Lyle in his seat holding his two Ruffs. Amber bid her parents goodbye at home, permitting her to go to work for a few hours. Armand brought Lyle to work with him for a time.

Lyle thought his house was nice, but the building with the *Rambulet* name, where his mom and dad worked, impressed him. He had never been in a building so large. He was shown his grandparents' offices. In a special location on his dad's desk, Lyle spotted a picture of himself. He squealed, "Hey, that's me!"

Next they went to his mom's office. When he saw her, he dropped his dad's hand and ran around her desk. She lifted him onto her lap. He held cuddly dogs in his arms. Kissing Lyle she asked, "Can you play here while I finish what I am working on?"

Armand had gone to his desk to check phone calls. Lyle grew restless, left his mother's room, and walked around in the upstairs hall. He went into his Uncle Ronald's and talked briefly with him. He still held his cuddly dogs.

The stairs interested him. He thought they were pretty. He looked down and realized he could not reach the hand rails. While his parents minds were occupied with work, he decided to back down the stairs. He was having a difficult time trying to bring his toys with him as he began to scoot down the steps.

On the second floor, Florence picked him up and took him to his mother reporting, "He was playing on the stairs. I thought you would be worried." Amber thanked her and seated him in her lap and explained a little of what she was doing. When he saw the numbers on the computer screen, he became interested. "Mom, those numbers are really long," he exclaimed.

Recognizing what he was seeing, she asked, "Do you recognize this number."

"That's a four."

"What's the mark before the four?"

"Is that a dollar sign?"

"Yes. What is the next number?"

"A four."

"How about the next number?"

"That's a five."

She announced, "The whole number is four hundred forty five thousand dollars."

"Wow. That's a lot."

"It certainly is." She helped Lyle move the mouse to another place. His action was too animated. She helped him back up to where she needed to be. Their morning continued until lunch time.

Amber asked him to put his toys into her car before they left to eat. His dad came to his mother's office. He embraced and kissed her. Lyle asked, "Me, too," and received his hug. He walked between them on this spring day, happy as could be. He was wearing his blue hat, shorts, short sleeved shirt, white stockings, and gym shoes. He told his dad about the big number he had seen on his mother's computer.

In the restaurant, Lyle sat on a booster chair opposite his mother on the inside of the booth beside his dad. He wanted a hamburger with french fries. That was fine. Amber also gave him her green beans.

After lunch his mother drove home with Lyle in his seat, clutching Ruff and Ruff-Ruff. At home Lyle went to his room and carefully placed his toys on his pillow.

At supper time he heard the garage door open and waited by the kitchen door for his dad, who picked him up while Lyle kissed him on the cheek. Holding Lyle, Armand kissed Amber. Lyle was beginning to understand his parents loved each other very much. He had never been around people with so much love to share. In past years, more often he had heard angry voices raised.

After their meal, the family went for a swim. Lyle was learning how to coordinate his feet and arm movements to help him negotiate the water.

Amber had showered and gone into their bedroom. When Lyle grew tired, his dad and he showered and toweled the shower stall dry.

After Armand locked the door to the pool, they proceeded to Lyle's bedroom. In the room before they dressed Armand explained the difference between his penis' appearance and Lyle's. "Son, you can pull skin back from your penis. I cannot, because my skin was removed shortly after I was born."

"Next Tuesday morning we are going to take you to Dr. Peterson's out-patient services where he will cut that skin away. It is important for us to keep our penises clean."

"Will it hurt, Dad?"

"Yes it will. When you grow older and see other boys' penises, yours will look like theirs," Armand related.

On Tuesday morning, Amber and Armand took their little guy to the out-patient department. In a special room Lyle was placed on an operating table. Dr. Peterson explained what he was going to do, so as not to frighten the little lad. A green drape was placed about Lyle's chest. His parents were seated by his head. They talked to him. His dad held his right hand.

Lyle felt a prick then numbness. Amber and Armand kept their eyes focused on Lyle. In a short time the surgery was finished. The doctor pulled Lyle's partially bandaged penis, upward in his briefs. Amber went for the car. Armand carried him to his own seat and handed his son his precious toys putting one in each hand.

Lyle went to sleep on the way home. He was quietly put into his bed to continue his recuperation. Armand and Amber ate lunch with Jessica, then Armand went to work. When Lyle awoke, he called for his mother. She went to him hearing, "Mom, I have to pee." His mother helped him with his clothing. "Mom, I hurt."

"Of course you do. Let's wash our hands and I'll make you a peanut butter and jelly sandwich." Lyle asked, "Can it be toasted?"

With an affirmative nod, she helped him into his booster chair and kissed his cheek. As she made his sandwich, he asked, "Mom, why do you keep bread in the refrigerator?"

"Store bought bread is loaded with preservatives. We make our own bread and must keep it cool to prevent it from spoiling." He devoured his toasted sandwich and Amber gave him some applesauce and rice milk, which he enjoyed. After he ate they went upstairs for Amber to work at her computer while he lay on the couch.

"Mom, my crotch hurts," He began to cry.

"Lyle, what's the matter?"

"I don't have my toys."

"I'll get them for you. Which ones do you want?"

"Ruff and Ruff-Ruff." She went to his room, returned with his toys, and dried his eyes, "They will help you feel better."

While she worked at her computer, Lyle talked to his toys. He told them quite a story. When he told them, "My 'pisser' hurts." Amber realized she needed to correct his language. Kneeling at the sofa she put her arms around him. Their faces nearly touched. "Lyle, the body part of yours which hurts is your penis. Please do not use any other word for that part of yourself."

"Why, Mom?"

"That's the name which is used in medicine. Dr. Peterson would use that word."

When Jessica left, she announced, "There is a salad in the refrigerator, and a hot dish in the oven."

"Thank you so much. We'll enjoy them," Amber replied.

The sound of the garage door opening announced that his Dad was home. Lyle forgot his pain and holding his toys in both hands, met his dad on the stairway. Lyle laughed and raised his arms, while Armand lifted him onto his back, toys and all, and carried him to the den where Amber was concentrating at her computer. He kissed her and she returned kisses to both of her men.

"Dad, I need to go to the bathroom," Lyle stated. The males urinated together. "Dad, does mine look like yours, now?"

"Yes, indeed. However, I know yours is sore." He sat on the sofa holding Lyle and speaking softly to him. "Right after most male babies are born, they are given the operation you had. As males grow older, that surgery is more painful. I'm sorry you have pain. I'll give you some medicine before you go to bed tonight, so you'll be able to sleep."

"I had a nap."

"That's good."

"Mom toasted bread with peanut butter and jelly for me."

Amber closed her computer and arose to give Armand a kiss and embrace. Armand held Lyle's left hand and Amber's right as they descended the stairs to the kitchen. Armand put Lyle into his seat as Amber prepared their meal.

All the conversation concerned Lyle's operation. His father explained. "As you grow older you will understand why we had that surgery done."

Chapter 32.

Armand continued to work, while Amber carefully researched where Lyle would go to school. She felt a private school, which stressed the basics, would be needed. She and Armand realized that their son was extremely good with elementary math. His addition and subtraction was fascinating for a lad so young. He grasped multiplication without difficulty. They both realized he was truly a gifted child, particularly with mathematics.

After their son was in bed, they often discussed his progress. They felt it would be wise to notify the judge who had heard his case, about Lyle's progress.

Amber spent some time every day working with him in arithmetic, and simple reading and writing.

Lyle was adapting very well to his immediate family, their house, and his many relatives. He enjoyed being with his cousin Floyd. Though the two boys shared no direct blood relationship, he now had a cousin whom he liked better and better each time the boys were together. He was especially fascinated with a bright blue sports car toy resting on his night stand, which Floyd had given him.

Jeffory talked with Armand about what he had discovered regarding Lyle's early abuse. Roslind had learned that other children had been abused by the couple who injured Lyle. Jeffory was in the process of having them prosecuted. When Armand gave this news to Amber and Lyle, big tears welled in their son's eyes. He begged, "Don't let them hurt any other kids."

Armand picked him up and holding him tightly, asked, "Do you remember any other times when a child was hit, shouted at, or touched inappropriately?"

Lyle began to weep. "PLEASE, DAD--NO!" he cried.

Armand remembered this was the second time Lyle had refused to answer questions about abuse.

After Lyle was asleep, Armand and Amber discussed what they needed to do. Amber suggested, "I'll call Dr. Peterson tomorrow to see who he would recommend for a child psychologist." She did not want Lyle to be stressed any further.

The next day she called the doctor telling him she was concerned about Lyle's reluctance to be questioned about foster care, and his firm refusal to discuss the subject of abuse. She told the doctor, "The family where Lyle had sustained his head injury while in their care, is being prosecuted.

Dr. Peterson replied, "Amber, let me make a phone call. I'll get back to you." In his return call he reported, "Amber I made an appointment with Dr. Melvin Anthrews for tomorrow at ten o'clock." Amber called Armand, who said he was anxious to be present for this appointment.

The next morning the three went to the mental-health doctor's office. The physician interviewed Amber first, then Armand. He wanted to see Lyle's reactions when both parents were present. His father held Lyle while the doctor asked questions. This MD could see that Lyle was more threatened with Amber around, but the lad felt comfortable with his new Dad.

In private conversation with him, Amber had mentioned to the doctor that she had observed Lyle acted very comfortable around his dad, but seemed more distant with her. The doctor signaled his receptionist, who asked Amber to step into the outer office. He could focus on Lyle and Armand more comfortably.

Lyle's visits with this doctor continued. Armand would often drop Amber off to work before taking Lyle to the appointment. Other times, Lyle was questioned with his mother present, and sometimes only with his dad.

When the doctor talked with Lyle without his mother being present, he carefully noted Lyle's reaction when her name was mentioned. Lyle's eyes brightened when asked about his mom. He admitted he loved her. He told the doctor she was kind and loving.

The MD then asked, "Will you tell me about the women in your foster homes."

Lyle began to weep, saying, "No, I don't remember," while he shook his head vigorously. Armand hugged and kissed him asking, "Lyle, please tell us what happened to you besides being slapped and pushed into the door frame. My dear son, please relate what happened to you. I'm holding you. Don't be afraid."

Lyle wiped his tear-filled eyes with the back of his hand.

"She did not like me! She was mean and yelled very loud. Whenever Roslind came around Marie was very nice."

"Are you telling me that she changed her personality?"

"I don't know what personality is, but yes, she sure did change." His father hugged him and gave him a kiss. Armand thought, *My god! What has Lyle gone through?* He was beginning to appreciate the wonderful parenting he had received at this age.

"Son, don't be afraid to tell us what happened."

The doctor asked, "Did Marie touch you in an inappropriate way?"

Lyle shook his head, *yes*, with more tears. Hugging him, his dad was crying, too.

The doctor obtained a small boy figurine from his desk asking, "Please show me where Marie touched you."

Pointing to the figurine's groin area, wiping tears away, he cried, "She would take my *weenie* and hold it, then pull it up and down."

Armand was horrified. He grasped Lyle saying, "Lyle, I love you. Your mom loves you. What Marie did was wrong and against the law."

The doctor quietly stated, "We understand how you feel. Not all woman are like Marie. She will be punished."

Changing the subject the doctor asked, "Lyle, do you like your home?"

With arms around his dad's neck, he answered, "Yes. My daddy wears a suit and tie to work." The conversation moved to favorite toys, color, and food. They left with Lyle in his father's arms. He was gently put into his car seat.

In the *Rambulet* building, they went to Amber. When she saw Lyle she began to cry because Armand was weeping, too. She picked Lyle up, kissing him saying, "My son, I love you. We will love the bad things away. Honey, you are with us now. Let's go home."

Amber took him home. In the car she asked, "Lyle, would you like to have Floyd come to our house for a sleep-over?"

"Yeah, I'd like that."

After Armand returned home and embraced Amber, he picked up Lyle and praised him saying, "Son, you are very brave."

"Dad, Marie touched me when I was going to bed."

With a shock, Amber began to understand the trauma her son had experienced. She began to weep. At the sink she splashed water on her face to rinse away her tears.

Armand did the same thing as Lyle stood beside him begging, "Dad, don't cry."

Before they ate, Armand, Amber, and Lyle went in to the living room. She took off her shoes and sat on the floor in a lotus position. Shoeless, Armand had Lyle sit between them with their arms enfolding him. Sitting in the same position, Armand gently asked Lyle to close his eyes as he began:

Oh Energy of Love, enfold us, especially Lyle, so he can feel your Great Love. Oh Great Energy of Protection, enfold us, and especially Lyle, with your Great Guardianship. Surround him in Blue. Oh Blue Angel, help him and us overcome impure thoughts. Finally we ask that all which has happened to Lyle and to us be transmuted into pure Light to guide and protect us. Oh Energy, Greater than we understand and be with us. We thank you. We thank you. We thank you.

Armand and Amber kept their eyes closed for a long time. When Lyle opened his eyes he exclaimed, "I saw the Blue Angel."

Amber then spoke, *"Dear Blue Angel, we thank you, we thank you, we thank you.*

Amber urged, "It's wonderful to see your *Blue Angel*. Remember prayer, Lyle."

"I forgot."

"Let's eat. Jessica has our food prepared," Amber invited.

Their evening went well. Amber asked Lyle to call Aunt Jennifer. Amber had told her earlier to expect a call.

"Aunt Jennifer, can Floyd come over after school on Friday?"

"I think that could be arranged very easily. Certainly, Lyle."

Floyd's visit and sleepover made Lyle very happy. The boys stayed up late. Amber kissed the boys goodnight and Armand tucked them in bed.

In their bedroom, Armand helped his love remove her shoes. He embraced her fondly. They admitted they needed each other while removing their clothing. Putting her arm around Armand's neck, he placed her in the middle of the bed. Amber's embraces and kisses revealed affection which Armand sorely needed.

Following their emotional encounter, Amber remained in Armand's arms while they discussed the trauma of the week. He assured her that his brother would make certain that Marie was put in prison.

Roslind had called Armand at work, insisting she did not know of any problem until Lyle came forth. But since then, she discovered that other children had experienced problems with Marie. These children had been adopted, so Roslind contacted those parents, making certain all such children received therapy.

On Saturday afternoon, Floyd's parents came to swim and take him home after an evening meal. Amber had baked chocolate brownies for Lyle.

Armand laughed when Lyle took two, saying, "Thanks Mom."

Chapter 33.

The Armand Rambulet family settled into normal living with Lyle being encircled by love. Jessica expressed her kindness toward Lyle by often making chocolate brownies for him.

Since Amber was home most of the time, she assisted Armand when possible. So far they were managing well. Barbara Bentley, the new-comer at work was doing fine. She helped when and where she was needed. Armand thought she was a brilliant businesswoman, almost the equal of his wife, but not quite. In his eyes, she was not nearly as beautiful.

A search for a pre-school for Lyle took most of July. Amber did not want him going to just any school. She finally found what she felt was a good one. He would start in August. She knew it was her responsibility to drive Lyle to and from school.

One day Armand surprised them by going to school carrying a prepared lunch for the three of them. This kindness brought tears to Amber's eyes.

One evening, a week before their eighth wedding anniversary, they lay in each other arms, wondering what to do for this celebration. "Do we take Lyle with us? He would be bored." Amber changed the subject, asking, "What would you like?"

Looking into her eyes he purred, "Just your love."

Armand was at work the day Amber took Lyle shopping for his Dad's anniversary gift. Amber drove to a specialty stationery store. Hand in hand they walked through the store. In the desk accessories area, they discovered a collection of lighted world globes which attracted Lyle.

"Mom, here is our country. Mom this would be a good gift for Dad."

She twirled the globe looking at other countries. She noted that the African countries were difficult to identify, but found Mount Kilimanjaro on the equator. "I think you're right, Lyle. This would make a wonderful gift for your father."

She purchased the globe and some computer ink, thinking, *These inks are not particularly personal, but as time passes, he is becoming more difficult to buy for."*

Amber stored the globe in the girl's bedroom closet because Armand never looked in there. She stressed to Lyle not to mention what they had done.

When Jennifer called asking, "I know your anniversary is coming up. How would you like us to keep Lyle overnight? He could eat and sleep here. Perhaps you could pick him up and take him to school. Would that work?"

"Jennifer, how thoughtful. Of course that would be fine. Armand will be thrilled for us to have some time alone. Thank you." The ladies discussed children, schools, and the news.

When Armand came home, Amber was preparing their evening meal. She had allowed Jessica to leave early. Lyle was waiting for his dad to open the door and to be picked up. He knew his father would take him to his mom and would kiss her, followed by a three-way kiss. Lyle was being caught up in his parent's love.

The next thing Amber knew, Lyle was questioning Armand, "Dad, do you know what we did today?"

Still holding him, Armand's eyes became wide as he looked at Amber. She had told him they were going shopping that day. He made-believe he didn't know. "What did you do?" he asked.

"Lyle, remember we have a secret," Amber directed.

"Mom, Dad needs to know we bought his present today,.' Lyle reminded his mother.

Armand put Lyle in his booster chair and washed his hands. "Mine too, Dad," Lyle begged. Armand picked him up and went to the laundry sink. He held Lyle so he could soap his hands and rinse them. "Thanks, Dad."

"You're welcome," Armand responded as he put Lyle back into his chair. As they ate Lyle told his dad what he had seen on their outing and grocery shopping.

When bedtime came, Amber kissed Lyle, then left.

His dad listened to his story about the day. Lyle revealed, "Dad, your present is a globe."

"Hey, that'll be nice."

"Don't tell Mom."

"Okay, this is our secret. Goodnight, Lyle."

Their eighth anniversary occurred on a week-night. Amber took Lyle to Jennifer's house. She came back quickly to prepare for a work-out. She was excited. When Armand came home, he embraced her, then shaved, added new shave lotion, and donned a different suit, shirt, and tie. Arm in arm, they went to the car. He kissed her as he bent to fasten her seat belt.

At their favorite eating establishment they were seated in a booth. After champagne arrived, Armand presented her with gold dangling earrings for daily wear.

"I thank you so much, sweetheart. Your present is at home."

"My real present will be at home after our dinner," he smiled.

"Well, that too, of course."

He acted shocked. "My present is at home, but it is here too? Wow, I really must be on top of my game."

Back home after a good meal, Amber asked him to follow her as she headed for the girl's bedroom. In the closet she presented a large box to him. He carried it to his desk in the den. Upon opening the box, he found the spectacular globe. He took it to the other bedroom, where an electric outlet was near the dresser. He kissed Amber and thanked her. She then handed him the computer inks, saying, "I believe you can use these, too."

"Thank you my love, may we share each other shortly?"

"Yes, sweetheart, I thought you would never ask," she smiled as she began to remove her clothing. Their evening anniversary interlude was gently and lovingly shared.

Amber then asked, "I'll bet you knew what your present was."

"Of course. You know kids can't keep secrets."

The next morning, Armand left for work while Amber went to Jennifer's house to pick up Lyle and take him to school.

Lyle loved his school. His intensity to learn convinced his teacher he was definitely ahead of his school mates, particularly in math.

A few days later, Roslind stopped by for a visit.

Lyle asked her, "Why do you come here? You don't need to."

Flabbergasted, she answered, "I'd like to know what I could do better."

Lyle answered, "You need to watch other kids more. Don't let them snow you." She quickly understood she had been chastised by an intelligent child whose parents were a wonderful guidance for him. She recognized that his pre-school was giving him a great foundation for regular school. Thanking Amber, Roslind left.

Lyle knew his mother was devoted to him but like any child, he could be demanding. He pressured her more often, due to the fact that they were together during the time after school. Amber realized what was happening.

One day while grocery shopping, he demanded to see Floyd. She asked, "Lyle, why are you demanding something that you know I would say *no* to? If you were to ask your father, what would he say?"

Lyle repeated, "I want to see Floyd."

With groceries in the trunk, Amber put Lyle in his car seat. She was beginning to feel manipulation, which she did not approve. She explained what he was asking was not possible to carry out. "You know Floyd is in school all day."

While driving home, Lyle began kicking his seat and being a little brat. Amber parked the car in a parking lot, took him out of his seat and held him firmly in her lap. She kissed him saying, "I am disappointed in your actions, but no matter what, I love you."

A thought came to her. *I wonder if he sees some of the qualities of Marie in me? Is that a reason he is acting up?*

In Amber's lap, Lyle began a tearful session.

"Dear Lyle, please express your feelings. Do you dislike me because you are remembering the actions Marie used when you were with her?"

With big tears in his eyes, he shook his head, *yes.*

Still holding him tightly and fondly, she explained, "You started this unhappy event when you knew my answer would be no. We could not go into Floyd's school. He would be studying in class. The school would not permit us to enter unless his mother had written a note approving the plan for him to go home with us. My dear and loving son, please let your father and me know what you would like. Most of the time we try to satisfy your wishes, because you are special. Do you think we are special?"

He put his arms around his mother's neck saying, "Oh yes, Mom."

She kissed him saying, "I love you, sweetheart. Please believe me."

This episode was the beginning of a closer bonding between Lyle and Amber. After Armand arrived home, she explained what had happened that afternoon. Armand took his son on his lap. They sat on the sofa with

Amber next to them. Armand explained, "Lyle, I want you to understand, when your mother is upset over something you do, so am I. Please realize you are with us partly because you chose us, just as we chose you. Your mother and I love each other deeply. When one of us is hurt, so is the other one.

"Lyle, you are a very privileged youngster. On any question your mother and I will agree. We are one. That's what a real marriage is all about. Because you are now with us, we must act in harmony, or you would be confused. When you are older, you'll realize how important agreement is."

He continued, "I may be sedulously occupied at work, but that is not as important as my family. If a difficulty occurs, we'll talk about it and eat later. Nothing is more important than to discuss the sharing of our ideas."

Amber then questioned, "If there is someone at your school you would like to invite here for a sleep-over, that would be fine. We want others to enjoy our home as much as we do."

Lyle developed friendships in school. Amber and Armand encouraged him to be outgoing. Often when Armand played with Lyle in his room, he talked with his son about what to say to other boys in school, how to ask friendly questions, and how to respond to something he didn't like.

Once Lyle asked his Dad, "How come we live in such a big house?"

That question led Armand to discuss all the things his parents and especially his mother had done for him, to help him become a partner in the business. He then mentioned extended families who came to visit or to play in the pool. "We really needed a house large enough to have all our families here at once."

That led Armand to tell Lyle about how he had met Amber. "The first time I saw her I knew I wanted her to be my wife, but it took awhile."

Lyle's response was, "Mom is pretty. Why did it take a long time?"

"Your mother wanted to obtain her degree. I had to fly way down to El Paso, where she was going to school, in order to see her."

"Dad, where is El Paso?"

"El Paso is in Texas. Let's go to the globe where we can find it."

Armand showed Lyle how far it was between the two cities and continued, "After flying down there, I rented a car and went to her apartment to take her out to dinner. The next day we would visit museums, the zoo or other unusual places. It's an interesting city. I flew down every three weeks, until she graduated. We were married shortly after that.

"Before you came to live with us, your mother worked in her office. You know where that is."

"Yeah it's nice, but so is yours."

"My brother works in the same building. Aunt Eleanor worked with him before they had your cousins, Gilbert and Gabrielle. My sister, Aunt Jennifer, worked in the business until Floyd and Desiree came along. Your grandmother, and my grandmother Alma worked there after my grandfather started the business. If we had not worked hard, the business would have suffered and we would not have a nice house. This house was your mother's idea. Now, Lyle, it is time to get you ready for bed."

Lyle asked, "Could Floyd stay over here tomorrow night?"

"Let's ask your mom."

Amber's answer was, "Fine Lyle, you can tell me tomorrow what food you would like." Amber kissed their son goodnight. Before he shut his eyes he saw his dad embrace and kiss his mother.

The house alarm was set and the house was checked. The two parents went to the den where they worked for a short time before they retired.

This was the way the three lived, birthdays, anniversaries, and holidays were spent having fun, enjoying each other, and being with family.

Chapter 34.

Life was filled with daily routines. There were times when he and his mother went to work. Toys were brought along, so he could have something to play with. Lyle found it interesting to see his uncles' offices and those of his grandparents. He occasionally would play in his dad's office, but his father spent more time on the telephone or on the computer than his mother did. He was able to talk to his father when he was free. Often Lyle was able to sit on his father's lap and look at the computer, especially when there were all sorts of numbers on the screen. Lyle did the same thing in his mother's office, though most of the time Amber did not work more than two hours.

With all of this interaction with his parents and family members Lyle became a loving member of the Rambulet family.

Amber spent some time at his school and often invited Floyd to stay over on Saturday nights. Then on Sundays Floyd's family came to swim and take him home, because of school the next day.

Lyle comfortably finished his preschool. He became a well adjusted little boy, who was learning his numbers rapidly.

Before he was to start first grade he and Amber went to his new school to meet his teacher, Mrs. Melodea. Amber took an instant liking to her. The teacher was enthralled when Amber told her she would like to spend four hours a week helping children read or do math.

Mrs. Melodea asked Amber to talk with office people. Amber was warmly received and met the principle and the assistant principle who named Mrs. Delena. In conversation with her, Amber found they did not live very far from each other.

On his first day of school, Amber let Lyle board the bus alone. She then drove to meet him getting off the bus. Hand in hand, they walked to his room. Mrs. Melodea was standing at the schoolroom door to greet the students. Amber greeted Lyle's teacher then left for work, Amber was home to greet Lyle when he stepped off the bus. She had punched a button on the keypad in the house to open the gate which was always closed even when there were guests.

Because of the time Amber spent at Lyle's school she grew to know the staff, especially Mrs. Melodea and Mrs. Delena.

The rest of Amber's time was spent at work. When she came and went, she always greeted her husband even if it was with a blown kiss when he was on the telephone.

There was interaction between Amber and Armand during the morning or afternoon, just like their days were like before Lyle entered their lives.

Lyle never had a problem finding his bus which was number four.

He knew that number because his parents worked math with him a great deal. They also read together, in fact there were many times when his parents kissed each other and him, too. Their life was enjoyable.

When errands needed to be done on Saturdays or after their evening meal, Lyle went with his dad who still wore his suit. Armand never took off his business clothes until he prepared for bed, or if swimming was planned after supper, was a time for Lyle which improve his swimming. He and his dad played in the water while his mom stayed away from their water splashing.

Lyle developed into an outgoing child, who became friends with Peter Barnes and Philip Denmoor, who spent overnights and swam, which was a thrill for Lyle.

At holiday time Amber invited the school faculty to the house for a swim or just conversation. Jessica had prepared food which she loved to do. Lyle spent that night with his cousin.

On a warm, calm, spring day, Lyle emerged from the bus extremely happy. Amber bent, hugged him, and kissed him on his cheek.

"Mom, guess what?"

"I can't guess, Lyle."

"When I was doing math today I saw the Blue Angel. I really heard him speak. The Blue Angel told me someday I would be working in an office close to Dad."

Amber embraced Lyle with tears in her eyes. She spoke in halting words to him saying, "Your father, grandfather, and great grand father will be enormously pleased".

In another dimension, very similar to what we recognize in areas covered in this book, especially New Mexico, there is more love and beauty than we presently know or enjoy.